<u>Nascence-1</u>

MW00934961

Edited by Clayton Oliver Rutschow

clayton-oliver.yolasite.com

ISBN-13:
978-1482648768

ISBN-10:
1482648768

Table of Contents

NASCENCE
The Story of Ferroc

By:
Clayton Oliver Rutschow

To Jane,
For all of your help and love.

To Mom, Dad, and Cohlman,
For your unending support.

And to Danielle,
For never giving up on me.

Prologue

There's a beautiful landscape in front of me. The vegetation is lush and healthy, proudly wearing vivid greens. The sky is a crystalline blue. The clouds are white as mountain snow. Everything is pristine. There's so much life. Like the animals that are so fruitful they almost overwhelm the local ecosystem. But there's balance to this immaculate, natural world. Everything has its place. Predator, prey, plant, air, and soil. It all belongs.

It's all cohesive.

It's symbiotic.

It's a world filled with air I can't breathe, fruit I can't eat, growing from fertile earth I can't feel, all of it saturating the atmosphere with scents I can't smell...

This isn't the apocalypse I was expecting.

Then again, there's no one else; no others around to appreciate this beauty before me. What that means regarding my perception of the world's end, I have to wonder. Maybe the apocalypse and the human concept of it are two different things. That could explain what I see versus what I feel. There's so much...opportunity here, if only there were others around to benefit from it.

But there aren't. They're the endangered species; the humans. I don't qualify anymore. Or, I don't *think* I do. I'm in a world that has no use for me, or so it seems. So I try to find a use for *it*. Most of the time, I just try to find a reason, not knowing how long that's going to take. I wander, hoping...

I guess I don't know what to think anymore. It's why just moving helps. Progress is progress, even if it's pointless. With the others gone, I'm left alone, gazing out over a landscape that holds so much promise, but given my circumstance, is a wasteland. Or might as well be. The animals in front of me...The deer, the rabbits, birds flying from tree to fruit bearing tree in this supposed "Eden" I hold within my view...They're the imps from the reality of *Faustus*. Or maybe I think that's what I could compare them too. I haven't been able to find a copy of that book in a long time. I've read many and learned so much. History, poetry, astronomy, physics, art, patterns, codes, languages...I only have the memories now. The memories that I hold to, even if they have a way of haunting me with things that once were. Memories like

Faustus, or the smell of an autumn morning. The taste of an apple or a cold beer...

My memories are all that's left. I'm the only one remaining to describe what they felt like. Someone has to keep those facets of humanity alive, even if only in memory. It's ironic that the thing doing that isn't human itself. Then again, better *something* than nothing since there's no one left to speak of the memories with.

Yet...

That's my hope anyway.

It's been over 23 years by my counting. My chronological protocols are still accurate to my knowledge. I've recorded the sun and stars as they rise and set every day. I've watched them trace their telltale tracks across the sky, signifying the seasons. And in all that time, I found so few survivors. I tell myself I'll find more, but that hope is diminishing, even as much as I'd like to hold onto it.

Combine this expanding sense of despair along with my deepening absence of humanity and I'm beginning to wonder if I'm even *living* anymore. Humans are meant to thrive and thus, truly *live* as opposed to just exist. It feels like I'm only doing the latter. And that, to me, is no way to live a life. Even one as mechanical or artificial as my own. There's still a soul or spirit...or will to believe there's such within me. I know I have that. Even now as I look down at my robotic hands covered in metal, I remember this. Titanium, steel, and other alloys compose me now, but they are *not* me. I have to remember that. Even if there's no one else to remind me this is so. I'm not just a machine.

But I can't neglect the reality. I'm not human either.

My thoughts come full circle. It means it's time to keep moving. Why?

Because it's something else to do. Anything but live in the cycle of endless, despairing contemplations.

To my left there's what's left of an aging highway. The rusted signs tell me it was once Interstate 90. I've made it to Washington. I'm a little further south than I thought. I'd gone north thinking the damage wasn't as severe up there. I thought maybe the cold had slowed or stopped the micro-genocide inflicted upon the human race. I should have known better, but a small hope is still a hope. I had to see for myself that the entire world was affected. Besides, I had plenty of time to make the trip. I think I got as far as Alaska, now completely frozen over. Without human industry influencing the atmosphere, the frigid north had expanded its borders to cover the whole state.

6

I didn't find a single survivor. The only thing resembling a human was me, wandering the world, and marking the fifth year since I last saw a living person.

Five years since I spoke with someone.

Five years since I felt human again.

Five years since I'd been able to live.

So I came back south. Going further north didn't seem sensible. It was too cold to support life beyond the animals adapted specifically to the arctic. Now, I'm heading for what's left of Seattle. After that, I'm going south again through Oregon to northern California. I've been this way before, though never through the city. Maybe other survivors have surfaced. Maybe they haven't been hunted and eaten. Maybe they found a way.

Or maybe there's another like me out there.

If nothing else, the mountains, for whatever reason, bring me some level of comfort in this solitude. Their soaring peaks remind me that there are things left to be seen. If they've remained in this world through all that's happened, so can I. So could someone else. It's nice having that hope when I look at them, even if I'm just passing by. I've seen many of their summits, yet there's so much left to explore. I still have yet to get across the ocean. If I don't find anyone else here, maybe I'll head over to Asia. I need to stay moving.

It's something else to see and something else to do.

But I need to stay focused on the task at hand. Interstate 90 winds toward the horizon, or what's left of the road does. The birds, alighted on decrepit power lines watch me as I follow its crumbling path. The other animals don't seem to mind my presence. They never have. They don't have much to fear from me, and maybe they know it. They simply watch for a bit, then go about their lives, feeding on the abundance of plant life that surrounds them. I guess, with the absence of humanity, they've regained their confidence. They just watch as I walk past them, following the road. After a few hours, I see an old gas station. The pack I keep strapped to the small of my back is almost devoid of items. A few spare mags for my .45 and a whetstone. That's it. I don't need much from this place, but it's worth a look. I stop to investigate, peeling away wrist-thick layers of vines and overgrowth to get to the door. Hoping to find old batteries or something else that contains a charge, I enter.

It's dark. I give my "eyes" a moment to adjust spectrums. I switch to night vision. I see a grouping of what I think to be small animals. Uncertain of what they are, I switch to infrared. I find a nest of bats hanging in the corner of the building above what used to be the refrigerated section. There are still a few bottles inside that look distinguishable. Everything else has molded over or cracked. I approach slowly, not wanting to disturb the bats, switching back to night vision. I open the door to one of the racks. Or try to. The handle, rusted over time, breaks off in my hand. I wonder if I gripped it too hard or if my mechanical arm pulled back too swiftly. Then I remember this isn't the first time this scenario has played out. Some things have reached a state of irreparable decay. I debate breaking through the glass to get the bottles of fruit juice. The chemicals have separated and it looks like the pulp has settled on the bottom of each container. They still look consumable however. Even if I can't drink them, I might find someone who could. I decide otherwise about breaking the door though. If the bats are disturbed and fly out now, it might be enough to draw some attention to me. Attention I don't need.

I remember this as I make my way out of the gas station, unsuccessful in my search for anything useful. Even if people are gone and the animals generally don't care if I'm here, I'm not the only one carving out an existence in this world. There are others who want me dead. I need to be careful not to bring them to me. I look down at the sword I keep on my hip and the .45 I keep strapped to my armor-plated leg as I remember that. The two weapons have truly served me well over the years.

The .45 I was familiar with. I'd bought it on advice from a friend, familiarized myself with it, then enjoyed recreational shooting before things went to hell. I learned quickly that tranquil target practice goes out the window when your life is at stake. Such was the case every time I pulled the trigger in this world. And beyond that, there was no sport shooting when your targeting protocols could calculate wind, velocity, and gravitational influences in milliseconds. Firing a weapon was more of a program, even if it was still somewhat emotional to initiate the sequence.

The sword took some getting used to, but given I generally had nothing but time, I taught myself how to swing it properly and well. Coordination and artificially enhanced limbs helped with that. I was no Samurai or anything, but I was capable. I'd found the weapon at what looked like a forge or something. Maybe one of those places where they manufactured equipment for martial arts suppliers. Straight-bladed with a groove down the middle. The guard and handle were never finished. I took the liberty of completing the weapon. I didn't need a guard. Metal hands offer their own type of protection. I'd wrapped the handle in tight fitting wire, coarse enough for me to grip. It was crude, but I wasn't worried about ornamentation or comfort when I made it. Besides, it was damn effective, and I'd cut down enough enemies with it to know that for a fact. So I kept it sharp, and my ability to use it sharper.

Putting these two items together usually made life easier for me, but I'm reminded anyone can be overwhelmed if the numbers are large enough. I've learned to resist and evade capture from sizable groups, and I don't try to wage open warfare with gun or blade. That mindset has kept me alive through the years.

I pause.

"Alive..."

Why does it always seem like such a strange term when I think about it now?

I don't have time to contemplate the subject when something crashes loudly from inside the gas station a hundred feet behind me. The bats fly out as I hear panting and growls. More destruction is wrought inside the overgrown convenience store when I hear glass breaking and shelves being overturned. Something is frustrated. That tells me "something" is looking for me.

I drop down low into some bushes along the road. They don't provide much cover, but it's something. The illusion of security dawns on me, but I shrug the thought away with the danger at hand. I draw my sword, not wanting to waste ammo or bring any more unnecessary attention if it comes to that. I wait for a few moments, then have my fears realized as I watch a very large, male Rantir exit the gas station. He's following my trail. I can see he's tracking me when he holds up his hand, using his ultra-sensitive pads to feel any vibrations in the air. Meanwhile, he keeps his other limbs on the ground, using the pads upon them to do the same thing, feeling for any seismic vibrations his prey might cause.

I can't hide from him for long. I know I'm in for a fight.

I look closely and see the blades strapped to his prehensile appendages extending from his shoulder blades. When Rantir do that, I call those extra limbs "scythes." Seems fitting because of what they use them for. He made the attachments himself out of scrap metal a while ago from what I can tell. They've corroded over time, looking very weathered. He also has seasoned blades strapped to his wrists. Judging

9

from the jagged scars dotting his gray hide, it looks like he's used to brawling. He probably thinks I'm another human or animal to make a meal out of.

To top it all off, he's feral...

...Fantastic.

Now grasping the fact that a fight is inevitable, something shifts within me. I remember all the humans killed by his race, putting myself in a mood to confront him. I wonder how many humans survived just to be mauled by the feral Rantir left behind. The more "civilized" of their kind decided humanity wasn't worth giving a second look to, turning our world into a land of exile for their undesirables. It was these pricks who decided that pushing a button and unleashing a devastating weapon that would annihilate a sentient race was the best choice. One press of a button that unleashed genocide on a species that was once mine.

Those were my friends.

My family too...

And me? What about me? I didn't exactly belong with humanity anymore, but I did once. These Rantir assholes took that from me.

Maybe a good fight is exactly what I need. Even if he wins, he's going to feel it a lot more than I will.

Hell...I won't feel a thing. Except satisfied when it's over.

I step out from amidst the bushes and reveal myself to him. He stands up, walking on two legs instead of four, displaying his full, seven foot height. Obviously, with the noise he just made in the gas station, he's not concerned with the quiet approach. But what he lacks in subtlety, he makes up for in brawn. That much is clear from my analysis. He sees me, exposing his shark-like teeth and prominent underbite with a growl. After that, he's on all fours charging straight for me, reverse-jointed legs hastening his approach. In less than a second, we'll be face to face. I take that time to ready my sword.

He dives at me, thinking to tackle me to the ground like a tiger, scythes leading the way attempting to impale me on impact. I quickly duck underneath him, mechanically enhanced legs and body helping me stay perfectly balanced and coordinated as I do so. I make a downward slash when I shift, keeping the movements linked to save momentum. I'm up instantly, tensed, and ready for his next approach. He lands and pivots, but doesn't charge again.

He might be feral but he's smart. He knows I'm a capable opponent after a dodge like that. Plus, the cut to his abdomen is proof enough I won't be easy prey.

He starts circling me now, still on all fours. I stay motionless and tense, ready to react to whatever move he makes. I have to play it defensively. He's got the reach on me with those scythes of his, and it's going to be hard for me to get inside his guard for a clear slice. I debate using my pistol again, but think otherwise. I don't need to waste the ammo now.

No...I can handle this without the gun.

He stops circling me, then makes another lunge, pulling up short as I make a defensive sweep with my sword in front of me. His right scythe whips out, aiming for my neck. I duck under it, then flip over the next attack coming low for my legs. My orientation programs help me summersault through the air. Instead of ears to help me balance, my cybernetic functions, such as gyroscopic programs, take control of coordination. Tracking my revolutions, I know I'll land right on top of him if he doesn't dodge. He does though, skirting out from underneath me. He rises to two feet and takes a swipe with one of his wrist blades. I step into his swing as he aims for my chest, sword leading the way as I slice into his arm and make the block at the same time. I lower my shoulder and drive into him, forcing him back. I get my other arm cocked, give my hydraulics a moment to charge, then unleash a punch into his chest that takes him from his feet, launching him back into the wall of the gas station some eighty feet away. The hit doesn't do much damage to him. Neither does the impact with the wall. His bones are too dense to break, even from a hit like that. They offer his internal organs similar resilience. But it does send a message as he bounces violently off the concrete.

Now he knows who he's fucking with.

He gets to his feet, snarling as he does so. Then he gets an idea. I see it by the way he looks over to the gas pumps. I'm not sure what he's up to, but it can't be fire. There's no gas left in the lines. Instead, I watch, not wanting to fall into a trap he might be setting. My advantage is in the openness of the road and the ample maneuverability it provides me. I want this field to be on my terms, so I wait for him to come to me again.

He walks over to a pump, then starts ripping it apart, hurling chunks of it at me. He's not the most accurate given the distance, but it's a smart move. If I took a shot from something he threw, it could do substantial damage. I either have to walk away and let him hunt me later, chancing an ambush, or come at him now to stop the barrage.

Not being one to look over my shoulder, I accept his challenge.

I start walking toward him slowly, letting him know my intention. There's no reason to hide it. He keeps up the assault, forcing me to dodge a few times, but not slowing my advance. I know he's going to lash out with his scythes when I get close, so I need to play this one carefully.

I wait for him to throw another chunk of metal at me. When he does, I anticipate its approach utilizing speed assessment and trajectory programs, then block by shielding with my forearms. I get a minor abrasion to my metal exterior, but that's all. I collect the piece and hurl it back at him, forcing *him* to dodge for a change. Then I charge him, sword behind me and ready to strike. Propelled by the hydraulics in my legs, I close the gap faster than he thought, but he still has enough time to attack with both of his scythes. I have to leap over him to avoid the low angled strikes. As I do, I don't see that he's grabbing for a gas hose. When I land and turn, he has it swinging out at me. I can't dodge in time. The nozzle weights the end of the hose as it swings about me, wrapping around my neck and cinching tight. The Rantir yanks me toward him, launching me off my feet. I fly past him as he moves aside, allowing me to go crashing into the stone pillar near the gas pumps. I slam into it with my back, taking a large chunk of concrete out of it. Diagnostics are performed, informing me I've sustained minimal damage to my external structure. There's a slight puncture in my outer shell which exposes one of my circulatory tubes, but he doesn't know that. And I don't need to think about it now.

I cut through the gas hose, then get to my feet quickly, moving my sword in front of me to block a drawing slash from one of his scythes. The next attack comes from above with his right scythe, trying to split me down the middle. I step to my left, then duck under his right handed jab as he aims his bladed wrist for my face. I grab his arm as it passes by with my left hand, planting my feet and digging my metallic toes into the earth. I twist my body for full leverage, forcing him off-balance as I pull him past me. He takes a step to steady himself with his right leg, which I guessed correctly he'd do. In less than a heartbeat, I release his arm, withdraw my feet from their anchored position, spin, and cut him deep on the side with a backhanded draw of my sword. He continues to stumble past me, gripping his side as bright, blue blood pours from the wound. His bones stopped me from doing serious damage to his organs. It would take a much stronger cut for that. But he'll still bleed out if I land a few more slashes on him like that, and he knows it.

He turns and faces me, holding his side and growling. He starts to curse at me in his own language; a sequence of glottal noises, growls, and snarls when it's not syllabic. My translation programs kick in, informing me he's saying less than kind things about an "abomination." I guess that fits with their theology. Their "Great Creator" would consider me some kind of demon given what I am. It shouldn't affect me, but I can't help but wonder how right he is at the moment. Even I don't know what I am anymore. Abomination could be just as likely as savior.

But then he calls me something I've heard a few times before. "Ferroc." I've never been able to find a translation for it. Still, it's what I call myself now, because every Rantir has called me by that title.

It's better to have a name you don't know the meaning of than no name at all.

He eventually stops the string of curses and squares off against me again. I'm thinking he's going to be overly aggressive this time. He knows he's outmatched, so his only options are to run or really step up his game. The way he's stood his ground so far and tried to come at me, I know he's too prideful or consumed by his savagery to retreat. Now I have to be even more cautious. There's no telling what he might try to do out of desperation.

"Cornered foxes" and all that.

I'm correct in my assumption. He comes out swinging with every limb he has. I'm forced to retreat as I block an attack from his right scythe, and yet another from his left arm while dodging an overhead chop from his left scythe. Again, his right arm comes at me with a jab, but this one isn't as heavy, so the opportunity for me to grapple isn't there. He retracts it after I avoid the blow, then follows up with a series of quick jabs that I evade. Dodging or blocking the simultaneously attacking scythes, both of which are making quick thrusts at my abdomen, is proving difficult. I'm retreating heavily now, forced back onto the road. Evading or backpedaling more than I'm blocking, he understands his advantage and presses all the harder, thinking to overwhelm me. I accept the fact that in order to win this fight, I'm going to have to bleed a little.

...So to speak.

I leap away from him, creating some space between us as I sheathe my sword. Then I wait for my moment. When he approaches and attempts a diagonal slash with his left hand blade, I bend and lock my left leg, anchoring my toes as I did before while I deliver a kick into his gut with my right. The hydraulics are now charging. Unable to halt his forward momentum, he barrels into me, but I'm not going anywhere. His scythes slam into my torso at the same time I catch him. One breaks through my armored exterior. A quick red flash within my vision is followed by damage analysis. One of my processing compartments has been compromised as well as a severe laceration to a coolant tube. Micro-robotic cells are being administered to contain damage and stabilize energy dispersal, which could melt through me if left unchecked. It's OK though. This fight will be over long before that happens.

I "feel" him sense that he's impaled me with one of his scythes, and he tries to pull away. I've already reached out and locked my left hand onto his shoulder, digging deeply into the flesh with metallic digits. Holding him steady, I give the hydraulics in my right arm and fingers a second to lock and charge before I punch him hard in the ribs. I aim for the cut I made before, fingers extended like claws. With individual poundage of pressure on each digit, I bury them between his ribcage. I then release my hydraulic charge, clamping my hand down tight onto one of his ribs. Once I'm sure my grip is secure, I mechanically lock my fingers into position.

They're not going anywhere now.

He roars in pain and flails at me, but I'm inside his guard with his scythes still lodged in my torso. Each hit he lands on me with his wrists is minor. I'm too close for him to put any real momentum behind each strike. Diagnostics inform me he's only causing cosmetic damage.

I now release the charge in my right leg. Using him as a brace to launch from, I accelerate backward at approximately ten G's of force. The hand locked around his rib stays clamped tight to him.

His rib and a lot of his flesh don't.

The bone comes with me in my retreat, tearing through his flesh and opening a gaping wound in his side. He roars in agony, then falls to his knees as blood pours uncontrollably from the injury. I realize then that the scythe that impaled me accompanied my retreat as well, still buried in my abdomen. I pull the bladed appendage through me so as not to disrupt more functions by tearing a wider hole. Then I look back to my enemy. He's moaning in pain on the ground, succumbing to

14

shock. I approach him, dropping his rib next to him and drawing my sword.

"Great Creator," he prays softly. "May I find you among the stars."

It was a typical Rantir last request. I've heard it several times before. I hold my sword above my head, charging my arms as I do so to come down with enough force to cut through his neck.

I speak in his language. The noises produced by my audio capacitors actually read the words my mind wishes to speak, then tunes my vocal components to the proper frequency, producing pitch and sustained sound patterns. It's my voice, but I can't speak it. I just tell my body to make the sounds.

"I can end your suffering," I tell him.

He turns his gaze to me, a look of surprise on his face, but I can see he's still suffering through the astonishment. He gives me a slight nod. It's as much as he can muster through the pain.

We share a moment of respect for one another. A moment I've had with others of his kind as I've fought them over the years. They may be merciless in war, but they do believe that even enemies can show respect. After they decimated our species with their micro-robotic plague, they started to see our propensity for valor and self-sacrifice when their sweeper teams fought directly with humans. This one, apparently, was familiar with humanity's sense of courage. I might have hated them for what they did to us, but we were just trying to survive now. That meant something. There's an unspoken respect between all in war, I've come to learn. If nothing else, for the fact that we all have the power to kill one another. He and I had just fought in what I'd consider to be an "honorable" way. That deserved to be acknowledged. Given the fact that a sentient being was now dying right in front of me, by my hand, I thought it important to show as much mercy as I could. Even if our history as a species was unfavorable at best.

I bow to him, a signal of respect he'd understand, then bring my arms down, powered by my mechanical enhancements. The blade cuts through clean, and it's over. I take a moment, looking at the lifeless corpse in front of me, letting the weight of the moment sink in.

I've grown accustomed to the task of killing. War was war and survival was just survival. I don't blame myself for what I have to do. Most of the time, the lives I end are justified. I feel no remorse for that. But with the world gone to hell and nothing to do but wander, it always makes me lament the act of terminating someone or something else. After all, the moment with the alien I just had was the first intelligent and compassionate dialogue I've had in years, one-sided as it was. And I just fought and killed him for no other reason than the fact he was hunting the wrong prey when I was in the mood for a fight. Some might argue it was self-defense, but I wouldn't have provoked him so openly if that were the case.

Guilt starts to sink in.

I try to remember what his kind did to mine. I try to, but then I remember he's been banished here. Ostracized by his own and driven to a feral state in order to survive. It was in his nature, and nothing more. Only in his death throes did he regain his mind. What a sad situation that was. Right before he died, he was able to fully comprehend his own demise. At least he'd met it bravely. Maybe he even considered it a good death. A lot of Rantir seemed to think dying in combat against a worthy opponent was the way to go. I hope, with respect to my enemy, I'd given him that.

Mourning isn't what I need right now, however. I have repairs to make. After a moment of acknowledgment to the fallen Rantir, I set about the task. My internal systems are busy trying to contain the damage, and they all need components and materials for my micro-robotic cells to utilize and assimilate. My restoration protocols inform me I require substitute metal for the ruptured containment tank in my processors to sustain balance in "cellular" power generation and dispersal. I require atomic substance that can be broken down and reformed into compounds of elasticity and proper density for fluid transport. (My "veins.") I need various fluids for filtration of proper molecular compatibility and conversion into coolant or micro-robotic lubricant. Miscellaneous substances are required for production of further nanorobotic cells lost in initial damage reception, as well repairs to my exterior.

I check the alien's scythe and find I'm in luck. The metal it's composed of is compatible with my systems. I open a compartment in my chest which houses my atomic recycling chamber. There, my nanorobotic cells can break down the material in a safe containment area. Each cell is a hive-minded A.I, programmed to exercise whatever protocol necessary to ensure the sustainment and structural integrity of the host vessel. The ones inside me make repairs by mending metal and transporting fluids or molecular compounds to necessary locations in my body. In groups, they're capable of amazing things. In this case, repairing me by reducing the alloy into molecules, then redistributing those molecules to the places requiring maintenance. In others, building more of themselves to replace damaged or lost vessels of their kind. With mechanical strength and hydraulic assistance, I bend the metal into the appropriate size, place it in the chamber, and let the nanobots get to work.

I then approach the body, retrieve his bone and break it in half, placing it in the chamber next. The calcium, iron, and other minerals can repair any coolant or circulation tubes that have been damaged once they're decomposed. I reach into the deep laceration I exposed when I tore his rib out. I withdraw some of his organs. The tissues and fluids can assist in further repair. Whatever isn't useful can be filtered out in gaseous form from vents scattered throughout my robotic body. I also take some of the metal off his wrist blades and add it to my materials for good measure. Lastly, I go back to the gas station and retrieve more bottles from behind the refrigerator door I broke the handle from before the battle. The various fruit juices will suffice for what remaining fluids my body requires.

I run a scan of the materials in my de-atomization chamber. All requirements are satisfied. Estimated time of full assimilation and maximum repair: 45 hours. This requires me to remain mostly inert during the repair process, otherwise the duration of restoration doubles or triples due to micro-functions being directed elsewhere.

Looks like I have some time to kill. The very worst kind. I see my reflection on the glass case as I realize this. Noting my sleek, angular, and flowing design, all composed of metal, cables, tubes and the like, I see myself for what I am and what I must now come to terms with. I'm the sentient machine, eternal in body but mortal in thought, left to the elements for reasons I still haven't discovered. And I have all the time in the world to contemplate this subject.

I look into my visor, or "eyes," noting the vision strip running from one side of my head to the other, a prominent optic processing center in the middle of it. It glows green, flaring brightly every now and then as regular system functions are performed.

I wonder what's left of the soul behind the visage.

Whenever I'm left alone with my thoughts, it's always a scary thing to me. It's been just these meditations and I for years now, and always they seem to be frustrating, depressing, or just forlorn. I try to remain hopeful. After all, there is natural life here. Abundant life. And in the absence of humanity, it has been allowed to flourish to an unprecedented level. I've seen the most remarkable vistas. The sunrise greets me every morning, casting its golden glow upon an Earth that is so picturesque now that the most brilliant of artists couldn't capture its sheer beauty.

But there's no one here to know that.

Except me.

I read once that missing someone isn't how long you've been apart, but experiencing something and wanting them there with you. I guess I'd have to agree with that. I miss my family. Constantly. My mind finds its way back to Angie, my wife, and Cassie, my daughter. I never even got to say goodbye.

I remember trying to fight...The moment I died...

An intense firefight. Rantir sweepers cornered us and some other refugees when we were trying to get to a fallout shelter. They'd been hunting us. When we got close to the refuge, they opened fire with disintegration rifles. The weapons tore through flesh and de-atomized organic material, much like my own decomposition chamber, but lethally and violently with extreme heat and kinetic destruction. The first ambush took down over half of us. The survivors withdrew into the shelter. We didn't stand a chance. If they didn't shoot us, they tore us apart with their blades. When it was down to just me, I was out of ammo. I stepped out from cover, knife in hand because it was the only thing I had left. I didn't know what I was trying to accomplish, but my family and others cowered behind me. I wanted to give them hope at least.

I remember watching the blades come down on me...

...Feeling them as they ripped through my body...

I force away the memories of what happened next. It's too painful for me to think about. I don't want to anymore. Images of my dead and rotting family fill my mind to replace the horrible recollections, and I wish to God I could make them stop. I can't even fall asleep to forget them. At this point, I'd give anything for one good dream. Something. Anything to make this constant world of limbo disappear for just a moment.

But I can't...

Memories of Ryan and his death are prevalent, which leads to recollections of Jaclyn and how she died right in front me. More people I couldn't save. I try to carry their memories with me, hoping to keep them alive in that respect. But now, when those memories are coupled with the stinging images of death that have become my recurring nightmares, I feel only emptiness and despair at the losses my life has incurred. And I can't escape them because that's the life of a machine. There is no indulgence to ease my troubled mind. Not even sleep.

A thought occurs to me. One that's run across my mind many times before. A thought I never like, but one I always acknowledge. It happens when I grasp the handle of my .45, slowly drawing it from the holster. I look at the weapon, remembering how much I've needed it. How much I've used it. How much I've seen it as a way to survive. Or in this case, the only way out. The only salvation.

I cycle a round into the chamber and turn the safety off. It's ready to fire. Only this time, as I consider my options, it's not meant to fire at an enemy. I slowly raise the gun to my head, not with any real intention of pulling the trigger, but entertaining the thought as I've done before. Reminding myself that there's a way out is comforting, even if I'm not going to take it.

...Yet.

I wonder if this would be better. I can't imagine anyone was meant to live like I am now; trapped inside a body that can't die but wishes it could.

I tap the gun against my head, confused, alone, and angry. This isn't fair, but it's life. And I'm living it one day at a time, trying to find reasons not to pull this trigger. It's getting harder and harder to remind myself not to think like this. I lower the weapon after a while, shaking my head in frustration. I made it through this moment, but I know there's more like it coming. It's inevitable in this world. I'm not sure if I hope I'll endure the next as stoically. Or maybe I'll just follow through with suicide.

It's a vicious cycle; being trapped in this cybernetic shell I now inhabit. There's always a war going on within me. So much of me just wants to die and make it all stop. The endless wandering, the constant loneliness, and the longing for a family I'll never see again. But then there's the other side of me. A more fatalistic side that says I was brought back in this form for a reason, trite as that logic may be. A side that says I have to stay strong for some reason unknown to me. A side that has hope left, even amidst the desolation of reason to possess that virtue.

I'm at war every day when I journey this earth. Just not physically. The stillness of waiting for my body to repair itself is a painful reminder of that. But this is my life. It's the one I choose to live.

I remind myself of that as well. It's always my choice to keep moving forward. Just like I will when these repairs are done.

God...I hope I find someone soon. Anything really. I just need a reminder that what I'm doing isn't delusional or in vain.

Seattle is a couple days away by my standards of travel. That's my guess anyway. I'll need to be careful to avoid more Rantir. Even though they're renegades, they don't like finding their own killed by anything other than their kind. No need to draw unwanted attention, so I'll take my time.

For now, I just have to wait.

Part I

Threshold

Chapter 1

My repairs complete, though the process is dull and grueling as always. I'm no worse for wear. Better than before, actually, though I'm loathe to admit it. In the end, it's just some lost time, and time is something I have plenty of. All the same, I'd rather just get to where I'm going sooner than later. It helps me just knowing what's out there, even if all I've seen is so much bountiful desolation. Right now, Seattle and what I might discover there seems like a good place to find serenity. I start moving the moment my repairs are finished.

The first day goes by uneventfully. I don't bother following the road. My internal navigation systems guide me west. I'll know if and when I reach Puget Sound where I need to go from there. Cutting through the mountains would be a time consuming and exhausting process for anyone else, but a machine doesn't tire. When there's a cliff or exceptionally steep incline, I just climb it by burying my hands into the stone with my augmented arms and legs. Following a straight course saves time, and staying up high allows me some good vantage points to assess any threats in the area.

Scaling a mountain rock face, I see a large swath of storm clouds heading my way. The animals below me start to scatter, looking for a place to weather the gale. I enhance my vision, further assessing the landscape. I don't see anything that poses a direct problem, but I do discover evidence that a Rantir has taken up shelter here. There are telltale tracks and assorted animal bones lying around. I can't tell if it's gone feral or just trying to survive off the sustenance provided by its chosen habitat. Either way, it's something I'll need to be wary of when I pass through. I don't want to go around, and I see no need to do so. If it wants to find me, then let it. I'll be ready if it comes to that.

For a moment, I contemplate that thought. Having just emerged from an encounter with one of its brethren, being in a confrontational sort of mood then didn't help me get to Seattle any faster. I don't think it will again, so I decide to be a little more cautious. Still, I'm not going around unless the threat presents itself. It might just leave me alone after all.

Wouldn't be the first time that's happened.

Fortunately, I traverse the area without an incident. I'm beginning to wonder how much of me just wants to fight after getting through the Rantir's territory. Maybe even how much of me wants to die as well. I'm not suicidal. But I suppose, as I reason with myself, saying you're not suicidal after holding a gun to your head for the better part of forty-five hours seems a little contradictory. I guess I'd say I'm not opposed to the idea of dying. Maybe I share a common Rantir belief...

Death in combat. The appeal of the idea goes both ways, apparently.

...I'm having a hard time figuring things out in my head lately.

After a few more long days, I finally see the ruins of a city silhouetted against the gray sky. The dark clouds make me think it's going to rain, as is typical in this place. I'd visited there a few times before the Rantir came. Whenever I went it was precipitating something. Everyone told me that's what you can expect from Seattle. The Emerald City. It was certainly greener now. Even from a few miles away, I could tell without optical enhancement that the skyscrapers were overgrown. Vines and moss clung to the sides of the stone towers, only leaving the occasional window free of their roots. It amazes me how much has changed since last I was here.

I make my way towards the city, following the highways still littered with abandoned cars and trucks, some filled with the skeletal remains of their owners. People who were trying to escape the city but didn't realize they were already dead from the air they breathed. I meander past an oil rig, tapping the side of it to see if there's anything left within. I can tell from the sound there's some fuel inside, so I pop a hole in the container large enough to fit my hand through. I can use some oil down the road for cleaning my weapons or for fire if needed. Beyond that, there are a couple other things I could do with it, and it never hurts to be prepared. I dip my arm inside. When I pull it out, it's covered with the familiar brownish-black substance. I look around for a container, eventually finding a plastic bottle inside one of the forgotten trucks. I fill it up, put the cap on, then place it in my small pack of possessions.

Continuing on, I reach what was once the docks of Seattle. Ships, or what's left of them, litter the bay. Some of them are still seaworthy. Others are capsized or sticking straight out the water, like mournful headstones paying tribute to the unforgiving sea. I debate for a few moments whether it'd be worth it to look inside them for anything ,then think otherwise. I came here to find survivors if I could, not supplies. The cold waters and only somewhat hospitable vessels aren't the best place for any human to live.

I work my way downtown, picking a path around the regular discarded items like cars and rubble, and the bones that accompany them. The plant life has really taken hold now. Trees maintained as saplings when humans resided here are now fully grown, some reaching heights of over eighty feet. I stop for a moment to admire them, marveling at how nature has truly thrived in such a prominent way.

Then, the ground where I would have been had I not stopped explodes in a shower of concrete and dust, followed by a shot ringing out.

My instincts kick in.

Whether it was good fortune or miscalculation on the shooter's part, I'm glad I wasn't hit. I look back at the damage done to the road I was just walking on, seeing a significant portion of it torn up by the impact of the round. It tells me what I need to know.

The shooter was firing a high powered rifle. The bullet hit before I heard the shot, which means they were over eight hundred yards away.

And they were good with a human weapon. Even though they missed, that was *damn* close. This is a first for me since Rantir don't utilize human technology.

Or they haven't until now…

I move behind a nearby van as another shot impacts, pelting the ground right behind me and sending a shower of dirt and leaves into the air. Again, the report comes after, making it difficult to track the origin as I scurry for cover. Another shot hits the corner of the van as I try to peer out from behind it in an attempt to find the sniper. From the ensuing sound, I think the weapon is military grade. The Rantir might have gotten ahold of it in an armory. Whatever the case, it's trying to kill me with it. It's also popping off rounds with abandon, despite the accuracy. Evidently, it has ammo to spare.

Ammo that I want, with I rifle I could definitely use.

I switch my vision over to thermal for a moment, hoping to get lucky and find a heat signature. When I peak my head out, I get grazed by a round, forcing me back behind cover. No significant damage but if I still had a heart, it'd be racing.

That was too close.

The shot does provide me some valuable insight into the situation. Diagnostics provide information about the angle of the groove on my head as well as the required velocity of the round to make it. I was right. About eight hundred yards out, an elevated position of approximately one hundred and thirty-seven feet based off calculations from the gathered information. The sniper is in a building straight ahead of me on the seventh floor.

I'm stuck in a street between two buildings. The nearest entrance to the structure on my right is about one hundred feet away. Too far for me to reach safely, even with mechanical assistance, and the stone walls of the structure are too thick for me to break through. An entrance is available directly across from me on my left, but I need to expose myself in order to reach it. Crossing the thirty-four foot expanse could be risky. Still, it's the best bet. I set a charge in my legs to launch myself out, then make the dash. A shot strikes the earth as I leave the van, but it's behind me. The shooter was waiting to ambush me the moment I left, anticipating my intended escape. Perceptive as they were, they couldn't have predicted I'd be capable of accelerating from zero to sixty miles per hour in under a second. I make the distance safely.

Smashing through the doors of what I think was an office building, I find myself skidding to a stop in the dark, even with my thermal vision activated. No heat here. Just cool, vegetative dampness. I shift spectrums, going to night vision. I need to find an exit that's out of my attacker's line of sight. Right now, since they've lost me, they're going to shift locations. That's what I'd do anyway. They're probably expecting me to go looking for them, so the best bet and clearest shot for them would be a new position in my direction with a clear view of their old vantage point to ambush me when I arrive. They'll need a spot that they can get to fast enough without me noticing them as I close the distance.

I change my mind. Instead of going directly for my enemy, I need to be somewhere high. This building is fairly tall. It'll do.

I make my way over to a window that's facing away from the sniper. I break through it, turn, then start burying my fingers and toes into the plant-covered concrete wall. I charge my arms and legs as I do so, then launch myself upward, making a giant leap up the vertical surface. I catch myself by anchoring into the wall at the peak of each jump, then repeat the process. In under a minute, I climb nearly two hundred feet to the roof of the office building.

Toward the sniper is a series of rooftops, some of which require further scaling, all of which provide me perfect vantages of the ground below along with adequate cover if I need it. The sniper would need to move out of the building, probably on the side not facing me so as to avoid any chance I'd have of spotting them. Regardless, they'll have to exit the structure, and I'll see them do it from a nearby perch. I need to get close enough without letting them know I'm there, however. And burying your hands and feet into solid concrete isn't exactly a silent endeavor, expeditious as it is. If they haven't heard me already, I'll be lucky.

Doesn't matter. I need to close the gap.

I start sprinting toward the nearest rooftop, leaping once I reach the end of my present structure. I soar through the air, easily clearing the gap between my previous rooftop and this one. The landings would be rough for a normal human, but I just leave a swath of shattered concrete where I touch down and keep running without losing momentum. The next rooftop is twenty feet above me. I sprint to the end of my current location, then set my legs for a charge. I release it, leaping the height and landing lightly as I jump exactly twenty-one feet high and sixty feet in length. I keep moving, repeating this process and improvising when needed. In one case, I use the remnants of an old crane to swing over a gap, cross the street, all the while maintaining my steady forward charge uninhibited.

Within three minutes, I close the gap and get to a vantage point of my choosing. I'm about eighty-five yards away from my attacker. I lay prone on the edge of the building, waiting for a chance to spot them. There's no way they could've navigated seven floors of a nearly ruined building in the time it took me to reach my perch. At least, not without me seeing something. There's also no way they could've known I'd be able to close the gap this fast.

But they might have heard me. If I were them, I'd be taking my time moving positions, just in case. And I wouldn't want to make a dumb mistake and give away the element of surprise. Turns out, my instincts are right again.

After a few moments, I see a small figure emerge from the corner of the building. They come out a side exit, like I'd anticipated, and they're heading to a different position. My logic is flawless thus far, save for one thing.

It's a woman I'm looking at. A living, breathing, *human* woman!

The fact that she was trying to take my head off with a powerful rifle suddenly disappears from any logical thought process.

A human! I can't even wrap my mind around it for a few moments as I watch her duck inside the building I'm perched on top of. I almost can't believe it. The very thing I've spent years searching for just ran into the building upon which I now sit. Normally I'd be about as giddy as a cybernetic organism could be.

Normally, people I meet don't try to kill me with powerful rifles too.

And she came close. I might be resilient in terms of structure, but a bullet to my head is just as lethal to me as any human if the round penetrates.

At least I think so.

She'd already grazed me once. The mark would be there for a long time to prove it. Directly above where my right eye would have been and running past my also absent ear. It's the first time I've been damaged by a human.

I almost don't mind.

I wait for her to get inside the structure, then slowly start making my way over to the crumbling roof access. I remove some debris from the rusted door, then check to see if the stairs are still intact. I find they are, so I start cautiously moving down them, hoping they'll support my weight. I have no way of telling what floor she's on, but I need to find her regardless. Unfortunately, I can't sense vibrations as well as the Rantir, or this task would be easy. Sonic registers are another story though, so I crank up my audio sensitivity and activate my sonar.

I hear all the animals moving through the structure down to the high-pitched whine of a mosquito meandering about the remnants of whatever kind of building this place was. At first I can't zero in on her location, but then I start to notice there's a lot more animal movement about a hundred feet below me. I wait for a moment, then listen to the same animals moving up the building. Either they've all taken to interspecies migration, or they're moving away from something.

Apparently she's working her way up the building, but in a very meandering and unpredictable way. Her erratic movements could be for a number of reasons. There could be debris preventing her from taking the maintenance stairs I'm currently utilizing. Maybe she's just being cautious. Whatever the case, the fact that the animals are scurrying away from something tells me there's someone there moving quickly enough to scare the creatures to safer locations throughout the edifice. And I sure as hell don't think there's another human around who just happened to enter this building the same time she and I did.

I start moving toward her, conscious of my well-being but still eager to find the survivor. I work my way down the steps with practiced precision only a machine can apply. Still, I'm in a hurry to be sure. After all, it's been years since I've seen a living human. And part of me is giddy at the prospect of having someone to talk to. I'd also really like a dialogue about more than how my conversation partner is going to kill me. Or how I need to finish them off like the Rantir outside the service station on I-90.

I reflect on how much I *need* this. How much I have to talk to them or at least just have someone else in my life. Especially in this world that seemed so pristine and perfect, but to me, couldn't be more dystopian or barren. There has to be more than just me journeying from one place to the next, finding one disappointment after another.

This is my first chance in years to confirm that theory.

I get down to her level, or at least what I think was her last location judging by the movement of the animals. I don't dare send out a ping for sonar, lest I give away my position. So now I return my audio sensors to standard sonic detection. (Which is still heightened compared to human standards.) I cautiously open the weathered door of the floor I think she's on. I find myself in what looks to be some kind of office building again. Cubicles and dividing walls litter this place along with the typical refuse and decay of the years. It all serves as a bleak reminder of the state of things, just like the ships at the docks. It seems like these testaments to human ingenuity are now nothing more than somber cairns marking the rise and fall of their makers.

But at least some of those makers are left, like the one I'm tracking right now. I hear a small shuffle from off to my left, but I don't see anything. There's ample shade and darkness in this place. The rain and veiled afternoon light add to this. I stop moving for a moment and just listen, hoping to hear something else, but there's only silence. I switch my optics to thermal settings and scan for any heat signatures. There's a few scattered animals here and there, per typical of the abandoned buildings of once great cities, but I can't make out a human shape. I continue to scan and finally see what I'm looking for.

There's a large heat register behind a section of decayed cubicle, curled up toward the edge of the building where a section of the wall has crumbled away. It reveals a clear line of site to the street below and also a perfect visual of the sniper's previous position.

29

However, I'm surprised to discover she isn't looking out into the street waiting to ambush me. She's looking in my direction. Or rather, she has her gun leveled at the position where I'm going to be if I take two more steps forward.

I have no idea how she heard me or how she knew I was here, but in this moment, I have bigger problems than figuring out her methods of perception. I know how accurate she is with that rifle at great distances, so it doesn't take a genius to know she could hit me easily from here. I change my approach, but draw my .45 and keep it pointed in her direction, just in case I can't convince her I'm not here to hurt her.

"I'm no threat," I call out.

There's a moment of silence and I watch her visually tense behind the cubicle wall.

She wasn't prepared for that.

She takes a breath, then gets to her feet, keeping her rifle leveled on me the entire time. She emerges from her hiding spot and my primary functions begin their full assessment of a possible threat.

Five foot six, one hundred and twenty-four pounds. A lean and fit physique with an elevated heart rate at the moment. No debilitating wounds or conditions. She's in perfect health and excellent physical condition.

That's what the machine part of me saw.

I saw a strong woman with strawberry blonde hair, hazel eyes, and genuine fear tempered with resolution in what she was doing. The way she controlled her anxiety denoted years of training and discipline, and I wonder what she used to be before the attacks, especially if she's carrying a rifle that I now confirm is military grade. I see a woman who's been crafted into a perfect survivor for this world. She wears a tactical vest, cinched tight to her and loaded with extra magazines, a 9mm sidearm, survival knife strapped to her leg, cargo pants, leather boots, and all of her shrouded in a homemade ghillie suit that's been modeled into a hooded cloak reminiscent of the medieval ages. She stands sure and confident in front of me. She's unshakable, and I suppose she's had to be over the years. I don't think she's over thirty-two, which tells me she's been surviving in this world for a long time.

No simple task, even for me. The fact that she could do it was impressive.

"No threat huh?" she asks, daring to take a step forward.

I shake my head.

"Kinda hard to believe," she states.

I almost chuckle. "I can understand that."

"You can?" she snaps. "You understand something moving as fast as you on foot *and* climbing up the side of a building is no threat? Even though it's pointing a gun at me right now?"

The way she says "it" stings me, even though I can't blame her for it. Again I'm reminded of my current circumstance, despite the fact that I'm granted so many physical advantages.

I have to wonder for a second how well my psychological state is faring.

I shake those ideas from my thoughts. "I'll lower mine if you lower yours."

"That's not gonna happen," she answers.

"Then we're at a bit of an impasse."

"I guess so."

There's a tense, awkward silence.

Then I speak. "Why were you shooting at me?"

"Wouldn't you? I don't even know what you are and you're coming towards me like you have an agenda."

I shrug, then decide I need to play the diplomat. I lower my gun, then holster it. "That proof enough I'm not here for you?"

"Hell no," she shoots back. "But it's a start."

"I'm here looking for survivors," I state.

"Survivors?" she asks. "Not much left to survive for. The robot plague is gone. Just a few pockets of it left here and there. Mostly underground. Whoever hasn't survived that has been wiped out by those bastards they left behind."

"The feral Rantir," I inform her. "I know. But that's why I'm looking so hard."

"So what does that make you?" she interjects.

What *does* that make me? In truth, I haven't been able to answer that question in a long time. I honestly didn't know anymore, just like I'd thought a couple days ago at the gas station where I killed the Rantir. But that wasn't much of an answer to give her. After all, I needed to convince her I wasn't her enemy.

"No threat to you," I answer as honestly as I can.

"Right," she reluctantly concedes. "You wanna take off that armor now? That's some pretty serious hardware."

If I could sigh, I'd do it. "That's...complicated."

She eyes me warily now, and I can see her grip tighten on her rifle. "You some kind of government secret or what?"

What do I say? How can anyone answer this question properly?

"The short version of it is I can't take the armor off, all right? I don't really know what I am."

"Then you'll understand when I keep my safety off," she adds. "Are you with them? The Rantir, or whatever you call them? Some kind of diplomat?"

"No, I'm not," I reply. "I've been against them for going on twenty some years. Just trying to survive out here."

"You know, I've seen a lot of weird stuff," she begins. "But you're at the top of that list so far. Even more than aliens. You're something different."

Tell me about it.

"I know," I answer. "I wish I could tell you more but the truth is you know about as much as I do concerning what I am."

"I still don't trust you."

"Haven't tried to kill you yet, have I?"

"'Yet.'"

"You're four up on me in that department. How many more rounds do you have left anyway?"

That lifts her eyebrows. I guess she never thought about it until this moment. Again, I can't blame her for that.

I start again. "Look, I know you're right to distrust whatever isn't human. But I *was* human once. That much I do know. Whatever happened to me that turned me into this...I can't say."

She tilts her head, analyzing me for a moment. "I'd say that makes the most sense right now, oddly enough." She lowers her rifle. "I guess I'll know pretty soon if you mean what you say."

"How's that?"

She starts moving toward me. "Because you have a really good chance to kill me right now. I'm coming in for a closer look."

She's true to her word, approaching me with that same tempered discipline over her fear she's held this whole time. I don't know what she's been through to gain that much composure, but it shows. She walks right up to me without hesitation, though I can tell she's ready to react if I make a move. Fortunately, even though she doesn't know it, she has no need to worry.

When she gets closer, I keep my gaze locked with hers. I track her with my "eyes," even though I can't emote. Not with an armored metal mask. And at this moment, I sure wish I could. I start to see the shape of her face with its angular, pronounced features. She's not malnourished. It's clear she's eating well and her chiseled features aren't a result of a poor diet. I can tell she's been carved and formed from a life on the move. The constant state of urgency that has become our world has taken its toll on her, but it could be just as easily argued that it's developed her into something more...enhanced.

Like me maybe.

Her eyes, with their sharp edges, scan me thoroughly. She goes up and down the creature that is me standing before her, and I see her noting anything she finds unique. She lingers for a bit on my sidearm, then locks her gaze on my sword. She pays particular attention to my hands, noting the individual, mechanized digits I possess, equal in number to her own. She shifts her focus to my face, then gets close enough to touch me. As she does this, I notice her finger never leaves the trigger of her rifle.

She puts a hand on my face, and though I can't feel it, there is a great relief that comes with recognizing human contact after years of its absence. She turns my head to the side, running her hand along the groove recently put there by her marksmanship. She then brushes her palm along my shoulder, scraping off some dust and bringing it to her nose. She takes a few sniffs, then lightly tastes a bit of it.

"You don't smell like one of them," she says. "But you've definitely been around them, haven't you?"

"I think they made me," I answer honestly.

"You said you were human once," is her reply.

I shrug again. "Right. *Once*. I remember dying. Then I remember waking up like this."

She looks into my visor. "Really?"

I see what I believe to be a trace of sympathy there. Maybe even pity. I'm somewhat surprised I don't see skepticism. Then again, I don't have a reason to lie.

"I had a life," I tell her. "A family..."

"Had?"

I nod, casting my gaze in any direction but hers. The memories are still fresh to me. They might as well have happened yesterday. "My name is Ferroc."

She eyes me curiously. "'Ferroc?' That sounds like something they would say."

"Because it's what they call me now," I explain. "The Rantir, I mean. And they're the only things I've had any dialogue with for a while."

"You'd think you wouldn't want to name yourself using the language of a species that wiped out ours," she points out.

"I use it because it's been said by every one of them I've killed. No one else around to call me who I once was either."

That gives her pause, but not for long. "You hunt them?"

"Not 'hunt them,'" I explain. "I defend myself. They have a knack for finding me."

She seems to glare at me, though I can't quite make out if she's uncertain or hateful of what I just said. "There's one more thing we have in common then."

"What do you mean?" I ask.

"They both seem to find us. Or in my, case, I want them to think they have." She taps her rifle suggestively in her own threatening way.

It's my turn for a moment of surprise. I'd like to think I give off the required energy from behind my stoic visage. Even if I can't emote the way she can, she gives the impression she understands what I'm feeling. A human who ambushes Rantir is no small thing considering the distinct advantages their species possess over our own. It's already a miracle she's survived this long on the surface among the feral aliens and what's left of the robotic plague. Now, I learn she's killing Rantir when she can, and that's a good reason to be more than a little surprised.

Well, she did nearly kill me, so I can't say I'm totally taken off-guard by what she spends her time doing.

"What you mean is *you* hunt them," I state.

She nods. "On occasion."

"That's why you asked me, isn't it?"

She shrugs. "It would make the most sense to me, given what you are."

I let out a helpless chuckle, turning my head away from her to some unseen focal point.

"Something funny?"

It's my turn to shrug. "Just the way you say 'what' instead of 'who.' I guess I'd do the same."

She narrows her eyes at me. Not threateningly, but inquisitively. I think she's trying to get a real bearing on who *and* what I

34

really am. I can't help but feel like she's done that ever since she closed the distance between us so we could speak face to face. It seems like she's always observing, analyzing, and calculating. I can understand the mindset. I've done the same thing many times.

I'm shaken from my contemplations when I hear a disturbance on the street below us, followed by the familiar roar of a Rantir; a noise akin to a lion's cry blended with a screeching undertone. She and I both ready our weapons. She shoulders her rifle as I draw my sidearm. The two of us carefully work our way to the edge of the building, trying to obtain a visual of the target. We reach the edge and see three Rantir circling one another in a less than friendly manner. They're speaking with one another, so I activate my translation protocols.

"Stay out of my way and you won't get hurt!" a large female states. With her blue toned skin, I see she's fully matured and even bigger than the one I fought on I-90. It looks like she and a male are together. He's wearing a helmet with a large spike on it and he's slightly smaller.

Another female across from them isn't fazed. "I'm only hunting. I'm no enemy!"

"I've been tracking this prey since the mountains," the large one claims. "He killed one of ours."

"Ours?" the smaller one asks. "You mean those that abandoned us here with the humans? I don't see how they're still our kin."

"Regardless..."

The sentence finishes the moment a loud shot interrupts the Rantir female. The ensuing bullet tears through her eye socket and into her brain. I turn to face the woman next to me to discover she's already cycled another round with one fluid motion of the bolt-action. She's never taken her eyes off her target and she fires again. This shot isn't as accurate with the other Rantir already moving. Still, that first shot was amazing. Even with a rifle like that assisting her, she needed to hit the eye from a distance of more than a hundred feet from an elevated position.

That's damn impressive. No wonder she's survived out here.

She stops firing and slings the rifle over her shoulder, running off to the western side of the building. I follow. We come to a halt at the edge of the structure where the wall has crumbled away. It looks like it was destroyed by some kind of explosion. Possibly a remnant of Rantir sweeper teams clearing this area.

"You think that was smart?" I ask, still trying to figure out what her angle is. I can hear the Rantir below us tearing their way through the building and I know we don't have much time.

"You say you're not here to hurt me?" she responds. "Prove it. Follow me."

She pulls out a small backpack from under her ghillie suit and withdraws what looks like some kind of gear and pulley device. It must be custom made, because I've never seen anything like it. She points to the building across from us and I notice another hole in the side of that structure. More importantly, I see there's a cable running from our position to that one. She's got some kind of zip line system developed.

"Done this before," I say more to myself than her.

Still, she hears me. "You think I didn't have a plan?" And for a moment, I swear I see her crack the slightest of grins. It's almost like she's enjoying herself now.

She finishes rigging up her trolley, then clips a line to her belt.

"By the way...You make it through this, I'm going to have a lot more questions," she says as she pushes off, soaring away from me over the street below.

"Me too," I reply, though she can't hear me for certain this time.

I wait for her to finish her journey across the span before attempting to do the same. I wonder where my trolley device is for navigating the expanse. Then I remember I'm a machine and grabbing the line won't hurt.

Funny thing to forget...My life is so confusing sometimes.

Locking my hands around the cable, I glide over the street below, a trail of sparks blazing behind me. I land, finding my new companion crouched and ready to fire at the opening where we just were. I look back with her, leveling my .45 and acting as her spotter. I enhance my vision and set it to thermal spectrum. The cracks and breaks in the windows of the building provide enough openings for me to track our enemy's movements.

"One target on the floor," I tell her. "Back of the room, approaching the opening."

"You can see that?" she asks, eyes unflinching from the scope.

"Yes," I reply. "The other one is on the floor below tearing up the place."

Now we wait for them. This woman and I know we're better off letting them come to our position.

Silence, at least between she and I, sets in as we wait for them to give us a target. We sit completely still, listening to them rummage through the building we just occupied. Finally, after what seems like an eternity, I see the enemy on our previous floor moving toward the opening where the zip line originates.

"Target approaching, twelve o-clock," I tell her. "Thirty-seven feet away from the opening."

"Got it," she calmly replies, adjusting her scope. Then we wait some more.

Thanks to my thermal vision, I watch as the Rantir stops, almost as if it sensed our ambush. It holds up a hand, indicating it's "listening" for vibrations through the air. The only noise I can hear beyond the ambient wind is the very soft and steady breathing of the woman next to me. That silence ends the moment the Rantir roars, charging for the opening and leaping toward us. It's the other female. A shot cracks the air. I see it connect with her torso, blasting right through her belly. That doesn't stop her though, and she lands right in front us.

I was already in motion after she went airborne. When she lands, she lashes out with her scythes. I have my sword ready and slash upward, cutting into the two appendages lunging for my new companion. They're not bladed, but they could still strike her, crush her, or if they grabbed ahold, throw her off the ledge we're precariously close to.

I couldn't put my full, mechanical strength behind the strike, but I still give the alien a deep cut to both of her scythes. She reels back as I raise my left arm, leveling my .45 on her face. My targeting programs line up the sights in under .01 seconds as the Rantir regains her composure. I squeeze the trigger four times and four bullets tear through the Rantir's eyes. She spasms for a few moments, then staggers back off the building, lifelessly falling to the street. A dull thud echoes from below a few moments later.

The other one, having heard the commotion, appears in the opening a shortly after. Another shot is fired.

I have to give credit to the woman I've just met. She hasn't even flinched during the skirmish I'd had in front of her. Instead, she's been covering the opening, never taking her scope off the potential area of opportunity. She doesn't hit her intended mark, but I couldn't expect anyone to make that shot with the short amount of time she'd been allowed. The Rantir does take a round to the head though, even if the bullet didn't penetrate his helmet. The impact staggers him backward. He then crouches low, out of our line of sight.

"He's not going to come back out," I say. "He'll wait for his moment."

"Then let's get down to the street," she replies, rising to her feet.

I stop her. "No. Then he'll have elevation on us."

She eyes me curiously. "Then what do you want to do?"

"The roof." I point up. "No ambushes. You can put your rifle to work."

She looks up, then back to me skeptically. "Not a lot of room up there. I'm not exactly comfortable with close quarters."

"Don't worry about that," I comfort her, gesturing with my sword. "He'll have to deal with me if things get tight."

"Pretty confident, aren't you?"

I'm not entirely sure why, but I'm pissed off at that remark. It might be her mocking tone. Maybe it's the way I've just defended her even after she'd made several concentrated efforts to kill me, and now she won't even listen to a strategic suggestion. It could be how my gestures of cooperation have been met with disdain. Or maybe it's the way I'm still treated as an "it" when I feel I've given her sufficient evidence I'm a "who." Whatever the case, it's time to make a point.

I march over to the stone wall, sheathing my sword and holstering my .45. I charge the hydraulics in my arm and unleash a devastating punch that takes out half the barrier, further exposing the side of the building as the rain pours in. As the dust begins to settle, I turn back to her, hoping she grasps a fraction of what I'm capable of when I'm in a weaponized mindset.

"Then stay," I offer. "Make shots from here. Because this would be better than getting ambushed on the street."

Silence.

"No?" I ask. "OK. Then listen. I'm here to help. You may hunt these things, but I sure as hell know how to *fight* them. Right now, you have no element of surprise. So, you can trust me when I say we should go to the roof, or we can take our chances on the street and let him get the drop on us. The second option isn't going to end well, but I won't force a decision on you. Just know what you decide matters to me because you may be the only human left in the country. Believe me, I've looked. Don't get killed over a stupid call when someone else is offering you the solution."

There's a long, awkward silence between us.

"And it's not overconfidence or bravado," I continue. "It's a certainty I've earned after fighting these things for years."

"What are you?" she asks, her tone heavy with incredulity. "Some kind of robot protector?"

I shake my head in disgust. "Won't make much difference if you're dead, will it?"

She scoffs. "I'm heading to the street. You might know how to fight them, but how do you think I've survived this long?"

Damn it.

"Fine," I concede. "But is it going to kill you if I tag along?"

She gives me a very sarcastic grin. "Not at all. Will it kill you?"

Maybe...

I also entertain fantasies about what telling her "I won't say I told you so," is going to feel like.

She moves out with efficiency, in a hurry to reach the false sanctuary she believes lies on ground level. I keep pace easily enough, though I have to will myself to take every step since I know I'm going right into a trap. This Rantir is pissed, ready, and fully aware of what we're capable of. He's not going to give me an opening like his companion did. He knows not to sit still long enough for either of us to line up a shot. And he's got that helmet that even a rifle couldn't pierce. I'm betting he's going to come in hard and fast. On the roof, this wouldn't have been an issue. We'd have open visibility to every possible line of attack. On the street, he's got the high ground, and we're running blind.

Doesn't seem to matter too much. I'm going along anyway, following this woman who I'm glad to see but want to grab and shake at the same time. She's got the escape routes out of this building down, and we easily exit the premises in under a few minutes. We get to the street through an emergency exit, only to be greeted by ominous silence, save for the ambient noise of rain.

I could set my audio sensors to sonar, but to do so would probably do more harm than good. He'll just hide behind a wall and be that much more aware of my capabilities and the fact that I'm actively scanning for him when he hears the ping. So, I accept that this isn't exactly going to be a good day. Whatever happens from here, I just hope I can keep her safe. It's about all I've got going for me right now.

We make our way down the street with her on point and heading north. She motions to me with simple but clear hand signals as

I keep an eye above us at all times. Whenever she stops, I take a moment to adjust to thermal vision and scan the floors and rooftops.

I know we're being hunted. I can just...feel it. There's a lingering sense of tension in the air. The only thing that could make things more ominous would be a clap of thunder or gust of wind. It feels like some kind of standoff against an unseen entity.

I'm truly appreciating the full, deadly capability of Rantir evolution now. Before they became so technologically advanced, it seems like their predacious stature was suited for hunting prey even more dangerous than themselves and in perfect anonymity. The soft, ultra-sensitive pads not only received kinetic signals, they silenced the Rantir's footfalls completely. They were also incredibly versatile. I'd seen Rantir climb trees and rock faces with ease, almost as if their pads melded with the surface they were scaling for increased adhesion. I think about that and realize the only way we're going to hear him coming is if he's clumsy enough to step on some crushed glass or rubble.

Real good chance of that happening.

I move up behind her. She's crouched behind an old tow truck, leaning against one of the large tires and peaking over the bed of the vehicle.

"Still thinking we should've gone to the roof?" she asks.

"Yes," I answer flatly, too distracted by searching for any possible threats to take her jab the way she'd intended.

She's being a cocky little bitch right now anyway.

She shrugs, then goes back to scanning the street in front of us. She moves off again, running for a tunnel. I'm glad to see that's where we're going. At least then it'll be that much easier to anticipate an attack.

She makes it to the lip and waits for me. I stand to run after her, then get pummeled from the side and down onto the concrete. Whatever hit me grabs onto me, rolls with our momentum, then uses it as leverage to throw me into the side of a building. I leave a spider web pattern on the concrete where I impacted, then try to grab onto something and stabilize myself when I feel I'm being lifted off the ground. It's too late, and I'm flung across the street again, slamming into the tow truck I was just hiding behind.

I get to my feet and face my attacker. As I do so, analysis of structural damages flash across my vision. Diagnostics inform me of a deep puncture to the upper left side of my chest. Hydraulic systems to my left arm are disabled. Nanobots are being administered to halt excess fluid leakage. Other than that, internal scans inform me I'm functioning as nominally as possible.

When I find my target, I see him waiting for me, crouched down and ready to pounce. He's got his bladed scythes up in the air, ready to strike. I notice he doesn't have any blades on his wrists, but he's got that custom helmet with a large spike at its center. That explains the damage that I took from the initial hit.

I reach for my .45 but it's not there. I look around for a moment, then see it lying at the base of the building I was slammed into. Now I expect to hear a shot, as has become so regular during these encounters on the streets of Seattle, but there's only the breathing of the Rantir in front of me. I look over to the lip of the tunnel and find that she's gone.

Gone...

I feel so betrayed. She was looking right at me. She couldn't have missed the attack. Even if she'd started to leave, she'd have heard the commotion behind her. The only explanation I have for her disappearance is that she ditched me. She took the opportunity to leave and save herself. In her mind, I was probably nothing more than a "robot protector," as she called me.

Apparently, I was expendable.

The Rantir snarls, slowly stalking toward me. "I saw what you did to my kind, Ferroc."

If I could glare, I'd love to do so now. I activate my linguistics programs, speaking in his native tongue. "More than your kind did for mine. At least I offered mercy."

"You humans should have thought about that before starting a war you couldn't finish," he counters, continuing his advance.

"You guys jumped in the middle of a human conflict," I counter. "Then you never listened to our pleas for understanding." I advance a step myself. "Looks to me like the war between our kinds is pretty finished. Aren't many humans left, are there?"

He growls again. "Why do you seek to rejoin your race, Ferroc? You can never be one of them again."

He may be right. "Why do you keep calling me that? That supposed to be some kind of insult? I'd like to know since I've taken it as a name."

He snarls in response.

41

"I gather that offends you," I continue. "Guess the name is something complimentary then, huh?"

That gets a reaction. He leaps for me, aiming low to sweep my legs. I jump up and slightly back, letting him slam into the tires of the tow truck as I nimbly land on top of the vehicle. He quickly regains his feet and makes a sweep for my legs with one of his scythes. I leap back again, then notice the cable and winch from the tow truck is still fully intact, albeit a little rusted. Without the full enhancement of my hydraulics working in both arms, my swings and cuts with my sword won't be as powerful. So, I rely on physics to help me out.

I rip the cable and hook out from the winch, then snap off a thirty foot length and the hook. The Rantir is already closing on me, so I set the end to swinging. Motion tracking and proximity sensors tell me how far the hook is from me, as well as its speed, giving me the information I need to make this improvised weapon as lethal as possible while avoiding damage to myself.

I spin, snapping the hook out at my closing enemy. He ducks underneath it, so I spin again, bringing the hook back around for another attack. The Rantir doesn't expect me to be this quick, and catches the hook to the side of his face as it comes around for its second revolution. The force of the hit is enough to send him reeling back and off the bed of the tow truck. I pull the cable tight, grasping the hook and ready to set it into a deadly swing once again.

He shakes his head and glares at me. Only now do I notice the dent I've put in the side of his helmet. If I could grin, I'd do so. I feel pretty accomplished with what I've done. Besides, he already left a mark on me. It's only right to return the favor.

He makes a good focal point for my ire.

He stays crouched on all fours, ready to pounce at me. Without hesitation, I begin to swing my improvised flail. If I'm going on the offensive, I'm staying on it, otherwise stopping could give him an opening I can't afford. And I'm not seeing much choice other than attack. These Rantir seem to recognize basic and effective means of melee combat, even if they're prone to anger and aggression from years of exile on Earth.

At least he's not throwing things at me.

I spin again, building the deadly force I need. The hook sails toward my enemy. He ducks underneath, then leaps toward me, horn leading the way. I dodge to my right as he lands atop the bed of the tow truck and pivots, lunging toward me again. I keep my spin going, performing the same maneuver I did before, pulling the hook in tighter. Again, my enemy avoids the hit, this time dodging back, but now I adjust the angle of my attack. I tilt my body, leaping off my right leg and performing a barrel roll as the cable launches from me. The hook goes up and over my spinning form, plummeting down toward the Rantir as I guide it back to earth. He dodges back again, and the hook slams into the bed of the tow truck, splintering the wood and breaking clean through our platform.

He lashes out with one of his bladed scythes, attacking my right shoulder. I pull the cable tight and block the attack, then block another coming from my left with the same tactic. He presses his advance, attacking my torso with another swing of his scythe, and yet again with a slash for my legs. I dodge the first and jump over the second, giving the cable a good yank as I do so. The hook catches on the planking of the tow truck bed, pulling a board with it as it snaps up and out from under the Rantir. The hook clips him under the chin as I pull it to me, giving him a solid hit as it does so. I land on the roof of the truck, hook in hand and ready for him once more.

He snarls, then leaps for me, scythes leading the way this time. I duck under him and his two horizontal cuts as he flies overhead, standing my ground atop the tow truck. I take this opening to make a lasso out of the cable by latching the hook onto it, then wait. He lands, pivots, and launches toward me with the same alacrity he did before. This time his horn leads the way, scythes cocked and ready to attack the moment he gores me. I leap up and over him, summersaulting and tossing my lasso for his head as I do so. When I feel I've snared his neck, I tuck my feet under me and pull as hard as I can, cinching the cable tight around his throat.

He pulls me with enough force to drag me along for the rest of his leap. I hit the ground hard. So great is the impact I actually break through the tarmac and leave two long grooves in the street where my feet grind it to pieces. I'm forced to engage the hydraulics in my legs after my toes have locked before I can finally stop. Now we're in a tug of war, and I'm not exactly sure what I can do beyond keep my distance from him. He'll just come towards me if I try to choke him out, but at least I have some level of control with the leash I've put him in.

He starts circling me slowly with a very displeased expression on his face. That's what I can tell from behind his helmet anyway. I keep the cable tight, not wanting him to slip from the lasso. He takes a few swings at it with his scythe, but they don't cut through the wire. Then, with a growl, he circles me, seeking an opening. We eventually switch positions, and now I notice the street sign arching over the mouth of the tunnel and indicating the roads that lead to the remains of interstate 5 and a few others. The steel structure has held up well, and the sign looks like it could support what I'm about to put it through.

I charge the hydraulics in my legs, still keeping the cable tight as I do so. At this point, my enemy knows better than to come at me so aggressively, so there's opportunity for what I'm hoping to accomplish.

I leap into the air, accelerating up and over him toward the street sign at seventy miles per hour. He holds his ground as I crash into the sign, hand extended and leading the way. My hand, arm, shoulder, and body break through the sign as I continue to torpedo past it. Damage analysis confirms only cosmetic destruction to my exterior. I twist my body to face my enemy, then lock my hands around the cable and charge my legs for another leap when I land.

The cable goes tight, and the remaining force I have from my leap is enough to yank the Rantir into the air and towards the sign. The hole I punched through it isn't big enough for him, so he catches himself against the sign with his hands and feet just over the opening. This stops my initial flight and I fall to the street below, still grasping the cable. The moment my feet touch, I release my charge and accelerate back towards him as quick as I can, pulling the cable to me to keep it tight, and more importantly, keep him pinned against the sign. I can already see him tugging at the noose he's in, so I need to be quick. Once I get underneath him, I leap straight up, still reeling in lengths of cable as I do so. I end my jump right next to him, giving one last tug to pull me to the metal framework holding the sign and landing upon it with my back to my foe.

I essentially have him stuck in an improvised pulley system now. He's the weight with a lasso around his neck, and I'm the force. I want to keep him like this, so when I get close enough, I throw a shoulder into him to pin him against the sign still further. I lock my left hand around the cable, hoping my compromised hydraulics will hold as I strain to keep it tight, then draw my sword with my right. I charge my right arm for a moment, then shove him hard into the sign to create distance and give me the opening I need. With the line still tight, he's too busy trying to free himself from the cable to dodge or block when I unleash my charge with as much force as I can. I'm trying to sever his scythes at the shoulder as I make my cut. I feel the blade impact the bone and fortunately I have enough power behind the swing to slice through them both. His appendages fall twitching to the ground below as he starts to howl, but I cut that cry of pain short when I throw my shoulder back into him and lock my toes around the frame of the sign arch. I'm not moving now, so I pull with all I've got. My mechanical gears strain against his strength as he tries to break free of the noose I have around his neck.

The sign begins to bend, metal groaning in protest as the resistance applied against it is multiplied. Still, the opening I created is too small for my enemy to fit through. The cable is straining, and I can hear it audibly twanging as the tension increases. I also hear the Rantir start to gurgle, then nothing but silence as I start to win in our tug of war and his airway is blocked. I notice blood starting to flow from his neck as the cable bites into it. I begin to stand up straighter as more length of cable is freed, which means the noose is getting tighter and tighter. I hear a pop as I feel even more length of cable release. His windpipe is crushed from the gradual constriction. The resistance on the other end of the line is lessening. His movements are getting sluggish. Finally, he goes still altogether, and there's only silence.

I release the cable. The body of my enemy and I both fall to the street below. I land on my feet. He lands limply with a sickening thud. I don't want to turn around and look at him. It's been a brutal fight and I'm not proud of it. Even though I provoked him, the magnitude of taking a life like this again makes me feel disturbed by what I am. It seems like even if I'm trying to survive in this world, I'm almost too well-suited for it. I'm the perfect fighting machine, in any situation, with whatever I can find. The body I inhabit is engineered for war. My mind is starting to think like a weapon.

And this time, I have to wonder if that's exactly what I am. I told myself just a few days ago that I'm more than just the metal and alloy that composes me. I don't know if I can believe that in this moment after I've just savagely ended the life of another Rantir. Especially after a human abandoned me, despite my efforts to save her.

So...What *does* that make me? Sitting here alone, unfeeling despite the damage done to me... That is, unfeeling in pain or sense of physical affliction. I'm certainly hurting emotionally. But does that make me more than a weapon? Especially if I'm so good at being just that? It seems like that's all that I've been since I've come back from my trip north. The one time I meet a human in five years, and she leaves me without hesitation to a Rantir bent on killing us.

I feel angry and deceived. My head tells me I should just let it go and continue on my way. If she wants to take her chances out here in this world, fine. She's survived this long. And she's proven she doesn't need me around to protect her. Let her go her own way. Then again, my instinct is telling me to pursue her because I'll never get the chance to again. She probably isn't worth this much effort if she's willing to sell me out like she just did. But then, what else am I going to do? For that matter, what's so pressing anywhere else that I need to keep moving?

I know I should stay here and initiate repairs, but I can't afford to give her that much distance. My internal systems are functioning at eighty percent capacity while secondary repair protocols are in effect. This means I can still cover a lot of ground and not have to worry about stopping all activity for restoration. Fixing myself is going to take longer if I keep moving, but that's a small price to pay.

What the hell...What's it going to hurt?

Besides, I have a few choice words I'd like to say, and that alone is reason enough for me to go after her.

I retrieve my .45, then go back to the tunnel and activate thermal vision. Any residual heat she could have left is gone, so I switch over to night vision. There's a layer of dust on the tunnel floor, along with a well-worn path leading through it. I start to follow her.

A thought occurs to me.

She could be setting a trap. For the Rantir or myself...I'm not sure. Whatever the case, if she wants me dead, I doubt she's going to miss this time. But, I don't really care anymore. I've had my gun against my head on more than one occasion thinking that would be the best course. What's the difference if she just pulled the trigger for me?

Chapter 2

Tracking her isn't difficult. The path has been used many times before, and anywhere it branches in a different direction my night vision easily spots the floating dust particles left by someone recently passing by. I follow her trail through the tunnel, over and under the remains of cars and trucks, through a maintenance corridor, and up a ladder to the surface. I emerge a little beyond I-5 towards Capitol Hill, or what's left of it beneath the overgrowth. Her trail isn't as easy to follow anymore now that we're on the exposed tarmac and concrete. There are no heat traces and no dust to track her with. Instead, I resort to the animals around the area.

They're not afraid of me. For one reason or another, I can always pass by without them minding too much. Usually they just go around me or get out of my way, maintaining visual contact to ensure their safety. But they never outright *run* from me. However, from the few people I've been with over the years, I've noticed animals generally harbor an old fear of humanity from before the Rantir attack. The woman I'm tracking may have already passed, but the animals should still be spooked. Or at least, a little on edge as I make my way through the area.

Sure enough, I start to notice signs from the wildlife. The birds don't provide much assistance. They sit on the rooftops, safe from any threats from the ground. However, as I look upward for any clues to the woman's whereabouts, the squirrels give me insight into her direction. In front of me, they're up in their trees or just coming out from their holes. On my left, they're on the street, foraging for food and going about their daily routines. To my right, it's the same. As I follow signs like this, I start gaining confidence as my theory is confirmed. Rabbits are doing very much the same as the squirrels, and a group of deer immediately freeze the moment I make myself known. Normally they wouldn't have cared if I was there or not. Now, they need to confirm I'm not hunting them like a human. For all I know, she may very well have stalked these animals before, which only helps me in this situation.

The rain has been reduced to a light mist as I track her to a housing area. They're not easy to spot, but I can see faint footprints going across a yard. They disappear behind the wooden fence of a house next to it. When I approach, I notice the boards are set in place, but they're loose. I move them aside, then replace them after I step through. On this side of the fence, there's another worn path amidst the overgrown grass leading to the back of the house. It's underneath a thick canopy of saplings and bushes. It's completely invisible to any view from above, and without entering through the fence, would have remained just as unseen from the street. I follow it, arriving at the back door of the house. I twist the knob, but find it's locked. Or barred. Part of me wants to just kick it in because I could. I'm not exactly pleased with her, after all.

But I take a different approach. I just knock, waiting to see what she'll do.

I enhance my audio sensors, listening for any movement inside. I do so in time to hear the sound of a bolt slowly sliding a round into the chamber. This is followed by the sound of a sidearm cautiously being wracked.

I chuckle softly, still irritated with her but amused by the whole situation. "You really think a Rantir is going to knock?" There's silence inside the house now. "I know you're in there. If I wanted you dead, you'd be dead already."

I hear her stand up, then come to the door. "How am I supposed to know you weren't followed?"

"I don't know. You didn't stick around to find out. You going to open this door?"

I adjust my audio sensors to their default level when I hear metal grind against metal, then slide across what I'm assuming is some sort of locking mechanism. When the door swings open, I can tell it's been reinforced with iron or steel by the way it slowly but steadily pivots on its hinges.

"What do you want?" she asks, stepping into the threshold and looking into my "eyes." She's standing stiffly, almost like she's a soldier at full attention. I can tell I'm making her nervous. Maybe she's ashamed of her actions.

Good. Nervous, afraid, embarrassed...I can't say I care so long as she's uncomfortable. I want her to know I'm pissed, even if I act with a sense of temperament.

"I just want to know why you left me to die," I answer. "Then I'll leave. You seem like you prefer solitude anyway."

"I think you're being a little dramatic," she replies.

"Am I? From what I can tell, you took an opportunity to save your own ass at my expense. I stuck my neck out for you, *after* you shot at me, then you just ditch me as a distraction for the Rantir that you picked a fight with. How far off am I?"

She's silent.

"Yeah...That's what I thought. The street might have been your best option. I can see that now. You had your escape planned from the start, which you could have just told me. But the rooftop could have helped us both out. At least I was thinking of you when I made that call."

She looks sincerely hurt by what I've said, but she remains defiant. "Well, aren't you chivalrous. Just so you know, I didn't ask for your help."

I snort. Or make the noise that resembles that. "Right. You didn't. But I gave it anyway. Glad we got that cleared up."

"So you tracked me down just to say this?" she asks. "You are the weirdest fucking thing I've ever seen, you know that? This making you feel better? Because I'm not sure I give a shit."

She's really pissing me off.

"No," I begin. "I didn't come here to say that. I came here because after five years of searching for a single survivor, I finally found one. And she left me to the Rantir the first chance she got, even though, from what I can tell, I'm the first thing in years that hasn't tried to kill her outright. I just want to know why you did that, then I'll leave you alone."

She's silent again for a few moments, then responds. "I don't trust you, 'Ferroc.' That a good enough answer? I don't even know what you are."

I guess that's as good of an answer as any, but I don't find it sufficient. We've already established that neither of us know "what I am." That didn't stop her from having me follow her across the cable, then provide cover. It didn't stop her from starting a fight with the Rantir that I then had to spend valuable resources finishing for her.

"I don't know what you want from me," I tell her. "Clearly I'll never be able to win your trust with any action, even though they've been backing up my words pretty well. But fine. Your answer is fair enough."

A wave of hopelessness washes over me as I comprehend the reality of my circumstance. The cold, hard truth is now I actually believe what that Rantir told me on the street. He's right. I can't return to my own kind. No matter what I do or how many humans I protect and save. The reality is I'll always remain what I am. I'm stuck in this body until I'm killed or until I finally just kill myself. As I look at her, I only see the same desolation that I find in the bountiful and overgrown world I've wandered for years. All these things that, if I were human, would be a veritable paradise with boundless opportunities for growth and renewal.

To me, they're just bleak reminders of a human life I once knew but I'll never again call my own.

I turn and start heading for the fence, making sure I take the path she's carved through the grass after many trips to and from this place. I don't want her to be found and killed because of me.

"Wait!" she calls out. "That's it?"

I don't turn around. "That's it."

"That's all you wanted?" she asks.

"That's what I said, wasn't it?"

No answer.

Now I do turn. "You know, there's still one thing I don't get. I don't even know what I am or what I'm here for. It's like I just don't belong wherever I am or whatever I'm doing. Fighting seems to be the only thing I'm good at anymore. I guess that makes me...a weapon. But why does a fucking weapon have a deeper sense of humanity than a living, breathing person? That's what I don't get. Because I didn't leave you to die, even though I could have. I've spent years alone looking for someone living and worth fighting for. I've stayed alive just for that reason. And now, all you've done is prove to me I've wasted my time."

I start to leave again.

"Hey, wait..."

"No!" I snap, wheeling around and facing her. "I may be just a machine but at least I know what's right. You go ahead and do what it takes to survive, but you leave me out of it. I don't need to be around someone like you. Have a nice life."

I duck under the fence, then before I set the boards back, say one last thing.

"Or what's left of it, anyway."

The planks slide back into place, and I stare out at the street, slowly turning back towards the skyline.

All this time...I finally find what I'm looking for, and it's nearly destroyed me.

Be careful what you wish for.

But what am I supposed to do now? For the first time, I honestly don't feel like moving forward. With nothing but inertness awaiting me while my body repairs itself, the only thing I feel is desolate.

Barren. Empty.

Mechanical.

I start moving toward the highest building I see. I don't know why.

But I do...

I reach it, then dig my hands and feet into the stone, climbing to the top, wondering with each hand and foothold if this is a good time to let go.

The rain, no longer a light mist, falls steadily after my slow climb to the perch I now stand on. I look upon the ruined city below me, the same disheartening thoughts on my mind. Fog rolls through the forest of concrete and vegetation, occasionally blocking my view behind its gray veil. When it does, for just a moment it seems like I'm in a world where none of my troubles exist. It's just the clouds and I.

It's endless.

There's some comfort in that. With nothing but the grayness around me, it feels like I'm doing more than just...this. It feels like I actually belong. It feels like those thoughts of suicide I entertained with every handhold I took on my climb don't matter. It feels like every other time I've felt so alone haven't hurt me as much as I know they have.

But the fog dissipates. I see the world for what it is. Those thoughts I have do matter. And they still haunt me.

This is how life is.

I can't get beyond how much I wanted to find someone. I remember thinking about how I'm only existing when I started walking I-90. That seems fitting right now. I realize that in order to live, I have to do so through others since I'm incapable of performing that basic human ability. I *can't* live. I can't experience life like a human anymore. I can see it and I can perceive it, but I can't experience it. I can't relish it. Everything goes from one moment of analysis to the next, serving as data to enhance my mechanical sense of preservation.

When I'm around someone else, my actions are defined by that person and what they're experiencing because I have to act and experience it with them. I'm defined by what they feel because I share in that feeling. I can remember those sensations of happiness, fear, anger, and peace. And in those moments, I feel like my life and theirs meet a mutual goal. I can live through them, but I can also ease their lives, enhancing them beyond the mere act of survival. I can protect. I can guide. I can provide. I can be more. I have a reason to be on this earth besides just killing. I'm more than a weapon. I'm more than...

...me.

Even if I'm only living by what they dictate, it feels better to do that than feel nothing at all. And we both *live*.

Feelings of sorrow well within me, but I have no tears to cry. I have no deep, mournful breaths to take. I can't exhale a lamenting sigh. I can only mimic the noise through my audio systems. Everything is just a program or routine. It's all so *machine*. Even standing on the edge of this building, viewing the world below is robotic. I look at a world that I know doesn't need me, but one I've tried to survive in for years nonetheless merely as protocol.

Is this what it's come to?

I don't want to think that.

Or maybe I do...

Is this the way?

I just can't do this anymore...

I'm so tired...

I should end it. Finally. Maybe the fall will kill me. If it doesn't, I'll have to do it myself, because I'm not going to sit and wait for my body to repair itself for days. I couldn't stand that now. Hours upon seemingly endless hours of waiting with the same thoughts tormenting me over and over again. And all the while, I'm powerless against them.

I can't face that anymore.

I can't do this anymore!

I'd give anything to make this stop...

An hour passes. Then two. Then three. The rain stops, but the gray sky remains. I look over my shoulder, hearing the wind but unable to feel it. It pushes against me, but my orientation systems preserve my balance. For just a moment, I see the misty outline of the Olympic Mountains, then they're swallowed up by the clouds again. I wonder if maybe there's something out there atop their peaks or within their valleys. Maybe there's someone else tucked safely away within the confines of their wilderness.

But then I remember how the last encounter with a human went for me.

The words of the Rantir I killed echo in my mind for a second time. I enhance my audio sensors, hoping to drown out the relentless voice with ambient noise. Another hour passes and the rain returns, but the thoughts remain. I reflect again on the fact that he's right. He's absolutely right. I can't go back. And now, with full sincerity, I ask myself...

Is there a point going forth?

Forth to what?

I lift my right foot.

"Please don't," a voice calls from behind me.

I anchor my left foot into the concrete, cracking the stone but halting what was going to be my last step. I regain my balance, plant myself on the edge of the building, then look back over my shoulder to see the woman standing behind me. She must have climbed the stairs while I was listening to the rain.

"Please don't," she repeats, taking a tentative step towards me.

I can't say I'm pleased to see her. I'm not sure I care. Part of me wants to throw myself from the ledge just to spite her, but suicide was never about petty grudges when I first considered it. I'm even a little irritated that she's here ruining my attempts at self-termination, but there's another part of me that's curious why she's here at all.

Still, I don't feel like speaking to her. I turn back to the streets and cityscape below me, my thoughts still swimming.

"Can you step down from there?" she pleads.

Why should I?

"What are you doing here?" I ask.

"I followed you," she answers.

"No shit. But I asked what you're doing here. Not how you got here."

She pauses, probably taken aback by my sudden sharpness.

"I came because I knew you were right," she answers at length.

I know I was. At least she's honest. But that only makes this harder.

"A little late for an apology," I reply.

"No it isn't. It's never too late."

"You come across pretty rigid," I comment. "It's hard to believe you have a sensitive side. Especially now. Seems pretty convenient when you want to alleviate the guilt you're feeling."

"And those are bitter words coming from someone who claims to know what humanity is," she retorts.

And now I feel a sense of shame when she points that out to me. Even more so because she said "someone" and not "something."

53

I hang my head. "I thought I knew. Now I'm not so sure."

"You and me both, Ferroc."

There's a pause between us, and only the sound of the wind and rain is audible for quite a while.

"Look," she begins again. "What I did was pretty pathetic."

"'Pretty?'"

"I'm trying to apologize! What do you want from me?"

That's a good question. What do I want from her?

"I don't know. A reason to live would be nice."

There's another lingering silence in our conversation. I would guess she's never had someone ask that of her. I know I haven't. I wonder if even I could give someone what I've just asked her to give me. But I don't really know what else to say. I truly do need that specific thing in this moment.

"Is it true you've been searching for a living person for years?" she asks.

My mind is still at war with itself over whether or not I want to talk to her. But eventually, the thought of having nothing better to do than kill myself wins me over to initiating conversation. I nod in confirmation of her query, finally turning to face her but not stepping down from the ledge. I notice she's a lot more relaxed now, though not completely so. She stands with her arms crossed as she leans into her left hip. I can see some reservation with the slightly closed off nature of her posture.

Then I do something I didn't think I'd ever do again. Something that hurts but grants me catharsis at the same time. Something I'm almost not sure as to why I do at all.

I begin my story.

So many memories are accompanied by a myriad of emotions as I recall each one of them in detail.

Still, it feels good to talk about the ghosts of the past.

"Five years. Her name was Jaclyn. Before her I tried to save Ryan."

"What happened to them?"

More painful memories come to me, but I can't see a way to block them out. Not if I'm going to tell her the truth. And I've wanted to tell someone for so, so long. Maybe it's finally time to face it.

As I remember those events, it feels so good to finally speak to someone about what I felt. What I feel...

And I wish I could cry *so* much.

I see his face. I see hers. And I see this woman in front of me now. All the while I'm wondering if she's going to join those who I've met before. Is she going to be just another painful memory of a better time in my existence? Or, maybe a span of joyful years that I can carry with me. Maybe if my life is defined by those I live with, that same rule applies to the memories I hold close. Even if I can't die with them, they live on through me, at least in memory.

It's not a great comfort to me as I wonder what future awaits this woman I've just met, but it's something hopeful. It's better than thinking only on the pain of the past. And it helps me tell the story I've longed to share.

"Ryan died when two Rantir ambushed him," I begin. My life with him, while brief, is easier to speak of. Mostly because its ending fills me more with anger than pain, and that sense of ire forces the words from me when I remember the events of that fateful day. "I was out hunting with him. He was an Army Ranger. Knew how to survive pretty well in the wild and worked better on his own. He survived the plague with the rest of his unit in a sealed shelter. His family and friends were wiped out when they tried to counterattack the Rantir after the nanobots were gone. He escaped and survived on his own for ten years."

It all seems so distant when I remember it. Ryan was just twenty-four when the initial wave of micro-robotic death from the Rantir was unleashed upon the Earth. He'd lived a long time by the standards of this world created by the hostile aliens. Then he met me...

"We first met in Michigan, near Lake Huron. He was fishing. He shot at me when he first saw me too."

She laughs at that. I even spare a chuckle at my own expense.

I continue, taking a moment to scoop up a broken chunk of concrete. I hope that by squeezing it, it will alleviate the grief associated with the events of that day even though I can't feel it.

"We were separated trying to find some deer in Wisconsin. Neither one of us knew that a pair of Rantir had been stalking us, waiting for the right moment." I pause for a second, shaking my head at the helplessness of that day. "He survives the whole damn invasion...Even the nanobots. Then a Rantir rips his throat out the day after he meets me."

Something breaks in my hands, crumbling out of my grasp. I look down and realize I've pulverized the concrete I was holding just a few moments ago. It's nothing now but a faint trail of dust wafting through the air before it disappears amidst the rain.

"I'm sorry," she offers.

I wave her off. "You didn't do it. Don't be sorry."

She gently nods. "What about Jaclyn?"

Ah...Jaclyn. Her death was something I couldn't accept for a long time after she was gone. It was so sudden and so simple...I think that's what made it all the more unbearable. Especially because she always had a way of viewing the world as it should have been. Not as it was. She was an optimist at heart. She learned from *Don Quixote*, quoting the novel often. The fact that we'd spent months together and not just a day added to the grief of her loss.

"I made it to Texas with Jaclyn," I begin. "I found her outside Charlotte. She'd been living in one of those government fallout shelters since the invasion. The Rantir had overlooked it and she'd had enough supplies to last for a few years. All of her family had died one by one of starvation or dehydration."

It's difficult to go on. I pause to collect myself, not having felt this vulnerable in a very long time.

"When I found her, she was almost gone, but I brought back food and water. Things were good for a few months. When we decided to move out, we made our way west."

Telling this part of the story is harder still. But I force myself to make it through.

"When we got to Texas, we found an old armory. When we went inside, there was still a pocket of nanobots."

I replay those events in my head, remembering the feint shimmer that was the cloud of the mechanized, microscopic killers. The robotic form of a deadly biological plague. I remember the moment before that when we crawled through the fence. And just before she died when I opened the door to the armory.

"She was dead a few minutes after we went in. Since then, I've never forgotten what the air looks like when the nanobots saturate it."

Again, I wish I could weep for my friend. I swear I can feel a deep pain in my chest. I swear I can feel *some* sense of physical affliction.

I want to so much.

"I buried her there. There's a rifle marking her grave."

Just for the sake of doing something I'd once done as a human, I sit on the edge of the building, facing her. As I look into her eyes, I see that same hope I had when I looked into Jaclyn's or Ryan's. That hope that only exists when I have someone else around helping me live as I help them survive. That hope that only exists when I have a reason to keep going beyond it merely being something to do, as has become the typical motivating factor in my life.

"Why do you care?" I ask after I finish the stories.

She takes a few more steps closer to me, then kneels down so she can look directly into my "eyes." "Because I believe you now. Because I can see you're more than a weapon."

"Yeah? How's that?"

She tilts her head to the side like she did in the building. I can't tell if she's confused or if it's a mannerism of hers. "Weapons don't try to kill themselves."

I shake my head, chuckling helplessly. "That's not why I came up here."

I'm lying more to myself than her.

"Yes it is," she answers. "I know it is."

"...How?"

"When you said you've been living for nothing after you found me, I could tell you meant it," she replies. "Machines don't say things like that. They don't feel defeat. And weapons don't think like that, even if you claim to be one."

"Apparently, that's all I am," I reply. "It seems like it's all I can be."

"I don't think that's true."

"Isn't it?" I ask. "I don't even know what I did for Jaclyn or Ryan beyond hunt for them or protect them. And I couldn't even save them when the time came for it. I could just *avenge* them."

She keeps her gaze locked upon me, even when I look away from her. "Do you blame yourself for their deaths?"

Yes...

...No.

...It's hard to figure out.

"I don't know," I tell her. "Sometimes I wonder if they would have been better off without me. Maybe they would have lived longer."

Another silence, then I hear her take a deep breath, considering her words. "Ferroc...I don't know if that's true either. I've only known you for half a day and you've already made my life pretty interesting. And that's just from what brief talking we've had. I already know you're damn good at fighting Rantir."

57

I wish I could grin. "But if that was the case, you wouldn't have left me."

She hangs her head, stung by what I just said. "I'm sorry I did that. I thought you were just…"

I look back at her with as much intensity as I can muster in my green, illuminated visor. "Just a machine?"

She keeps her head hung, but nods ever so slightly.

I can't bear to look at her anymore. And not because I'm angry with her. It's because I can't blame her for that. I've even admitted to being only a weapon just a few moments ago.

"Granted, you were the most interesting machine I'd ever seen," she goes on. "Or met for that matter."

For the first time in our conversation, I actually snicker out of sincerity. "Not too many cyborgs running around out there, I would guess."

"Is that what you are?" she asks honestly. "That would make sense to me."

"I don't' think a lot of things *can* make sense in this world," I point out. "But yes. That's what I think I am. It's why I feel what I feel. It's why I'm not some mindless robot. Or at least, that's why I think I can still be somewhat human. Why I still have emotions." I look at my hands and other parts of my body that are visible to me. It makes me pause to consider my words and their origins. I'm a machine, but I was human once. "I think there's still some part of me in here somewhere."

She nods. "There is."

"I truly hope you're right." I stand and walk to the other side of the building, hoping to catch another glimpse of the mountains through the clouds. "So what did you really hope to accomplish by following me?"

She walks up next to me. "At first, I just wanted to watch you. See if you were what you said you were."

"What changed that?" I ask, turning to look at her.

"When I saw you standing on the edge," she replies. "That changed things. I knew who you were then."

I'm truly touched by that. She said "who." Not "what."

"'Weapons don't try to kill themselves,'" I quote her.

She shakes her head, looking into my visor again. "No they don't. And another thing; I needed to prove you wrong."

I keep looking at her. "About what?"

58

"About me not knowing what it is to be human," she answers. "Because I do know. Maybe not as well as you, but I do know. You got me to think about it after you left. It's the first time I've been able to feel remorse in a long time."

I tilt my head, mimicking her mannerism. "I know you at least have an idea. You took the time not to shoot me again. That shows it. And I know you're not as heartless as I said you were. I was angry." I feel a sense of remorse of my own as I speak the words. "You followed me, and not because you were hunting me or needed to soothe your conscious. That means something."

"Yeah?"

"I think so," I say. "For what that's worth."

"It's worth a lot," she informs me. "Because you're the first person I've been with since my parents died. You made me feel like a human again too. I guess you don't need to be turned into a machine to make you forget what actually does help you feel that way."

It's just a matter of reference, but being referred to as a person instead of anything else is still refreshing and encouraging. It feels increasingly pleasant being discussed as a living, feeling, *human*. Even if it's only a term. It means far more than that to me.

My thoughts shift to something she said that I'm curious about. "May I ask you about your parents?"

Her expression grows very distant. Her skin seems to pale. "Sure."

"What happened?"

She sighs. "Pretty much the same story as your friends." She walks to the edge of the building, leaning over it and looking down. "They weren't the only ones who made it to the shelters only to die later."

I stand at her side, keeping my gaze on her. "Did the Rantir find you too?"

"Not like you," she answers. "We were one of the few who made it past the invasion. We were in touch with a few other shelters with our radio. Who would've thought an old C.B would come in handy?"

She stops after that, no doubt ruminating on what had shaped her into the woman she was now.

"How did you learn to survive?" I ask, wanting to change the subject.

She turns to me. "Mom was a park ranger. Knew pretty much everything about the outdoors you could imagine. She taught me what I know about the wilderness out here. We lived in Issaquah, so there was plenty to do outside. Dad was a cop. Taught me how to shoot. Both he and Mom liked to hunt, so there was no shortage of boom sticks in our home. And we all knew how to use them. They also believed in being prepared for anything. They even taught me Morse code, but I've never used it. Still it's good to have, like everything else they taught me. I guess that's all I could tell you. Their lessons have kept me alive."

I nod meekly, understanding the importance of that last statement entirely. In the days before the invasion, wilderness survival wasn't exactly a critical factor for everyday life in the states. Before I found myself in my present misfortune, I had deigned to undertake some of that outdoor wisdom myself, mostly just for camping or similar naturalistic activities. I never knew just how much I was going to be utilizing those skills in my future. Or how much time I was going to have to perfect them. It's something she and I both must practice daily to survive, albeit in far different measures. I'm glad we possess that knowledge. Like her, even I took the time to learn obsolete methods of survival or communication just in case. Though I'd learned most, including Morse code, as something to do more so than thinking I'd ever utilize it.

One never knew, however...

"We heard a few things from the other shelters," she continues. "From what we gathered, the Rantir were rooting us out, so Mom and Dad opted to take their chances with me in what was left of the world once the Rantir pulled that robo-plague out of the air. We left the others. Never heard from any of them again. They all decided to stay put."

I tilt my head slightly downward. This story was familiar wherever I went. And now it continues with her.

"How old were you?" I ask.

Her answers aren't so readily available to her, but she forces them out. "Ten."

That isn't a familiar part of the story. "And you survived with your Mom and Dad out here?"

She nods. "For the first few years, things weren't too bad. Without anyone else around, we stayed low and most of the Rantir didn't find us. Eventually the sweeper teams left."

"How long was it like that?" I press, very much intrigued by her life. The way in which her family adapted and survived gave me hope others could have done the same.

"Two, maybe two and half years," she answers. "It wasn't a picnic by any means, but it was better than what we kept finding in the shelters. And we learned to avoid the places where the plague might be." She pauses again. "It was a harsh world. Scary as hell to live in too. But we made it. And you know what? Those are actually some of my best memories...living with Mom and Dad out here."

I see her wipe a tear away from her eye.

It's not easy for me to ask, but I feel I must. "What happened?"

Her face goes cold and rigid. She's locked these memories down well, but I just brought them back to the surface. "Eventually we couldn't hide. Mom and Dad did what they could to keep me safe..." She looks out to the horizon, perhaps trying to catch a glimpse of the mountains as I had done earlier.

"You don't have to tell me," I say, placing a hand gently upon her shoulder. The gesture probably doesn't feel like much to her, but I think she might need it. I know I do, even if I can't "feel" her. The act of performing this gesture of affection isn't easy for me since I need to calculate precisely how much force I put into each gentle squeeze on her shoulder. I could break her collar bone or worse if I don't work my mechanical grip in the proper application of strength.

Fortunately for us both, I do none of these things since I do know how much external pressure the typical human would consider a comforting gesture. It took some practice, but it boils down to basic mathematics in pounds per square inch.

She shakes her head. "It is what it is. I was only hearing what happened anyway." She sits on the lip of the building now, legs dangling fearlessly over the side of the skyscraper as she delves deeper into her memories. Memories that scar her maybe even more than mine do me.

"Mom was outside when the Rantir found her," she starts. "She was gardening. The first Rantir pounced on her and the other three closed in..." She looks down, another tear dropping from her eye. She takes a moment to gather herself, then looks directly to me. "Dad was going out with the shotgun but made me swear to just stay in the basement. I didn't want to. I thought I could help. 'No matter what you hear, you stay down here, Sasha,' he said. 'Just don't come up. I

61

want you to sing your favorite song in your head. Sing it one hundred times, OK? Then come out.'"

She has to stop again. I watch her wipe away more tears. Tears that flow freely from unrestrained memories.

She forces herself to continue. "I told him that was for children and I wasn't a child anymore. Then he said 'you're my daughter, Sasha, and you *stay alive.*' He told me he loved me. Then he made me promise not to let them find me. He went outside after I went into the cellar."

This pains me to hear. I can tell she'll never forget the last words her father said to her as she was listening to the screams of her mother. Those moments in her life will forever be ingrained in her mind. Even more so would be the moments after her father gave her those instructions. I knew she listened to him after her initial protests, and she went into that hiding place and sang whatever her favorite song was one hundred times *exactly*. She sang it over and over again while she listened to everything that was happening outside. This girl was twelve when that day began. Still a child. When she finished singing her song for the hundredth time, she was a woman, made so by the harshness of the world we call home.

Her breath quivers as she wipes her nose. "I don't really want to talk about what happened next."

"Then don't," I add quickly. "You don't need to."

She wipes her eyes, looking up at me once more. "You've probably seen something like that, haven't you?"

I nod solemnly. "Yes. More times than I should have."

"Did you have a family?" she asks. "Before all this?"

I nod, not wanting to disclose far more painful memories any more than she did. "Not very pleasant conversation material."

She nods as well, still fighting back tears. Then she rises to her feet and turns to face me directly. "Tell me something…What's your real name?"

"My real name?"

"Yeah," she confirms. "'Ferroc' is what the Rantir call you. What do *you* call you? What's your real name?"

That's something I haven't thought about in a long time. As my life has progressed in this world, the only thing I've thought about is the current state I find myself in. Living each moment, day to day as what I am. Not who I was. It worked better this way with my intentions of moving forward, accepting what is and not what has been. My old name just reminded me of what I'd lost. But now, because of her question, it stood for something again. Now it brought me strength and hope to remember who I once was.

"Nathan Oscar Williams," I tell her.

She smiles, and I smile in my heart with her. "Sasha McKelly." She extends her hand.

I find the gesture old fashioned in a very endearing way. With no less effort than it took to place a hand on her shoulder, I calculate the proper amounts of pressure to return her gesture firmly, but without breaking any of the bones in her hand.

As we shake hands, she says something else I don't expect. "I wish I would've found you sooner."

God I wish I could smile. Not a full, ear to ear smile, but a sincere and heartfelt expression of gratitude.

"Me too. I've been through Seattle before. How come I didn't see you?"

She shrugs. "I don't stick around any one place for too long. Dead Rantir attract other Rantir. No good for survival. I've been hunting all over the Pacific Northwest with that in mind."

"Hmm…That's a lot of ground to cover," I comment.

"So is going to Wisconsin, to Charlotte, to Texas, and wherever else you've been," she shoots back. "I would've thought I'd have seen you along the coast somewhere."

I shake my head. "Big, shiny thing out in the open isn't a good idea for me unless I'm inviting trouble. We think alike in that regard."

"Avoiding trouble?" she asks. "Yeah we do." A small smile lingers on her face. "To an extent, I guess."

For a moment, there's this sense of levity between us, and I feel like we've both needed it for a very long time. She needs it because she's been a participant in this cruel game of survival that has been her life for the last eleven years. Worse than that, she was forced into it after the brutal slaughter of her family. I can imagine one would need a reason to smile after years of having none to do so.

And me…I needed this levity because I felt I was going insane. I mean, I'd held a gun against my head as a habit. Only after Sasha had left me to the Rantir did I finally find the motivation to end my life. It seemed like things were so completely different and so quickly. I feel strange because of that, almost like it's another one of my mechanized quirks that conflicts with the remnants of my humanity. The ability to

63

switch from utter despair to unwavering hope is something I know Sasha can't do. Or anyone else for that matter.

Then again, Sasha doesn't have the body of a machine.

Or is this just part of the human condition?

I guess I need to take these things as they come. It's better than thinking about putting a bullet in my head anyway.

"I'm assuming that house you were at is your shelter for the night?" I ask, breaking the silence.

"Yeah," she confirms. "I have supplies and weapons there."

"More ammo for that, I'm sure." I gesture to the rifle slung over her shoulder. "Where did you find it?"

"Dad had a friend in the military," she explains. "We went over to his house after we left the shelter. There wasn't much left of the family, so we took what we needed." She slings it off her shoulder, examining it as she recalls the events of that day. She then slides the bolt back, confirming that she's chambered a round. "And yes, I have more ammo for it. A couple other things too."

That was good news to me, as only now do I realize I still need to repair myself. If she had any type of mechanical gear or maintenance chemicals, they were going to be a huge help for me. It meant far less time sitting inert while I waited for my systems to restore themselves.

I run a quick diagnostic of what components I'll need. For full repair, I require sixteen fluid ounces of oil and eleven of water, both of which I can cover. My inner workings require some kind of elastic material, which I can acquire from the Rantir bodies or car tires. I'll also need a small amount of replacement metal for the puncture damage in my side.

Estimated time of complete system restoration: seventeen hours, thirty-three minutes and twelve seconds.

"Thanks, by the way," I say to her.

She tilts her head to the side again. "For what?"

"For following me up here," I tell her. "Thanks for not letting me..."

She reaches out for my shoulder, the slightest hesitation of doing so washing over her, as if she's confused by whether or not it's a good idea. She follows through with it anyway, wears that small smile she did before, then nods ever so slightly.

"Thank you for talking some sense into me," she says.

Another moment of levity passes between us, and for that moment, the hardships of the lives we live don't seem to matter so much. We found each other, and that's given us more hope and peace than we've both had in years. Strange as it might seem for a grown woman and a cyborg to be sharing a moment like this, it makes perfect sense to us if for no other reason than the companionship we offer one another.

"How did you get up here anyway?" I ask.

She laughs. "I've been running through the woods for years and I'm still not in shape for hiking up God knows how many flights of steps! That really sucked."

I actually laugh with her. "I won't put you through that again."

She smiles in that way I'm beginning to feel is just for me. "And I won't leave you again, Nathan."

It feels so much better than I ever could have imagined. Her promise, as well as her use of my real name.

"Thank you Sasha," I say. "Ready to go?"

She nods, and we make our way to the door. The hundreds of steps down get easier and easier with each one we take.

Chapter 3

We return to her hideout with little trouble, but as we walk together, the things that I've taken for granted in my current form amaze me. Only when I see her struggling to keep a footing on the muddy earth or streets do I realize the problems I don't have to manage. I never lose balance due to my movement and coordination protocols. My feet never slip because of my inherent robotic enhancements like pressurized toes and friction plates. Every foot I place on the earth is calculated for perfect weight distribution and balance. I don't even need to control it. The system reacts to my needs artificially. As I watch her slip, fall, and right herself, rare as it is, I'm given a stark contrast between the two of us. Her, so alive yet so...mortal. And me, nonliving metal, but so untouchable and seemingly without weakness.

Now that I'm with someone, my metal form is a benefit to my existence. When I'm with her, I begin to appreciate all of the perks of an artificial build. Thoughts of my attempted suicide still linger, but I set them aside to reflect on how I've often thought of my body as a tomb for my soul. But that only applies when I'm alone it seems.

When we reach the house, I ask her why she chose to hide here. She tells me it's the closest thing she's had to an actual home since her family was killed. She'd rather be living inside a building that made her somewhat happy than feeling scared and isolated every night. I agree with her logic. I would have done the same if I had need of sleep. Most of the time, I kept moving for days at a time before I'd take a moment to consider where I was.

We go inside and she bolts the door shut behind me. I now see I was right when I assessed it was reinforced. There are several pieces of thick steel that have been pieced together over the door. I can see where they've been welded. When I look around, I discover the remains of an old oxy-acetylene unit.

She notices me assessing the welding supplies. "Dad always believed in being somewhat of a renaissance man."

I nod in approval. "You know a lot."

She smiles. "Yeah...There's a lot I don't too."

She leads me down to the basement where I see she has some candles burning. No chancing a larger fire here. The smoke would give away our position to any Rantir. So she's made due with the dim illumination provided by the burning string and wax. The light isn't much, but I don't require much to see the armament she's stockpiled in this place. A quick scan reveals there are thirty-one different firearms within the confines of the room. Everything from pistols to shotguns along with boxes of assorted ammunition befitting the caliber of each weapon.

I look to her, wishing I could wear an expression of pleasant surprise. "You stay busy."

"I try to," she replies. "You're not the only one with time to kill."

She sets her rifle against the wall, then begins to take off her ghillie suit. It's warm enough in the cellar that she doesn't need it. She folds it neatly, then places it on what looks to be a bed that's been assembled from the remains of other furniture. She undoes her belt and removes her equipment, placing it on the bed as she does so. I notice she keeps her handgun tucked into her pants as she begins aligning a set of four candles. I continue to observe her, learning later that she's preparing to cook when she places bricks around the candles, then a pot across the bricks. Her task complete, she retrieves a can of some unmarked food from the back of the cellar, pours its contents into the pot, then settles onto the bed. The whole routine seems so ritualized even though I know she's been on the move for years. I wonder how many other places like this she has out there in the world. Places where she performs routines similar to this.

"You just going to stand there?" she asks when she notices I've been observing her this whole time.

I snap to attention, not even aware of what I was doing. "Sorry. It's been a long time since I've seen anyone...live." I withdraw the juice bottles I found at the gas station from my pack, placing them on the table where she's prepared the pot and candles.

She nods in gratitude. "I won't say I understand, but I can imagine. Still, it's a little unsettling with you just watching me."

I laugh. "I would assume so." I unstrap my small pack, then begin removing a few items. "You have any .45 ammo?"

She nods, pointing to a few of the boxes stacked neatly against the wall to my right. "Help yourself."

I say thank you, then move over to the munitions depot she's acquired. I quickly sort through the many containers of bullets, finding what I need. I reload the four rounds I spent on the Rantir, then place a box of bullets inside my pack. As I do so, something catches my eye amidst the many rounds and cartridges. It looks like parts for an old car battery along with battery acid. I remove a few more containers of ammo and verify that's indeed what the assorted materials are.

"Have you used these?" I ask, holding the battery parts out to her.

"No," she answers. "Just found it a bit ago. Older car garage. Looked like they specialized in 70's and 80's models. Some of them still had parts that were usable."

My morale soars with that answer. "Perfect."

"Why?" she asks.

"Watch," I tell her, then begin to assemble. I piece together the unused battery, then pour in the acid. System analysis confirms that the battery is now sixty percent charged.

More than I need.

I place my left hand on the negative node and my right on the positive. There's a few sparks at first, but then the flow of electrical energy finds its way into my internal systems. Soon, the current is absorbed into my host of micro-robotic cells and utilized to enhance all primary functions. In this case, repair protocols. I now place my bottle of oil, a handful of shell casings from the floor, and some pieces of the tow truck's tire into my decomposition chamber.

"Do you have any water?" I ask. "Or more oil-based chemicals?"

She takes a moment to observe me, genuinely intrigued. "I have both."

She rises to her feet and makes her way over to an old bin. There, she withdraws a few cans of rust preventative and lubricants. She also reaches into an old tote next to the bin and withdraws a bottle of water. She comes back to me, handing them over.

I hear her giggle as she gives me the items.

"What's funny?" I ask.

She grins at me. "No offense, but the fact that you need oil. Don't want you to rust or anything. Seems a little...funny."

I just look at her.

Is that funny? I'm not so sure. I'd offer her a confused look if I could. Instead, I nod.

"Ah," is all I say, then get back to work.

She keeps giggling. I'm glad she's amused.

...I guess I am a little too.

System analysis confirms that with the components she's given me, I'll have everything I need for full repairs and performance. The puncture to my hydraulics systems will be mended and lost fluids will be replaced by assimilated chemicals from the oils and other liquids. All other structural damage will be broken down and reformed by existing materials and those provided by the shell casings.

Estimated time of full repair, now accommodating accelerated system functions due to electrical stimulus: twenty-two minutes and four seconds.

She watches as I remain still and allow my optimized systems to go to work. The nanobots, now powered by the electrical charge of the battery as opposed to their own static conductivity literally "heal" me at a pace that is visible to her.

"Do you always need these things when you're...hurt?" she asks.

I keep still but allow engagement of vocal functions. "Not the battery, but it helps."

"How?"

"My internal systems are self-sustaining," I explain. "The micro-robotic cells that reside within me generate enough kinetic energy and static charges to remain active and perform basic necessary functions. However, when optimized by outside electrical influences, they carry out functions at an accelerated rate and higher efficiency. This repair would have taken me seventeen hours to complete without the battery."

She seems surprised, and still very intrigued. "How long will it take now?"

"Twenty-one minutes and six seconds," I tell her.

"Electricity helps you that much?" she asks.

I nod very slightly, not wanting to disrupt system repairs. "It's what we all sustain ourselves with. Energy, I mean. I'm no different from you in that regard. It's my 'food' when I can get it."

"Does that work with any kind of electrical charge?" she inquires.

"I would imagine so," is my answer. "There hasn't been anything electrical yet that I couldn't utilize. This world doesn't offer much in terms of electricity though."

She thinks for a moment. "What about solar?"

I shake my head slightly. "I've tried. Solar panels aren't efficient after twenty to twenty-five years. The solar cells I've found so far didn't make it this long."

"Well, that sucks."

I chuckle.

"So you just put some stuff inside your chest and your body fixes itself?" she asks.

I think about that for a second. "I guess you could say that. Anything that matches the molecular structure of what I require is compatible. Sometimes, even things that don't can still be broken down into useful components. Coal, for example, is carbon, and carbon is a basic structural element of many compositions. I can use those molecules. The nanobots inside me piece them together as needed."

Her eyes widen. "They know how to do that?"

I shrug. "Apparently. I have no idea how many applications the Rantir use them for. From what we know, they were used to wipe out a species, assimilate atmosphere, and now, perform robotic repairs."

"But wait," she starts. "Didn't you say you were a…cyborg? Doesn't that mean there's something human left inside you?"

"My brain is," I tell her.

"OK," she says. "So how is that staying alive? You don't have blood, right?"

Again, I shrug. "Your guess is as good as mine. My theory is that the nanobots are preserving my flesh as well as my metal. All my brain needs is nutrients and oxygen. The nanobots can provide that from the atmosphere and from the components I place inside my decomposition chamber."

I can see her still trying to grasp the whole concept of just how complicated I really am.

"Don't think about it too much," I tell her. "Trust me, it's hard to comprehend."

"I guess so."

We both chuckle.

She tilts her head to the side, analyzing me still. Now I know what she meant when she said having someone just "watch" you can make you feel uncomfortable.

"You have to stay completely still?" she asks.

"No," I inform her. "For maximum efficiency, I stay still so all primary functions can be reprioritized to repairs. Makes the process go faster. I could move, but that would prolong the ordeal."

"What's the longest you've had to wait?"

"Four days," I answer. "Give or take a few hours."

Her eyes widen. "You didn't move for four days?"

"I didn't see much choice at the time," I tell her. "I fought off two Rantir and buried Ryan. I wasn't in any hurry."

She's thinks hard on that for a moment. I'm not sure that was the explanation she was expecting to hear. "It's hard for you, isn't it?"

"Waiting?" I ask.

"Yeah."

I would sigh deeply were I capable of doing so. "It is. I don't like being alone with my thoughts. I've had enough time with them already."

"And if you kept moving while the repairs were underway?" she presses. "Would that be worse?"

I shrug minimally. "It would be if some Rantir found me in a weakened state."

She nods, but remains confused. "It almost seems like you wanted them to find you. Almost like you were hoping to die, Nathan."

I'm impressed by her perception.

"Maybe I was," I answer honestly. "I'd always hoped to find someone again. That was reason enough to stay at optimum performance levels as frequently as possible. It had just gotten harder and harder to do that. Especially after coming back from up north."

"I can understand why you would though," she offers. "I would do the same."

I tilt my head, growing comfortable with the gesture I've acquired from her. "Would you?"

"If I was looking for someone as much as you were, I'd want every reason to be alive for them," she replies. "Able to protect them."

"You haven't tried to find anyone?" I ask.

She shakes her head. "I don't think we all have the option to wander the world like you do, Nathan. Except for you, we all need to sleep sometime. And the Rantir don't need to as much as I do." She sighs, still watching my body mend itself. "No. It's rough in this region, but it's safe." She thinks for a moment. "Relatively."

"What were your plans after coming through Seattle?" I ask.

She shrugs. "Keep moving. Keep hunting." She looks into my eyes. "What about you?"

"Now that I've found you, I guess I'll go where you go if you don't mind," I answer. "I really don't have anywhere else to be."

"Putting a lot of pressure on this relationship already, don't you think?" she jokes.

I laugh with her. "I guess. Maybe I should have put a ring on your finger before we took that step."

That gets her to laugh out loud. The sound of it is enough to bring me peace of mind for years if I hold the memory close. It's so soothing to hear the emotions expressed by humans once again. Rantir aren't without their expressive moments either, but I haven't seen anything from them beyond hate, anger, or remorse. Seeing Sasha laugh, hearing it, maybe even feeling it as my own feelings react to it, are like medicine to me. Almost "soul food" I guess.

"Well, now that you're here," she begins when her laughter dies down. "I wouldn't mind seeing the world a bit. As long as that's alright with you."

I'm confused. "You just said it was relatively safe in this region."

She agrees. "I know. But I've been here for the last twenty some years, Nathan. It's been the same thing, and I haven't been able to leave it behind because of that sense of safety. But..."

I keep my gaze locked upon her. "But what?"

She looks right back at me. "You're a kind of safety. No offense, but you are. It's not like I'm helpless out there, but you don't need the things I need. When I need to sleep, you can look out for us. I can hunt, and I know you can too, so it's not like I'm going to be starving either."

I begin to see her point, and I'm more intrigued than concerned with her proposition. Staying on the move is appealing to me. Still, I feel I must ask something to satisfy my curiosity.

"So why stay moving?"

She thinks for a moment. "Same reason you've kept moving too."

"But you said yourself I have a distinct advantage in this department," I point out.

She waves me off. "Look Nathan, don't get protective on me, OK? That's not what I need. I know you're asking this because you're worried about me dying. You can't be worried about that."

My, is she perceptive. Even more so than I thought just a moment ago.

"But I am, Sasha."

She takes a deep breath. "I can't presume to understand what sense of 'mortality' you have to deal with, Nathan. For all we know, you can't die."

"I can die," I cut in. I wonder what relevance that statement bears concerning this conversation. For a moment, I wonder if I'm trying to prove something.

Again, she waves me off, irritated. "The point is, you have to accept that people around you are going to die, Nathan. From the Rantir, from sickness, or accidents. And there's no step you can take to avoid that. *You* don't have to deal with at least two of those things. So you better get used to the idea that I do, and that's how it is every day for me. Why would traveling with you to wherever we end up going be any different?"

I think on that for a moment, realizing she's absolutely right. Even more unsettling to me is her observation about my own 'mortality,' if I can call it that. For all I knew, I might be able to piece myself back together even from serious damage. I've reattached limbs to my body, mended unstable power sources...even performed surgery on my brain after receiving serious trauma from a Rantir attack.

Could I die? I wasn't sure. But she was right when she said a day for her out in what was left of this world was just as risky as living in the Pacific Northwest. I couldn't be protective of her like I was just a moment ago. That would belittle the person she'd become and the life she now wanted to live.

As I contemplate this, I'm amazed at the impact I'm having on her just a few hours after meeting her. We've certainly covered a large emotional spectrum, and we've provided such a sense of purpose and drive in the other just by making our existences known and significant. I want to be with her to have someone in my life again; providing me with a reason to feel alive. She wants to be with me because she was just as lonely as I was. And knowing her years on this earth are finite, wants to maximize the life she can have, dangerous as it may be.

I very much respect that. And though we aren't the closest of friends by any means, we are the most the other has at this point and time. That's a good enough foundation to form a relationship with someone in my book. With that thought, I set my mind to thinking about the future road with Sasha instead of keeping her from it. I'm not opposed to having someone to travel with either.

If I could smile, I'd do so now. "Where would you like to go?"

She's stunned for a moment, not expecting the question. "What do you mean?"

"I mean," I begin. "You have the choice to go wherever you like. What would you like to see? I can navigate for us to go wherever you'd like in the world."

"Really?" she questions.

I nod. "I've been a lot of places, Sasha. I've seen the majority of this country and a bit beyond it. If we can walk to it, I can get us there. Maybe even across the sea if we find the right transportation."

She grins ever so slightly.

"So," I start again. "Where would you like to go?"

She thinks it over for a long time, perhaps cherishing each second of rumination upon the many possibilities spanning the proverbial horizon. Then, at length, finally makes her decision.

"Vermont."

Vermont sounds fine with me, although I'm interested in what made her choose that.

"Why Vermont?"

She starts smiling wider, and I truly enjoy seeing a sense of eagerness and hope so openly displayed on her face. "Have you been there during Autumn?"

I nod.

"I bet it's beautiful."

"It is," I tell her.

"Then that's where I want to go."

I wish I could wear an expression of skepticism to make my point. "That's a good trek. It's going to take us a long time."

"You in some sort of hurry?" she asks.

I wish I could grin. "Good point."

"Thought so." She wears a coy smirk.

"I just have one question," I state. "If you don't mind?"

"Is that your question?" is her sarcastic response.

Her levity and sense of humor is greatly appreciated. How I've yearned for this kind of interaction! But I stay focused on my query.

"You seem so quick to warm up to me now," I begin. "And granted we are starting over to some extent since our first meeting...But I was just wondering, why come with me at all? Why trust me? Given what I am..."

She shakes her head. "To me, *Nathan*, it's not about what you are. It's about who you are. And I'm just as curious about your origins as I am the rest of the world."

She gives me a moment to think on that.

"Or maybe," she starts again. "It's a matter of having nothing better to do. Or maybe I just want to get away from this place. Or maybe it's because staying with you helps me survive longer. Or maybe I've needed to be around someone for years. Or maybe…"

I break my typical protocol and hold up a hand to silence her, adding another twenty seconds to my restoration period.

"I understand," I tell her. "I see your point."

"But my first answer is the one you should remember," she adds with finality.

"Then I'll remember that one," I tell her.

I begin to enjoy these moments of contentment we have after conversations like the one we've just had or previously on the rooftop. It seems like we can be together and just share in one another's company; a trait I much admire. I'm growing fonder and fonder of her since I never had a bond like this with Ryan or Jaclyn. But I suppose everyone's interactions and relationships are going to be different and special. Mine with Sasha is no exception. I'm very glad of that.

"Alright," I say. "Just one more question then."

She rolls her eyes, maintaining that smile she seemingly saves for me. "What now?"

"Would you like to leave tomorrow?"

While my repairs finish, she eats her meal, then sleeps. It's night now, and setting off through the darkness wouldn't be smart for her, so we decide to stay in and wait for morning. She can sleep easier tonight with me around anyway. I feel like maybe it's the first time she'll actually remain slumbering through the whole evening if I give her the peace of mind she says I do. I help myself to more of the weapons and ammo, keeping myself busy. Thinking ahead to any future conflicts we might have, I decide to strap a shotgun to my back, keeping it loaded with the safety off but with no round in the chamber. It's a security model with a pistol grip. I take three extra boxes of shells for it as well, two of them slug ammunition. I also strap a survival knife to my leg, not knowing when it will come in handy, but fully trusting it will.

The night passes while I inspect and clean my equipment. I also check the current status of all my systems. Navigations, translation, targeting, restoration, gyroscopic, coordination, motor, circulation, conductivity, hydraulics, processing, decomposition...the list goes on for a while. However, everything checks out and is functioning at one hundred percent. I'm ready for the road. As soon as she wakes up and gives me the go ahead, we'll be off.

I don't think the time could pass any more slowly given how eager I am to get moving. It does give me time to reflect on the complete attitude shift I've undergone. There's this drive and determination regarding everything I'm about to do. A "come what may" type of mindset that, before, was only a bleak "whatever" disposition.

I'm excited. Maybe even giddy. The world is fresh and new; filled with life and adventure.

I almost don't believe these are the thoughts I harbor. I'm glad to be this optimistic for a change. All because of this woman...

Eventually, the sun rises and Sasha along with it. She gathers her things into a large rucksack. She slings her rifle across her back, straps her 9mm to her leg, her knife to the other, packs cans of food and MRE's, bottles of water, paracord, sleeping bag, one pot, some eating utensils, fire starting materials, and more ammunition. She then asks me if there's anything else I'll need. I request what remains of the rust preventatives and any other oil-based compounds she might have. She gives me a few other cans of lubricant, some 10w-30 motor oil, and some caulk. All of this could be useful to me in the future. Maybe even for her. I place them all in my pack, which is now becoming full of all the essentials I would require. I offer to carry her pack as well since I don't tire, but she refuses, wanting to keep her own equipment close. She says she's used to carrying her stuff anyway. I then ask her to lead the way out of the city.

We set off, working our way through the rainy, overgrown streets of Seattle. It takes us about two hours to reach our intended destination of I-5, but they're hours well spent. We seem to work in concert with one another. We take on different roles. I walk in the open while she travels from one hiding spot to the next, leading me along. Any time I lose sight of her, a quick switch to my thermal or sonar functions reveals her location, showing me the way to go. We see this as the best way to travel. Not that I can't be stealthy if I choose, but I'm considerably larger than her, standing nearly a foot taller and weighing a couple hundred pounds more. I'm almost inviting an attack, but that's the point. If we were to be ambushed, I'm best suited to fight my way out of it. Not her. Beyond that, she's accurate enough to provide excellent cover and "overwatch," as the military would call it. I trust her implicitly already.

After the majority of the day, we get outside the city and begin working our way back to I-90 via I-5. Knowing this road to stretch across the states all the way to Minnesota, we decide this will make the journey go fastest. I'll set waypoints accordingly with my navigations systems, allowing us to stay along the interstate for guidance while avoiding the dangerous exposure that traveling directly on the pavement would yield.

The sun sets, and we stop for the night in the thick wild before the Cascade Mountains. It's cold out, so we need to get a fire going. I gather some firewood for her after we find a hole produced by an uprooted tree. She begins laying pine boughs over the top of it for insulation. I stay relatively close, turning up the sensitivity on my audio sensors just in case a Rantir decides to come after us. I'm not going to make the same mistake I did with Ryan.

After about an hour, we reconvene, and I find she's already gathered a bundle of tinder, ready for my supply of firewood. She also has a ferro-cerium rod ready when I hand her the materials. She places each piece neatly around her fire bundle, then strikes the rod with her knife. A fire sparks to life. It's small enough not to draw attention with excess smoke, but large enough to cook with and keep warm. Given how insulated the little hole is going to be with the pine boughs laid across it, I assume she's going to be comfortable enough. She withdraws a sleeping bag from her backpack and nestles in. I spend a moment admiring her resourcefulness, then say goodnight. She smiles at me in that way I've come to cherish, then says goodnight as well.

"Wake me if you need anything, OK?" she says as I head outside the temporary shelter.

I look back, then give her a nod of my deepest appreciation.

I stand outside the shelter, not wanting to crowd her, scanning the nearby area with night vision, then thermal, switching between spectrums every minute and thirty seconds.

It's easy to pass the time this way. I have a duty to uphold and someone to protect. I'd done the same for Jaclyn when I was with her, all with the same vigilance. There's a part of me that thinks that perhaps this was my intended purpose. Maybe the Rantir engineered me to be some kind of robotic security role with a more human sense of self-awareness. It makes sense to me, especially since what I'm doing now is fulfilling the purpose of that theory. It's nice to think of myself in roles such as these. Capacities that surpass that of an offensive weapon. I'm not just engineered for war, even if security is a part of warfare.

At least when I'm guarding Sasha, it's about protecting my fellow human. My associate.

Dare I say, my friend.

On my watch and ventures to collect more firewood, I see only the usual wildlife in the area. Some rabbits, a fox or two that's aware of me, owls, and a few others. I watch them all curiously, now trying to figure out ways in which I could utilize their indifference to me so as to benefit Sasha. I don't wish to abuse their nonchalance regarding my presence, however. It's been a useful tool to me; the animals paying me no mind. It certainly helps when the Rantir are around since they run when something other than me is in the area. Maybe it can help Sasha so long as it doesn't come at the cost of the animals fearing me.

Morning approaches, and once again I find myself anticipating the day's travels. We make our way through the Cascade Mountains, stopping periodically by the occasional stream flowing from the melting snows above us. Were I on my own, I would have taken a very direct route through the mountains, even if that meant scaling the cliffs or rock faces that comprised them much like I'd done on my trip into Seattle. However, with Sasha along, it's far safer and much more accessible for her to stick to a lower route. It's warmer and there's more game, some of which we hunt in the afternoon. Not to mention, it saves precious energy for her by not climbing mountainsides.

She sets snares for something small, baiting them with portions from MRE's she's brought with her. She doesn't like how they taste, she explains to me, but they come through when she's in need. For now, she knows she can get something bigger. Checking the snares is something I can do after sunset for her since traversing the forest in the dark is far more hazardous for a human. I appreciate the thought and the chance to lend a hand.

We make another temporary shelter as daylight begins to wane. This time I help her construct a lean-to amidst a copse of saplings. They provide protection from the wind, and with our added materials, will insulate warmth. When she no longer needs my assistance, I venture to a nearby meadow, gathering large armfuls of grass for her to further insulate the shelter. It's nice knowing she's as comfortable as possible. I aim to make it so physically and mentally.

We spend some time talking about our lives before she goes to bed. She tells me about what her father was like and some of the stories he'd shared with her when she was just a girl. She tells me he'd only had to draw his gun once, and even then, it was never pointed at anyone. It was just to make a statement. She appreciated how prepared he was but how he'd never had to do anything drastic. She was glad of that. His life was peaceful for the most part. She also tells me of her mother and how they would go horseback riding together. It was something she greatly enjoyed. After hearing that, I make a note to myself to find her a horse. It's not a bad idea as far as transportation is concerned. And ever since the Rantir attack, horses had returned to a more wild and roaming way of life, becoming numerous in states like Wyoming. If we could find one, the benefits from having it would far outweigh the cons of time spent looking for it.

She finishes her story and asks me about my life before the Rantir came. I tell her about my childhood. I tell her about my favorite places I'd like to go to, riding my bike to get there with my friends. I tell her how we used to catch frogs by the creeks and ponds, coming home covered in mud, much to the chagrin of my mother. I tell her about high school and how I played football. I was a fullback. I lettered. We went to state, but lost my senior year. I tell her how I went to college and met Angie in a sociology class. She laughs at the irony of that. I tell her about how we had some rough times after college when I tried to start my own business, but we got through it together. I tell her when we had Cassie, my beautiful daughter. I tell her about the first time I held her and how I felt. I tell her about the day the Rantir attacked and how we fled like so many others, trying to find shelter in a place that could offer none. I decide to stop there, saying she knows the rest.

"What kinds of things have you seen since you've become 'Ferroc?'" she asks after I finish my stories of the past.

"What kinds of things have I seen?" I repeat, uncertain as to what she means.

She nods. "Yeah. You said you came back from up north. What was that like? I've always wanted to see Alaska too."

"Ah," I understand. "It's..." I take a moment to think on how to explain it to her. "The mountains there soar into the sky, almost like they're trying to reach out to the stars. It seems like they could. I've climbed up a few of them."

Her eyes widen. "Really?"

I nod. "It was something to do. And it helped me survey the land around me. I even spent a night at the peak of Mount McKinley."

"What was that like?"

Lonely is what I want to say. But it was more than that. "It was a perfect night because the northern lights appeared. I swear I've never seen anything more beautiful than that. The colors...every one in the spectrum, all the brightest and most vivid I've ever seen. Golden yellow, crimson red, sky blue...And the patterns...So many shapes, almost like the lights were taking it upon themselves to form every object imaginable and some that weren't...All of it against a backdrop of thousands of the brightest stars..." I almost get lost in the memories as I recall that beautiful sight, solitary as I was atop the mountain.

"You talk about everything in so much detail," she notes.

"The memories are all I have, Sasha," I tell her. "Memories are what give me hope."

She grins. "I hope I can see them one day too."

"You will," I promise her. Then I offer a reassuring nod. "You will."

She smiles her smile, then yawns. I take that as my cue to let her sleep. She says goodnight. I say the same. I then leave to check the snares, discovering one of them has captured a rabbit. I'm happy she'll be able to eat well in the morning. I skin it and clean it, analyzing it for any infection or bacteria. Confirming it's indeed healthy and sanitary, I bring it back to the camp, venturing into the shelter to smoke the meat. Periodically, I check on it between scanning the area in thermal and night vision. It's prepared by dawn.

As we ready ourselves to leave the next day, she's grateful for the rabbit. The meat doubles her spirits during our journey and we make excellent time. We cover nearly as much ground as I did when I made the trip into the city, and after a few more days, end up near the gas station that was the sight of my battle with the Rantir.

As we approach, I warn her this was where I fought and killed the alien, so it may be best to avoid the area. She agrees but wonders what else might be of use in the gas station. I tell her there were a few more bottles of juice that looked preserved enough of drink if she thinks it would be worth it. She says yes, telling me it's unlikely there's any feral Rantir in this area. They probably found the body and decided to move on. And we knew for a fact that at least those that were following me previously had been dealt with in the streets of Seattle.

We make our way down the road cautiously. She keeps her rifle ready, a round in the chamber and her eye looking through the scope. I fulfill my typical role, ready to manage whatever danger there might be in a more direct fashion. I keep looking to the sky, finally spotting some crows. However, I notice they're circling instead of descending. There's something else feasting on the corpse of the alien.

Or something else keeping them from doing so.

I keep this in mind as I make my way down the road, trusting that Sasha is somewhere nearby. When the service station is finally visible, I see why the crows are circling.

There's something there, hunched over the body. There's two other things flanking it on its left and right, both of which look like humans.

Both of which look like me, I realize.

I keep walking closer, now seeing the thing hunched over what remains of my former opponent is a Rantir itself. However, unlike the normal kind I'm used to dealing with, this one is dressed and equipped with full battle equipment and armor standard to the race. It's something I haven't seen since the invasion.

The battle suit is almost like a second skin. Contoured smoothly to cover the Rantir's entire form, layered to compliment its movement perfectly and provide flawless mobility while still providing complete protection from all but the most powerful of rounds. Not to mention there's a plethora of internally and externally integrated Rantir tech, some of which glows from the power sources within. All of its joints are sharpened to fine points. From its elbows to its reverse jointed knees, it's a walking death machine. I notice both of its scythes have long, curving blades attached to them as well, contoured to fit the natural curve of its "feelers" in their resting position. It keeps them neatly folded on its back for now, resting above what looks like a large disintegration cannon. Along with these enhancements, I have no doubt its armor helps it with sensing vibrations and other methods of detection. It's good to note every asset it possesses. Even if it just seems to *be* one itself.

It stands up and turns, and the two humanoid creatures next to it do the same, revealing them to be eerily like me, but with subtle differences. The same robotic design and structure comprises them, but they seem thicker. A little more bulky than me. Their visors glow yellow as opposed to my green viewport. They also carry no weapons or supplies. There's one more crucial difference between these two and I. One that I note after I enhance my optics to get a better view.

They stand like machines. Unmoving in the slightest. There doesn't seem to be a trace of humanity in the way they hold themselves. Almost like a soldier that had trained his entire life just to stand at attention. I can't explain it, but I can sense it. There's something *different* about them.

I wonder what's going on, and I'm answered in a way I don't expect.

"Ferroc!" the Rantir calls out...In perfect English. "I've been looking for you."

Chapter 4

I'm not sure I hear correctly. I wonder if I've been going crazy and just crossed the threshold into insanity. Maybe I can't handle the idea that my life has turned a bit of a corner these past few days and that the recent events have been some cruel joke of fate.

...So I gave myself a completely illogical occurrence to make myself focus on anything but my solitude?

I'm really reaching for excuses to disprove what's happening...

I'm not sure what to make of this. But I know that there are three creatures standing in front of me. I know one of them is a Rantir. I know Sasha is watching, probably wondering what I'm going to do next. I know this isn't a dream or figment of my imagination. This is real.

This just happened.

I take a very tentative step forward, hand going to the shotgun strapped across my back. I notice the Rantir watching me, and I swear he grins through his helmet when my hand grips the stock of my weapon. The two other versions of me stand as still as they were just a moment ago. It continues to bother me just how statuesque they appear. I'm not sure if advancing on these three is the best course, but it's the only one that gives me answers to the many questions I have right now. It also keeps their attention on me and not Sasha, who I hope they are oblivious to.

In front of me there's someone who could know the answers to questions I've had for years. I've wanted to know who made me, what I was, what I was meant for, and just a simple explanation of *why* I am what I am would put down some very troubling demons for me. However, I keep in mind I can't allow my desire for those answers to jeopardize Sasha. I didn't spend years wandering the earth trying to find someone just to watch them die a few days after I met them.

...Again.

I think maybe diplomacy is as good a choice as any, though I keep my finger on the trigger and cycle a round into the chamber. When I do so, the other versions of me, both with perfect synchronization and timing, take one step forward on their right foot, raise their right arms, and aim at me with what appear to be wrist mounted disintegration weapons that fold out of their forearms. The tell-tale cyan glow is something I've seen as the precursor to a lot of destruction when those weapons were charged.

I wonder if they really are just machines modeled after me.

"I wouldn't advise you to fire your weapon," the Rantir states, again in English. It's a little muffled due to his large teeth and pronounced lower jaw. He has a harder time pronouncing p's and imagine would with other plosives, but it's clear enough to me what he's saying.

I'm not even sure if I should talk, but I see no other choice. "Don't give me a reason to."

"That depends on you," he tells me. "We understand one another?"

"Perfectly," I respond.

"Good," he states.

Now that we've gotten the pleasantries out of the way...

"You've been looking for me?" I ask.

He nods.

"Why?"

"Because," he begins. "You hold a key to something I've been researching for some time."

"And what's that?" I ask.

He looks me up and down, beginning to circle me. I keep my eye on him, but keep my weapon trained on the two other things pointing guns at me. I'm not comfortable at all, but again, I have no choice. Not if I want answers.

"Do you have any idea what you are?" he poses after he's finished with his examination.

"I've been trying to figure that out since I woke up like this," I tell him. "But, apparently, you think I'm some sort of key. Key to what?"

"A key to the future of my world," he states. "And a forerunner to achievements I've put into motion many long cycles ago. Maybe even 'years' by your measurements."

"I don't have time for metaphors," I tell him. "Speak plainly."

"Very well," he states. "You were the first of your kind ever created. And you were an accident."

"I was supposed to be a machine then?" I ask, discouraging as it is to do so.

He shakes his head. "Not just a machine. A cybernetic enhancement of both worlds. The human brain contains enormous

84

potential for the integration of advanced robotics. With the right nurturing, it's a self-sustaining processing center as well as an infinite memory bank."

"So I was an experiment?" I question, nearing anger as I do so.

"An unforeseeably, incredibly successful experiment," he confirms. "Albeit, one that didn't follow its intended course, but the deviations of protocol were for the best, as you can see."

"So what was I supposed to be?"

He shrugs. "What I speculate you were supposed to be, was more like them." He points to the other two still leveling their weapons at me. "They were once like you. Everything about them is based off their human evolution. Anatomically, your bodily structure allows you to adapt to a myriad of different conditions. This is why your structure was incorporated into the final design of what you are and what you see before you. Your physical evolution makes you the perfect masters of any task. However, it's your mind that is the key. The human mind, like a Rantir's, is special because of its longevity, adaptability, and many other qualities. A machine influenced by a human mind demonstrates lateral cognition; problem solving abilities. And, with the correct applications can reach unknown and exciting potential. Even after it's decomposed and an artificial processor takes its place to manage the nanobots within the vessel."

"What do you mean, 'after it's decomposed?'"

"There can be no mechanical preservation of the human brain," he explains. "Only a replacement. Our micro-robotic technology is capable of the latter but not the former. However the schematic or structure of your brain is still required first for them to carry out their programming for sustaining the structure of a host vessel. Only then can a compatible, robotic replacement be implemented into said host vessel."

Now I'm starting to get really pissed off. It seems like everything he's telling me has all been an exploitation of the human race. "So why didn't you do this to your own kind?"

"Do you understand what I'm saying to you?" he responds.

"I asked a question regarding the subject for further clarification, so clearly not."

He sighs. "Organic material, having been replaced with mechanical and digital composition, is no more than a machine. A very powerful, infinite machine that can store vast amounts of data and functions, but still just a vessel awaiting commands. Such cybernetic methods have been tried on Rantir before, and I discovered the same results as I later did with humans. However, since humans don't have the best diplomatic standing among the Rantir...Let's just say it's easier to acquire human subjects for scientific advancement."

"So humans are expendable?"

"Your words. Not mine. That is the correct human phrase, yes?"

I want to teach him another none too pleasant human phrase by demonstrating it to him. It involves my foot penetrating one of his orifices.

"Why did you make those two?" I ask, gesturing to the *things* flanking him on either side. "They just servants now? Is that why was I made?"

"You, I did not create, so I know not what your purpose is," he starts. "But I am the maker of these two, and from original human vessels as I stated. 'Expendable humans,' as you said. They serve me in roles such as protection, labor, or whatever I would ask of them. And thanks to their brains, can be repurposed for any task, so long as the nanobots ensure the welfare of the host."

"Let's get right to point," I say, pointing my gun at his head. "Why do you want me?"

"Very well." He takes a deep breath, as if he's annoyed. "You are the first of your kind. The 'prototype,' if you will. The fact that your emotions and memories were left intact along with your brain, all of which was integrated into the technological body you now inhabit, could lead to other monumental advancements beyond your present state. Things like programming our cellular robotics in a multifunctioning, intelligent way. Repurposing the technology that has allowed the Rantir race to become as advanced as they are will only enhance the future of my species. You, potentially hold the key for that."

I can't believe what I'm hearing. Apparently, he can sense my apprehension.

"Think of it," he continues. "Your species has researched the cure for diseases that have plagued your world for years. Thus far, no suitable solution beyond exposure to radiation, vaccinations, or invasive treatments has presented itself from what I've learned from human medical archives. With the micro-robotics introduced by my kind, you would have your solution to all of this. Malfunctioning cells will be destroyed and removed from the body by the microscopic machines.

Broken bones will be mended when these nanobots bring the proper nutrients to the injury. Healing rates will exponentially increase. Imagine the potential for any living species."

I shake my head. "I still don't get it. How do I factor in?"

He sighs in that same, irritated way he did before. "Your micro-robotic enhancements are programmed to maintain the body of the host. However, have you not noticed how they do more than just that? You've maintained yourself well enough, so you know your robotic cells break down matter to fit the purposes of the mechanized body. But yours also have left your mind in its original state. They are in fact nurturing it. *Preserving* it."

It's crazy to me that I'm listening to this Rantir at all, but I'm starting to see what he's talking about. I was aware of the fact that my brain was still intact and fully functional, though I'd never considered the significance of this fact until now.

"You're aware you have some organic material left within you. That brain of yours, yes?" he asks.

I nod.

"Then that is proof enough of your robotic cells and their multi-purposed programming," he says. "They maintain both organic and inorganic substance."

I shake my head. "That doesn't prove anything. Your race has programed those things for any number of functions. You even engineered them to wipe out my entire planet."

"Not all of it," he reminds me. "Those nanobots were only programed to deny the human body of oxygen. Programmed to deny a preset structure of a basic component. They carried out a very simple, cellular function that nearly annihilated your species. Those robots were programmed for a *singular* function, Ferroc. Much like the ones I now use to breathe your atmosphere. But even the nanobots I possess can't create compatible, organic material for my body. They can create a molecular compound similar to my flesh, but not entirely replicate it. The manipulation of subatomic activity concerning the biological realm is a technology that the Rantir and I have not yet mastered in the field of nanorobotics. The sole function of my nanobots is to transport nitrogen and helium to my bloodstream, and they do so by breaking down the atomic substances introduced through my respiration. Those molecules of nitrogen and helium are then distributed. They don't know it's for my respiratory functions. They are just programed to perform the task. Much like yours would go about their task if you placed any piece of metal within access of your robotic cells."

"You're still not making it any clearer for me," I growl.

"Simply put, the nanobots within your system were similarly programmed for a singular function to maintain the host," he tells me. "This is a broad program to be sure, but simplistic in essence considering your mechanical nature. Metal can be mended, circuits reformatted, and necessary components transported to areas of utilization. Any machine can be repaired with the right tools and instruction. Those nanobots are your tools, Ferroc, complete with their own set of instructions which is a schematic of your physical being along with all mechanical components. Still, it's a singular function, as I stated before. *Maintain the original structure of the host.*"

"So you're saying mine are doing more than that?"

He nods. "Yes. Don't you see? Your brain is capable of human emotion, and thus we can conclude that it is still, in fact, preserved due to synaptic activity. But how, Ferroc? It should have decomposed long ago without human blood and circulation. Why hasn't this happened? How, when the nanobots within you are only programed to maintain the host on a purely molecular scale? Moreover, only on a mechanical basis..."

If he's about to say what I think he's going to say...

"The answer is, your cellular robots learned not only to preserve organic material, astounding enough alone, but also to *create* compatible, living, renewable tissue. Not just elemental substances. Your brain is thriving and renewing. This means your nanobots have adapted to generate fresh biological material. Even replicate subatomic activity within that material. And they did that on their own."

That...I wasn't prepared for.

"Do you understand now?" he asks. "You are the first artificial intelligence ever created that is fully self-aware and fully functional in both a mechanical and organic existence. You are the embodiment of combined biological and artificial evolution. Yet we have no idea how this came to be. Your nanobots hold the key."

My mind is reeling from this information. I never expected a concept like this. I thought I was some Rantir experiment or toy that one of them had misplaced. I thought I was a project created by humans trying to fight back against the alien invaders. I thought maybe my life in this mechanical form was an act of God!

Not the culmination of evolutionary science for two different forms of existence.

If he was right, then there was no telling what I was capable of. I'd never even thought about it before, but he was right. How was I still alive? How was I still *me*?

It all made sense now. *He* helped me see that. Scary as that was.

"And you're telling me all of this," I stated, still trying to believe what he'd just said. "Why?"

He keeps his gaze locked on me as his entire body goes rigid. "Because, you know what must be done."

I perform the equivalent of narrowing my eyes as the intense glow of my visor dims. "Enlighten me."

"Your robotic cells must be extracted," he answers.

"Which would kill me," I add.

He shrugs. "Not necessarily."

I shake my head. "If I'm the host vessel, that means any extracted nanobots will cease their function of preserving the host once separated from the host vessel. And without my own host of robotic cells, my brain goes dead after about six minutes without oxygen."

"It's a theory," he replies. "But a very real possibility. Small price to pay, don't you think? You are in fact aiding the evolution of my species with your sacrifice."

"And what about my species?"

"I would think that what the Rantir has done to your race is evidence enough of my disposition on that subject," he answers. "Humans are beyond saving."

I audibly growl. "Not much of a moral complex among your kind is there?"

He waves me off as his helmet folds into place over his head, his four eye ports glowing brightly with violet light. "I didn't come here to debate ethics with you, Ferroc. I've tracked you down with the hope you'd willingly surrender yourself for the betterment of another race. You may not be able to save the humans but you can spare many Rantir lives."

"And you actually thought I'd just give up, huh?"

He retrieves the weapon strapped to his back. A large, two handed cannon resembling a human machine gun, but with more bulk and a less rigid theme. The weapon contours from trigger, to chamber, to barrel, containing no magazine except for a large glowing power source situated near the gun's core.

"I thought you'd appreciate the chance to exhibit some selflessness and potentially save another species from civil war. The advances you could bring would stifle a brewing conflict. If you willingly offered yourself for study, I could benefit much more from undamaged samples. This option is still available if you wish. If you resist, there will still be something of you left I can utilize. But it would make a difference to be sure."

"So my choices are die, or live as a lab rat, huh?"

"To enhance the lives of the Rantir," he clarifies. "A noble purpose."

"That what this is about?" I ask, anger boiling. "Saving your species from war? I sure as hell don't see any Rantir enacting genocide on each other like they did to my kind. What are you really after?"

"Irrelevant," he replies. "What's your choice?"

"Go fuck yourself."

He scoffs. "So be it."

I'm acting on instinct the moment he finishes his sentence. I fire a round into the face of one of his robotic compatriots, dropping to my knees as I do so and avoiding the fire from the Rantir and other cyborg. The slug impacts my enemy, snapping its head back as the bullet penetrates through its visor and tears into its artificial brain. I see its body spasm, then lock in place as its systems shut down. It falls heavily to the ground, and I'm already on the move by the time the round struck.

Two blasts of disintegration energy soar over me as I roll to my left, powering my legs and tucking them under me as I do so. The anti-material projectiles interfere with my internal systems and vision, causing static and impaired coordination for a second. I make it a point to be nowhere near their blast radii lest the energies inhibit my combat capabilities. I complete the roll and leap straight for the second robot with a deadly pounce. I leave my shotgun behind knowing I won't get the drop on them like my first shot. I reach my enemy before it can react, both arms outstretched. I collide with it, gripping one hand under its jaw and the other behind its head. We both skid along the pavement for several yards, leaving a trail of sparks and metal as we're powered back by my momentum. It's stuck underneath me, but that doesn't last long.

I'm trying to rip its head off, but can't find a foothold for leverage with the two of us struggling for control. My enemy takes the opportunity to slide further beneath me, creeping its legs up behind me and locking its ankles around my neck as it does so. I'm wrenched from my feet by the powered effort of my foe and slammed into the ground with such force that I shatter the tarmac. My vision blurs for a moment, afflicted by static from the impact, but clearing a moment later.

No exterior or internal damage detected.

I roll backward, trying to get to my feet as quick as I can lest I be blown away by the Rantir, who I'm sure is drawing a bead. The moment I turn to see any incoming threat from him, I hear a shot from a rifle pierce the cacophonic sounds of battle. Almost at the same moment, sparks fly off the helmet of the Rantir as his head is slammed forward, impacted from behind by Sasha's round. He roars in protest, then turns and fires a blast at where I pray Sasha isn't.

He couldn't have spotted her. At least, that's what I'm telling myself for now as I deal with the present threat.

I quickly turn my attention back to my robotic enemy as it levels its wrist-mounted weapon at me. I power my legs, draw my sword, and cock my right arm back, keeping the weapon ready and my intended attack charged for the moment I'm hoping for. I dodge to my left, hoping that accelerating at such high speed will prove too much for its targeting systems. As I see the glow of its weapon intensify in preparation to fire, I drop to my knees again, sliding along the ground and hoping to duck underneath the incoming blast.

It's close. Had I not anticipated its accuracy this would have been it for me. Fortunately, I avoid the blast by no more than a few millimeters as my internal systems begin to short, almost malfunctioning completely. Again, I recover from the interference quickly enough, plant my feet, charge them, then leap back as another blast sunders the earth on which I was just standing. I prepare another leap while flying backward, immediately changing direction upon landing, then spring forward toward my enemy, making an attack of my own.

My initial intention was to cut the thing in half as I passed by in a summersaulting vault. That changed the moment I saw how accurate it could be, even against my enhanced speed. So I improvise. I begin my flip by acquiring a mark for a calculated throw. After my aiming systems give me a lock, I unleash the charge in my right arm, hurling the blade at the cyborg with a powerful snap of my limb. The weapon whirs through the air horizontally, spinning so fast it appears to be a flying circular saw. The weapon strikes true, and thanks to my calculation and targeting protocols, hits my enemy square in the chest, the tip of the sword leading the way. It impales my foe, staggering it back and disrupting its shot. My flipping approach brings me to my target not even a second later.

I perform a flip and half twist, gyroscopic and coordination programs assisting me once again. As I fly over it, I reach down with my foot, grasp the hilt of my sword with robotic toes capable of performing such a feat, and rip the blade from my enemy as I pass by. I tear through its internal workings, nearly slicing it in half vertically as I complete my pass. I can't put my feet under me as I reach the ground, and because of that, spring off my hands while releasing my sword. As I flip over to my feet, I catch my blade as I stand straight. Now upright, I see the enemy robot is dispatched. The left side of its body hangs limply and its head rolls to the side where the blade passed through its shoulder, unable to function. Its systems shut down like its counterpart before it falls heavily to the ground. I turn to square off against my last enemy just in time to see his disintegration cannon fire at me.

I have no way out this time.

Except for Sasha.

Another shot cracks the sky almost a hundredth of a second before the disintegration cannon is fired.

She saves my life. It's all the time I need.

I try to drop to my right and roll away as fast as I'm able, but even though his shot has been disrupted, it was only partially so. He's still accurate enough to clip my left shoulder, which turns my entire left arm to ash that floats away in the breeze. Warning indicators and lots of red flash across my vision as I see he's ruptured my decomposition chamber, compromised administration of nanobots, and damaged propulsion and hydraulics to the majority of my left side from my waist up, compromising my movement. My legs are still working fine and I'm glad of that. If I'm going to survive, I need to keep moving.

He roars again and fires another shot at where he believes his attacker is. I take the moment to charge my legs. He turns back to me and fires again, but I'm ready. I dodge the attack, leaping almost fifty feet to my right. While airborne, I sheath my sword and draw my .45. I fire a few rounds upon landing, aiming for his weapon. I know I can't penetrate his armor. Sasha's rifle couldn't even do that. But she has the right idea. Maybe we can destroy his weapon and make the fight a little more even.

I fire three rounds, then leap away. My fire disrupts his shot and he has difficultly drawing a bead on me. I can only rely on this tactic a limited amount of times though, for my magazine is going to run dry after a few attempts. I pray that will be enough to compromise his weapon.

I land, legs charged, and I'm forced to dodge again as another blast explodes where I just landed a moment ago. I fire from the air, targeting systems guiding my hand as I arc to my next destination. I fire two shots, both of which connect with his weapon. I notice some sparks flying off the side of the cannon, confirming I'm doing something disruptive to it.

I land again, ready to spring, firing three more rounds aimed for the power core. I connect with one round, but miss the other two as his body flinches to avoid the incoming fire. He recovers faster than I thought and levels his weapon as I leap away, tracking my movement. Another rifle shot pierces the chaos of our battle, connecting with his weapon and saving me once again.

There's an eerie, keening noise coming from the weapon now. Almost like air escaping a taught balloon. That's the only warning we get as the weapon explodes in a brilliant display of green and blue light. I'm tossed back from the concussive force of the explosion. The Rantir is enveloped in the blast and disappears from my vision.

There's a heavy layer of dust in the air as I rise to my feet. I draw my sword and slowly begin to stalk through the haze. I look for my enemy, seeing nothing but the shroud of particles. I switch over to thermal vision and find the glowing center of the whole mess, still hot from the blast. It's all one big blob of heat, so I can't tell if my enemy lies somewhere within.

Only one way to find out.

I keep advancing on the center of the heat source, switching back to standard vision and charging my arm for a slash if necessary. I'm hoping he's alive, even in light of everything that's just happened. There are a few more questions I'd like to ask before I rip his throat out. Eventually, I see his blackened and charred form lying near the outside of the crater formed by the explosion. I hear him wheezing. I guess the explosion took its toll on him. I approach, but I'm forced to retreat shortly after as a scythe snaps out from his back aiming for my head.

I react quickly enough, but get grazed atop my artificial skull. I swing my sword upward, stopping his blade from cutting any deeper into my head. I then block a second attack sweeping for my legs. I jump back before he can ready another slash. I can't afford to be caught off-guard or overestimate my capabilities. My body is heavily damaged and functioning at about sixty percent combat capacity.

He's definitely got the advantage.

Suddenly, a blue glow is emitted from his armor. Something folds out from his back, revealing the source of the illumination. I hear what sounds like miniature jet engines firing, then he blasts away from me, rocketing into the air and breaking through the sound barrier soon after. He disappears over the horizon.

He's running.

And I'm pissed.

But just like that, he's gone.

I stand watching him long after he's out of sight, wondering what else he knows that I don't. I question all the things he and I just discussed, knowing in my heart I shouldn't be doubting them because they make sense. But I feel like I have to in order to keep some semblance of a grip on the situation. My ability to question and analyze this from a perspective other than a mechanical one is important to me right now. After all, it seems like what was left of my humanity was something that evolved the nanobots residing in me.

Turns out, I've been more human than I've given myself credit for.

I hear Sasha running up from behind me.

"Nathan!" she calls out, about a hundred feet behind me.

I turn, waving her in with my remaining arm after I sheath my sword. I notice her ghillie suit is burned on her right shoulder. It looks like her skin is red near her neck and on the right side of her face, but she's no worse for wear.

She closes the distance, face twisted into a grimace of surprise, concern, and fear all at once. "Oh my God..."

"I'm all right," I tell her. "Are you?"

She leans in and inspects the damage. "Yeah, I'm fine. But are you sure? This is..."

I hold up my hand. "I can't feel it. Don't worry. I'm fine."

Some of the metal comprising my exterior is still red hot. I shy away from her touch after realizing this, not wanting her to harm herself. I assess the damage more thoroughly now that I have time.

There's a fairly large, charred hole where my shoulder should be. Circuits and tubing have melded together from the effects of the disintegration cannon. Some interior power surges spark and fizzle even now as I look at them.

To me, it's nothing but an inconvenience. To Sasha, I'm sure it looks ugly.

"What are you going to do?" she asks.

I gesture to the other two robots. "I have everything I need." I then make my way over to the bodies.

My systems get to work on scanning the husks of the former humans. However, instead of assessing them for compatible materials, my systems run diagnostics and threat assessments first. I discover that the two are still very much alive, albeit in a hibernating state. Their internal systems are continuing to function, busy trying to repair the host vessel. Meanwhile, all exterior functions have been terminated to expedite the restoration process.

"If we run into any more of these, make sure they're dead," I tell Sasha.

She eyes me curiously. "You mean they're not?"

I nod.

"Then how do we make sure?"

"I think I know," I tell her.

I kneel down next to one of them. Analysis of the body informs me they have internally stored power cores containing vast amounts of residual electric charge. I rip through the cyborg's metal exterior, then remove the cores carefully. I then begin detaching its left arm. Further investigation reveals the limb to be comprised mostly of suitable replacement metal. Even better, diagnostics inform me the disintegration weapon attached to the right arm is compatible with my current systems. My available power is capable of sustaining the weapon's function upon integration. With that knowledge, I remove the right forearm as well.

Looks like I'll have some Rantir tech to play with soon.

"Residual power is stored in containers like these," I tell Sasha, holding up one of the power cores. "Without them, the nanobots within the vessel need to generate their own power, lowering their overall productivity exponentially. Maybe even ceasing their function altogether if the host vessel can't operate. It's interesting though..."

"What is?" she asks, analyzing the robotic husk.

I turn to her. "I don't have storage systems like this. I generate my own modest, but self-sustaining power. These two can save vast amounts of energy through a more advanced power generation system at the cost of cellular longevity. So long as they have access to energy reserves, they're capable of rebuilding expended cells."

She nods as I explain, and I can only assume she understands.

"It seems like a more efficient power system than mine," I begin again. "That makes sense if I was the prototype. Looks like these two might be better models of what I was supposed to be. Except if that's the case, the more potent energy system they possess is only useful if the system isn't compromised. At least my power supply is self-sufficient."

"So what do they do with all that extra energy?" she asks, perhaps thinking out loud more than asking me.

"The excess energy is stored and can then be transferred elsewhere," I tell her. "Maybe for their restoration subroutines... "

She gestures to the weapon mounted on the forearm. "Or maybe those?"

I nod. "I think you're right. So I guess I'll have to be careful if I use it."

She looks to me. "Wait, you can use it?"

"Analysis confirms my system is compatible with the arm and the weapon," I tell her. "So, yeah."

She shrugs, but grins. "Works for me. So what about these two?"

"Without their power storage, I'm noting an exponential decline in nanobot efficiency," I inform her. "Calculations indicate they'll be out of commission for at least a week, and functioning at twelve percent capacity after that. That's only if they get their power cores back. But I can see the energy levels within the storage vessels starting to decline as well, so these power cores will only be useful for a limited time."

"So take away their power cells and they're done?"

I nod.

"Is twelve percent dangerous if they ever got back up?" she asks.

"Only if you're a bug and they happen to step on you," I offer. "They'll barely be able to walk. Besides, we can make sure it's even longer before they're useful."

I start ripping the thing apart, scattering its many components all around us.

"Whatever works," Sasha notes, then approaches the next one.

I go to the other robot with her, remove its cores and any other components I need for repairs. Everything essential to my recovery is provided by these two robotic drones. Everything else I discard. Only then does it occur to me that, in a way, I've just committed murder if these things were once human. Now I'm scavenging their bodies like some robotic vulture.

It's not a pleasant thought, but I quickly shake it from my mind. I need to survive and so does Sasha. We need these parts to do that. That's what matters. Beyond that, I know now isn't the time to have a crisis of morals. There's a whole lot that's just been introduced to my world, making it exceedingly more complicated than it already was. Suddenly there's a Rantir who is producing assembly line versions of me by converting living humans into robots. That same Rantir is hunting me to harvest my evolved and self-developed micro-robotic A.I's. And, apparently I'm the first and only one of my kind in this world.

...This galaxy.

...This universe?

Yeah. That's a lot to soak in right now. Scavenging parts off things that were once human isn't such a big issue by comparison. Especially since they're not human anymore. At any rate, that's how I'm going to rationalize it and deal with the bigger threat.

Things got a lot more complicated indeed.

"So what was that all about anyway?" Sasha asks, breaking my focus from the task at hand.

I audibly chuckle at the bizarre and suddenly drastic situation.

"What?" she presses.

"It's just that I don't even know where to start," I tell her. "Do you want the long version, or the short?"

She puts on a quizzical expression. "Is there a middle ground for those two?"

I laugh again. I figure I might as well since the whole situation needs a little humor to balance out the gravity of it. At least for me.

"Apparently," I begin. "My nanobots are evolving inside me. They've gained some form of sentience."

Pause. "What?"

I shrug. "I can't tell you how, Sasha. But that Rantir claimed I was the first A.I ever created, and my micro-robotic cells hold the key to that type of evolution. If he's right, there's a whole lot that I'm capable of."

She looks at me with more concern than curiosity. "Like what?"

"Cure for cancer, for starters," I tell her. "Cure to *every* disease for that matter. I could lead to unprecedented advancements in most scientific fields. I'm the perpetual motion machine. I may even be the first form of immortal life. My robotic cells can *learn* to do anything so long as it benefits the host."

It looks like she doesn't know whether to nod in comprehension or shake her head in disbelief. It appears she's trying to do both at the same time, so instead she just ends up rolling her head around rather humorously.

She eventually finds the words. "Do you have any idea what you're saying?"

My tone gets very stern and slow. "I'm fully aware of what I'm saying, Sasha. All of these theories apply to his kind too. Whatever sickness they have, my cells know how to overcome it biologically. Whatever technology they possess, my cells can assimilate it. Maybe even improve it. And if he ever gets his hands on me, I know he's not going to make peace with the human race. He's already turning us into..." I gesture to the two husks. "Them."

Now she wears an ashen expression. "They were people?"

"Yes," I answer. "'*Were.*' According to him, our brains can lay a blueprint that robotics can follow and duplicate in a mechanical state. These two had their minds wiped and were then transformed into his pets. Apparently, that's what I was made for, but my memories were never erased. My mind was preserved. And my nanobots learned how to do that on their own. Combining that with my human ingenuity..." I shake my head at the situation, not even sure I'm believing what I'm saying. "I'm still trying to get a vague idea of what that means to the advancement of life as we know it."

"You're absolutely serious?"

I don't blame her for having a hard time grasping the whole situation. I'm having difficulty with it too. "It's not easy to accept, but why else would he be here? Especially with these two in tow..."

"I mean this in the best way, Nathan," she begins. "But what the fuck are you? It almost sounds like you're a type of god."

I shake my head at the whole situation for another time. "Wish I knew, Sasha. But from what I do know, I'm the first of my kind ever made. And the *only* one that is self-aware. I'm no god, but I'm getting the impression my ability to adapt is almost god-like."

She thinks for a moment. "If that's the case, Nathan, that makes you a pretty wanted man."

I nod. "That's for sure. But maybe only by him. He said he wanted to use me to advance his species. He even alluded to there being a Rantir civil war in the works. But whatever he's up to, it seems like he's going it alone. He's got an agenda."

"What makes you say that?" she asks.

"If he had backing, he'd have showed up with them if I was as important as he claimed," I explain. "He brought his own creations with him. Evidently, his resources are limited. But he's well-informed. Apparently I'm being watched. I'm not sure how."

She looks at the two drones, then back at me. "Whatever's going on, we need to figure out how to avoid him again. He'll be back."

I nod in agreement. "We hurt him though, so it may take a bit. He was wheezing pretty good before he took off. Whatever that explosion did to him was significant."

"You think he's close?" she poses.

A thought occurs to me. "Maybe we can find out."

I begin disassembling the armored head of the drone I cut with my sword. It's not easy work with one arm, but I manage. When his artificial brain is exposed, I begin scanning it for any information. I touch it with my hand and absorb some residual charge, but more importantly, establish an electrical connection to access its programming. My nanobots begin assimilating its protocol files. Most of them are the same as my own, however there's something unique. It's some kind of "eventuality protocol."

SYSTEM DIRECTIVE 0003-45911-09E. SEPARATION FROM USER COMMAND: RETURN TO PLANETARY POSITION 40.714623 BY -74.006605.

Latitude and longitude. I know where that is.

"New York," I say softly, not surprised.

"New York?" Sasha asks.

"That's where this thing was supposed to go in case it got separated from its commander," I tell her. "He's going back to New York."

She looks from the drone back to me. "You have any idea why?"

I shake my head. "But maybe we should find out."

Chapter 5

There isn't much more to discuss after my proposition. New York isn't too far out of our way since we're heading to Vermont. Sasha doesn't mind a little detour. In the end, it all boils down to a simple matter of us having nothing but time. More importantly however, and Sasha is openly receptive to this, it's a chance for me to find out my origins and maybe even save remaining humans from a fate of artificial servitude.

She's more than happy to agree to this.

It's all a waiting game for the moment. I need to repair myself and that's going to take time. The damage to my structure is significant. Even with the power cores and necessary parts from the two drones, it's still going to take at least four hours. We arrived at the service station in the afternoon, so pressing on in the dark doesn't seem like a good idea. We make camp in the ruined structure. The bats don't seem to mind as long as we don't get too close. Sasha finds some more juice bottles, much to her delight. She's glad to keep me occupied with conversation while she enjoys her beverages.

We're not worried that our enemy will return or that he'll send some of his drones. We don't know how many more he has or if he has other allies. And beyond that, there's really nothing we could do. The countryside is fairly open here. The surrounding area isn't ideal for hiding. Mostly plains and rolling, non-forested hills. So, we make do with what we have. Besides, it's comfortable for Sasha, and we both need her rested in case something finds us again.

We talk mostly about what we're going to do and what we think we'll find. We both have a lot of questions about the strange Rantir who suddenly made himself quite the presence in our lives. We wonder what he's up to and what he's been up to. We wonder if there's more like him out there and if he was telling the truth about there being a schism among the Rantir race. If that's the case, maybe they have the same problems among members of their society that humans did. These are things we hope to learn to enhance our knowledge of them, perhaps exploiting any weaknesses later.

She asks me what I'll do if I find out who made me. I tell her I'd like to track that specific Rantir down and question him myself. Not in any hostile way. I just want to know the particulars of my creation.

"What would you ask him first?" Sasha questions.

It's something I've asked unseen entities for years. "'Why me?'"

"Yeah?" she probes.

I nod. "I want to know what made me special. What was it the Rantir saw in me that they decided to turn me into what I am now?"

She tilts her head. "You said you were the last one between your family and them when they attacked, right?"

"Yes."

She shrugs. "They seem like a pretty warrior-oriented society. Maybe they respected that about you."

"There's plenty of soldiers out there for that," I dismiss. "I'm sure they all exhibited valor."

"But only one Nathan," she's quick to reply. "And someone who's not a soldier, by their standards, doesn't show valor as openly as someone trained for war I'd guess."

I laugh weakly, helpless against her logic. "I guess that's another reason why I want to know why they chose me."

Her expression suddenly becomes ashen. "Do you think it was him?"

"Him who made me?" I shake my head. "He said he wasn't. And I think he'd know a lot more about me if that were the case. I think he'd also have known where to find me a long time ago."

"Hmm," she thinks aloud. "Wonder what took him so long anyway."

"True," I agree with her. "It's not like I'd be difficult to find. The population isn't exactly saturated with either species. But if there really is a civil war among the Rantir, that could mean he has enemies after him, so he'll need to mask any movements and the activities he's attempting."

"'The enemy of my enemy...'" she begins.

"'Is my friend,'" I finish, nodding my head in agreement. "Let's hope so."

We let things be at that. There's only so much we can confirm from the information we have. For the most part, all we can do is speculate and make educated guesses, and thus far, it isn't giving us a lot of hope. Granted, there are beneficial possibilities for us in so doing such theorizing, but we won't be able to confirm anything until we actually have reasonable evidence to support such hypotheses.

So we wait, making small talk to distract ourselves while my repairs finish. While they do so, I attempt to assimilate the power core technology of the two drones, thinking that maybe I could utilize such a method for my own system regulations. I discover that the process of power storage could indeed be integrated, however I'd need to rearrange my inner components to install the upgrade. This would be a very time consuming process. All the while I'd be vulnerable as my power was rerouted to the new storage units. However, there were many benefits to this if I ever finished the procedure. For one thing, I'd be given reserve energy to repair myself expeditiously. For another, my nanobots, while self-sustaining and self-sufficient in their kinetic energy production, would also have access to a reserve storage facility in the event of surplus energy generated by regular or irregular activity.

The question is: is now a good time to perform the procedure?

Considering Sasha now relies on me while she sleeps, I decide against attempting such enhancements for the present. She isn't opposed to the idea after I explain it to her. She encourages it, in a point of fact. Just not now. Not after what we've just gone through and discovered. She says we've learned too much for me to be captured or destroyed while in such a helpless position.

I agree with her.

Instead, when my repairs complete and my arm is whole, but with an interesting addition, we have something else to manage. It's one of those "good problems to have" kind of moments.

"So you're saying you have one of their weapons now?" she asks shortly after I confirm the assimilated ordnance.

I'm a little stunned myself with how quickly the weapon was integrated into my own system, but I nod. "It would appear so. One moment..." I didn't think things would go this well when I took apart the weapon and integrated it into the repair procedure. There's a lot I need to learn about it.

I run a quick scan and perform necessary diagnostics on weapon compatibility along with operating procedures. It seems all that's necessary for the user to fire the weapon is something as simple as a mental command. The electrical impulse would travel through my systems much like the nerves of a human. The end result, of course, would be the discharge of disintegrating energy.

A display of the weapon's schematics appears in my field of vision. It's in the Rantir language, so I need to run translation protocols on it, however, an error indicator flashes in red. Apparently, there is no available translation for such a device as it was custom made.

I get that. Seems like our new enemy doesn't have any friends among the Rantir after all.

I turn to Sasha. "All assessments confirm full weapon incorporation, including compatibility with targeting procedures. I have detailed schematics of the weapon's structure and function. Evidently, it utilizes gathered particles from the air which are then super-heated through a smaller type of nuclear fusion. Just before the energy becomes unstable, it's discharged."

She narrows her eyes as she tries to follow along. "So you're saying it has no magazine? It just fires stuff from the air?"

"Yes," I confirm. "However, energy consumption is enormous. Firing one burst from the weapon drains nearly a third of a power core's energy."

"But you don't have a power core inside you," she points out.

"Which is why I'll have to be careful if I ever fire this thing. I'm not sure, but I think it could kill me if I discharge it without sufficient energy."

"So…" she says, trailing off in midsentence.

I eye her curiously. "Yes?"

"Do you have enough power?"

"Internally? Yes," I tell her, a little confused by her question. "What are you getting at?"

"Well," she starts, uncertain of what to say. "Might be kinda fun to put a few rounds downrange, if you know what I mean."

Even in light of the fact that it's my well-being at stake, I can't help but giggle at the mischievous grin she sports now that she's voiced that thought. But I feel like we need to exercise the necessary caution for the situation given the consequences of unforeseen and unfortunate happenings.

"You don't think that's going to draw unwanted attention?" I ask.

She rolls her eyes. "We just have a miniature war right outside the place where we're spending the night and you're worried about drawing more attention? If anything else, I think it'll discourage the curious from getting any closer. And, this spot is our best bet at making a stand. I don't want to get caught out in the open." She rises to her feet. "You have a few power cores from the two drones, right?"

I nod.

"Then let's find out what you can do!" she says. "Better to learn now when we have the chance. We may not get another shot in a controlled area like this."

I guess I can't argue with that logic. I also can't deny I'm a little curious as to what the weapon will do now that it's integrated with my systems. So, I get up and follow her outside.

This whole thing is actually pretty exciting, and we're acting like a couple of giddy kids. But we're not being *that* stupid about it. We pick a target against a backdrop, exercising all the firearm safety procedures we've learned over the years. After she places a tire against the embankment, we both move back about fifty feet. My targeting protocols acquire the intended object after I level my newly installed arm and weapon toward it. However, I don't fire right away.

All precautionary measures aside, it feels good to just *play* again.

"All right," I begin, almost laughing at the situation. It's funny how excited we are to try out a new weapon. Apparently, we both like guns. "You have the other power cores?"

"Uh huh," she replies nodding.

"You know what to do if I lose too much energy?"

"Put the power core in your hand and let your system do the rest," she answers. "Will you just shoot the thing already?"

"Yeah sure," I mutter. "Not like I could die or anything..."

She rolls her eyes. "Oh, stop being such a pussy."

Ah yes...There's the Sasha I first met.

Alright. Firing.

For a second, there's nothing significant as the weapon whines and collects energy. Then all hell breaks loose as I'm torn from my feet and thrown to the ground a split second after a deafening blast.

I didn't expect the discharge to be so thundering, but that's really the only way to describe it. From what I can gather, the drones have better blast containment or energy management than I do. When they fired at me, the results weren't so dramatic.

"Jesus Christ!" I hear Sasha yell.

I just lie still for a second, mostly because I'm stunned at what just happened. Also because my vision is clouded with static and distortions. I certainly wasn't expecting an explosion of that magnitude. The nighttime air is saturated with dust and assorted debris. I hear what I think is Sasha coughing and trying to call out my name. The noise is distorted and muffled, almost like a radio broadcast trying to get through on the wrong frequency. I don't respond, but instead sit up sluggishly and survey the damage.

There's a gaping hole in the embankment; the edges of which are red hot with melted sand and liquefied rock. Saplings and grass are burning and there's plenty of smoldering remains lying about the crater. The ground is charred and blackened where the blast struck. It's starting to form a glossy sheen as the melted stone and dust begin to harden.

There's nothing left of the tire.

I do a quick system check to make sure I'm still alive. I discover I have nearly twenty percent power to function on. My nanobots are quickly generating more kinetically formed energy. I'll return to nominal performance levels within five minutes, so there's no permanent damage.

But holy shit!

"Nathan!" Sasha calls, genuine concern in her tone. Her voice is getting clearer. I think my audio functions are returning to normal.

I can't see her, so I wave her over to me. "I'm here. I'm fine." My voice is distorted too. Like some kind of record playing faster and slower all at once.

She runs over to my location. All I see is a blob of darker static.

"Whoa," she remarks.

"What?"

"Your arm," she tells me. "It's red hot."

I command the weapon to stand down and watch as it neatly folds back into my arm. I think it might be best to not have any accidents for a bit.

"Well that's interesting," I note.

"You sure you're OK?" Sasha questions. "That was...uh..."

I chuckle. "You wanted to see what it did. That what were you expecting?"

"Hell no!" she replies. "But it was fucking awesome!"

Now I give a good, full laugh. "Glad you approve." I look back over the damaged landscape. "Satisfactory performance from the new firearm. This will be a useful tool in a pinch."

She gets a little more serious for a moment. "Did it do anything to you?"

"Yeah," I tell her. "My power is drained nearly eighty percent. I'm running on primary functions only. I'll be fine and back to full strength in a few minutes, but there's no way I could do that twice."

"So what does it mean if you're drained?" she inquires.

"Impaired vision, hearing, speech, and movement to start," I inform her. "Internally I have only basic functions. My body is performing only the tasks necessary to prevent complete system failure. Self-sustainment is the priority, so my cells are generating more static energy to compensate for the loss of power. But I'm getting stronger by the second."

"Oh," she replies. "Well that's good news then. All good things to know."

"You know," I say. "There's a part of me that should blame you for this."

"Oh no," she answers between laughs. "Don't pin this on me. I just did you a favor, if anything. It was your call to listen to me. I just nudged you in the right direction."

"Peer pressure, peer pressure, peer pressure," I chide.

She laughs, then offers to help me up. "Hey, if you wouldn't have done it, I wouldn't have been angry..."

I accept her hand with my non-heated arm and a lighthearted laugh, rising to my feet with her help.

"I just would have been disappointed," she finishes.

"Oh, like that's supposed to hurt even more?"

"Doesn't it?"

I shake my head.

"Oooo...Cold, Nathan. Real cold."

"Funny," I comment. "I feel anything *but* in this moment."

She laughs. "Let's get back inside."

I'm glad that even amidst the dire nature of our situation, we can spare a few moments to put a damper on what is usually the bleak demeanor we must carry in order to survive. We just made it through quite the ordeal, yet we can still have fun like normal people.

Normal people...

God it feels good to be thinking things like that again. It feels good to be with someone and laugh with them, even if I'm physically incapable of doing so. It feels good to provide that kind of happiness and joy to someone. It feels so good to have someone here with me, sharing the experience even after such monumental and life-altering revelations.

I feel better for it. I *am* better for it.

God, how I've needed it. And now, here I am, groggily walking back to the place I'll call home for the night, assisted by my friend who

106

takes it upon herself to provide a shoulder to lean on. Literally. Even though I weigh a good four to five hundred pounds. She doesn't care about that. She doesn't care about the fact that I've just enhanced myself into an even more deadly and capable machine. She only thinks about me as the person trapped inside the robotic shell. We can even joke about my circumstance now. Almost as if we were old friends before...all of this.

We make it back inside the gas station. A few minutes go by and I don't need her help moving anymore. She still wears a broad smile as she gathers wood. She's about to get a small fire going, but then puts her Ferro cerium rod away. Instead, she approaches me with a dry stick, and presses it against my heated forearm. The twig immediately catches flame, and she quickly brings it back to the pile of firewood she's made.

"Ha. Ha. You're so clever Sasha."

She bats her eyelashes at me. "If you say so, Nathan."

I wish I could roll my eyes. "I guess, if nothing else, we discovered I can start fires for you."

She giggles. "I'll remember that next time I have a barbeque. I'll let you cook."

"Ah yes," I say. "Just how I like my meat...Carbonized."

She giggles again. "You have a favorite meal before the Rantir came?"

I find the question to be a bit of an odd segue, but I indulge her. "Yeah, but you're going to laugh."

"Try me."

I dig into my memories of the past, remembering something from childhood that stayed with me into my years as a man.

"Mom's mac and cheese."

She wears a very skeptical but amused look. "Mac and cheese?"

"Yeah," I answer. "What's wrong with that?"

"You could've said anything and I would have believed you, but you say 'mac and cheese'," she remarks between laughs. "Steak, risotto, burgers...But mac and cheese from a box?"

"Hey, not just any box," I clarify. "I said *Mom's* mac and cheese. She always made it differently. Better than I ever could."

"Yeah? How so?"

"Good God...I don't know! Didn't your Mom and Dad ever make something differently than you did? Even if it was just canned soup?"

"Well, I wasn't exactly at the age where I was making stuff in the form of meals," she tells me.

I grow a little somber at that statement. "No. I suppose not."

She nods, her own spirits dropping for a moment.

"Did you have a favorite meal?" I ask, wanting to change the subject.

"Yeah," she answers. "Dad always grilled amazing elk burgers. I like venison too."

"Venison is good," I agree.

"Man, that'd be nice right now," she states.

I tilt my head as I look at her, wondering if she performs this mannerism when she's being critical or pensive. I know I'm utilizing it for that at the moment. "Maybe we can get some."

"You're saying you want to do some hunting?" she asks.

I shrug. "If we get the chance. Wouldn't hurt."

She smiles. "If we get the chance."

We both experience another moment of contentment, simply glad of the other's company and this night with each other. It's that type of unspoken bond and respect you rarely receive from another person. I'm not sure how she and I have so quickly established such a connection. Maybe it's the lack of options, or maybe it was the circumstances upon which we became acquainted. Regardless, I find myself increasingly grateful for every moment I spend with her.

"Today has been one crazy day, hasn't it?" she asks at length.

"Yes it has," I agree. "I'm actually looking forward to tomorrow though."

She grins. "Me too."

Sasha falls asleep shortly after our conversation. I can tell she's resting easier each day the more that I'm around. Again, I find myself glad I can provide that kind of comfort. I take only a moment to watch her as she drifts off, then go outside the station, marching around its perimeter and switching back and forth between spectrums.

The night is rather still. Just the chirps from crickets. An occasional gust of wind adds to the nighttime symphony. Then I hear an odd noise similar to the jets of the strange Rantir's combat suit, followed by a piercing thunderclap. It's a long way off, but I know it's getting closer. I run a quick scan for the origin of the sound which informs me the source is several miles away. However, I remember that when the enemy Rantir took off, he broke through the sound barrier. It was impossible for me to mistake the sonic boom for anything else. Wherever the approaching thing is, it's closer than my scan tells me since it's traveling faster than sound.

Sure enough, as I'm considering this very possibility, I see two lights on the horizon. They're feint, almost like dimly lit stars, but they're moving toward my location in a very direct manner. From what I've seen not but a few hours ago, they can only be one thing.

More Rantir.

More *outfitted* Rantir.

I run back inside, waking Sasha as gently as possible given the urgency of the situation.

She snaps up, finger on the trigger of her pistol and whispering to me. "What?"

"Two more approaching from the east," I tell her. "They'll be here soon."

"Two more Rantir?" she asks.

I shake my head. "I don't know. They're flying like the last one did."

Her eyes widen. "Two more like *him*?"

I nod.

She's quick to accept the situation, which I'm glad of since we don't have much time to consider options. "Well, good thing we tested your new gun."

Despite the gravity of the moment, I laugh. "Yeah. I'll have it ready."

"What's the plan?" she asks.

"You stay inside," I begin. "Find a good vantage but stay out of sight. I'm going out there."

"You sure?" she questions. "They might just bomb you."

"No," I deny. "They won't. They need me alive. That's why you need to stay hidden." I look directly at her. "They're not after you. That means they'll just kill you, Sasha. That's why I want you to stay hidden."

She returns my gaze, then nods.

"No matter what happens, just stay hidden," I instruct her, reflecting on my poorly chosen words the moment I speak them. I resolve I'm not going to make her relive the events that took her family from her, then close the distance between us, gently grasping her hand in mine. "I'll come back. I promise."

109

She looks at me for a moment that seems to last much longer than it actually does. Just looking at me. As if she's trying to say something without saying it. I see it in her eyes. Then, she nods and pulls her hood over her head and moves off to a crumbling corner of the station.

That pause was invaluable to me. She didn't have to say a word. I already knew what she was feeling.

She cared. She cared a lot.

So did I...

This is one of those moments where I wish I could take a deep breath to just embrace the inevitable chaos that's about to ensue. I wonder if we made the wrong choice by sticking around here, but then remind myself the surrounding area wouldn't be any more beneficial to our present situation. If these things could fly around us all day, we'd just get picked off in a matter of seconds out in the open. The station prevented that, assuming they didn't bomb it to dust. My mind tries to think of things we could've done differently, but then I remember events were set into motion beyond our control the moment we first saw the strange Rantir yesterday.

There's nothing left to do but just face our fate. Come what may.

I step outside, activating my disintegration weapon and drawing my sword. I don't point a weapon at them, thinking it unwise to adopt a "shoot first, ask questions later," policy. It only meant I'd put Sasha in more danger. So I wait, displaying my weapons and my desire to resist capture if that's what their intentions are.

I watch the two glowing lights approach. When they come within a reasonable range, I enhance my optics to get a clear view of them. They are indeed armored Rantir. One of them is smaller. Female, from what I can tell. She looks to be about six feet tall. Her armor is sleek and angled like the one we met yesterday, but she sports blades on her wrists, shins, joints, and of course, her scythes. The other one is larger. Well-built and looking to be about eight feet tall. His armor is bulky and squared, almost as if the extra metal incorporated intentional redundancy. I can see it would offer full protection, but for some reason I feel like his movement will be limited. Not that it would matter a whole lot. I note he has two disintegration weapons mounted on his scythes instead of blades. I'm sure he has more hardware to match.

All good to know when things erupt as they have a tendency of doing.

I expect them to fly over us, circling a few times before making their initial assault. However, I'm surprised when their altitude begins to drop. They're still heading right for me, but not in any threatening way. They're also slowing down, which confuses me further.

They land. Then they just watch.

The silence is...awkward, if anything but tense.

I'm hoping and praying Sasha doesn't fire. These two are outfitted for an all-out war. At best, I'm outfitted to survive, even with my newly acquired disintegration weapon. If one side ignites the proverbial flames of conflict, it's clear to me who's going to walk away when the dust settles.

"Ferroc," the female calls out in the Rantir language, visor glowing with cyan light as she does so. Her voice is a little smoother than I thought it would be. Almost as if there's a refined quality to it, much like a singer or public speaker.

Man, am I popular.

"Yes?" I inquire.

"I am Andizha," she states. "This is Marukarn." The large male next to her remains still, yellow light illuminating his visor and various points on his armor. "We're not here to fight."

What the...

Why is life so complicated? And it became even more so in the last twenty-four hours.

"You here for something else then?" I pose. "Like the last one?"

"Last one?" the large Rantir, Marukarn, asks. He looks to his counterpart. His voice is very much the gravelly quality I've come to expect from the Rantir. However, if his brethren's voices were like gravel, then his voice is the equivalent of boulders with its deep, rumbling quality. "There was another like us?"

I hesitate to give any information freely. I have no clue what these two are up to or what their true intentions are. For all I know, this is just a ruse to get me to expose Sasha. They may even be attempting the diplomatic approach much like the one we met yesterday.

"What's it to you?"

"Please, Ferroc," Andizha pleads. "There are things at work you do not yet understand."

"Clearly," I remark. "But you'll forgive me if I'm a little paranoid. That last one took my arm off."

"You appear no worse from it," Marukarn observes with a hint of sarcasm.

"Doesn't justify him shooting at me, does it?" I fire back.

The two of them look to one another, seemingly confirming something unspoken I'm not yet aware of.

"Ferroc," Andizha begins again. "The one you encountered yesterday is no friend to us. He is a criminal. A murderer. A blaspheme upon our beliefs and exile from our kind. He is not what the Rantir stand for."

"Really?" I ask, unconvinced. "And what do the Rantir stand for? Because it's definitely not for humans, is it?"

Marukarn growls, tensing. "Your kind struck first, Ferroc. Our Archon was killed because of your species' reckless propensity for war. We would not let such a crime go unpunished."

"Irked" would be a good word to describe my attitude. "So I saw. So I've seen. But you didn't take the time to ask about the confusion amidst our global conflict either. We were going through World War Three and you got caught in the middle. We never intended to attack you."

He relaxes a bit. "That was many years ago, Ferroc. Perhaps there can be peace between our races. Or at least, between us."

I'm disinclined to oblige him, but he does have a point. That was a long time ago. Things have most definitely changed since then. The more advanced Rantir that landed on Earth are something I haven't seen since the invasion. I'm sure there was a reason for that. I'm also sure that reason is less than complimentary to our species and planet. However, that matters very little in the situation I find myself in.

I've seen enough death. As much as I distrust and perhaps dislike the Rantir, I'm not against a peaceful renewal between our species. Even if it begins small. Two Rantir and a cyborg who was once human just being able to talk would be a good start.

I fold my disintegration gun back into my forearm with a thought, but keep my sword drawn. "That's a step in the right direction."

"May we approach?" Andizha requests.

I nod. "But we stay out here. I don't want any surprises."

Both nod in acquiescence. They then close the gap between us. I feel almost foolish for letting them get this close, but the reality is, I don't have much choice if I wish to discover more about recent events. And Sasha and I both very much need to know.

"Andizha?" I ask for confirmation. "And Marukarn?" He gives a slight bow. "How do you know me?

"There are many who know you, Ferroc," Marukarn answers. "Particularly among the Rantir. You are 'Retribution Incarnate' to them. There are even whispers among the humans of a strange protector, neither man nor Rantir, who wanders the earth."

I'm stunned. "Wait...'The humans?' You've found others?"

Marukarn looks to Andizha. She responds. "We were under the impression you were searching for other survivors. Where have you been for the last few cycles?"

"Cycles?" I ask.

"Apologies," she replies. "The last few years?"

"North," I answer. "I thought the robotic plague may not have struck as severely up there."

Marukarn nods. "We too have been searching for survivors. We've found several. We've liberated even more."

I'm still reeling from how all of this has so suddenly been made known to me. "What do you mean, 'liberated?'"

"The Rantir you encountered yesterday is called Gahren," Andhizha informs me. "He has been on this planet for nearly seven years. Recently he has come to this region. Our sources indicate he resides in what you call 'New York.'"

I'm growing even more intrigued. "I scanned one of his drones yesterday. It had a location subroutine instructing it to return there if ever separated from its superior."

"Drones?" Marukarn asks. "What do you mean?"

"Another like me," I clarify. "Only with no mind. Just a robotic shell formed from a human body."

"The remains?" Andizha inquires.

I nod in the direction of the two fallen enemies. "Back there."

"We must examine them," Marukarn states. "If his designs..."

"Just hang on," I interrupt. "I'm not going along with this blindly just because you say so. There's a lot that I've yet to be made aware of. And I have a lot of questions that need answers."

"Ferroc," Andizha begins. "We will be happy to answer any and all queries you possess, but there is urgency to this matter for both of our races. Gahren endangers both of our kinds with his ambitions. We must be swift."

"Then take a few seconds and explain the situation to the one who can help you the most," I reply. "I'm not asking either. I'm telling you. Your kind nearly erased everything that was humanity. I think, as long as I still have some part in mankind's future, I'm allowed a few moments of clarification. I'll get those moments, or you're on your own." As the tense silence sinks in, I look directly at Marukarn. "You're right, you know. About there being peace between us. I've wanted that for a long time. I've killed too many of your kind to know that the war between us hasn't solved a thing. But I can never forget what your kind did to mine, or what you took from me." The three of us stare intensely at one another. "So help me forgive you. Give me a reason to start over with the Rantir."

Andizha seems to be scrutinizing me thoroughly at this point. "You speak as one who has seen the hardship of many years."

If only you knew Andizha…

I give a meek nod.

"Very well Ferroc," Marukarn says. "What do you wish to know?"

Chapter 6

Marukarn and Andizha are both very cooperative after my little speech. They seem genuine with their cause and their intentions. The moment they see Sasha, they're both elated to find another surviving human. They even switch to speaking passable English for her. Sasha is a little quiet and dry in her responses, but one can hardly blame her. She's suffered just as much as anyone at the hands of the Rantir. But, like me, she's willing to let the past stay there. After all, if the human race wants to start over, we need all the help we can get. If the Rantir extend a hand, she knows we need to take it. So we both listen to what these two have to say.

It turns out Gahren's implications about there being a Rantir schism in the making were true. It had already happened on a grand scale. We learned there were a few Rantir who opposed the obliteration of mankind, and those few had caused quite a stir amongst the political rankings of the alien society. It didn't help that the higher-ups of the Rantir social order were basically using Earth as a prison or place to banish their undesirables. So, as time went by, more and more Rantir had become dissatisfied with how things were being run as far as Earth was concerned. Some of their more religious types thought that their "Great Creator" would have wanted them to help guide humanity on their journey to salvation. Other's just thought giving peace a shot would be nice since we never really had a crack at it in the first place. Besides, it wasn't like humanity was going to have much choice in the matter with so few of us left. And the numbers were dwindling daily. Humans certainly didn't pose as much of a threat as we once did.

This was where Gahren came into play. He was one of the leaders or "Seraphs" as they called him. He strongly supported the complete annihilation of the human race and had spearheaded several of the sweeper incursions himself. However, when he was tried for war crimes involving the elimination of insubordinate or human sympathizing troops under his command, he was stripped of rank and all possessions, and sentenced to banishment to Earth. He went rogue shortly after, taking a ship, as many weapons and supplies as he could gather, and fled to Earth for refuge. Several of the Rantir were worried about what he might try to accomplish with the other criminals on Earth should he ever give them a cause to unite under. However, a full-fledged pursuit couldn't be orchestrated, as there were still several sympathizers with Gahren's cause on the Rantir homeland. This sparked small-scale skirmishes that the Rantir government was presently trying to control. Any open and non-diplomatic action taken against Gahren was deemed a possible provocation for further violence.

Enter Marukarn and Andizha. They had been dispatched to Earth on a covert mission to find Gahren and eliminate him if possible. They were to do so quickly and discretely, and to make it look as "accidental" or "incidental" as possible. Killing Gahren in this manner was the only way to deter the already developing schism among the Rantir. Thus far, no opportunity had presented itself. But, while they hadn't accomplished this goal yet, they were also instructed to protect any humans that may have survived to help win the favor of human sympathizers. Their commander, a Seraph, also thought it best to preserve what was left of humanity if given the chance.

Apparently, the war that was waged on Earth wasn't the Rantir's finest hour.

So, Marukarn and Andizha had been trying to locate Gahren for the last seven years over in Asia. That's a lot of ground to cover, and as such, they'd had little luck. The fact that Gahren had his own fully equipped Rantir vessel and lots of advanced Rantir tech at his disposal didn't help matters either. It was technology Gahren was outfitting the renegade Rantir of Earth with. He was using them to run his ship or track down other humans. Andizha and Marukarn had only suspicions of this until they were able to confirm it was true during a recon mission to Gahren's ship. It was one of the few occasions in which they'd been able to locate him. But they couldn't infiltrate or sabotage his vessel due to the sheer number of enemies inhabiting the transport. And placing any kind of tracking device was too risky lest it be found and used as political leverage to fuel Gahren's cause. If he could prove there were attempts on his life, he'd really gain some clout with any sympathizers for his cause.

And he was already building himself an army.

So the two Rantir in front of me thought it best to observe, waiting for another moment to strike.

"Do you think he had anything to do with my creation?" I ask during their explanation. "I know he wasn't directly involved, but indirectly?"

Marukarn shakes his head. "You were created at the beginning of the invasions. Long before Gahren betrayed his people."

116

"Whoever created you did so for a specific purpose," Andizha adds. "Yet we know not what."

"Don't suppose you'd know *who*, would you?" I pose.

"Apologies Ferroc," she replies. "But we do not."

That's a bit of a blow for me. It would help me make peace with the many feelings I have regarding the point of my existence if I knew simply *why* I was here. I'd spent several long hours contemplating the subject with nothing but fatalistic results. Having something a little more reasonable or logical to go off of would sure be nice. It'd make me feel more like a man than a machine.

But it looks like I'll have to wait for those answers.

Marukarn and Andizha then switch topics to Gahren's sudden reprioritization. Something had driven him to make the journey overseas, and it appeared to be an interest in cybernetics. The two proceed to tell me that ever since Gahren came to the U.S, he had been gathering humans wherever he could find them. Using them as test subjects for his robotic conversions was a frequent application. There was no telling how many he'd gathered thus far, but it was likely he'd holed up in what remains of New York for the purposes of gathering materials as well as human survivors. Since the two drones were programed to return there, we all agree to this scenario.

I ask them about how he could have found me, thinking that perhaps the discovery of my existence was what prompted him to make the journey, and worse, start experimenting on humans.

"His ship contains many instruments of detection," Marukarn replies. "Perhaps he found your energy signature in this fashion."

Andizha speaks. "And as Marukarn said, you are well-known, especially among the Rantir. Many go out of their way to avoid you. It is very likely those same Rantir are among his ranks. With the information they could supply him, he would know where to search for you on this continent."

That makes sense to me, especially if he's been roaming the country.

"As for his experiments on the human race," Marukarn adds. "One can only speculate, Ferroc. Regardless, that is something for which there is no blame to place beyond Gahren's own disregard for your kind. You take needless guilt upon yourself if you accept the responsibility of his exploitations."

Andizha and even Sasha nod in agreement with those words. They make sense to me too. I had bigger things to focus on than the reasons of a renegade Rantir. Since when did renegades with dark ambitions need a reason?

"And what about you guys?" Sasha cuts in. "How did you know about Nathan?"

"Nathan?" Andizha inquires, curious about the word.

"Me," I clarify.

Marukarn observes me for a moment before answering. As if he's getting a feel for the human word that describes my identity. "There are Rantir roaming these lands that know of you and take no sides. We have questioned them. In their minds, if they haven't joined his cause, it matters not who they share their information with. So long as they are left in peace."

"Why would they do that?" I press.

"Some of us are more bound by honor than others," Andizha informs me. "They choose their exile as willing punishment for their crimes. So long as they are left to live the rest of their lives, it makes no difference to them what happens in this world."

I'm beginning to see some of my theories on Rantir psychology are proving true.

The discussion continues at a gradual, but informative pace. I ask about why I couldn't have seen the vessel he pilots, but they tell me it's equipped with a type of camouflaging technology Gahren adapted from the chameleons and other reptiles of Earth. It made his movements incredibly difficult to track or predict. However, Marukarn and Andizha had managed to stay ahead of him as he made his way to and from each city by researching human history and geography. They knew where he would go based off of population densities before the Rantir attacks. That was until they lost him in Kansas. They were sidetracked when they found a few humans. Instead of continuing to tail Gahren, they focused their attention on a safe place for a colony of survivors while staying beyond their enemy's reach. Hoping to shelter the remaining humans from any feral Rantir and Gahren himself, they stationed themselves in northern Minnesota. Duluth to be precise. What was left of the military installations there, coupled with the resources of the surrounding area, made for a viable location to start over. The humans had even organized their own militia and stood ready to fight alongside the two of them after they had won each other's trust.

This was all incredible news to me. I'd never dreamed that there would be this type of organized renewal for the human race, especially with such dangerous threats like the feral Rantir roaming the Earth. Yet it was the help from the Rantir themselves that gave these survivors a chance to start over.

"You said 'liberated' before," I note. "What do you mean by that?"

"There are humans Gahren takes as prisoners for his labor or future tests," Andizha explains. "He does not always convert them immediately. He's found uses for them other than experimentation or labor. Some of them he employs as agents to find other humans with promises of freedom or shelter. We try to emancipate them from the fate of betraying their own."

I'd twist my face into a sneer if I could. "For one who hates humans so much, he sure makes a good diplomat doesn't he?"

They both nod grimly.

"He is not to be underestimated," Marukarn declares. "His application of physical ability, political charisma, and inherent intelligence are among the best of the Rantir. I have seen his prowess in all three fields firsthand."

I tilt my head. "You knew him?"

"We both did," Andizha tells me. "He was our instructor."

The revelations just keep coming. The last day and a half has been one hell of a ride.

"Sasha and I managed to drive him off once," I tell them. "We compromised his weapon, which then exploded and injured him."

"Was that the blast we saw earlier this night?" Andizha asks. "We had been following him for days, uncertain as to why he was covering this ground so thoroughly. Only until tonight were we able to close the distance. But we discovered you instead. Has he fled?"

Sasha, to her credit, suppresses a giggle.

...Mostly.

Behind their armored masks, I'm sure Andizha and Marukarn wear expressions of curiosity.

"He did run," I tell them. "But that was hours before the last explosion you heard."

"What caused such a blast then?" Marukarn presses.

I unfold my disintegration weapon for them to see. "We were curious."

"You assimilated its components?" Andizha asks, very intrigued.

I nod.

"You are unique indeed," Marukarn comments. "Your importance and involvement with Gahren cannot be overlooked."

"He said I was the culmination of biological and artificial evolution," I tell them. "A merger between the two, even."

They both look at each other intently. They seem like they're stunned, but in a good way. Almost as if they need to process what I just told them.

"*Ferroc*," they both whisper reverently.

"What?" I ask, not sure I heard correctly.

"That's precisely what you are, Ferroc," Andizha confirms, ignoring me. "We'd only *heard* you were capable of such things. Never had we even dreamed of our technology reaching such levels as the kind you now possess. The robotic cells within you were never engineered for a purpose as advanced as the direct creation of atomic or subatomic material. Or the assimilation of systems foreign to your own."

"The robotic cells help you breathe though," I point out. "How are they not directly involved in your body's preservation like mine?"

"They are only instructed to introduce certain elements into our bodies while diverting others," Marukarn explains. "It's a very simple directive. Your robotic cells are far more advanced."

"He said something similar," I tell them.

Sasha, who has been mostly quiet during the majority of this conversation, looks from me, to Andizha, and up to Marukarn.

"So what does all of this mean to you two?" she poses. "We know if Gahren ever gets Nathan, he's going to use him to build more robots. He'll kill whatever's left of humanity, and then, I'm assuming, he'll turn those same robots loose on the Rantir?"

"A full scale incursion on our home world would be unthinkable," Andizha replies. "At least for now. You may be correct with your theory however. It may only be a matter of time. If he were given access to Ferroc's cellular structure, he would have the power to reshape any energy he saw fit for whatever purpose he desired."

I look at Sasha, then back to the two Rantir. "He could live forever, couldn't he?"

They nod.

"It's possible," Marukarn acknowledges. "He could heal wounds almost instantly, expand cerebral functions, increase muscle capacity, heighten bone density....And those are only the evolutionary and biological applications. Artificially, he could very well *create* life were he to reprogram your existing cells."

"It is all feasible given we don't know what even *you* are capable of, Ferroc," Andizha adds. "Your cells, with their learning capabilities, contain endless possibilities."

I'd suspected as much, but I'm taking all this in with a sense of resolve. I feel like all of this has been dumped on me rather suddenly. But considering the world I've survived in for years, this isn't the strangest thing that's happened in my life.

In a way, this is what I've been hoping to find as I've wandered the world for years. I'd been looking for some kind of purpose or reason to be here. Even though I was no closer to discovering my origins or why I was made, I was now capable of making a difference if I so chose. I could prevent Gahren from harming any more humans. I could help stabilize a budding conflict among an alien race. Granted, it was the same race that had wiped out humanity, but it was the only race capable of helping us rebuild.

"Nathan," Sasha interrupts my thoughts. "What are you thinking?"

I've grown to admire how she speaks for my contemplations. As she gives them a voice, my thoughts become reality.

"I think," I begin. "The only way humanity can start over is with some help." I look at Marukarn and Andizha. "And I think the only way for you to stop Gahren and balance out the schism among your people is with *our* help."

"Both of our causes are satisfied with Gahren's defeat," Marukarn states. "I believe the human expression is 'the enemy of my enemy is my friend,' yes?"

I nod. "Right." I turn my gaze to Sasha. "Any thoughts of your own?"

She holds a glare against Marukarn and Andizha for a second, no doubt ruminating on the origins of her hatred for the Rantir, then her expression shifts to a neutral theme.

"I guess you're right," she begins. "You both are. But what about me? What about the rest of humanity? How do we fit into this?"

"If you intend on recolonizing your planet, you'll need to fight for it," Andizha claims. "If you help us, we will fight and die by your side to assist you in this endeavor if needed."

Sasha is still confused. "So, what? We take the fight to Gahren in New York? Find him and kill him?"

121

I'd grin if I could as I voice another thought. "Seems pretty suitable for a hunter."

She stifles a smile, not wanting to let on too much. "What about the other Rantir? Could we get help from them?"

Andizha nods. "It is possible. But given they are either outcasts from our society or willing recipients of discipline, you should not depend on any other Rantir but the two of us. However, now that we've found you, Ferroc, our Seraph will be far more open to sending assistance. The ramifications for lending aid to Earth would not outweigh the benefits of cooperation with someone as important as yourself. We could very well supply the human survivors adequately by the end of this cycle."

It's all starting to fall into place. At least to me. The hoops Andizha and Marukarn had to jump through, the tasks that lay ahead of all of us, and my own duty throughout all of it to the human race and those I would call allies.

It all seems like I'm suddenly promoted to a commander without any prior experience. I guess it really isn't up to me though. All I needed to worry about is stepping up.

"All right," I say. "Then let's get started. Sasha and I will start heading back to Minnesota."

"We will accompany you," inserts Marukarn.

I shake my head. "No. We hurt Gahren last time. Now is a perfect opportunity to see what kind of resources he really has. He won't be in any shape to deal with threats directly. I'd say now is the time for you two to dig up some real solid intelligence on him."

"We don't know where to look," Andizha argues. "New York is a vast ruin."

I start analyzing their armor systems. "Do you have any ports I could electronically interface with?"

Marukarn opens a panel on his chest near his right shoulder. "You have his location?"

I nod. Then, I extend my hand to the exposed wires and circuits of his battle suit, making contact and passing the necessary information to him. As I interface with his systems, I'm also allotted a glimpse of Rantir battle technology. I learn these battle suits they wear enhance every sense they possess. It seems like their nervous systems are melded into the suit's schematics, making both machine and Rantir a symbiotic unit. Not to mention the extraordinary nature of physical augmentation. Rantir were strong enough even without this type of mechanical assistance. But with it, I knew now Marukarn could snap me in half like a twig if he wanted to. He could also pick up a city bus and toss it with one arm.

I'm glad I had Sasha with me to help disarm Gahren when I fought him. I had no idea what I was up against at the time.

We got lucky. We shouldn't be alive.

Through the electrical connection I establish, I copy the existing location of the drone's rendezvous point into Marukarn's data banks.

"Do you have it?" I ask.

He takes a moment, then nods. "Yes. Thank you Ferroc."

I nod in turn. "We'll leave in the morning then."

"We can leave now," Andizha replies. "But would it not be safer for you to come with us?"

Sasha laughs. "Neither one of us can fly. And Nathan might be fine, but I don't think I could survive a trip going as fast as you guys go."

"If anything comes our way, you'll be able to see it," I respond. "I'm sure you can handle any threat that's heading for us. And, with Sasha and I traveling in the open, you'll have a clear shot if Gahren makes another move for me."

Marukarn is amused. "Your faith in our abilities is appreciated. But what if something should arise that we can't handle ourselves?"

"Then, at the very least, you can fly back and warn us," I tell them. "We run the same risk if we travel together. I know it's not always smart to split up, but we have limited resources. And if nothing else, we can cover more ground this way. There's no telling where his ship is if it isn't back in New York."

They both look hesitant.

"Look," I tell them. "I know it's not fair to ask this of you, but you're best suited for it. And I'm not leaving Sasha behind. If you guys pull your load now, I promise you I'll do my part later."

After another moment, Andizha nods in agreement. "Indeed. But there is one pivotal thing involved in all of this, Ferroc. Something you need to recognize as your duty. You *must* survive. So much depends on you."

I don't entirely like hearing that considering I just tried killing myself recently. But I accept it with what grace I can. "I'm also the only way we're going to truly discover what Gahren is capable of if he's as bent on capturing me as you claim."

"But do you understand your significance?" Marukarn presses. "We do not seek a plan to defeat Gahren, Ferroc. We seek an acceptance of the responsibility you now carry. You are the future of both of our species. This is not meant to be taken lightly. Show us you are capable of bearing that mantle."

"Then I'll stay alive and meet you in Minnesota," I answer. "Where are the other survivors?"

"Just travel north until you reach the ruin of 'Duluth,'" Andizha explains. "From there, they will find you."

"Sounds good," I say. "We'll get there as soon as we can. Come get us if you need anything."

They begin to leave.

"Hey, wait," I call after them. They both turn and face me. "One last thing. What does 'Ferroc' mean?"

They look to one another in confusion.

"You don't know?" asks Andizha.

I shake my head. "There's no Rantir definition for it. All of my translation programs can't give me an answer either."

"That's because the word is not particularly defined," she answers.

"It is part of our beliefs as Rantir," Marukarn explains. "Some say it is sacred while others whisper it is an abomination. It is rarely spoken of. We thought you'd have known since you've taken it as your title."

"I need a little help understanding it then," I tell them.

Andizha turns to Marukarn for help. He obliges me with an answer.

"'Ferroc,' means 'fused wrath,' or 'avenging hybrid.' It is the source of balance the Great Creator will place in this universe. 'Ferroc' is neither an executioner nor savior. It is a neutral force between the two. But he is harbinger of transition nonetheless."

I wasn't expecting that. For a moment, I feel a flash of guilt over having chosen a title that could be the equivalent of the Christian "Jesus," at least to their religion. I get over it quickly though, as I see they don't mind too much.

"So how is this 'balance' involved in your theology?" I inquire.

They both hesitate, as if they're uncertain they should disclose such information about their religion. However, Andizha tells me.

"Ferroc is the precursor to great change. Whether that change is for the better has always remained uncertain. The prophecy is open to interpretation."

They weren't kidding when they said I carried a heavy mantle.

"Your actions will dictate our futures and their evolution," Marukarn tells me. "And their consequences bear more weight than you know."

I can't say anything to that. So I nod and give a slight bow.

"A question for you," Andizha poses. "What does 'Nathan' mean?"

I feel like the answer I'm giving them isn't going to be sufficient. But it's the truth.

"It doesn't mean much," I tell them. "It used to be what I was called."

"Sasha still addresses you as such," Marukarn observes. "It's still who you are. Perhaps you are more of the hybrid than you realize."

And with that last statement, they both turn, activating their thrusters and blasting off. Sasha and I watch them disappear over the horizon. I don't know what's on her mind, but mine is preoccupied with a strange blend of concern and hope.

Concern for the enemy out there waiting for us. Hope of a new beginning for the human race. Concern for what my part in all of this will be. Hope for the potential of a life I can actually live out of my own desire to explore it.

"What do you make of all this?" Sasha asks at length.

I shrug helplessly. "I truly hope they mean what they say. I hope it isn't a trick."

"You know it could be," she says.

I audibly sigh. "I know. But if we do something now and they're telling the truth, we have a legitimate shot at starting over with the help of an advanced race. If we don't take a shot with them, nothing happens, and humanity withers away."

"So we pretty much have to roll the dice then," Sasha concludes. "Gotta tell ya, it doesn't sit well with me."

"It's no easier for me," I reassure her. "But again, do we have a choice?"

It's her turn to sigh. "No. I guess we don't."

The two of us sit in silence for a bit, looking out to the point where the last traces of Marukarn and Andizha sparkled against the silhouetted arc of the horizon. I would guess it's never a fun thing for anyone or anything to bet their future on a measure of uncertainty. It was especially hard for me if I was indeed the key to all of this.

A cure for any disease, a source of renewable and sustainable energy...

But also with a sense of self-awareness, responsibility, and temperament. All of this came wrapped into the proverbial package that was me.

"What will I have to become before all of this is over Sasha?" I ask her. Perhaps more because I needed to hear it out loud than pose the question.

"What do you mean?" she asks.

"I mean," I rephrase. "I'm already a machine in body. I wonder what choices are ahead of me...Choices I'll have to make that mean so much suffering or growth for those around me."

We're both silent. It's not exactly an easy question to answer. It's an even less thrilling concept to fathom.

She places her hand on my shoulder. "Just be you, Nathan. Remember that."

Her touch and her words are all the comfort I need. For a few moments, nothing else matters as I gaze out at the night sky. Then, the faintest rays of morning light begin peeking through the black haze of darkness. The signs of morning are a thing I find most fitting considering the events of the last twenty-four hours.

The world is starting over again. A new day is dawning. A new day for everyone upon this Earth.

Including me.

"'Ferroc'," I say out loud, rolling the word through my mind now that I know its true meaning.

"'Great force of change,'" Sasha quotes. "I'd say it suits you."

I laugh weakly. It's all I can do for the moment.

"Just make sure you're the change you want to see, Nathan," she continues. Then she leaves me alone in the waning darkness. She goes back inside the service station, and I hear her packing her things.

"'Be the change I want to see,'" I repeat.

I feel like wiser words have never been spoken to me, though I know she was quoting Ghandi. (I'm not sure if she knew she was.) I feel like I have to remember this wisdom through all that's about to happen. I believe amazing, life-changing things are about to make themselves known in my existence. But I can't help but feel these great things will be accompanied by horrific events that are going to test me in every way I can think of, and more that I can't. I feel like I'm going to have to give so much more than I already have.

And I feel like, no matter what, in the end, I'll still be alone when it's all said and done. All because of what I've become. All because of what I am now. A product of a life forced onto me, with an evolving power I know so little about beyond that which was explained to me.

And there's one other thing I've realized on my own…

If my cells are renewing themselves in both the biological and robotic realms, what does that mean in regard to my lifespan on this earth?

I'm going to be around for a long…long time.

It's something I'm trying hard to focus on. It's important. I could be selfish and lament my situation. I could despair at what was taken from me and what I can never get back.

…Or…

I can remember that there are others out there. There are those who need me. To help them live, to protect them, and to give them a second chance. To be a force of change for the better in the future.

It looks like I'll have plenty of time on my hands. Why not put it towards something higher than myself?

…Especially if that's the only thing I have left to live for.

Part II

Purpose

Chapter 7

"What do you think?" she asks me.

I've run about every scan or precautionary sweep I can. Still, I see nothing. No heat registers, no sound indicators, not even seismic or impact tremors when I attempt to detect them with a little finagling of my systems. In the quiet, fall air, I was hoping something would stand out a little more.

Wherever these survivors were that Marukarn and Andizha told us about, they were hidden from every type of prying eyes. I guess that would have to be the case if one was trying to hide from the Rantir. Against the perfect predator, you required the perfect camouflage. I wonder if even that will save them from Gahren. Feral Rantir reduced to a ravenous state of mind were one thing. An advanced alien armed with unknown but incredibly sophisticated technology…

That was something different. There wasn't a lot of hiding from that any way you spin it. There isn't much fighting against it either.

Unless you're me, I suppose. Or another Rantir comparably outfitted.

"I think," I tell her. "We listen to what Marukarn and Andizha said. We let them find us."

She flicks a loose braid out of her eyes as she chambers a round into her rifle. "I'm not sure I like that plan, Nathan."

"We don't have much choice," I point out.

"I shot at you the first time I saw you," she reminds me. "Don't you think they might do the same?"

I give a small laugh. "Believe me, I remember." I trace the groove running from the front of my face along the side of my head. "But you were alone. They aren't. They might be curious before they're hostile. Especially from how Marukarn and Andizha describe them."

"That seems like a pretty risky guess," she comments.

"It is. But again, we don't have a choice if want to find them."

She turns to me, concerned. "Nathan, we can't have you getting killed. Even if it's an accident. If Marukarn and Andizha are right, you're the only thing that'll keep people alive on Earth, even if you're just a diplomat to the Rantir for humanity."

I nod, genuinely touched by her concern but unwavering in my resolve. "I'm aware of that, Sasha. I've had plenty of time to think about it these last few weeks. You and I have discussed it in detail." I gently place a hand on her arm. "But remember how you told me I couldn't be protective of you when we first set out? That applies to you too. You can't fight all my battles for me."

"I know Nathan," she tells me. "And it's not even about you being some kind of advanced, evolved being either. I don't want to see you hurt. I need you around, and I don't feel like taking unnecessary chances."

With words like that, I can't help but think of Angie. She used to say things like that to me. She used to care in such a way. She would have thrown herself in front of a train for me if that's what was needed.

Sasha and I have only been with each other for about two months, yet the bond we've formed is so strong it's like we've known each other for years. We've both suffered. We've both persevered. We both can just *be* around one another. We seem to exist as cohesively as a human and a cyborg can, yet our relationship seems almost symbiotic at this point. The way we rely on one another in such an unspoken manner. The way we seem to continuously learn from each other too. We both know how to fight, but we offer unique qualities to the other person. I share my vast knowledge with her, compiled from years of exploring, scavenging, reading, studying, and experimenting in mechanical and physical applications. She shares her wealth of wisdom with me forged from years of hunting, stalking, observing, foraging, and evading. She doesn't just help me in physical conditions, but in spiritual practices as well.

She never lost her sense of personality. I never lost my sense of practicality. And we're teaching each other something new in those fields every day.

Beyond that, she's always there. When I sit patiently through the evening hours, watching the stars trace their journey from one end of the sky to the other, she sleeps nearby. Her rhythmic breathing has grown increasingly softer and smoother as I've shared the days with her. Her eyes don't fidget through their lids as much. She drifts off deeper and deeper, fully trusting I'll be there to protect her while she rests.

I wonder what she's dreaming. I wonder what she sees when she escapes this world and ventures into the unknown of her mind and imagination.

I wonder if I'm there with her.

Because she's always here with me. She always wakes up in the middle of the night to talk to me, even if only for a few minutes, no matter how soundly she sleeps. We've learned each other's hopes and dreams. We know of the other's past in such detail that we might as well have lived the events together. As I protect her from the dangers of this world while she rests, so she protects me from the dangers I hold within myself. She keeps me focused. She gives me hope. She gives me reasons to think of the future involving more than just an endless journey.

And she does this for me even when the sun is at its zenith too.

We've become the spiritual sustenance the other has needed for many years.

I had that bond once...

Granted I was a normal human then. But all the same, I'm so glad I have it again, even under far different circumstances.

I have to shake these thoughts from my head, grateful as I am that Sasha is in my life. I can't afford to think like this. It's a line of thought that will only get me into trouble if I entertain it too much. The bond we have can never grow beyond what it is now.

No...I have to accept what I am. I have to accept what must be. I knew this the night I watched Andizha and Marukarn leave.

There are things that must be left as they are in this world. And more things that I must allow to develop, remaining absent of their evolution.

"Sasha," I begin again. "The feeling is mutual. Don't doubt it for a second." I look into her eyes, hoping she finds my visor a worthy equivalent for her focus on when she gazes at it. "But you know we have something that needs to be done. It's not about us. And it's definitely not about me."

She sighs. "I just have a bad feeling about this, Nathan."

I shrug. "I appreciate that, but we have to keep moving."

Clearly, she's not eager to accept that, but she nods, quickly regaining the demeanor and mentality that's helped her survive alone for years in this hostile world. That posture, focus, and expression that denotes she's no ordinary woman. She's carved from resiliency that's endured every hardship and still stands ready for more.

Those moments of vulnerability are rare with her, and I'm so glad I can see them. I'm so grateful this world hasn't taken that from her. She's still a person. She can still feel those things that make a human who and what they are.

I have to wonder if I can say the same. My ability to flip a switch and turn my emotions on and off, even if it's in the name of a higher purpose is becoming unsettling. I've been monitoring it for months now, and time has only indicated this behavior is becoming more prominent.

I'm not the metal that composes me...I'm still me...

I keep reminding myself of this, perhaps hoping instead of knowing it's true. But the proof will lie in my actions here on out, not in my hopes.

We make sure we have all of our things in order, then take one more breath before facing whatever potential threats there may be from the survivors near Lake Superior. Marukarn and Andizha, as far as we know, were still scouting Gahren's location or waiting for us here. I'm hoping it's the latter of the two, but not holding my breath.

...So to speak.

"You going to hang back?" I ask. "Cover me?"

She shakes her head. "Not this time. I think it would be good for them to see you're walking with a human. It'll let them know you're safe to be around."

"I hope you're right," I speak softly, concerned for her safety.

"They've been teaming up with two Rantir armed to the teeth," she points out. "I think there's a chance they'll be open to accepting you if I'm out there with you."

"My previous statement still stands," I tell her.

"Now don't you get all protective on me," she chides.

I'd roll my eyes now. "Fine. You want to lead?"

"Hell no!" she replies. "I'm not going first and getting shot. You take point."

I'm glad some things never change.

And I wish I could roll my eyes again.

I begin making my way towards the shore of Lake Superior. We're a few hundred feet away after having navigated through the remains of Duluth. Again, the forces of nature have prominently taken hold as they are wont to do in this ravaged, fertile world. There's ample coverage from bushes, trees, and other plant life that has grown unchecked through the years. It aids us now, to some extent. At least we'll be able to disappear quickly if things don't go as well as we're hoping.

I keep my hands far enough away from my weapons to demonstrate what I hope is a peaceful disposition to anyone watching. I know I could reach my sword and gun in milliseconds if I so chose, but my enemies don't, and I like to maintain their ignorance as much as I can. We weave through and around the plants, abandoned cars, and the occasional pile of rubble. There's only the sound of our footfalls for what seems like hours. Then I hear the telltale sound of a bullet sliding into a chamber as we move down a street lined with buildings. There are a few cars around us and an alley or two. Plenty of places to hide. So, I stop, hoping I haven't walked into an ambush.

It sounded like a rifle. I turn to Sasha. She's clearly not liking the situation and tensing her grip on her weapon while actively scanning her surroundings. Again, all she has to do is read my body language and she knows. There's no way she could have heard the cartridge slide into the chamber. Her ears aren't sensitive enough. But her perception is invaluable and just as effective.

I face forward again, then project my voice. "We're not here to fight!"

I hear some shuffling of feet, which is enough for me to zero in on the thing's location. Using my sonar, I find the would-be sniper on the second floor of a building ninety-three feet away and to my right. They're looking out the second to last window on the eastern facing side of the structure, and they've got three friends.

Normally, I'd be more concerned with the situation, but then I realize it's a human waiting to ambush Sasha and I. I think we may have found the survivors. Then I hear them squeezing the trigger with a sound that's a combination of creaking and grinding metal.

And I know they're not aiming at me.

Now I'm more concerned.

I snap into motion in an instant, leaping in front of Sasha as the shot is fired. The round streaks toward its intended target, impacting my back hard enough to cause a significant dent to my exterior and making me stumble forward. The bullet doesn't penetrate, and Sasha sits safely within my arms. I keep her wrapped in my protective embrace and charge my legs. Another shot rings out and impacts off the back of my head, launching my face forward and into Sasha's.

My vision blurs with static and red warning indicators flash across my view from the force of the bullet, but I'm not concerned about that. The impact against Sasha's forehead was significant. I didn't hear any bones break, but I know I could have given her a concussion or worse. When my field of vision clears, I see a steady stream of blood flowing from her forehead and her eyes fidget rapidly.

She's regaining her composure but still wincing in pain, only adding to my worry.

I release the charge in my legs, leaping thirty feet into the air and to my left, carrying Sasha with me and landing gently atop a nearby building. I set her down and watch as she grabs her head. Her fingers are instantly coated in blood as she continues to grimace.

"You OK?" I ask, anger welling within me. I'm furious that someone tried to kill her. I'm pissed that someone tried to kill me. But I'm irate that in trying to protect her, I accidently injured her.

I hate being reminded I'm a machine when every day I try to convince myself I'm not. It's difficult to think that way when I felt no pain from both bullets, but Sasha is in agony from my good intentions. I may have saved her life, but she's going to feel it the morning. Now, my only concern is getting to that shooter.

I'll make sure the little prick doesn't get another shot off.

"Yeah," she manages through the anguish. "I just need a second."

"Some kind of rifle," I tell her. "Not as strong as yours. Maybe even a lever action. Enough to have some stopping power though. He's in the building up ahead about one hundred feet. Brick exterior. Second floor, second window from the left, east side."

"Alright," she says, getting to her feet and wiping some blood from her eyes. She takes a moment to tear a piece of cloth from her ghillie suit and wraps it around her head. "I'll have you covered. Make sure…"

She has no time to finish the sentence as I hear the roar of a Rantir coming from the same direction as the shooter. I wonder if it was hunting nearby when it heard the shot, and I hope we may have some lucky intervention from it if it decides to go for the human sniper.

"They're on the rooftop!" I hear a gruff human voice yell. "That building!"

I'm thinking he's yelling at some of his allies, perceiving us to be the bigger threat. Maybe a few more humans were hiding around the area. That doesn't last though, because a few moments later, I hear the sounds of a Rantir running full speed through the street. I take a chance wandering to the edge of the building, confirming the Rantir is indeed heading our way, but there's a twist.

I wasn't counting on it being armed with what appears to be a partially completed battle suit. There are no outer plates on the defensive coating, but I know the internal portion of the suit will still protect it well enough as it covers the entirety of his body. He also has a disintegration weapon strapped to his back. The blades on his scythes and forearms are also going to be an issue.

Before I have time to contemplate why a Rantir would be working with a human, another shot is fired, but the bullet streaks wide of me as I duck behind the lip of the building.

"We've got problems," I tell Sasha as I approach, drawing my sword. "Stay ready and cover me. He's coming."

She doesn't ask questions or hesitate. She gets her eye to the scope and faces the same direction as me.

Almost as soon as I finish the sentence, our enemy crests the edge of the building. The second he plants his feet on the roof, he slings his weapon from behind his back and takes aim with it as it glows with cyan energy. As it starts to hum with an increasingly high pitch, Sasha opens fire. Her shot slams into the left side of the Rantir's partially covered head. Had he not been wearing his lighter but effective armor, the shot would have penetrated his eye straight to his brain. However, he rotates with the momentum of the bullet, spins, and opens fire upon completing his revolution. The weapon screeches as it discharges a wide blast of energy that sizzles the air around it. His shot isn't particularly well aimed, but it's enough to force Sasha and I to dodge aside.

I complete my evasive roll, charging my legs as I do so. Sasha immediately returns fire as she recovers from her own dodge. Her shot isn't as accurate as the first, but it does strike the Rantir in the shoulder, throwing off his aim.

Just as I knew she'd do...

My charge releases and I blast toward my target. He turns and faces me, whipping his scythes out to intercept me with horizontal strikes aimed for my neck. I quickly lean back and skid along the ground with my knees, leaving a trail of sparks and torn concrete as I duck underneath his blades. I've set a charge in both of my arms, but lead in with a strike from my sword first. My right arm aims for his belly, intending to slice through his suit and into the flesh beneath. He intercepts my attack by blocking with his rifle, but in so doing, exposes the right side of his body. I plant my feet under me for maximum leverage, then release the charge in my left arm, driving home a devastating strike to his belly. He's hurled backward off the rooftop. During his flight, he slams through the brick siding of the building across the street, disappearing into the darkness behind a cloud of dust and debris.

I hear another shot, then I'm spun around from the force of a slug connecting with my left shoulder. Again, the bullet doesn't penetrate, but it dents my exterior. Damage assessment informs me there's no internal damage, but the fact that there's another human shooter armed with a shotgun doesn't encourage me. I quickly withdraw toward the middle of the rooftop to break line of sight and return to Sasha, only to see another Rantir rise over the edge of the building behind her. This one also wears what appears to be some kind of partially completed battle suit and has two curved swords in both of its hands. I can see the circuitry and wiring of the armor clearly exposed, but it's well integrated into the protective coating the armor provides. I also notice now that he seems to move with surprising alacrity and agility as he makes a dash straight for Sasha.

She fires, then begins to retreat to me. The shot doesn't do much as it bounces off the chest of the Rantir in a shower of sparks, but it does slow it down enough for her to create some space between herself and her enemy.

I charge my legs, calling out to her. "Down!"

She obliges, displaying complete trust in me as I release my charge and soar an inch over her head, foot leading the way straight into the lunging Rantir's chest. My kick blasts him back, but he wraps one of his unarmed scythes around my ankle, pulling me with him. He tries hoisting me skyward, but I lash out with my sword at his grabbing appendage. I manage to connect with a lesser swing. Enough to cut into him, but not enough to sever the scythe completely. It does force him to release me though, and we both come skidding to a stop at the edge of the building.

I hear footsteps retreating toward the edge of the building facing away from the snipers. I know Sasha is taking this time to relocate and find the two hidden enemies since there's not much she can do in the fight with the Rantir. She'll take this opportunity to hide while I draw out our foes. It's a tactic we've used before. I know she'll be watching my back, but right now I need to be more focused on surviving the battle at hand.

So, I grip my sword tighter, grasping it in two hands and squaring off against the new threat. It growls at me, taking a ready stance of its own and pointing both of its blades toward me. I can't help but feel like some kind of Knight in this moment, and I hope whatever wisdom they held in combat will assist me here as I face my equally armed opponent.

He strikes first, lunging with his left blade for my torso. I turn his weapon aside with my own, then block a follow up attack for my shoulder from his right hand blade. I duck under his next swing from the left, then dodge a lunging strike from his right aimed for my head. I take the opportunity to counterattack, striking for his side, then for his legs after he parries my first attack. He jumps back, then both of his scythes lash out. I turn them skyward with my left arm, but again, he uses them to grapple me as they wrap around my forearm. Anticipating his next move, I charge my legs. Then, the moment he pulls me toward him, I tuck my feet under me, curling into a ball. As I fly at his upraised swords, aimed to impale me on impact, I swing my sword out in front of me and under the tether of his scythes, deflecting both his blades. Then I unleash the charge in my legs. The powered dropkick slams into his chest. He's blasted backward at nearly sixty miles per hour while I fall to the ground, planting my sword into the concrete as I do so to anchor myself. His grip upon my forearms remains strong, and he's whiplashed severally when he reaches the ends of his scythes' length. However, he lands gracefully on his feet, maintaining his hold upon me. I pull my sword from the ground, charging my arm. I then take a fully powered swing for his scythes once again as they try to pull me towards him. At the last second, he releases his grasp and pulls his scythes out of harm's way, then lunges for my torso with both of his blades yet again.

My guard is wide from my last swing, and I can't get a fully charged counter attack ready. But then, I don't have to if his momentum will do the work for me.

I begin recharging my arms, leaping up and forward as I do. I land a flying knee squarely upon his face as his blades both go harmlessly wide of me since I've foiled his intended attack. I hear metal crunch and grind, knowing there's no damage to my robotic form. Only to his armored face. Now, as I begin to fall back to the earth, I release the charge in my arms in a forceful, downward chop. The blade splits the thin metal coating he wears along with the dense skull beneath his skin. I don't sever him in two, but my sword still slices clean into his brain. His nervous system forces him to tense and twitch in protest as he dangles from the edge of my blade. I raise my foot to his stomach, charging my leg. I release the hydraulically powered kick, pushing him lifelessly from my weapon with a loud screech as the bone of his skull grinds against the metal of my sword, unwilling to relinquish its hold.

He falls limply from the edge of the building, and with my weapon free, I turn to face a new threat.

I suspect to find the Rantir I'd previously sent careening from the rooftop, but I'm greeted with another surprise instead. There are two drones, very much like the one's Gahren had as his entourage, poised on the rooftop across from me. The same rooftop now supporting a very angry Rantir.

So there he is...And now he's up there with his firing squad, all of whom have disintegration weapons aimed at me.

It doesn't look good.

Then a sharp crack of a discharging rifle shatters the stillness of the moment. Not a split second later, one of the drone's heads lurches to his left as a bullet careens through it. Mechanical components, circuits, fluids, and what looks like bits of rotted brain explode outward from the exit wound. The drone's body seizes for a moment before it crumples lifelessly to the ground. Meanwhile, the other drone, apparently programed with some kind of self-preservation subroutine, drops to the ground, scuttling along the lip of the building to safety, much like a roach fleeing from light. The Rantir, distracted by the bits and pieces of what was his former ally's head showering him, fires a poorly aimed shot that streaks wide of me by a few feet.

Thank you Sasha.

Knowing I can't get off the roof without presenting an open target and fully aware I won't get another opportunity like the one my friend just provided, I charge my left arm. I release the stored energy as I strike the ground with an open palm. My hand impacts the surface with meteoric force. The powerful hit shatters the concrete rooftop around me, forming an interweaving network of cracks and breaks in the structure before collapsing. I fall with the debris to the next floor below, landing nimbly and concealed amidst a cloud of dust. The moment my feet touch the ground, I'm already moving. There's a brick wall between my attackers and I, providing ample cover from their fire.

I'm safe from them here. But I want to make sure they aren't safe from me.

I know Sasha is keeping them pinned down. No doubt the Rantir is scanning for her. For a fleeting second, I wonder how many more enemies we're dealing with, but I quickly shake the thought from my mind. There are targets right in front of me, and they require my attention. I'll deal with them first.

I charge my legs and my left arm once again. I do a quick calculation for a jumping arch to clear the street, confirming I'll have enough speed and power for what I'm intending to do. Then, I sprint forward, powered by my enhanced legs to nearly sixty miles per hour in under two seconds. The brick wall is in front of me, still shielding me from my attackers. I should veer and go through a window. That would make for a faster advance upon my foes.

But they'll be expecting that. I can't risk exposing myself in such a way.

And I can't stop now.

I release the charge in my arm and legs the moment I get to the wall, lashing out with a punch that shatters stone while I leap forward. My fist blasts through the wall, leading the way as my body follows suit, carried forward by my generated momentum. I careen outward from the building, an explosion of dust and brick cloaking my position as the wall is reduced to nothingness. It's not subtle, but it gets the job done. And I incur no damage. I clear the street, entering my enemy's building through the same hole the Rantir produced with some of my earlier assistance.

Again, the moment I touch down, I'm already preparing for my next move. I'm not about to give my foes an open shot at me with weapons that could take me down in one hit. So, following a page of my newly formed playbook, I charge my legs and my left arm again. This time, I leap skyward, plunging my fist into the concrete ceiling above me. My arm tears through the material, body trailing unscathed behind. I break through the barrier with momentum to spare. I linger in the air for a second, which I take to charge my legs again. When I hit the ground, I launch myself straight for the Rantir who has yet to level his rifle at me through the environmental carnage I've wrought.

I fly at him faster than he can react, landing a hard kick onto his face and throwing him back. He rolls with the momentum, planting his scythes into the ground as a fulcrum to spring off of and regain his feet. He's still carrying a lot of momentum backwards, but as he completes his improvised tumble, he brings his rifle to bear, taking aim for me. I dodge to my left as he fires, rolling away from him and the ensuing blast. He continues to roll backward, and then I hear another weapon charging behind me. I look to see the drone aiming its wrist-mounted disintegration weapon at me. I put my feet under me, jumping and twisting into the air as I barrel roll over its shot. My vision scrambles for a moment as the blast passes by, but I focus my systems through the disruption. I put a charge to my legs and left arm, releasing the stored power in my legs as I land and closing the gap between my enemy and I as I lunge forward.

My powered journey brings me face to face with my opponent, and I take the sudden advance I've performed as an opportunity to swing at my foe's left shoulder with my sword. It raises its arm to block, but I step in even closer to it, releasing the charge in my left arm, landing a powered uppercut under its chin. The drone is hurled into the air a good fifteen feet as I hear metal crumple and groan in protest. Bits of alloy go flying from its face upon the initiation of its skyward journey, however, it's not finished yet.

The drone tucks its feet, flips, then rights itself in the air, drawing another bead on me from its elevated position. I hear a shot, but it's not from a disintegration weapon. A familiar report from a rifle cracks the sky as I proceed to watch the drone's head explode in a shower of metal and sparks; a result from Sasha's excellent marksmanship even against an elevated and moving target.

But then, another rifle discharge pierces the air. This one comes from somewhere to my left, close to where the original sniper was. The round slams into my right shoulder, sparking off again, but forcing me off balance near the edge of the building. As I right myself, I turn away from the ledge to face the enemy Rantir, who once again has a leveled rifle aimed for me. I hear the weapon's screech, indicating it's about to fire. Compromised as I am, I can't dodge or roll to the side, so I simply let myself fall off the structure. I take the forty foot plunge over being destroyed by the Rantir's weapon, but the landing only reminds me that I picked the lesser of two evils as I'm fully exposed now.

I hit the ground hard. The tarmac breaks under the immense impact, and I sink down into the earth as slabs of the street erupt around me. I rise from my knees amidst the rubble, then get hit by a slug in my left hip. This time, the round finds an opening in my defensive plating, severing a processing tube which leaks oily fluids down my leg.

These two snipers have to go. Though they're only minor irritations now, they could prove to be fatal distractions later.

Even a mosquito can carry deadly viruses.

I break into a full out sprint, heading straight for the building where I believe the sniper still resides. While moving at top speed, I hear the Rantir above me charging his weapon. I know he has me in his sights, so I take a few evasive maneuvers in the form of some robotically assisted acrobatics.

I sheathe my sword and charge my legs, leaping off the street and grabbing a tree branch at the crest of my flight. I then swoop my legs under me to build more momentum, releasing the branch and soaring even higher into the air, but angling myself to my right as a shot explodes behind me. I'm heading for the face of a building at an angled approach, so I tuck my feet under me, assisted heavily by my gyroscopic programs yet again, and strike the wall feet first. However, I don't let my momentum stop there. I start running down the face of the building, mechanical toes digging into the brick siding to keep me positioned along my intended path. My speed still intact, I run near to the bottom of the building, then leap away, aiming for the remains of an old sedan.

I land on the decrepit automobile as metal bends and twists around me. It fulfills its purpose of breaking my fall, but I don't stop there. I flip over the side of the car, then hoist one side of it into the air, using it as cover from the impending fire from the Rantir. He's not about to let something so trivial as a whole car stand between him and his prey however, so he fires a blast into my improvised shield.

I'm glad I have it there, because the ensuing explosion erupts with such force that I'm thrown back into the building behind me. I crash through a wall, rolling with the force of the explosion and hoping to evade any flying debris or burning particles. My vision blurs and static fills my sight for a moment. When all clears, I rise to my feet slowly, trying to assess my next move.

I hear footsteps on the floor above me, confirming the presence of one of the human snipers. I hadn't been able to run another scan for their position in the chaos of our battle, but I'm glad a little good fortune brought me to them. I can hear them coming down a set of stairs off to my right, so I silently move behind a wall they'll have to pass by if they're trying to get to me. It's also away from the Rantir's line of sight.

Now I wait. But not long.

After a few moments, a shotgun barrel pokes through the threshold first, and that's all the invitation I need to burst into action. My sword appears in my hand in an instant. Without any hydraulic assistance, I slice through the shotgun cleanly, severing the weapon in two near the chamber. I then spin around the corner, reaching out with my left hand and palming the skull of a small human, hoisting my attacker into the air. They scream, flailing wildly as they try to break free from my vice-like grasp. My digits aren't gripping tight enough to crush the skull, but enough to ensure they won't escape. I also make my point when blood starts dripping from wherever one of my mechanical fingers starts applying pressure.

The woman reaches for another weapon on her hip; a rusty hatchet.

"Wouldn't do that," I tell her as I raise my sword to her throat.

She keeps flailing and whining in protest, but stops reaching for the weapon. I take this time to note she's five foot four, weighs one hundred and ten pounds, and is Chinese in descent. She has black hair and brown eyes and is very malnourished.

I'm not sure what to make of her. But I haven't forgotten the multiple rounds that struck me either. Or the bullet intended for Sasha that I took.

She yells something at me, issuing orders in a language I haven't heard in a long time.

"Shut up," I snap, not bothering to translate her dialogue. "If you want to live, you'll tell me what you're doing here."

She screams at me, still struggling to break free but only causing further damage and pain to herself.

"Last chance," I tell her, squeezing a little tighter.

She yells something at me in Chinese. I activate my translation protocols this time and discover she was saying something none too pleasant.

"Fuck you!" she screams at me again. "Gahren told me what you are!"

That gets me to loosen my hold a bit. "Gahren? You're fighting for him?"

She answers me by spitting in my face, then continues to fight.

I hear more footsteps, this time approaching from near the other sniper's position. I'm surprised to hear four sets of feet, but even more surprised that there's a fifth set approaching from behind me in the direction I'd just come from. Knowing I'm about to be surrounded, I put my back to a wall and wait for them to get to me. The four reach the building fairly quickly. The other set of feet stops outside, then goes silent, even to my ears.

I turn my attention back to the four inside the building with me. The woman in my grasp calls out.

"I'm here!" she says, again in Chinese. "Help me!"

I don't know what I'm up against, but I decide if there's any way this can end diplomatically, it has to be determined now.

"Yeah, she's here!" I confirm, yelling in English. "And she's safe. For now. Come here so we can talk this out." All the while I'm listening for the Rantir as well, but I hear nothing to indicate he's even near. He must be watching instead. Though, if that's the case, I have to wonder why...

Has Gahren really solidified the use of humans and Rantir amidst his forces this well already?

I hear them make their way to my position, two closing from in front of me and two from behind. I decide it best to step out from concealment and into a more open room, still holding my captive by her head. I need to make a point that I won't be trifled with, but I'm not beyond finding a peaceful outcome despite being shot at.

Eventually, two more appear behind me. Both are men. One is slightly smaller than the other in frame, malnourished again with clearly defined bones due to this fact. The other is bigger in bulk, but I can tell it's been a rough couple of months for him too. He wears some outdoor gear. Hunting clothing mostly. And he's armed with a revolver. Magnum by the look of it. The smaller one has a snowsuit for clothing and carries a double barrel shotgun.

I turn and face forward, finding another woman also wearing hunting gear and armed with a pump action shotgun. There's a man next to her wearing what looks like military issue camouflage and carrying a lever action rifle. He also has a machete strapped to his right leg. I look around one last time and realize they all have a knife or blade of some sort.

"Lying in wait for my friend and I, huh?" I ask as they surround me and level their weapons.

The one with the lever action speaks. "Yeah. But you're all we want. Not the girl."

I look directly at him. "And why is that?"

"Because Gahren said so," he answers. "So how about you shut the fuck up, let her go, and give this whole thing a rest. We know what you are."

I don't particularly like being told how or when to remain silent. "Gahren left out a few details I see."

"Shut it!" the woman with the shotgun yells.

"Or you'll what?" I question, taking a threatening step forward and squeezing the head of my prisoner just a little bit more. "I know you need me alive if you're taking me back to him."

"No we don't," the man in camouflage says. "We just need to bring you back."

"Your guns aren't going to be worth much," I tell them. "Even at this range. You're going to die if you come at me. Did Gahren tell you that?"

For a moment, I see a flicker of regret in his face. "We don't have a choice."

I look around to the others. "I'm not your enemy. I was human once. I can help you get away from him."

"You're not human anymore," the woman with the shotgun says. "And we need to survive."

"He's not going to let you!" I snap. "If Gahren gets his way, humans are done!"

"Not if what he says about you is true," camouflage guy states. "And that makes you a hypocritical piece of shit in my book. You have the chance to save everyone who's left, but you don't."

"That what he told you?" I ask. "Or is there another reason?"

He glares at me, then takes aim at my head. "Go fuck yourself, dick."

I'm moving the second he starts squeezing the trigger. In my mind, there's no more reasoning with any of them. They've all cast their lot and declared themselves enemies to Sasha and I. They already tried killing her, and I know they'll try to do the same to me here and now.

I snap into motion, going into a dance of death I never knew I possessed.

The woman I'm holding is dispatched the moment my mechanical hand closes into a fist with her skull still inside. Her head splatters like a melon, showering me in blood and gore when I clench my fingers together. I roll forward to the man in camouflage right after. He tries to track my movement, but his shot goes over me and into one of his fellows who yelps in pain, clutching his belly. He and his revolver drop to the floor. I put my feet under me and swing my sword diagonally upward across my body. Without the aid of any hydraulic charge, I slice clean through the man. Again, more blood spills across the room, painting the walls red as thick coats of it drip from the point of impact. As the man falls to the ground in two separate halves, he

146

gurgles on more of the crimson fluid while it fills his mouth as his lungs cease to function.

I turn to the woman with a shotgun, getting a blast of birdshot to my torso as I do so. The pellets bounce harmlessly off me as I close the distance, charging my left arm. She tries to pump the weapon and cycle another round, but I'm already to her. I release my charged punch straight into her chest. I'm expecting to send her soaring backward as I'd done to many Rantir, but I'm dealing with a human. My fist goes right through her flesh and bones, impaling her cleanly. I withdraw my bloody arm along with a good portion of the organic material in her chest. She twitches, gasping for air in her death throes, then falls to the ground.

I turn back to my last enemy, who fires one of his barrels at me. I realize his weapon is loaded with slugs as the round slams into my stomach. I'm shoved back by the force of the bullet, but set my feet and give them a charge. I know he only has one shot left and he needs to make it count. As he aims for my head, I release the charge, sliding along the ground under his shot. I come up beneath him, sword leading the way straight through his belly as I impale him. He cries out in pain, clutching at the blade when I look him right in the eye, just inches from his face.

He's afraid, but he's still fighting.

He reaches for his knife, but never draws it. I grab him by the back of his neck. Then I break his spine with hardly an effort as I close my fingers around his vertebrae, digging deep into the flesh. Again, more blood rains down onto my hand and arm as I dispatch my opponent, and I cast the lifeless body aside.

I hear a hammer cocking, and I turn to face the threat. The man who'd been hit in the belly in the beginning of the skirmish holds his revolver, aiming for my head. I think to dodge aside, but never perform the action as I hear a shot from another small arm. A bullet tears through the side of his head, and more blood and brain matter is added to the ground and wall next to him.

I look to see Sasha standing near a window, weapon held level with the barrel smoking. She's distraught, looking at me with horror in her eyes. I wonder if she's ever had to kill a human before. Right as I contemplate this, I realize I've never had to either.

But then I see it's not this act she's afflicted by…

When I turn to look at the five slain people in front of me, I see my reflection in an intact window.

What I see is terrifying. Even to me.

I'm covered in blood, pieces of bone and hair, guts, and brain. The red fluid drips from me, especially from my left arm and hand. My visor is covered in a distinct splatter, but it still glows through the gore.

I've just taken five lives in less than ten seconds. The remains of my victims are the things I wear now. Granted, I'd tried to give them a way out, but it only stings all the more.

I'm the machine, built for war, and I've just mercilessly performed my function in a flawless nature. The image I see standing in the reflection and wearing such a macabre display of savagery is a perfect example of things I can't escape.

And I know there's more of this to come.

But they were going to kill Sasha.

They were going to kill me.

I don't know what Gahren had told them or what he did to them to make them this fanatical to their cause, but I know it was something monstrous. It was something so utterly manipulative that they believed it to the very core of their beings. Almost as if they had no other way of living.

I couldn't make them see reason. I couldn't show them I wasn't a threat. I couldn't sway their hearts. And it all had happened so fast. I reacted on instincts and my will to survive. On my desire to protect Sasha. All I knew was I had to stay alive. And if they got through me, Sasha was next. I couldn't allow that.

I *can't* allow that.

I just never thought I'd have to protect her from other humans. I never thought I'd have that kind of blood on my hands.

Not like this.

I'm staring into the lifeless face of the man with the revolver, an expression of shock still frozen on his visage. Sasha's voice breaks my line of thought.

"Nathan."

I can't face her.

"Nathan." This time more insistent.

Again, I don't want to look at her. I don't feel human in this moment. I wonder if I've lost a part of myself forever in the span of a few seconds; the time it took to end five lives.

"Look at me," she commands, and I'm compelled to obey.

Her eyes are filled with sorrow, but it's a pain she takes upon herself for my sake, almost as if she's suffering my internal anguish with

148

me. I can see myself reflected in her eyes, standing before her stained in blood, but still as the friend she's come to know and trust.

For a comforting second, I'm glad her perception allows her to see exactly what I'm feeling, though I have no way of expressing it. She knows me. I'm so glad of that. Especially now when I need someone to tell me everything will be OK.

"This isn't your fault, Nathan," she says.

I don't respond. I keep my gaze locked with hers, hoping and praying she's right.

"You didn't do anything wrong," she tells me. "You only did what you had to do."

Again, I want to believe her. Then I look down at my hands, now soaked with human blood. The realization returns to me. But again, seemingly knowing what I'm going through, she approaches me, taking my hand in hers and sharing the burden of guilt I carry with a smear of the blood.

"I want you to be right," I say to her, looking back at the bodies.

She grasps my face, turning it to look directly at her again. "I am."

I'm silent, wondering if this is something I need to take on faith and just believe in.

"I've never killed a human before," I state amidst my bewilderment. "I've never had to."

"Neither have I," she says.

I keep my focus on her eyes as they offer the emotions words can't express. Feelings of compassion and sympathy for me seem to flow from the gateways of her soul straight to my battered spirit, now ravaged by the unfair nature of this existence.

"I thought I'd only protect people," I start again. "It's all I've wanted to do."

"You didn't murder these people, Nathan," she points out. "You know they tried to kill us. They made their choice."

I can see she's right at this point. It's the same thoughts I had before I took action. And they also help me remember that I have to be there for Sasha in more ways than physical protection.

She's my friend. She's my family. I need to be stable for her just as much as she is for me.

"Are you OK?" I inquire, now genuinely concerned for her mental welfare.

She takes a deep breath, then nods. "I knew what I had to do. I didn't want them to hurt you."

I nod with her, confirming the mutual motivation for our actions today, and admiring her resolve and conviction. She openly bore the responsibility of her actions. Much better than I did too.

I feel like saying more, but we're interrupted as I hear the other Rantir on the move. Amidst the feelings of shock and regret, I'd forgotten about him. Sasha, in her concern for me, had made a choice in priorities. Now, however, we both need to shift gears.

"Thank you," I say to her as I ready my sword.

She pats my shoulder and offers a reassuring grin, then darts off out the back of the building, shouldering her rifle. I give her a few moments to relocate, then step out onto the street.

I thought my enemy was going to ambush me given how exposed I am upon exiting the building, but for another time today, my judgment is off. He's not running toward our location. He's running past us. I try to track his movement as best I can utilizing my sonar, but at his current speed, it's difficult to keep up. I run in the direction he's heading, but then I change tactics as I realize this isn't getting me any closer.

I head for a taller building to my left as I chase my foe down the street, ready to perform a familiar maneuver. I set a charge in my arms and legs. I leap almost forty feet into the air, and upon initial contact with the wall, plant my hands into stone, gaining a handhold. I then release the charge in my arms, pulling myself upward with such force I rocket to the lip of the building.

Upon rising over the edge of the structure, I now gain a clear view of my enemy as he flees from us, running on all fours at full speed. He leaps and bounds from rooftop to rooftop with ease, and I know catching him will be difficult, even for me.

"Sasha!" I yell. "At my twelve o'clock! Forty yards away! Get someplace high!"

I'm hoping she'll have time to reach a suitable vantage point. With as much confidence as I have in her abilities, I know that's still going to be one hell of shot, especially with how fast the Rantir is moving.

As I reengage my pursuit, I wonder what would make a Rantir flee like this. The one's I've battled before seemed like they'd rather die in combat than face defeat. Either that, or they wouldn't engage me as a target to begin with. Gahren was different when he ran from Sasha and I. He seemed more calculating than the typical Rantir. Given previous encounters with the alien foes, this one was behaving unusually. He was acting on something other than ferocity.

Whatever the case, I know it can't be good. The humans, the outfitted Rantir, the drones...Gahren has a very keen interest in this place if he's sending in a squad like this. I'm betting this one is returning to Gahren to report what he's seen. What was worse, if he returned with reinforcements (and I'm sure he would now that he knew I was here) there was the chance I'd be jeopardizing the human survivors that were supposedly located near this place. My pursuit becomes all the more urgent as I realize this.

I run as fast as I can, leaping, climbing, and hurdling every obstacle in my way, hoping to close the gap to my enemy. I soar over a street after releasing a charge in my legs. I grasp the edge of a building, then launch myself forward to build more speed. I've built up enough momentum to reach nearly sixty miles per hour, but still the Rantir keeps his lead. I'm not closing the gap, and we're farther and farther from Sasha's effective range.

In the end it doesn't matter as I watch him simply disappear. I slide to a halt in confusion, wondering if my optical programs malfunctioned. I switch to the thermal spectrum and see nothing. In a last effort to find some trace of my foe, I send out a ping for my sonar.

I discover something strange. Something I've never seen before.

My enemy is there, but he's come prepared.

There's some kind of transport vehicle where the Rantir used to be. It's alien in make and resembles a mechanical stingray. It's wider than it is long with multiple cannons mounted under the "wings." The weapons seem to be integrated human technology. .50 caliber machine guns and rockets from what once were fighter jets or helicopters. There's a clearly defined cockpit with a windshield shaped much like my visor and masked by an opaque, green tint. The whole vessel is cloaked with what I presume is the technology Marukarn and Andizha told us Gahren had developed from adapted chameleon evolution.

No wonder I couldn't see it. However, I'm more focused on what's going to happen next than anything else.

The ship's cloaking fades away, revealing it fully to Sasha and I. It then begins to lift off. The engines are much quieter than I'd anticipated. More so than the thrusters of Gahren's suit or those of the drones I've encountered so far. But they still sound like a jet. I wonder if he's going to keep running, but then watch as he pilots the fighter in my direction. I'm completely exposed on the roof, and given the opportunistic nature of the circumstance, I know he's not just doing a pass over.

I sheathe my sword and start running to my right where there are more buildings within my immediate reach. I could take my chances in the water of Lake Superior. It's relatively close and I could disappear beneath the surface. But as I'm unaware if the Rantir vessel is submersible, I'd rather not be caught in a helpless situation underwater. That, and I'm not leaving Sasha alone against the enemy craft. Instead, I'm hoping the remains of Duluth can offer me protection or temporary shelter from the incoming bombardment.

He opens fire with a stream of .50 caliber rounds that rupture the ground in a line in front of me. I run through the flying rock and debris to the edge of the structure, diving off the rooftop and aiming for the window of the building across from me. I make my leap, but I'm clipped by one of the powerful rounds. It's not a direct hit as the bullet glances off my left shoulder plating, but it carries enough force to throw me off my intended path. Instead of going through the window, I'm now headed right for a concrete wall and I don't have enough time to charge my arm and break through.

I twist in the air, trying to hit the wall flat with my back, but I can't maneuver in time. I connect with the back of my right shoulder unevenly, bouncing off and unable to gain a handhold. Now I'm falling, and my feet aren't under me. Gyroscopic protocols assist me in righting myself midair just in time to absorb the heavy impact on the street as I land on my knees. Again, the tarmac erupts around me as giant slabs of stone break and form an impact crater.

No structural or internal damage detected after a quick scan, and I'm on the move again. I duck inside the building by diving through a ground level window, tucking into a roll, then hiding in a room located toward the center of the structure after getting back to my feet. I'm thinking he might pass me by or hover for a bit before taking any drastic measures, but apparently he's not the patient type. He reveals he has another card to play, and it's an ace in the hole to be sure.

I hear a louder, screeching noise akin to that of a readying disintegration weapon. I can only assume it belongs to the ship, and it's aimed right at me. Or the building I'm hiding in anyway. I start running for the rear exit as quick as I can.

It's just enough to get me clear of the ensuing explosion.

Fire erupts around me. Were it not for my mechanical body, I would certainly have been consumed and destroyed. Brick, rebar, concrete and other debris bursts from the explosion of charged energy. Most of it bounces harmlessly off me. Some of it does minor cosmetic damage, like a piece of rebar that embeds itself into my calf. It's not deep enough to disrupt systems, but I take note of it all the same. It could have been worse if it had struck me in a more vulnerable area.

The force of the blast launches me forward and into the air. I emerge onto another street, moving with great speed toward another wall. Not wanting to take another hard hit, I twist my body in the air and face the ground. I slam my hand into the earth, shaping my fingers into claws that rend the tarmac as I drag them through the street, hoping to slow my advance. It does the trick, but I have no time to remain idle. Already there's another volley of machine gun fire ripping up everything in sight, vying for me.

I run down the street in a serpentine pattern, hurdling the remains of old vehicles and looking for an opening. I think to jump and perform the same evasive maneuvers I had before, but the arcing flight I would need to take would only provide a clearer target for my skyward enemy. I need to stay on the ground and hope for the best. If nothing else, I can keep this up all day. He'll need to sleep some time. And at least I'm keeping him away from Sasha. I just hope she doesn't try taking a shot at him. Her rifle won't do much but give away her position.

So I keep running down the street, doubling back when he gets near me. More bullets rend the area around me, showering me in sparks and bits of rubble. The loud and rhythmic crackle of automatic weapons fire ceases for a moment as I hear the emissions of propulsion systems. I know there are rockets inbound on my position, so I take a chance and leap skyward, hoping to clear the radius of the blast.

Again, the ground near me erupts in a shower of fire and debris. This time I avoid the kinetic force of the blast as I soar through the air. I twist during my flight, facing the next approaching missile. It has a lock on me, and I know there will be no dodging it. Instead, I calculate the rate of its approach and ready my hand. I don't charge my arm. Instead, I wait until the missile gets close. When the time is right, guided by precise calculations regarding the speed of the approaching missile, the speed of my intercepting hand, and the pressure required to not detonate the rocket, I palm the projectile away from me. My hand deflects the missile into a building to my left.

I twist in the air again, continuing my flight and heading for an intersection. I reach out, grabbing a nearby light post with my right arm, using it as a hinge from which to swing and angle my trajectory. I pull myself further along my flight from the post, now aiming for the corner of a building. When I get close enough, I bury my hand into the side of the edifice, performing the same maneuver to conserve my momentum as I round the corner.

Now I'm flying alongside the buildings with a full head of steam. I hear him behind me as I continue my journey, knowing he's getting closer. Hoping to create some space between us, I reach out with my right arm again, dragging it along the stone and bringing myself to a sudden stop. He flies past me, looping skyward to realign himself for an angle of attack. As he does so, I charge my legs, pressing them against the wall and launching from it. I clear the street, charging my right arm midflight, and break through the wall of another building with a powered strike. I tuck and roll to preserve my momentum, staying on the move while masked by a cloud of dust.

Now I change my approach. I check my power levels to make sure I have enough charge for a blast of disintegration energy. Analysis confirms I'll be at twenty percent power if I fire my weapon.

I'm only going to get one shot at this.

I'll need a clear target.

I start running through the remains of what I think was a medical facility. I build up enough speed to carry me over streets as I dive through windows, entering structures across or next to me through whatever portholes available. I can't take a chance on being caught in a collapsing structure, and by staying on the move from one building to the next, I'll ensure he doesn't waste valuable energy firing his primary weapon until he knows he has a clear shot.

He needs to be conservative like me. Otherwise he would have kept firing a weapon as devastating as his disintegration cannon.

I'm looking forward to showing him what I can do when I decide to be liberal with my resources.

I jump over an old desk, then fly through another window and into the one across an alley in front of me, entering another building. I take a moment to track his position after I move to the center of the structure for cover. I hear him passing over me. Apparently he doesn't know where I am as he takes his time hovering for a moment before going to his next destination.

Good. That's all I need.

I wait for a few more seconds, ensuring he's far enough away that I'll have enough room to run after I give him reason to chase me. Then, I run to the window, this time carefully and purposefully climbing out. I scale the wall by digging my hands and toes into the surface once again until I reach the roof. I climb over the edge and draw my shotgun. I load three slugs into it, then take aim.

I fire one round, cycle the next into the chamber, and wait for him to face me. The ship turns and I fire again, this time aiming for the center of the cockpit. Both slugs bounce harmlessly off the exterior of the fighter, accurate though they are. I wasn't counting on them doing any real damage anyway. I turn and run, charging my legs and firing one last shot before releasing the charge in my limbs. As I soar over the street, I sling my shotgun over my shoulder and do my best to make myself small as .50 caliber rounds streak past me.

I make it to the rooftop of the next building, landing nimbly while staying on the move. Upon reaching the edge of the structure, I leap straight forward, but this time angling downward. I'm heading directly for the wall of the next building, hands and feet outstretched to catch myself. However, before I make contact, I charge both of my arms and legs. When I hit, I dig my fingers and toes into the stone for a brief hold, then release my stored energy. Pushing off with all fours, I launch myself backward toward the building I just ran across.

My enemy is right behind me, piloting his craft overhead and beginning to adjust his rotation to track my position. I continue my flight backward through a brick wall, slamming the surface with tremendous impact. So much that a warning indicator informs me I've ruptured a containment tank. But my goal is achieved as I blast through the wall and into the structure, breaking his line of sight with me for the precious few seconds I need.

He has a clear shot on the building and knows I'm not moving at full speed since I couldn't recover from my tumble as quickly as I'd done before. With that knowledge, he starts charging his disintegration cannon, hoping to bring the building down on top of me.

The weapon's screech informs me he's taken the bait.

I regain my feet, set a charge in my right arm and both legs, then activate my disintegration gun. It begins to power up as I leap skyward, striking out with my right arm to break through the ceiling once again. I emerge through the stone floor in a shower of rock and dust, rising with enough energy to carry me still higher into the air some ten feet above the roof.

He fires, and in the .01 seconds it takes for his shot to blast the building below me, I have a target acquired.

I fire, immediately suffering the consequences of substantial power loss. My vision blurs and fades. My sense of sound no longer registers anything but muffled pitches.

I hear the explosion. I register that the external temperature around me is skyrocketing as I'm consumed by the flames of his blast. What little display I have left on my visor also tells me I need to right myself, as I'm falling at an improper angle according to my standard alignment. I hit the ground hard, then everything goes black as rubble falls atop me, burying me beneath the concrete and brick.

I hear the ship beneath my blanket of debris. The engine sputters and backfires, now unstable. I don't hear him crash though. Instead, I listen as the noise gradually fades away while he flies to the east.

I didn't take him out.

Damn...He's going to be back.

But there's nothing I can do. In the five minutes it's going to take for my power to regenerate, I know he'll already be long gone. Sasha and I could try and pursue him, but we'd only be exposed in the process of doing so.

So, I have to wait. Amidst a prison of stone and flame, I allow my power to regenerate. The concrete shields me from the majority of the heat, preserving my coolant tubes and transport "veins." Through the pops and hisses of the fire, I hear the sound of feet approaching after the passage of a few minutes.

Sasha is sprinting to me as fast as she can.

"Nathan!" she yells as I hear her pealing rubble away from the pile that was once a building.

"I'm here!" I shout back, hoping to calm her.

Apparently she doesn't hear me. "Nathan! Nathan!"

"Get clear!" I scream as loud as I can, amplifying my audio protocols.

She seems to hear that as I listen to her back away from the collapsed structure. I wait for a few more moments, allowing my systems to return to around sixty percent capacity, then set a charge in my arms and legs. I'm lying on my back beneath the rubble, so my first move is to bring my limbs to me. I release the energy, snapping my extremities to me against the pressure of the rubble and end up in a fetal position. Some of the stone shifts, but mostly my arms and legs just glide along the rock instead of dislodging it. That's fine as I set another charge, this time exploding my limbs outward.

All manner of building materials, some set aflame, are sent rocketing outward, and I'm free of my prison. When I see the light again, something is wrong. For some reason, I can't register depth or color. All I see is waving outlines in shades of black and white. However, I don't have time to process what this means as I must escape the fire. I quickly run through the flames, tripping and stumbling often without my ability to properly gage the whereabouts of most things around me. Eventually, I make it to the street, meeting Sasha. She reaches out to touch me, but I wave her off, knowing my exterior to be quite hot from the fires.

"Is there something wrong with...?" I begin, taking a minute to figure out what would best explain my request. "My 'eyes?'"

She looks closely at me. It's difficult to track her movements with my distorted vision.

"Yeah," she replies. "Half your visor is shattered. It looks like the wiring is pretty messed up."

Fantastic.

She continues to analyze me. "You OK?"

I nod. "Yeah. I'll be fine. It's hard to move around though. I can't see very well."

"I believe it," she comments. "Where do you need to go?"

"Back to the drones," I answer. "I need parts."

"All right," she says. "Here." She extends a piece of rebar to me. "I can't hold your hand. You're still pretty warm."

"Any chance he'll be back?" I ask after struggling to grasp the rebar and indicating where I think our enemy flew off to.

"I don't think so," she answers. "You got him pretty good. A lot of smoke and fire on that spaceship after you took your shot."

I chuckle. "Nice shooting on your part, by the way."

I wish I could see if she smiles or not. "It's what I do. But Nathan, you just took on a fighter jet or something, by yourself...and *won*."

Now I wish I could smile. I appreciate the levity given our situation. "That impressive?"

She giggles. "No. Makes you pretty badass though."

We share a laugh together, then start making our way toward the drones. I'm completely reliant on her during this process, and I find this to be strangely refreshing. It's not that Sasha is helpless by any means. I know this is far from the truth. But there are times when she is, like when she sleeps or has to relieve herself.

It makes me appreciate this moment as one of those things that helps me feel more like a human again. Every time I've had to repair myself and she's been there, I feel like that's the closest I'll ever get to dreaming. But even if this is true and this is the closest I'll get to those subconscious projections, I'm glad I have that. I'm happy I can feel something similar to what I once did when I was a man. Now, with her guiding me along the streets, I share an unspoken bond with her. A sharing of trust when I'm as vulnerable as I am now.

As odd as it is, I enjoy every second of the venture back to the fallen drones, even after what we've both just endured. She makes sure to lead me in a way that avoids the most difficult terrain or growth. The whole time, though it's hard for me to make out, she's scanning the rooftops and alleys. She checks corners and any potential point of ambush, just in case there's something else out there that would wish to do us harm.

We reach the drones in short order. Sasha brings me to the one in the street she'd shot through the head after I'd sent it airborne. I'm close enough to clearly see its outlined form. I make contact with it, scanning its functions and learning it's performing its repair protocols. Current functions are directed mostly at its central processing center. (The "brain.") I take the time to rip open its torso and remove both power cores, pleased there is still a large amount of residual charge left in them. I take plates off its armored exterior, placing them inside my decomposition chamber, along with tubing, fluids, and some of its circuitry for replacement materials.

"Can you get me some glass?" I ask Sasha. "I need some for my visor and situational displays."

"Sure," she replies.

I hear the sound of her wandering off, then the sound of a car window breaking. While this is transpiring, I'm busy absorbing the energy from one of the power cells. My systems have recharged from the disintegration blast I fired, so now it's time to speed up my recovery.

Diagnostics perform all necessary component assessments after Sasha returns with the glass I need. I've found all suitable replacement materials for full system restoration. Now, with the boost of electrical energy from the power core, what was once going to take nine hours and forty-two minutes, is going to take approximately fifteen so long as I remain idle.

Sasha and I move into one of the buildings that doesn't have a hole in it or hasn't been compromised from our battle. Then we both sit and wait.

"You should see what the place looks like now," she tells me. "You jumped it up a notch this time, didn't you?"

I look at my hands. Even though I can't clearly see them, I know they're stained with blood and burnt flesh. I wonder if the discoloration will ever be removed. "So did you."

She nods. "You do what you have to, Nathan. Don't forget that."

I know she's right. I feel it in what's left of my heart and soul that there was no other option and no better outcome than what we fought to achieve today. It's just hard to think like that. Especially with what seems like such a cold, *mechanical*, outlook.

But I reflect on the fact that, sometimes, the difficult path is the one that requires walking the most.

This path isn't going to get any easier. If I'm going to survive, I need to remember that. For myself, and for everyone else. I have to do what's necessary for Sasha and the rest of humanity if I'm going to give them another shot at life on Earth. This time without disease or medical inhibitions if research on my cellular activity leads humanity to such technological advances.

I have to do what's necessary for a future worth living for all of them.

It's not about me anymore.

Today was the first day in which I upheld that belief. Even if it's going to trouble me for a while, I'd resolved to make these decisions a long time ago. So, I suppose, today was also the first day in which I had to live with the consequences of being what I was.

Now I need to make sure those sacrifices and choices didn't turn me into something I didn't want to be.

Chapter 8

My repairs finish, though it always seems longer than it actually is. Sasha and I search the bodies once my restoration is complete. We take what ammunition we can off the humans. The drones don't provide much as far as useful items are concerned. There's really nothing we can take from them except parts in the event I'll need them, but it doesn't make much sense to lug around a spare arm and leg. So we remove their power cores and call it good.

While we're around the Rantir, we also have a chance to analyze their new armor more thoroughly. We can tell it allows the wearer an ease of movement with its relatively thin coating. It also doesn't seem to have any neural ports or integration systems like Marukarn's did when I accessed his systems. It didn't enhance strength or reflexes, but I discovered there was a shielding protocol embedded within the internal systems of the suit. A self-sustaining and maintaining system of nanobots creating what seemed to be an external layer of flexible protection.

I'm curious about it. Even though it can't help me, something like this could be of great benefit to Sasha. I take a sample from the suit and keep it in my pack for further examination and experimentation later.

After we finish looting the remains of our foes, I decide to head for the lake. I'm still covered in ash and blood from the fight, and if there are human survivors here, I don't want to make the wrong impression with my appearance. Besides, with the amount of gore I was covered in, I was going to start smelling rather foul. Sasha had been pretty polite, but I saw her crinkling her nose at the acrid scent of burnt flesh and hair I knew was emanating from me. I didn't want to discomfort her either.

I bathe myself as best I can. Sasha lends me a cloth to wipe myself down with, not daring to tread near the water, now frigid from the autumn air. I continue to clean myself as thoroughly as possible while the water turns an eerie maroon hue as the blood and remains of my victims is cleansed from my body. When I can't reach a certain crevice or break in my external plating, I sit underwater and just soak.

There's a silence that's almost serene beneath the surface. An emptiness where nothing matters but the gentle lapping of the waves.

I'm reminded of the grey veil of clouds when I stood atop the skyscraper in Seattle and the familiar tranquility of nothingness. I almost forget why I'm sitting completely submerged in the frigid waters of Lake Superior, unable to feel the biting cold and with no need to breathe. I can stay down here for as long as I want as I give myself a soak.

But Sasha is waiting and there's a lot left for me to do. I didn't come this far and survive this long to spend the rest of my life underwater, oblivious to the world around me. After a few minutes, I surface, scrub off whatever's left of the gore that once stained my body, and make my way back to the shore.

I'm greeted with rifles pointed in my direction from a group of humans who already have Sasha at gunpoint. They look organized and ready, all wearing detailed urban camouflage and brandishing assault rifles. They wear tactical vests and body armor. Some of them have helmets from various sections of the armed forces. All of them are geared for combat and stand with a composure I'd expect from a highly disciplined soldier, or someone else who's been trained to emulate that lifestyle.

Survivors have a tendency of exhibiting such self-control.

I'm shocked I didn't hear them. They must have been watching us for a long time, scouting us while waiting for the opportune moment.

I scold myself for remaining under the water for as long as I did, but quickly refocus on the present issue.

Sasha stands with her hands raised above her head. I watch as some of the men and women begin to search her. I count eleven total after doing a quick scan of the outlaying area in an attempt to find any more that may be hidden.

"Come out of the water," a masked woman in front of me calls. "Slowly."

I'm fighting an urge to deny her request, but I don't want them to hurt Sasha. Instead, I make a request of my own.

"Don't hurt her and I'll cooperate," I tell them.

The woman in front of me narrows her eyes, then waves me forward. "Deal. Now step out of the water."

I comply, watching as they strip Sasha of her weapons and rummage through her pack. When I get close enough, the same thing happens to me. Two of the men disarm me of all weapons and any equipment I wear on my exterior. I feel I don't need to tell them of the powerful weapon buried beneath the metal of my left forearm.

Just in case things get less diplomatic.

After the men finish searching me and stripping us both of our weapons, they regroup behind the woman who spoke to me. I'm assuming she's in charge. And now I realize the majority of this group is quite seasoned as far as age is concerned. They're not elderly by any means, but it's easy to tell they're middle-aged. Some perhaps bordering on their sixties.

"You're Ferroc, aren't you?" she says, lowering her rifle.

I can't say I'm not surprised. Clearly they had some clue I was coming, but I wasn't expecting this level of recognition.

I nod. "Yes. And this is Sasha. You've heard of us apparently."

The woman nods back, then takes off her mask. She's middle-aged as well. Streaks of gray run through a thick head of black hair. Pale blue eyes look at me with discernment, while a weathered but even and wrinkled face shows no emotion. "I'm Meredith. I stay connected with Andizha."

That was a relief. It's nice to have some good news at the moment.

"And you're in charge here?" I ask.

She shakes her head. "No one is 'in charge.' We're all fighting to survive. That's enough for us to get along."

"Fair enough," I say. "We've been looking for you."

"Yeah," she says. "And we've been waiting for you. You sure do make an entrance, don't you?"

"Whole goddamn world knows we're here now," one of the men to her left mutters.

I shrug. "I didn't try to draw attention. Evidently, Sasha and I weren't the only ones trying to find you."

Meredith narrows her eyes again. "That group you fought…They weren't after you?"

I shrug again. "I find it a little odd they'd know exactly where I was without any evidence to lead them to me. Especially if they were already here. I would have known if they were tracking us."

"You sure about that?" Meredith replies, skepticism dripping heavily from her words.

I do a quick scan. "You're five foot eight, one hundred and twenty-two pounds, heart rate currently at eighty-two beats per minute. I'm guessing it's lower than that when resting because you're not exactly relaxed around me, are you? And by the way, your body temperature is ninety-eight point nine degrees."

She doesn't know how to react to the information I've just given her. She just keeps her eyes narrowed and locked on me.

"Trust me," I tell her. "I'd know if we were being followed."

She thinks on this for a bit, then gives a nonchalant shrug. "Fair enough."

"Are Marukarn and Andizha here?" Sasha asks.

Meredith nods. "Yeah. They're in the underground."

One of the men approaches from the right. A tall and well-built man with a thick beard who wears a hood and some goggles. "Meredith, we gotta get moving. If that squad wasn't looking for these two, they're gonna be back with more of their pals."

"And now that they know it's here, they'll hit harder," another man adds as he gestures to me.

"*He's* here."

The tone was stern. Not a correction. Not a request.

A command.

And Sasha stands as defiant as I've ever seen her.

I didn't even have time to take offense before my friend did for me. There's a stirring in my being that I've never felt before. A swelling of pride and admiration for Sasha. Her steadfast loyalty to me even while at gunpoint surprises me in the best way. A way that tells me that she's not like anyone I've ever met or ever will meet again. Even when I was with Ryan and Jaclyn, I'd never felt such a heartfelt sense of gratitude. Granted, they'd never been put in this position with me, but I knew there was a difference in my relationship with them and the one I now have with Sasha.

I can't seem to place it. I'm just touched. Truly touched.

"What?" the man asks irritated.

"Now that *he's* here," Sasha reiterates. "Get it right."

There's one of those *very* awkward silences after that. The survivors before us are weighing their options on what to do about Sasha's blatant defiance of their tactical superiority. And maybe that was only an advantage over Sasha. I knew for a fact that whatever weapons they carried weren't going to be enough to take me down if things got ugly. But the fact that Sasha showed no fear even while at gunpoint was something anyone would take into account.

Especially defending a cause that wasn't hers.

"I'd appreciate being addressed as a person," I tell them with no uncertainty in my voice. "I was human once."

163

Meredith decides to follow my lead in an attempt to defuse the situation. "There's a lot we don't know about you Ferroc." She states it as a matter of tact, addressing the issue of the unknown.

"And now you know how I'd prefer to be addressed," I tell her. "And I'll extend the same courtesy to you." I look at the rest of them, paying special attention to the man now glaring at Sasha. "All of you."

That seems to do the trick. Meredith is taking the role of a practical commander at this point; doing what needs to be done in order to preserve her team. Most of the others with her don't seem to care one way or the other so long as they get moving. Even the man who Sasha berated relents.

"Come on," Meredith says, gesturing over her shoulder. "Underground is back this way."

"What about our weapons?" Sasha asks.

"You'll get them back once you're cleared with Marukarn and Andizha," Meredith replies as she begins walking toward her previously indicated destination. She turns back for a moment though. "It's standard procedure. Nothing personal. We need to make sure you aren't spies. That group you killed isn't the first one that's been looking for us recently."

I can tell Sasha is still unhappy with that, but I place a hand on her shoulder and give her a reassuring squeeze. "That's fine."

Meredith nods, then begins to lead us away. A few of the others fall in next to her while the rest take up position behind us with disciplined precision. Sasha and I walk side by side.

"Thank you," I whisper into her ear.

She looks up at me and offers a small smile. "No problem."

Then she nudges me with her shoulder. It's almost comical how little of a physical affect the playful action has on me, but the emotional impact is almost enough to make me stop in my tracks.

I don't though. And for the second time today, I remind myself to not let these things have such a large effect on me.

I focus on where Meredith is leading us. After a meandering way through the downtown waterfront area, we enter a particularly unstable building, then head into the lower floors. Everyone in the group ensures there's no trace of anyone passing through the building as we proceed. A good idea for any survivor to cover their tracks. When it gets too dark to see, a flashlight is offered to me, but I decline, though I'm pleased to see they have batteries.

They definitely have resources...

164

I tap my head, indicating to the group I'm fine as I switch to night vision. Sasha accepts the flashlight. Once we're equipped for the darkness, Meredith approaches an electrical box after we make our way to the building's mechanical room. I can't quite see what she's doing, but I watch her fiddle around with several switches. The way she activates and deactivates them, I know she's performing some kind of sequence. Shortly after I realize this, a section of the floor raises next to us. Two giant, concrete slabs lift and slide apart, hefted by a complex series of hydraulic systems. Before, they were so perfectly fitted into the floor that one couldn't detect a break between the stone slabs, much less the machinations beneath.

"This was a government shelter wasn't it?" I ask.

Meredith nods. "There's a couple reserve bases not too far from here. They helped get some survivors here before the first of the atmospheric attacks."

Sasha shines her flashlight down the revealed tunnel. "It's a whole lot more than that now."

"Yep," Meredith replies. "Come on. We've got a long way to go. Make sure you stay with us in the tunnels. Anyone who doesn't match a profile will be scanned and shot if they're not with someone who does."

"Daaaaaaamn," I hear Sasha whisper.

I couldn't agree more. These survivors were far more organized than I thought they'd be. I suppose that shouldn't be surprising if they'd had assistance from highly trained, advanced aliens like Marukarn and Andizha. All the same, the security measures were impressive given the limited resources any surviving humans have access to.

But the surprises don't stop there. We pass by the outer security systems which consist mostly of automated weapons and voice recognition scanners. I know Marukarn and Andizha had to have a hand in this since most humans wouldn't have the capabilities to program such complex computer functions.

"Things weren't always like this, were they?" I ask as we pass by automated machine guns. "You had help."

Meredith keeps her gaze focused ahead of her. "Yes to both. This network of tunnels and shelters was already established a long time ago. Most of the survivors down here had never even seen sunlight since the atmospheric attacks. Some of them have even been born down here."

I'm blown away. "How many are down here?"

"A couple hundred," she says. "Maybe more. There were a number of shelters under Lake Superior that made it. Once we'd received word the Rantir were sending in sweeper teams, they started digging to reach one another. Then they focused on escaping and evading the Rantir." She turns back to me for a second. "Not all of them made it, but there were enough survivors to start over."

I'm taking it all in, amazed these people have made it this long. "So you escaped them how?"

"Because of the reserve bases nearby, there was plenty of survival gear," she explains as we continue to make our way down the dark corridors. "We just played shadow tactics with them. A lot more of us were killed, but they couldn't catch us all. We had scuba gear and enough cold weather equipment to make it hard for them to find us. Eventually, once enough of us were dead, they gave up."

"So how many of you were there when you started to rebuild?" Sasha asks as she moves her flashlight from one point to the next, attempting to find any other hidden surprises.

Meredith shrugs. "Maybe fifty-two or fifty-three. I'm not sure. But more people came after the years started going by. More and more searching for a home."

"And here you're rebuilding," I comment.

"Yep," she answers, nodding. "There was enough food and supplies to get us through the beginning of the whole operation. Once the sweeper teams left, we struck out for the surface. We have a few hidden greenhouses up there, and hunting has never been easier for people. Plus, we have as much fresh water as we can use, so no one goes thirsty. Sanitation isn't a problem with some of the underground cisterns we've built. Power and electricity were tough, but thanks to our two mutual friends, that's recently changed. We're making it work."

"This is amazing," I say softly. "Really. I've been hoping to find something like this all my life. I've looked everywhere for it."

"Marukarn and Andizha told us that part about you," Meredith tells me. "There are even some survivors here who said they thought they saw you. No one ever tried to get close to you though. We all thought you were some kind of Rantir ploy. Some of us even got killed when the first of your kind showed up. We thought you were some kind of human reclamation effort that somebody got started."

I snap out of my sense of wonder for a moment. What she said confuses me. "What do you mean, 'my kind?'"

"The things that look like you," she clarifies. "The other robot people. They only showed up a few months ago, but when we first found them, they started killing or capturing us. We've had to lay real low with them around. If Andizha hadn't said otherwise, we'd have shot you on sight."

"How did you know not to?" Sasha inquires.

"Because of you," Meredith answers, indicating Sasha. "She said you'd be with...'Ferroc,' is it?"

I nod, then look to Sasha. "Good call on coming with me."

She gives me a grin, then goes back to actively scanning the tunnels.

Meredith looks at me. "Why Ferroc? You said you were human once...What's your real name?"

I look back at her. "Nathan is my real name. Ferroc is what I am now."

"You've really been out there in the world since the beginning of all this?" she presses. "I can't believe you made it."

I nod in agreement. "Neither can I." I reflect on that statement for a moment, remembering all the hardship and sorrow it's taken to get to this place. "It hasn't been easy."

I think I see Meredith's typical and hard expression soften when I speak those words. "No. I don't imagine it was."

We let it go at that and resume our march, passing other mounted gun emplacements, reinforced doors, or other armed guards along the way. Sasha stays close, continually looking over at me in an attempt to read what I'm feeling. That must be hard for her, perceptive as she is, given *I* don't even know what I'm feeling in this moment.

It's a mixture of amazement, surprise, hope, and loneliness. Amazement at what these people have done. Surprise that something like this is even here in the first place. Hope that there was finally a shelter that survivors could come to and start over. But loneliness throughout it all because of a strange feeling I can't shake.

I'm so glad these people are alive. I wasn't lying when I told Meredith I was looking for something like this all my life. And now that I knew it was here, I promise myself I'll do everything in my power to uphold and protect it.

But I just can't get beyond the thought that, no matter what, I will never be a part of it in the way so much of me yearns for. In a way that will make me feel I belong with the people here in a human capacity.

I can't quite pin the source of that lament either. It's not enough to cause me grave despair. But it's nagging enough that the concept won't leave my mind. Enough that I know this issue will arise at some point down the road. I hope I'm wrong, but I feel the thought deserves to be addressed all the same.

Finally, we come to one last door. It stands higher and thicker than all the others we've passed through. I can tell it's been welded together and formed from several different pieces of metal and scrap. It also has multiple locks and barriers and a slew of security details around it. Machine guns and heavily armed guards abound in this area. They're not taking any chances on someone unauthorized getting in. I can't say I blame them either. There was no need to be lax when you were protecting what could be humanity's best chance at a new start.

A few security scans, retinal identifications, voice recognitions, and confirmations from unseen observers gets us beyond the threshold. We step through the giant metal doors into a rather large, central cavern. I can see several passages, all illuminated, leading to a slew of different chambers.

And there's people.

There are people everywhere.

Even children.

I can't believe what I'm seeing. After years and years of searching with only the slightest hope that one day I'd see something like this if even for a second...

Here it is. It's real. People are starting over. They're living again. They're thriving.

Granted it's underground, but it's real!

And I'm here to witness it. I'm not waking up from some long, horrible dream. None of my programs are malfunctioning. My optical processors aren't misreading anything.

This. Is. Real.

I watch as two small boys run past me, too occupied by whatever game they were playing to notice the return of a handful of soldiers or even my presence for that matter. Many of the other inhabitants stop and look at me, most wearing curious or troubled expressions upon their faces. Most everyone is wearing some kind of amalgamated set of clothing stitched together from a few or many separate articles.

And, in a pleasant surprise, everyone is clean and healthy. Meredith wasn't lying when she said sanitation wasn't an issue, but I could never have suspected this level of sophisticated survival. Especially after the only other humans I'd encountered were most certainly roughing it in the wild. Sasha in particular. Here, though, there was proof that not only were people still alive on this earth, but they were beginning to repopulate and rebuild what was lost.

"Home sweet home," Meredith comments, breaking me from my sense of awe. "It gets a little dank but you get used to that."

I look at her, wishing my face could tell her what I'm having difficult putting into words. "...How...? How is any of this possible? How did you do all of this?"

"You know what it's like to find that drive to survive better than anyone, I'd imagine," she says. "Whoever was here when we first made this effort was intent on seeing it through. There's a lot of us here who were the first to start digging these tunnels and caverns."

"But how?" I ask again.

She shrugs. "With nothing but time, abundant food and water, and with enough manpower, what else are you going to do? Once we linked up with some of the shelters, we made runs to the surface for more heavy-duty equipment. And we only worked when we were absolutely certain there were no Rantir around to hear us digging."

"What about oxygen?" I pose.

"We have a network of airlines drilled up to the surface," Meredith explains. "The whole place is vented just enough to get fresh air in, but not enough to expose any carrying noises. We made sure to muffle any air tunnels we made."

I'm almost at a loss for words.

"It's beautiful," I tell her.

She smiles for the first time since I've met her. "Yes she is."

I look down at Sasha who shares the same awestruck state of mind. I know because of her expression. I've never seen her stunned before. Even when she met me she held her composure better than this. Now, she's almost as overcome as I am. Her eyes are slightly wider and unblinking. Her breathing is shallow and quick.

I put my hand on her shoulder and she meets my gaze. Neither one of us has to say it, but we know what's in our hearts.

It's a home. An actual home. A place of refuge where she can finally sleep in comfort and without that state of perpetual tension that comes from living among the feral Rantir on the surface. It's a place where she can start over. She can get her life back. There are people to talk to, confide in, form relationships with, and just be a human with.

169

It's everything she'll ever need. No more running. No more hiding. Food and water available to her.

...It's all here.

I wonder how well she'll sleep tonight. And for once, she won't need me around.

...And there's that nagging feeling again...

I can't get it out of my mind. For some reason, it's starting to sting a little more.

"I'm going to report to Andizha," Meredith states. She gestures down some corridors. "You two can do what you want for a bit. Beds are that way and food is down there." She looks at me for a second. "Don't suppose you need anything in particular?"

I shake my head, wishing I could display amusement in a more recognizable fashion.

"Good deal then," Meredith says. "We'll come find you when we need you." She turns and begins walking down a central corridor, the majority of our escort going with her.

Sasha and I linger for a few moments longer, just taking in the sight before us.

"A lot of people don't believe it when they see it," one of the soldiers who escorted us in says. "But it's real."

I look at him. He appears to be in his early 40's. Clean shaven, buzzed blonde hair, blue eyes, a long scar from some kind of blade running down his right cheek. He has a strong build, making it clear he's been eating healthily and stays quite active. The soldier life must be physically demanding here. He wears full camouflage fatigues and military issue boots and stands six foot two, weighing two-hundred and four pounds. He has a sidearm on his leg, a knife on his other, a scoped bolt-action rifle slung over his shoulder. It looks like the same model Sasha carries. He also carries an olive green backpack.

"It's so much to take in," I tell him, turning my focus back out to the thriving reestablishment of humanity. "I've wanted to see this for a long time."

He nods with a grin. "People will always find a way. So long as there are a few us left, we'll make it work."

I wish I could share his optimism. "Let's hope so."

"So you're Ferroc," he states.

I nod.

"I'm Jeff," he says. "People call me 'Free.'"

I turn to him, noticing his outstretched hand. I shake it with the same amount of precision and effort it always requires.

"'Free?'" I ask, puzzled.

"Yeah," he confirms. "Jeffry. Jeff-*Free*."

"Ah," I comment, getting the origin of the nickname.

"I've heard a few rumors about you," he goes on, taking a moment to notice Sasha behind me. As he does so, my sensors inform me his heart rate increases.

Curious...

"I didn't think I'd actually see you," he continues. "People say you're some kind of wandering ghost or something like that."

I shake my head, stifling a chuckle. It seems like I'll always be something foreign in this world. Machine, alien, and now "ghost." My list of titles was certainly broader than most.

"No ghost," I tell him. "Just me." I turn to look at Sasha. "And her. She's made sure I don't become one. This is Sasha."

She looks over at Free, and there's a shift in her demeanor.

It's subtle, as most things with Sasha tend to be. But subtlety is something that's hard to mask from something with advanced scanning and sensory procedures like mine.

Her pupils dilate ever so slightly. Her heart rate increases by a few beats per minute. In a millisecond, I turn to Free and notice the same fluctuations to his bodily functions. He's more in control, but I can tell there's an increase to his external temperature, indicating he's anxious.

There's an attraction between the two of them, if only physiologically at the moment. But it's an attraction nonetheless. Now I understand why Free's heart rate climbed just a moment ago.

And at that moment, there's a wave of jealously that washes over me.

Just as quickly as it arrives, I lock it away. Once again in my own convoluted sense of fatalism, I accept that some things aren't meant to be.

I choose to deflect the emotions instead. I *can't* feel this way.

"I need to speak with Marukarn and Andizha," I announce. "Free, it's good to meet you. Why don't you show Sasha around for a bit?"

Sasha looks at me with an expression I can't identify. I know there's a part of her that wants to go with Free. But her loyalty to me is fierce, and the suggestion I've just made is uncharacteristic. I'm sure it stung her more than a little.

"I can go with you," she tries to argue.

"It's fine," I tell her, deflecting her efforts. "Go with Free and learn about this place. I'll give you the details of my meeting later. You can fill me in on what we're dealing with here. Sound good?"

She's still confused. Maybe even hurt. But she nods.

"Is that OK with you?" I ask Free.

He nods as well, still a little nervous but eager to accept. "Yeah, that's fine. Why wouldn't it be?"

I shrug. "I hope you can trust us at this point. Besides, we need supplies for later. If she's walking around with you it won't be as suspicious as us snooping around by ourselves, right?"

He thinks on it for a moment, then nods. "Yeah. Sure thing." He turns back to Sasha. "You hungry?"

She looks back and forth from him to me a few times, trying to sort out what's going on. Eventually, she finds her answer.

"Yeah. Food would be good."

"All right," Free says. "Hope you like fish. Come on. Chow hall is this way."

He beckons her to come with. She hesitates for a few seconds, looking to me for an answer, as if she needs permission to go with this new man.

"Nathan…" she begins.

"Don't worry about it," I tell her. "Go ahead. You can get a full meal and whole night's sleep tonight. How good is that going to feel? For once, you don't need me guarding you."

I wish I could offer her a reassuring smile. Instead, I place my hand on her shoulder.

She grins hesitantly. "You're not OK."

It's amazing how I can hide so little from her. She has no mechanical enhancement like me, yet she always knows.

I nod. "I need to work some things out. I'll tell you later, OK?"

"You sure?"

"Yes. Now go ahead. I'll tell you what Marukarn and Andizha have to say later." I look to Free. "We'll meet up again once you eat and rest, OK?"

She doesn't want to leave me. She's almost fearful to, and not because of her own apprehensions this time. It's all because of her concern for me. I'm truly touched by her steadfast devotion. Her constant consideration of my feelings and thoughts.

But I need to be away from her right now. And I think she knows it.

She nods, then turns back to Free, following him down one of the tunnels and around a corner, looking back at me more than a few times. I watch them leave as they talk about the food. Both are nervous around each other, and I run another scan which tells me their heart rates have both remained elevated. They seem to like one another, though. That much is clear without sensory protocols.

Any forthcoming feelings of loneliness and abandonment are things I stifle quickly. They're frivolous desires I have no time for, and I can make no allowance for such notions. Things are what they are. No amount of longing can change that. I was human *once*. Not anymore. Love, romance, and jealousy won't do much but hurt me.

I turn, hurrying to catch up to the departing group of soldiers that brought us in.

Chapter 9

Meredith doesn't seem to mind me tagging along after I catch up to her. She inquires about Sasha, but I tell her Free is escorting her around the facility and, last I knew, they were going to get some food. She accepts that with a nonchalant shrug, then resumes her march, more of the soldiers peeling off from our group along the way.

As we wind through the corridors of this underground haven, I marvel at its immensity and sophistication. Not only have these people managed a method of air purification, they also have multiple piping systems for running water. Meredith informs me that the generators powering the facility are all based on hydropower from a channel they've dug to Lake Superior. They even have a pump system that returns the water to the lake via an underground line. The whole system is buried deepest underground, away from the keen senses of any prowling Rantir.

I wonder how good Sasha will feel after a hot shower tonight. And I realize, with that thought, how much I miss her already.

We proceed onward until we pass another heavily guarded security checkpoint. I discover this one is outfitted with Rantir technology after I run a quick scan of its schematics. Marukarn and Andizha had a prominent part in developing the fortifications of their own quarters.

Meredith stands in front of the heavy steel door and is visibly scanned by some complex network of blue lights and lasers. Immediately after the scan completes, the doors open, and there stand the two Rantir who changed my life nearly a month ago, both in their full battle regalia minus helmets. They look up, and I think I'm then privileged with the equivalent of two Rantir smiles. The expression is interesting as their already prominent underbite is further exposed. They still adhere to their regimented discipline though, going about formalities with Meredith before addressing me.

They discuss the events on the surface in brief. The two only want to know about casualties or wounds, sightings of other survivors, or other Rantir. With that being the focus of their conversation, it isn't long before I'm brought into it since I'm the most prevalent subject. At which point, I never thought I'd say that I was happy to see a pair of Rantir.

But I am. And they appear equally pleased to see me.

Marukarn extends his hand to me. "This is the proper human gesture, yes?"

I grasp it, giving him a firm shake. Thanks to his battle suit, I have no fear of hurting him. It's nice to not have to worry about something like that for a change.

"It is," I tell him. "Is there a traditional Rantir greeting?"

Andizha approaches. "It's similar to your custom." She holds up her hand, splaying her fingers so her sensory pads are picking up vibrations through the air more effectively. "Do your systems read vibrations?"

I nod.

"Then hold your hand to mine in this fashion."

I do so, tuning my seismic systems to a refined level. When my fingers touch hers, visuals flash across my visor, displaying her heart rate, so much like a human's. I can see her every function shown in percentages, pressures, and beats per minute.

I can't feel them though. Just like she can't feel mine. It seems to balance in a strange way. There's almost a mutual respect that comes of it. I'm glad to experience this custom. I find it quite personal. I'm sure if I still retained my sense of touch, I'd discover it to be even more so.

"Thank you," I say to her.

She gives a slight bow. "It is good to see you again Ferroc."

"And you also," I reply. "Sasha is getting food right now. I'm sure she sends her best."

"We will see her in due course," Andizha replies. "For now, there is much to discuss and even more to plan. You had quite the battle on the surface from what we've been informed."

I look to Meredith. "Were you watching the whole thing?"

She nods. "Pretty much. But whatever happened inside that building stays with you. We didn't see it, but after you came out covered in blood, that was enough for us."

"Gahren's human warriors?" Marukarn inquires.

My gaze lingers on Meredith, hoping her last statement wasn't a warning to me.

I turn to Marukarn. "Yes. Five of them. Poorly armed and malnourished. Apparently he doesn't have high regard for his human soldiers."

"We've seen increasing numbers of them," Andizha informs me. "They fight out of desperation. Gahren threatens them with death or worse, spinning tales about the abomination that is 'Ferroc.'"

"They didn't seem to take kindly to me," I remark. "Do you know what he's telling the humans to make them hate me?"

Marukarn growls lowly. "Radical lies. Things about your willing defiance to assist the human race. He tells them the truth about your cellular evolution, but twists it to suit his needs of manipulating the humans. They're already starving or near death as it is, so they are eager to join his cause. However, once in league with him, they are given an implant that they may be tracked or destroyed through a release of nanobots into their bloodstream."

A wave of panic washes over me as I turn to Meredith with urgency, thinking Gahren could use the corpses to find the exact location of this stronghold.

"We took care of it," she tells me, calming my anxiety.

That's a relief. These survivors really did have their stuff together.

"I suppose it's not going to matter much with the other Rantir escaping," I note. "They'll be back. And they're acquiring arms and modified armor. I fought two more of the drones too. Have you found out anything else about them?"

"Nothing more than we already know," Andizha answers. "We were able to locate his operation in New York City. He's utilizing residual power from the steel tunnels to power his assembly of fabricated humanoids and weapons."

I need clarification. "'Steel tunnels?'"

"Old freight lines," Marukarn tells me. "Transports for humans via linked metal containers running on steel tracks with an electrical current. All located underground."

"The subway systems," I say out loud as I realize what they meant. "He has them up and running?"

"There are vast amounts of electrical charge available to him," Andizha confirms. "And he's engineered a strain of nanobots to fuel such a large power source. They are almost like the fossil fuels humans once utilized, though they must supplied with energy as well."

"So you found his ship?" I ask.

Andizha nods. "He has it concealed within the ruins of the tallest structures. He's spent great amounts of time in his laboratory."

"Were you able to infiltrate the vessel?" I press.

"No," Andizha answers. "We were able to procure samples of this newly programed nanobot, which gave us the information we now pass to you. However, Gahren didn't leave the confines of his ship often. But when he did, he was always wearing his armor."

"How badly did you hurt him?" Marukarn interjects.

I'm not sure what he's getting at with such a question, but I oblige him. "He was wheezing and his armor was charred after his weapon exploded in his hands. That's all I could tell. He flew off before I could finish him."

"It would seem you did more than you realized," the large Rantir states. "His breathing was still labored when we observed him outside of the craft, though his armor is fully repaired."

"What's your point?" I ask.

Marukarn thinks for a moment before answering. "If he's hurt, that would explain his extensive efforts in the laboratory. He's researching more technology for his cause to be certain, but a permanent wound is something he'd need to address if attempting to assemble and lead an army."

"What else did you see?" I ask.

"His force has grown almost comparably to his operation," Andizha explains. She retrieves a strange metal sphere from a shelf nearby. She brings it back and squeezes it in a sequence I can't follow. The sphere splits open and I see a light source projecting illumination outward from its core. It forms a hologram between all of us, flashing images of drones, Rantir with the modified suits I saw before, a model of the fighter craft that Sasha and I encountered, and a few different images of human soldiers with various weapons.

"He's using every resource available to him," Andizha continues. "So long as it poses even the slightest form of lethality, he assimilates it into his ever growing force. When he arrived to Earth, he was already equipped with enough of our technology to lead a lasting operation with a force of fifty to one hundred Rantir soldiers. Since then, he's been gathering human weapons and vehicles. He can repurpose them in the ship's engineering bay, granting him a vast armory of both human and fabricated Rantir weaponry. And, with his operation located in one of the largest human cities, there's no shortage of parts or materials for crafting new weapons after decomposition through micro-robotic deconstruction. All he needs to do is program the nanobots to reassemble metal components into the form of a weapon through uploaded schematics."

"But he still hasn't figured out organic reassembly on a subatomic level, has he?" I ask.

"No," Andizha answers. "Which is why he still seeks you. And with the amount of followers he's gathered, it's going to be much easier for him to track your movements."

I'm starting to see the bigger, ominous picture now. "How many does he have with him?"

Marukarn steps forward. "Some ninety Rantir soldiers outfitted with his best equipment, nearly three hundred human soldiers, and over one hundred drones. All of his warriors are armed in some way or another, and all have access to vehicles. They are also organized into functions and groups, all answering to Rantir commanders who, in turn, answer to Gahren."

"And he has the ability to repurpose nanobots to fuel, equip, and sustain them all," I state, getting the picture.

This is going to be a complicated affair.

"Indeed," Andizha replies. "But it doesn't change our plan."

I nod in agreement. "We go right to him."

"After a few things are done, yes," Marukarn clarifies. "There is work to do here."

"Agreed," I say. "We need to be ready for his incoming attack."

Meredith speaks. "He doesn't know about us. He'll only be here for you. We could hide you."

Andizha, Marukarn and I all shake our heads, seeming in complete synchronization and agreement.

"No," I tell her. "I won't jeopardize human lives for my sake. Especially so many in a place that very well could be humanity's best chance of starting over."

"Beyond that, he was already aware of some level of human activity here," Marukarn expounds. "The squads roaming through this area must have been scouts. Now, his reasons for returning in force have only doubled. Even if Ferroc was gone, he'd wish to capture as many of you as he could for his purposes."

"How many of you are ready to fight?" Andizha asks Meredith.

Meredith thinks for a minute, then replies. "We have about fifty we can fully outfit. All with the best we have."

"And we will do our best to provide weapons and armor systems," Andizha informs her. "Ferroc, you said you encountered enemies using a new form of battle suit?"

I nod. "I have a sample." I reach into my pack and pull out the patch of modified armor I took earlier. "Is there anything you can do with it?"

Both the Rantir analyze the armor sample carefully, rotating it in their hands and holding it close to their faces.

"Perhaps," Andizha says. "Though time is short. We will do what we can."

"How much time do we have?" I ask.

Marukarn and Andizha look to one another, both seeking a mutual consensus without saying a word.

"Around this time tomorrow," Marukarn says. "Maybe sooner."

"You understand when he gets here, he'll know you're helping humans?" I pose to the two of them. "There's no telling what he'll do with that kind of information."

They fall silent for moment, as if they're fathoming the ramifications of revealing their presence to Gahren, who will no doubt use it as political ammunition to fire back at any who oppose him among the Rantir.

"I will not stand idly by and stomach another genocide," Marukarn boldly states after the pause.

Andizha nods. "Nor I. Gahren brought this conflict upon the Rantir. If defending the humans is the spark that ignites the flames of war, I believe that defense is still worth fighting for. There are many more like us who will believe the same."

I look to Meredith to see her beaming with hope. I find my own spirits soaring at the conviction so clearly displayed by our two Rantir friends. My respect for them has grown exponentially in the last few minutes. They are willing to fight for a species that wasn't their own. Even willing to give their lives.

I couldn't say I knew many who were willing to do that.

"Thank you," I tell them. "And I'm sure I speak for everyone here when I say that gratitude extends from all of us."

They bow humbly.

"Let us return to the issue at hand," Andizha shifts topics. "There is more to be done."

Right she is. I admire her focus on the current obstacle as opposed to bridges we'll cross later.

"Is there any way he would anticipate our defense?" I ask.

Meredith answers for them. "He doesn't know how many of us are here. We don't know what he'll send after you, but we can be sure he won't be as prepared as he'd like to be."

I give a pleased nod. That's good news.

There's a silence in the room as we all contemplate the options. Marukarn and Andizha are here to protect the humans and myself, and if they can kill or neutralize Gahren, that's the icing on the cake for them. As for me, I'm not leaving these survivors to fend for themselves no matter how important I may be to the future of the human race. I'm not going to start acting inhuman now. Not when I've survived this long looking for the very thing I've just found. And as for Meredith...I'm fairly confident she's content to defend her home and the home of so many others.

"What resources do we have available?" I ask. "You said there were a few bases near here that you gathered supplies from."

"We have lots of rifles," she answers. "Some heavier stuff too. .50 cals and grenades."

"Any other explosives?" I ask.

Meredith casts me a worried look. "You know how to use all this stuff?"

"My systems give me...understanding of weapons," I tell her.

She sighs, no doubt thinking about what she's getting into. "There's a couple bricks of C4 some other survivors brought in. They thought it would be useful. No detonators though."

"No problem," I reply. "Good to know."

"What are you planning Ferroc?" Andizha interjects. "You are not alone in this defense."

"My plan is to go up there, set the field in our advantage, and kill every last one of them however I can," I state.

The matter-of-fact nature of my declaration gives them some pause, however I swear Marukarn grins in a Rantir fashion. It's almost threatening but somewhat comical.

"Simple and effective," the large Rantir says.

"You seem well suited for this life," Andizha comments, also sporting that Rantir smile I'm becoming acclimated to.

Her remark stings. Of course she didn't mean it to. It was a compliment. But given how effective I've learned I can be in combat, I'm not inclined to entertain the idea of how good I am outside of it too. I didn't want my life to be one fight after another or planning for the next one, but it seems that's exactly the task for which I am best suited.

Andizha's compliment was well-intentioned, and I appreciate it. What makes it hurt is my own understanding of how right she is as much as I wish she was wrong.

"I've had a lot of time to practice," I tell her with a slight bow, mimicking their mannerisms of respect and acknowledgement. "Let's hope it's enough to see this through."

"How can we fit in?" Meredith asks. "We can provide cover and support for you."

I turn to Marukarn and Andizha for this one. I don't know much about troop placement or commanding.

They seem to take my hint.

"We will oversee the role of your troops in this fight," Andizha tells her. "Supportive roles would be best. Far enough away from any direct threat, but close enough for immediate assistance as needed."

Meredith nods, and I'm glad she accepts her part in this plan with grace.

The truth is, humans are fragile compared to what we'll be facing. If the rest of them are as understanding of this as Meredith, that will be fortunate to be sure.

I hope Sasha is as receptive...

Marukarn's deep voice breaks me from my thoughts. "Outfit them and prepare them. Then report back to us."

Meredith turns to me. "You know how to find the armory?"

"I'll manage," I reply.

She gives me a nod. "Good." Then she leaves.

"I'm going up to the surface after I get the C4," I tell them.

"We will join you when the humans are placed," Andizha adds.

A thought comes to mind. "How can I help you guys?"

They're puzzled.

"What do you mean?" Marukarn asks.

"I mean," I begin, thinking on just that. "When I fight, I adapt to the situation. I have no way of knowing what's coming next, so I just improvise. Sasha covers me from a distance so I don't get in her way. What can I do to adapt to you two when you're fighting? I don't want to get in your way or limit your capabilities."

Andizha chuckles. Marukarn laughs heartily.

"You needn't worry about that," Andizha answers. "Just adapt to us being beside you."

"We know how you fight, Ferroc," Marukarn continues. "We are similar. It is the Rantir way. Adapt, as you so aptly said. Combat changes, and so must we."

I wish I could return the grin they both offered me a few moments ago.

"I'm looking forward to actually fighting beside the Rantir this time," I say.

There's a lot of weight behind that statement. It could be one of the first open declarations of lasting peace between our species. More so than that, it's a declaration of our alliance.

Dare I say, a possible friendship.

"And we are honored to fight by the side of humans," Andizha replies.

The two bow.

I return the gesture.

"Then I'll go make what preparations I can," I tell them.

They nod again. I extend them the same courtesy, then depart. I hope to find Sasha before I head to the surface.

I want some time with her. Just in case.

What remains of the day passes into the night. I spend some time alone to sort through my thoughts, planning the best ambush strategies as I try to remember the waterfront area in detail. I then go to arm myself for the coming battle. In the early morning hours I learn Sasha was headed in the same direction I was. She wasn't comfortable without her weapons, and after an order was issued from Andizha that we were safe and to be trusted, she was allowed access to the armory. There is a very helpful guard waiting for me, my weapons in hand, who also informs me Sasha is currently sorting through the munitions, searching for something that could be of use. I thank him, then continue into the confines of the armory, strapping my weapons and supplies to me.

I find Sasha sitting on some ammunition boxes cleaning her rifle, checking every component to make sure it's in working order. She looks up at me for a second, giving me a smile, then returns to her work. As I scan my surroundings, I see every piece of weaponry the survivors have stockpiled through the years.

One hundred and twenty-three rifles, thirty-two hand grenades, seventeen assorted side arms, five heavy machine guns, and of course, the five bricks of C4 totaling six pounds of plastic explosives.

I don't know what we'll be up against tomorrow morning, or if our enemies will even show up for that matter, but I'm getting more and more optimistic about our level of preparedness.

"So what did Marukarn and Andizha have to say?" Sasha asks as I continue scanning racks of weapons.

"Gahren has already started making his army in New York," I tell her. "He has power to fuel his forces, enough materials to build more, and both human and Rantir followers numbering over three hundred when put together with the drones. And that number is increasing daily."

"That's encouraging," she mutters. "Any word on you?"

I tilt my head. "What do you mean?"

"Have they learned anything else of what you are?" she rephrases. "Where you came from?"

I shake my head. "Not yet."

"Ah," she notes.

Something tells me she's being guarded around me for a reason I can't quite place. There's an awkward silence between us, with only the sound of metal sliding against metal as Sasha goes about cleaning her rifle. I wonder how to break this tense stillness, but then think about whether or not I really want to know the answer to what's occupying her thoughts.

She speaks before I can.

"You heard about the order?" she asks.

I nod. "Odds are we're going to be seeing a lot more of Gahren's forces in the morning. Especially now that he knows we're here. Better mobilize."

"I intend to," she replies. "What are you going to do?"

I go to a nearby rucksack and start packing supplies into it. The C4, spare ammunition for an assault rifle and the weapon itself, then start strapping hand grenades to my body.

"I'm going up there to set the stage," I tell her. "Whenever he comes, we'll be ready."

"What if he doesn't show up tomorrow, Nathan?" she poses.

I continue going about my task. "Then I'll wait for him as long as I have to."

Sasha sighs in obvious frustration. "Nathan, I know you want to protect this place, but you sure seem eager to be outside of it."

That gives me pause. The remark stings and I don't know why. I'm not sure what she's getting at, but her tone told me there was a lot more meaning behind her words than just their grammatical properties.

"I'm going out there because I'm the best one to do it," I tell her with no room for argument in my tone. "Why else would I?"

She shrugs, turning her gaze from mine. "Maybe because being out there is easier for you than facing what's in here."

That ignites a fire of irritation within me. Mostly because she's right. Still, she's not *entirely* right, so I remain defiant. "And what am I not facing in here, Sasha?"

"You tell me, 'Ferroc,'" is her answer.

Years of wandering the earth, out of touch with my humanity, all the while developing borderline sociopathic tendencies to cope with my situation, along with years of fighting just to survive...All of that couldn't prepare me for the bite of having Sasha call me 'Ferroc' instead of Nathan.

I relent, allowing her to fully know the depth of my troubles if she chooses. "Sasha...I don't know if you could understand."

She stops cleaning her rifle. "Try me."

I don't want to answer. I want to leave and just go out to the place where I'm starting to believe I belong. Everything about me indicates I'm the perfect vessel for war. I can adapt to any situation, I can master any weapon, and I can effectively confront any opponent before me after a simple reading. I'm faster than anything on the field, most of the time I'm stronger, I'm incredibly fortified against most forms of attack, and I feel no pain. It seems like fighting is all I'm meant for now. Even after my time with Sasha and after I've discovered this new haven for human and Rantir alike, I still feel so *alien* to everyone and everything around me.

I can't function in a place like this in a way that would benefit the fragile society. Surely I could become a laborer or maintenance expert here, but to what end? As far as I knew, I wasn't getting any older. Did that mean I was to resign myself to that fate forever? Picking up my weapons again only when needed and the rest of the time just busying myself with mundane tasks?

But Sasha didn't know these were the thoughts on my mind. She deserved an answer, and no matter how much I didn't want to give her one, that didn't change this fact.

"I don't think I'm meant to be in a place like this, Sasha," I tell her.

184

She blinks twice, keeping her eyes trained on my visor. I can't tell if she's shocked at what I've told her, or if she simply doesn't believe me.

"What?"

I lament how hard it is to convey feelings when there's no possible way she could understand.

"I just…" I struggle. "I see you in a place like this, and I see you starting over. I see you with another chance with real people around. Not a…"

"Stop," she orders. "You're not a machine Nathan."

"Maybe," I grant her. "But that doesn't mean I'm entirely human either."

She sighs. "I know Nathan. But are you worried about your future here? There's so much you could do for these people. And lots of those things don't include fighting."

I wave her off. "I know, Sasha. I know. But how long is that going to last? Is that going to be my fate? Fixing the boilers over and over? Rebuilding the walls? Mining the tunnels? That's going to get old pretty quick."

"You don't like the idea of a quiet life?" she poses. "You've said to me, I don't know how many times, how tired you are of the fighting and struggling. Now you're going back on that?"

I shake my head. "No. I'm not. I am tired, Sasha. But I don't know what else to do. I don't see any other options. Because while a quiet life appeals to me, so does a life that's finite."

She furrows her brow. "What do you mean?"

I guess she hadn't realized it yet. Gahren, Marukarn, and Andizha didn't exactly say it out loud to me, but I knew what they meant with how limitless the potential of my robotic cells was.

"Sasha," I say, almost hesitating. "I'm not dying."

She remains confused. "What does that have to do with anything?"

"I mean," I restart. "I'm not getting any older. You're getting older every day. Your cells are oxidizing as your body continues to function. It's how humans age. My body isn't doing that. And that means my brain isn't either."

She grows very concerned for a moment. "Nathan…You can't die?"

I shake my head. "I can be killed." This is what's hard to tell her. "But I won't die. Not of old age or decay. Sasha..." I look her right in the eye. "Unless something kills me, I'm going to live forever."

...Or until I kill myself.

"Nathan, that's not true," she argues.

"Can you prove otherwise?" I ask.

"Well, no," she responds. "But neither can you."

"The proof is in the evidence, Sasha," I tell her. "Think about it. My body's micro-robotic cells are designed to sustain the host vessel and all functions. Since mine have learned to create organic material to sustain my brain, *which is part of the host vessel*, that means the cells and neurons in my brain are being renewed when the old one's die. My brain, the only living part of me left, is being regenerated daily, and given everything it needs to function at optimal capacity."

She's trying to keep up, but I can tell she gets gist of what I'm saying to her.

"How long do you think I have on this earth, Sasha?" I ask. "Couple hundred years if I'm lucky? Maybe more? Because I think it's going to be eternity."

"But you don't know for sure," she argues weakly.

"And you don't know for sure that you'll wake up tomorrow," I counter. "But all the evidence indicates otherwise. You go about your life with that assumption. Kind of like gravity. We don't *know* for sure that it's going to influence us, but we assume it will because everything tells us it will." I look away from her, sorting my thoughts to properly explain this to her. "Sasha, everything tells us that I'm going to outlive *a lot* of what happens on this earth if I'm not terminated by outside forces."

She seems like she's about to interrupt with another argument, but I hold up my hand, stopping her protests.

"Sasha..."I begin, hesitant of what I know I must say. "You once told me I'd have to get used to the idea that the people around me are going to die. I've made peace with that. But there's something you need to do now. You need to get used to the idea that I *won't*."

The two of us are silent as we consider that. For me, it's a mixture of emotions. It's truly hard to know what to think. The contents of this subject aren't pleasant.

"So, what?" she asks. "You're just going to fight for the rest of your life? There won't always be someone out there trying to kill you. And hopefully not everyone will need protecting."

I shake my head. "I think so long as there are sentient beings in this universe, there's always going to be conflict. And if that's the case, I'll always be needed somewhere. Right now, I'm needed here. I'm needed to help defend this place and give these people the chance they deserve." I take a few steps closer to her, kneeling down to her level. "The chance you deserve."

She reaches out and touches the side of my face. Again, though I can't feel it, the mere act of her doing so means *so* much...

"I want you to be a part of that chance, Nathan," she tells me, her face lined with worry.

I nod. "And I will be Sasha." I reach up and clasp her hand in mine, careful to avoid any excess pressure that could injure her. "But you have to understand something...I'm always going to be around. I'll be here to watch you grow older, hopefully find a husband, and have children. And I'll be there to help raise them and be a part of your family. Maybe even several others."

God I wish I could cry again...

"But when you get old and die, I'll still be here," I tell her. "And your kids will have children of their own, and then I'll be here for them. Helping to raise them. Look after them...But then they'll die too. And I'll remain. For generation after generation of your family until even your bloodline fades away. It's a precious gift; the chance to be there for every descendant of your family. But it's also the cruelest curse I can imagine, because it means I'll have to watch each of you die."

I see tears forming in her eyes.

I audibly sigh at the helplessness of my situation. "This is my lot Sasha. This is what I am. And that's why I didn't want to talk before. I saw the way you and Free reacted to one another, and as silly as it was, I felt jealous. But I can't feel that way. I can't let myself feel that way. Because it's a life I'll never have again."

A tear streams down the left side of her face.

...I wish...I wish *so much* I could do that just one more time.

But, despite my sorrows and troubles over a life that was thrust upon me, I feel a sense of conviction stir inside me. I realize here and now that I may very well be the embodiment of a perfect war machine, but there's nothing stopping me from doing good with that. Doing something other than the endless wandering. Doing something that will benefit everyone in this haven, including me.

And it all starts now. I'm going to remember the things that are worth fighting for. I want my future to be better than my past.

Even if I'm going to die trying to achieve it.

"I'm going to make sure that you get the chance to have a family," I tell her. "And that your children get to have one of their own. And that everyone else around me gets the chance to start over." I stand, releasing her hands. "That's what I'm heading up there to do right now."

I turn from her, armed with my assortment of explosives and firearms, heading for the exit. The guard steps out of my way with a nod. Before I leave her, I turn back one last time.

"You know something?" I begin.

She looks up at me, wiping a tear from her other eye. "What?"

"It'll be nice watching where humanity goes from here," I say. "I might get the chance to see how we evolve into a new life. I think I'll enjoy watching civilization grow."

She grows very serious. "Even if you can never be a part of it?"

That stings, but it's a good question to ask. I nod weakly after giving it some thought. "Better to fight for something, than live for nothing."

"You know I'm going to be up there with you," she says. I can tell there's no convincing her otherwise.

I wouldn't do something as foolish as that anyway.

"I'll be up front," I say. "Don't take your eyes off me, OK?"

She gives me a comforting grin. "You know I won't."

"And if things get rough..."

She cuts me off. "I said I'd never leave you again."

I think to argue with her, but know better. Besides, I don't feel concern for her well-being. I trust her to look after herself. The only thing I feel at this moment, standing beside my friend, is the utmost of gratitude in the depths of my being.

I look at her in a moment of the deepest longing for some better way to express how I feel. Instead, I approach her, then place my hand on her shoulder. She grasps it in hers. I then place my forehead gently against her own, holding this position of the deepest physical and emotional affection I can display for as long as I can. I pull away after a length of time unknown to me, finding a reluctant smile on her face.

I wish I could offer her some kind of comfort. Instead, I give her a nod and head for the exit.

It's somewhat of a lonely walk. And I can't help but reflect on what I've just said. Earlier in my life, I'd only thought about it. Actually hearing it had a much different effect on me.

Have I dehumanized myself in my attempts to help Sasha understand my circumstance? Or maybe I've come one step closer to truly accepting myself for who and what I am. Maybe now I can face the coming challenge of Gahren's force, and then Gahren himself with a renewed sense of purpose. And I need that. Knowing exactly what I can do for Sasha, her children, and her children's children, I feel a sense of hope beyond living to find another survivor.

I'm glad I adopted the attitude of playing a part in something much larger than myself when I learned of my true being from Gahren, Marukarn, and Andizha. It's a mindset I find invaluable as I walk through the tunnels with a slew of onlookers watching me pass.

It's about more than myself.

Maybe this is what I'm meant to do.

Chapter 10

The night is still. Only the stars seem to present any real activity with their intermittent sparkles. I've always liked looking at them. Without pollution in the atmosphere, their radiance shines with a luster I never saw in my previous life. There are millions of them in the sky with more appearing every night. They shine upon my way as I prepare the battlefield.

Without detonators, the C4 is unreliable at best. I need to place it all in one spot to maximize the effective blast. A smaller building, scarred from my previous battle in the downtown waterfront area, suffices as the most likely route in my enemy's search for the humans or me. If all goes according to plan, the building will be nothing but flying, deadly shrapnel when the blast goes off. That means, after I pull the pin on the trigger grenade, I'll have three seconds to clear the explosive radius.

For a normal human, that would be problematic. For me, it's all the time in the world.

After I finish setting my C4, I keep two grenades, my .45, my sword, and the rifle I picked up in the armory strapped to me. My shotgun I chose to leave behind, wanting the precision of the rifle over the stopping power of my former weapon. I have spare ammunition for my firearms; about two extra magazines each. After that, I'll have to rely on my sword and integrated weapons. That's fine by me. They've done the trick thus far.

I move back to a place near the entrance of the survivor stronghold. There's a taller building which is a perfect observation point. As I work my way up to the structure, I find a few other survivors filtering out from the building where the hidden entrance is located. They're fully outfitted and ready to go. A few carry the heavy machine guns, intending to place them in effective firing lines.

Marukarn and Andizha aren't taking any chances. Our retaliation to whatever comes our way is going to be…substantial, to say the least. The men and women all give me a nod, or at the very least, some look of acknowledgment as I pass by. I'm still not sure what they think of me. I guess I wouldn't know what to think of me either. In the end, the hesitant acceptance or even tolerance is enough for me. Yet another aspect of living this duel existence that requires stoic acceptance and not self-pity.

I find Meredith at the center of everything, directing positions. She sees me approaching. "All set?"

I nod. "The brick building off the waterfront, exactly .25 miles away to the southwest is wired. That's where the majority of my fight took place, so I'm guessing they're going to start looking there for any clues to my location."

She nods in acknowledgment. "Got it."

"My plan is to hit them hard and fast after the initial explosion," I tell her. "After that, we're each on our own."

"How many are you thinking we're up against?" she asks.

I look around at the men and women with her, numbering about fifty, just like she said they'd have. "Why don't you tell me? Looks like you're planning on quite the fight."

"Andizha wanted us prepped to take on a force of equal size but with better equipment," she tells me. "We're doing as much as we can. I'd rather overshoot them than undershoot."

"I can't argue with that," I comment. "Do you know where those two are? Marukarn and Andizha, I mean."

She points to the building I was intending on using as my observation point. "He went up there to get a vantage point. Andizha will be coming to join him soon. They also want to put Sasha and Free up there since they're the ones with the long guns."

"Free any good with that rifle?" I ask. "Looked like he was ex-military. At least the gun was."

Meredith nods. "As far as I know, that's what he was. Marine sniper."

"Ah," I note. "Glad he's on our side."

"You should be," Meredith says. "We haven't had a whole lot of action around here, but he's been a hell of an asset to have. He doesn't miss much."

There's a part of me that wants to argue on behalf of Sasha out of loyalty and pride for my friend. The marksmanship I'd seen her execute, even under situations of extreme duress was incredible. It was going to take a lot to convince me there was another as skilled with a rifle as she was.

I don't say anything like that to Meredith, however. There are bigger issues at hand.

"I'm going to meet Marukarn," I tell her. "Good luck when this whole thing goes down."

"You too, Nathan," she offers.

I hesitate for a moment, almost stunned by having someone other than Sasha call me by my name. It's a hesitation Meredith notices.

"What?" she asks.

I decide to be honest with her. "Only Sasha calls me that."

She narrows her eyes. "That needs to change. I'm pretty sure everyone here would rather call you by your real name. Not something the Rantir gave you as a title."

"It's truly nice to hear," I tell her. "But my title is fitting."

"Maybe," she replies. "But so is 'human.'"

That gives me pause. Meredith, content with her final thoughts to me, gives me a grin and extends her hand.

"No matter what happens out here, I'm glad I met you," she tells me. "You're proof there's a lot more going on in this world than just one bleak day after the next."

I graciously accept her outstretched hand, giving a firm shake. "So are you."

We part ways. She to go lead her troops. Me to consult with Marukarn.

I navigate the interior of the building, discovering it was once some kind of granary or factory for processing crop yields. There's plenty of open space within the confines of the structure with only a few conveyor belts and benches interspersed throughout. It makes me glad Sasha and Free will have easy access to a nearby exit in case we get pushed back in the course of the fighting. I find a set of stairs leading to the uppermost part of the building, casually climbing them as I notice the first rays of morning light creeping through the windows.

I reach the top, discovering it to be a long hallway with many windows, all of which overlook the potential battlefield. I see Free and Sasha setting up in the farthest corner from me. Both of them have their rifles mounted on bipods. Free has a spotting scope next to him along with a notepad I see him vigorously writing in, no doubt marking down distances from what landmarks are within his view. Sasha has a different approach. She adjusts her scope, makes sure her rifle is stable, and practices her breath control while squeezing the trigger and going through the motions of smoothly cycling a round into the chamber.

I appreciate both of their methods of preparation. Free's is methodical while Sasha's is organic, and both are just as effective. As I've learned from my years of survival, it's not just the skill of the warrior that gets them through a fight. A lot of it is their will to succeed.

That would certainly account for me on a number of occasions.

Marukarn, outfitted in his full battle regalia including his imposing helm with its angular yellow visor, notices my entrance. He waves me over. As I approach, he offers me a small computer chip no larger than the tip of my finger. A quick scan reveals it to be compatible with all of my current communications systems for both receiving and sending information.

It's a transmitter.

I remove an armored plate on the side of my head, exposing my audio receptors and their wiring into my brain. I attach the chip to the wires, allow my innate electrical energy to power the transmitter, then start broadcasting.

"Can you hear me?" I ask Marukarn. Oddly, I don't "say" anything to him. Instead, it seems like my thoughts are broadcasted instead.

He nods, then I swear I hear his voice in my head. "'Hear' wouldn't be as appropriate as 'sense.' But yes, I 'hear' you."

Amusing, Marukarn. Glad you're having fun with me as I figure out the intricacies of Rantir communications tech.

"This transmitter will allow you to communicate with Andizha and myself with a mere thought," he informs me. "It is like projecting your voice, but without sound. The transmitter has interfaced with your communications systems to project the information wirelessly to those with the same systems."

"Is there a chance Gahren could intrude on our communications?" I ask.

He shakes his head. "This is a specifically designed system. Andizha overlooked its entire development. Only she knows its true workings."

"You said Gahren taught you though," I point out.

"Indeed, he was our instructor," Marukarn admits. "But that doesn't mean he's the master now."

I like that answer.

"She thinks of you often," my Rantir ally segues abruptly.

"What?"

He motions to Sasha, still practicing her breathing and trigger control. "Your friend Sasha. You are a central focus of her thoughts."

I take a moment to observe my friend. Maybe "admire" would be a more applicable term. The way she sits with the utmost of composure and steadiness is remarkable. Her focus never shifts from the scope, and her movements of cycling rounds are flawless.

She's the perfect, human hunter. Instinct guides her hand, tempered with years of discipline. All of it so clearly displayed to me since I've had the privilege to live at her side.

I wonder what she thinks of me. I wonder if I'm held in the same regard.

"She thinks about me a lot?" I ask.

Marukarn nods.

"She can't hear us right now, right?"

He chuckles. "Why? Are there things you don't wish her to know?"

I suddenly adopt a more sedate tone. "She already knows everything."

"Does she?" he asks.

I look at him. "I may be a machine, but she can read me." I turn my gaze to Lake Superior as it's slowly illuminated by the unseen but soon to be rising sun. "We had a very…honest, discussion before we came out here."

"Indeed," he says. "She told me."

I look back to him, tilting my head. "She told you?"

He nods. "She is concerned about you."

I guess I'm not surprised to hear that. I might be too if my friend, the cybernetic future of evolution, was developing an immortal loner complex.

"What did she tell you?" I ask.

"Your sense of isolation continues to grow. May I ask why?"

I look at him. "How would you feel if you were the only one of your kind? And then, right when you found a friend that meant so much to you, you had to let them go because they're living a life you never can. Add to that the responsibility of being the supposed future of two races. How would that make you feel?"

That makes him think for a moment. "It is a heavy burden. But only if you choose to define it as such."

"What do you mean?"

"I mean, your life is only a curse if you believe it is," he answers. "You told Sasha you will live to see her descendants grow. Is this not a good thing?"

"I'm going to have to watch them all die too, Marukarn," I point out. "Even you."

He nods. "I concede that, Ferroc. But will you not also get to meet others who will mean as much to your life as those you hold dear in the present?"

"I suppose so."

"Then perhaps it is a matter of the quality of the cycles you spend with those you cherish that is of the utmost importance," he tells me.

"'Not the amount of years in your life, it's the amount of life in your years,'" I quote.

Even behind his armored helm, I can tell he's curious as he looks to me for an explanation. "Is this another human phrase?"

I nod.

"Hmm," he thinks aloud. "Wise words. The Rantir say, "Better to die on your feet than live on your knees."

I wonder if I should tell him he quoted *Agamemnon* or that humans have said something very similar. That wouldn't change my attitude though.

I tilt my head in skepticism. "Kind of bleak, don't you think?"

He answers me in earnest. "Ours was not a society formed of harmony. Not at first. Many of us had to fight for the freedoms and advancements the Rantir now treasure."

I analyze his body language for a moment when I notice he seems to go rigid as he withdraws into his memories.

"You're someone who helped earn that life, aren't you?" I ask.

He shakes his head. "Not I. But my family, yes. My line is composed of warriors. A proud lineage. And because of warriors like us, there is peace among the Rantir now. A peace that has lasted for many cycles."

"And Gahren threatens that now, doesn't he?"

He nods. "And I would see that his ambitions never reach fruition. Even if I must die on my feet. My life is one I can be proud of." He looks back at me. "Which brings me back to you, Ferroc. Can you say the same of your life? If this is to be your last battle, can you be proud of the legacy you've left behind?"

"What legacy?" I retort. "How can I leave a legacy behind, Marukarn? My family was killed and I was left like this."

"A legacy does not consist of offspring," he explains. "That is the passage of genetic material. How will others remember you? How will your name be spoken of in ages to come?"

"There aren't too many around to remember me, Marukarn," I tell him.

He points to Sasha. "What about Sasha? And her children you will be able to observe as they grow? Will they not remember you? What about your fellow humans here? Surely they will be able to give an account of whom and what you were."

"Maybe," I admit quietly. I take a moment to ponder the many different possibilities of how I *could* be remembered. The options were unlimited, and daunting as that was, I couldn't help but be a little exhilarated by it. I had so much opportunity to carve my own destiny, at least in the minds of any humans I would influence with my existence.

"Even if you are a memory, it is a memory that leads one to immortality," he tells me. "A legacy of your existence carried by those who surpass you in life is what you leave behind."

I'm pained by what I say next. "But I'm going to outlive so many of those who I share this life with, Marukarn."

"Then that is your gift," he replies. "For you are allotted much time to truly solidify the quality of your life. But that is only if you choose. As long as you are living, you have a chance to make the best of this life, even if it was thrust upon you."

I think hard on that as I look back to Sasha. She's taken a break from running through her motions of combat. Now, she's looking at me, not saying anything with word or action, but with her eyes, she tells me how much she cares. She just holds me in her gaze, leaving me to wonder what she's thinking. As I do so, I hope the memories I've given her are pleasant ones. I reflect on when we first met and the disaster that almost turned out to be. I remember when I lectured her on what it was to be human, thinking of how I'm nearly contradicting myself in the present as I'm faced with eternity.

Mine was not an easy balance to reach. Finding serenity in acceptance of my immortal, robotic form and my fragile, human spirit was going to be a lasting endeavor. I was sure of that. But as I contemplate Marukarn's words to me, I consider more and more of how very important it is to hold on to who I am and where I come from. It's the only way I'm going to have any "life" in my years, endless as they may be.

Then again, I may die here today.

I wonder how much life I've truly had…At least, in this existence I awoke to a little over two decades ago.

"Why are you telling me this?" I ask Marukarn when I stir from my meditations.

He tentatively places a hand on my shoulder, as if he's unsure it's proper human etiquette. "Because Ferroc, you should not feel as if you are alone."

"That doesn't change the fact that I am," I reply.

"But you needn't *feel* that way," he reiterates. "Do not impose this burden upon yourself needlessly. I find it curious you would do such a thing."

I tilt my head inquisitively. "Why? Don't I have the right to?"

"What I mean is this: I was born and raised as a warrior; a soldier in service to the Rantir. I earned every moment of peace I've ever known. You were born a human, forced to become a survivor of war in this form you now inhabit. Yet, it is I, the soldier who has known war his whole life that knows more of peace than you. Or at least, what to fight for. You seem to go from one conflict to the next, even if the struggle lies within."

There's a long silence between us as the stillness of waning night whispers of the impending sunrise.

"Why do you feel serenity will never be yours?" he asks at length.

I look at him as the weight of his words sinks in. "Sometimes I feel like I have more in common with the Rantir than I do my own kind."

"Why is that?"

"Because we're both strangers to the humans of Earth," I reply.

"Ah, but you are the harbinger of change," he replies. "The 'avenging hybrid.' You may be an alien concept, but you were born of something that makes you akin to both of our races. Perhaps your perceptions of foreignness are misplaced. You belong to both worlds."

That makes sense…In a way I'm not sure I understand. But all the same, it's comforting.

I feel like, oddly enough, I'm bonding with Marukarn. With the level of trust and openness we've so freely exhibited between the two of us, this may be the case. I wonder why I would be so quick to reveal so much of myself to him, especially when it was his kind that ravaged the world of man to begin with.

Then I remember there has always been respect. A very clear respect that accounts for a lot of things.

"It feels strange hearing these things from you," I tell him.

"Why is that?"

I think for a second. "There's so much your kind did to mine. To me. Now we're speaking as if we're old friends."

"Consider it repentance for past wrongs then," Marukarn tells me. "We can never be old friends. But new ones? That's a possibility."

I wish I could smile yet again. "That sounds good to me."

He gives me a nod. "Then let's both survive this fight that it may be so. For now, you should speak with Sasha." He looks at her as I turn my gaze back to my friend as well. "Let us hope this isn't the last time either one of us does so."

It's fatalistic, but he's right. I may never get another chance. Small skirmishes were one thing. It was up to me and my ability as a fighter to get through the conflict alive. Large scale encounters required a higher degree of situational awareness, combat aptitude, and more often than not, a significant amount of luck. One stray bullet, one wayward blade, one random piece of flying debris…All of these could end the life of the best of soldiers, no matter how well prepared they were. I knew I was ready and capable, perhaps even more so than anyone else setting foot onto the field this day.

But was I lucky enough?

That remained to be seen.

"Thank you, Marukarn," I express.

"Thank you, Ferroc," he replies. "For listening."

I give a nod of appreciation and offer to shake his hand. He graciously accepts my gesture, then goes back to survey the battlefield as I leave him and head over to Sasha.

She hasn't taken her eyes off me ever since they locked with mine a few minutes ago. She knows I have something to say to her. Once again, she reads me easily, though in this case, I'm sure it wasn't as difficult. I could tell she had a few things she wanted to tell me as well.

I take a moment to observe her vantage point. I even enhance my optics to simulate the magnification at which she'll be acquiring targets. She has a clear line of fire to the waterfront with several zones of opportunity presented at intersections between buildings. Assuming the enemy didn't zero in on her position, she'd be able to take out more than a few of them before they ever got close.

Hopefully, if I was doing my job, they'd be too occupied with me to notice the incoming sniper fire.

"Don't think you'll lose sight of me from here," I comment.

She grins. "Told you I wouldn't. But you didn't come over here to talk about that, did you?"

Always perceptive. And to the point at this moment. I respect both qualities of the conversation thus far.

"No," I begin. "I didn't."

"Then why did you come over here?" she asks. "To say goodbye? Because that's my guess after what you said before."

I take a moment to think on that. "It seems appropriate. Just in case."

"No it doesn't, Nathan. Not to me. Why do you think we're done after this moment? Do you really think you're not going to make it? We don't even know if they'll show up today."

"We know they'll show up today," I reply. "All the evidence supports it. Even Marukarn and Andizha agree, and they know Gahren best."

"I know that, Nathan," she says. "Don't change the subject. The heart of the issue is, at your core, you don't think you're going to survive. Am I right?"

I have to catch myself for a second. In truth, that wasn't my exact thought. But then I had to wonder why I was being so fatalistic just a moment ago with Marukarn. And earlier with Sasha in the armory. Maybe Sasha had put it best, though I'd never articulated it so matter-of-factly in my mind until she said it.

"Is there anything wrong with that?" I counter. "I'm not saying that'll happen, but there are no guarantees."

"You're right," she agrees. "There are no guarantees. And to answer your question, there's nothing wrong with that. What's wrong is that I think you *want* to die today."

That was unexpected.

"What?" I manage to ask.

"You heard me."

We sit and stare at one another for what seems like the longest of moments.

"You think because of what I said yesterday, I want to die today?" I ask.

She gives the slightest of nods. "It seems like it, Nathan."

It's hard to hear her speaking like this. Harder still because it rings of truth. Not entirely accurate, but true nonetheless. Also because, whether I can accept it or not, Sasha has made it clear she's not giving up on me. No matter how long I'm going to be here, no matter what I do, she's going to be a part of my life. With that in mind, I don't want to cause her pain.

I think back to the days when I was wandering the world alone. Before I ever went to Seattle and met her. I remember how I held my gun against my head, debating over and over again if it would be better to just pull the trigger. Then I found her, and despite a rough beginning, she talked me out of a fate that would have denied me a chance to see humans starting over. Then, I realized no matter how much I tried, I could never truly fit into this new world. My destiny seemed to be linked to that life of wandering I wanted so much to abandon. Because what could I do otherwise? I was meant for this world where survival and combat reigned. As I looked at Sasha interacting with Free, I knew this to be true. Yet I wanted to fight for a future Sasha could enjoy. I swore I'd give anything for just a glimpse of that reality coming to fruition for her, her family, and all the other survivors.

Did that now mean I'm trying to fulfill my own self-appointed destiny by making myself a martyr?

I'm not sure. Which is why I know there's truth to what she says. I can't outright deny her claim.

"I'm not trying to escape the fate I described yesterday," I tell her. "But...I can't say I'm not trying to prevent it either."

She keeps her eyes locked on mine, staring at me and penetrating my soul in a way only she can with those deep, hazel orbs. She then reaches out and grabs my hand. External pressure sensors indicate she's gripping it tightly. This isn't a casual gesture of affection. This is a sign of conviction and a placement of hope.

"Nathan," she begins. "I said it before, but don't make me say it again...I'm not leaving you. And I want you to promise me something..."

She pauses.

I squeeze her hand back, looking into her eyes.

"Promise me you won't leave me," she says.

I don't know if I can.

"Sasha...I want to..."

"Out of the two of us, I'm the one who could never promise that," she replies. "Yes, I'm going to die someday. Yes, you're capable of dying too. But we both know I don't have as much time here as you do, Nathan. And I want my years, however long they are, to include you. "So don't cop out behind something like you dying today as a way of saying goodbye to me. Don't be afraid of facing whatever life throws your way because you think you can't experience it like a human can." She holds our clasped hands in front of me. "*This* is life, Nathan. *This*, I know you can feel. In your heart, in your soul...I know you can feel it. *This* is your life now, Nathan. And this is something that's out there for you even years after I die."

The weight of that statement begins to resonate.

Sasha...You'll never know how much you mean to me.

"Promise me, Nathan," she pleads once again. "I gave you that promise back in Seattle. I want the same from you." She lowers our hands, then places her palms on the sides of my armored face, all the while never taking her eyes from mine. "You're my family now."

And in those words, I find something I never thought I'd be allowed again.

Home.

Home is with Sasha. Home is here and now, clasping her hand, "feeling" her touch against the sides of my face. Living this life, no matter how long or short the time given to me. Home is protecting this. Protecting her. Protecting her future and mine.

I never thought I'd have it again. Not since Angie and Cassie. But here it is. It fits. It functions. It's a world within this world.

And in this inner realm, our lives are cohesive.

They're symbiotic.

Our lives give us love that nourishes, hope that refreshes, trust that heals, and dreams that ease our minds.

No...This most certainly wasn't the apocalypse I was expecting. But dare I say, it's one I think I can get by in.

Now that I'm home.

I delve deep into the recesses of my mind, body, and soul for the words I'm about to speak.

"I promise I'll never leave you, Sasha," I swear. I hold her hands against my face with my own, treasuring every second of her contact.

She smiles that smile I know belongs only to me. An expression of her soul, gifted to my existence simply for who I was and because I was a part of her life. I wish so much I could do the same for her. But though I can't express these feelings to her through my face or body, she still knows. She senses it.

Somehow.

And that's enough.

"A lot can happen in a few months, can't it?" I ask her.

She nods with a contented sigh. "Yeah. Might as well live like we're going to die tomorrow since that could happen anyway."

God...I *wish* I could smile!

"Thank you, Sasha," I say with as much of my essence as I can muster.

She stands and hugs me. Deeply. Passionately. And she doesn't let go for a long time. Nor do I.

It's just the two of us, up here, on the top floor of whatever this building used to be before the world changed so radically. But even that great shift that altered our lives in such a drastic measure doesn't matter.

It's her and I, holding one another close. She squeezes me tight to her, and I, after a few calculations to ensure her safety, return the embrace with as much meaning and human effort as I can give her. She's so delicate and fragile in my arms. Arms that have crushed opponents far more formidable than her.

But then, in this moment, being held by her, I'm just as vulnerable. I'm just as fragile. I feel like if this moment was never given to me, I would have fulfilled the dark deed I'd intended just a few months ago, standing atop the skyscraper in Seattle. If this moment were never given to me, I'd have no reason to go on.

As a machine, I could crush her with the power of my geared and hydraulic arms.

But she...

She could crush me with a thought.

I want this moment to last as long as it can. It's been twenty-three long, painful years, but I've finally realized something that's so very crucial to my existence. And Sasha has led me to it. It's a lesson I've learned before, but forgot when this new chapter of my life began.

My purpose is what I choose it to be. I am who and what I *want* to be. I'm not defined by this world any more than I allow. And I'm not defined by anyone else any more than I permit either. My purpose is living, because even a life lived in adverse conditions can still be lived well. Even if only moments at a time.

But how beautiful those moments are. Even if they last only a few seconds, the memories immortalize them forever, just as Marukarn said they have a tendency of doing.

And he's right about another thing to: I'm born of both worlds. I realize now, in Sasha's arms, how much more expansive the scope of my life is because of those origins. Rantir and human...I walk the line, somewhere on the razor's edge between them.

Because I choose to. And my home is where I *choose* to make it.

And I find great purpose in that. I find great meaning in those choices that have led me to this place, holding Sasha tight against me as she returns the gesture. Even with Ryan and Jaclyn, I never felt this way. My time with both of them was filled with great meaning, but I never learned to live of my own accord. Perhaps that was because my life with them was short lived. Or maybe it was because I hadn't opened my eyes to the true reality of my existence yet. I was grateful for what I'd shared with them all the same. And I wish so much I could go back to them with what I've learned today, living and growing with them, all the while having a priority so much higher than just surviving.

I'm glad I can at least look back on my time with them, knowing what I could have done then, and knowing I can avoid repeating past mistakes with Sasha.

For a moment, I think of Angie and Cassie and the life I had before all this...

I can't go back to who I once was, but I can go forward to who I want to be.

Thank you, Sasha.

You've given me a life worth living.

And right there, in that perfect moment, we are abruptly reminded of how fragile it all is.

There's a deep, rumbling noise somewhere to the southeast. Sasha and I both snap to attention, our instincts kicking in as if the moment we just shared had never happened. As beautiful and serene as the time in our embrace was, we both know there are bigger things to focus on now. Things that will prevent us from ever sharing time like that again if we don't address them.

And it's very important that we give our full attention to the thing that now approaches, because it's something none of us could have prepared for.

I don't believe what I'm seeing, even with enhanced optics giving me a clearer picture of the encroaching horror. Marukarn gazes intently with me, scanning and analyzing; making sure he's not hallucinating much like I am. Sasha and Free look down their scopes, acquiring a target too massive to even scratch with their generally formidable rifles and deadly aim.

Slowly emerging from a line of clouds that faintly dims the morning sun, I behold a floating vessel shaped like a stingray, wings lined with cannons and assorted manner of firepower I couldn't even begin to guess the destructive capability of. I see more turrets and gun batteries located atop the vessel, swiveling and ready to acquire a target. I see a bridge, the windows of which are shaped like a thin visor much like my own. I see jets and thrusters firing all along the bottom and top of the ship, assisting the craft on its journey toward our location.

Analysis confirms the vessel is over a mile wide, half a mile long, and spans nearly four hundred feet at its thickest point.

I haven't seen a Rantir warship of this size. Even when they made first contact with Earth, the ship that brought them to us was only half the scope of the leviathan that now approaches us.

"Marukarn!" I call, running to him as fast I can. "What am I seeing?"

He's stunned. He doesn't respond immediately.

"That, Ferroc," he begins. "Is Gahren's retribution."

Chapter 11

It's a warship.

I can't believe it, but it's a giant, fucking, warship. No one can truly comprehend the magnitude of what we're seeing. Even Marukarn maintains his shocked demeanor. Sasha and Free are gawking with mouths agape. I'm sure I'd do the same if I still had that part of my face. Even when Andizha joins us, fully geared in her battle armor, her disposition is very much the same.

Gahren really pulled out all the stops on this one. He isn't here to negotiate or discuss anything.

He's here for what he wants. And he wants me.

I know it. Everything adds up to it. He'd been probing this area for a while. But when he found out I was in the vicinity, that was all the reason he needed to move out in force. Now that he was here with his full arsenal, it was clear just what his intentions were. I knew it in my heart, and it wasn't pretty.

There wasn't going to be much left of this place after he was finished. Not unless he got what he wanted.

That left only one choice.

"Marukarn," I begin. "Is there any way to signal him?"

He turns to me, stunned. "What?"

"You heard me," I reply.

Sasha approaches the two of us, Free tagging along behind her. "Nathan," she starts. "What are you doing?"

I look her in the eye. "I'm finishing this."

"And how do you intend to do that?" Andizha asks.

"By giving him what he wants," I state. "We all know he's after me. I have to get aboard that ship."

Sasha glares. "Nathan, we are *not* giving you over to him."

Marukarn and Andizha both nod. Even Free, obviously a bit lost on why I'm so important, utters his words of concurrence.

"We don't have a choice," I tell them. "Marukarn, Andizha...We know he's here for me. What other reason would he have for showing up like this? Even if he knew there was a colony of humans here, he wouldn't need to exert this much effort. He's making a point."

"Even if that's true, Ferroc," Andizha interjects. "We cannot simply hand you over to him. If you think he's a force to be reckoned with now, you cannot comprehend the extent of the power he'll possess when he harnesses the capabilities of your systems."

"I'm not saying I'm going willingly," I tell them. "And Gahren is in for a real surprise if he thinks I'll just hand myself over without a fight. But we have to make him believe that's what we're doing. We need to make him *think* I'm giving myself over to him, because it's the only way any of you survive this."

Everyone seems to think otherwise, but gradually, they begin to dismiss their arguments as they try to discern my plan.

"Ferroc, you understand the danger you place yourself in?" Marukarn asks.

I nod. "If I don't surrender and board his ship, I'm sure that behemoth is capable of leveling this whole city. Am I wrong?"

Marukarn and Andizha shake their heads.

"Then if I can get aboard that craft, I can at least buy us some time."

"Time for what?" Sasha argues. "If we're this outgunned, what are we going to do?"

The answers aren't coming to me easily. It's hard to make a choice that could get so many people killed. But I'm running on instinct, and since that's what's gotten me this far, helping me to survive, I'm hoping those instincts won't fail me or the people I would protect now.

I look at Marukarn and Andizha. "How difficult would it be to infiltrate his craft?"

Andizha shifts her weight. "We've done it before, but the vessel was grounded. With no way to reach him discretely from the terrain, he'd know we were there and the external defenses would render our attempts useless from an air incursion."

"Then we need to make him land or we need to create a big enough distraction that you could get inside unnoticed," I tell them.

Sasha nudges my shoulder. "And what do we do?"

I hesitate to answer because I know it's not what she wants to hear. "You guys need to hide. Every human needs to go back inside the tunnels and hold them. If he sends ground forces, we know where they're going."

"It would be unnecessary," Marukarn informs me. "The primary cannons of his vessel could easily destroy the entire network of tunnels."

"It's better than having everyone evacuate!" I counter. "Out in the open they'll get ripped apart!" I take a moment to calm myself as

206

everyone looks at me with surprise. I guess they thought I'd never get worked up like this given my generally stoic demeanor. "Look, this is our only chance. If I don't surrender to him, he blows us apart. If I do surrender, at least we get some time. Time to do something. Anything. It's better than just lying down and taking it." I look at Marukarn. "'Better to die on your feet than live on your knees,' right?"

Andizha recoils slightly in surprise at my quotation of the Rantir proverb. She looks to Marukarn for an explanation. He remains fixated on me, deep in thought. In a few moments, he comes to a resolute conclusion.

"Ferroc is right," he states. "The only way we have a chance is aboard Gahren's ship. We must bring the battle to him."

"I'm not staying behind," Sasha announces with no room for argument.

I look at her. "Then what are you going to do, Sasha? You going to come with?"

"I said I'm not leaving you, Nathan," she tells me.

"I'm not asking you to," I explain. "I'm asking you to defend what humanity has needed since this whole thing began. You're just as capable as anyone else here of doing that."

"You already tried to say goodbye to me once," she replies. "Now it's like you're trying to do it again."

That gets everyone's attention focused on me. Marukarn, Andizha, and Free all turn to me waiting for my answer. I wonder if they think the same thing. The odds of success aren't favorable. Even beyond *unfavorable*. And we all knew I'd utterly destroy myself before I allowed Gahren to get a hold of my evolved systems. Now, I was going into the belly of the beast alone.

I can see why they'd think I was bidding them farewell.

"I don't know what it's going to take to win today," I declare. "It doesn't look good any way you spin it." I turn my attention back toward Gahren's approaching warship, a feeling of determination welling within me. "But he's not leaving here today with what he wants. And he's not taking anything that everyone here has built with him." I look directly at Sasha. "And I have too much to live for to say goodbye now. I'm not going into this thinking it's a suicide mission. I'm going into it with every intention of seeing it through, no matter the outcome."

All of them give me a nod of approval as I look to each in turn. We all understand the danger we're involved with today. If things turned ugly with my plan to confront Gahren directly, Sasha, Free, and the rest of the humans were going to have a very one-sided fight on their hands. If I actually managed to get inside the ship or lure Gahren out, Marukarn and Andizha would have their hands full against the much larger forces of our enemy. And if I actually managed to reach Gahren, I was to face an adversary that, to my understanding, was the best the Rantir race had to offer.

I'm reminded of the Spartans at the battle of Thermopylae. I think of the seventy American soldiers at Mogadishu. I think of my last stand against the invading Rantir as they advanced on my family. All battles of great strife and loss.

But all battles worth fighting. And sometimes, it just boiled down to that very simple principle.

There are things worth fighting for. There are things worth dying for.

"I'm going to the C4," I tell them. "I need it."

"He'll know you've laid a trap with it," Andizha informs me. "You'll not catch him off-guard, Ferroc."

"I want him to know there are explosives," I tell her. "And I want him to know they're not meant for him."

That gets everyone to look at me again.

"Nathan...." Sasha begins.

I hold up my hand. "Don't worry. I know what I'm doing."

Her look of concern fades very slowly, eventually replaced by that mischievous grin I've come to appreciate so much. Right now, it means all the more as I know she trusts me, even through the dangerous game I'm playing.

I turn to Marukarn and Andizha. "You guys stay ready. Look for any opportunity you can to get aboard the vessel."

"We won't be far," Marukarn says, tapping the communications chip implanted in his armor.

I do the same to acknowledge the meaning of his gesture.

"If a rout of his forces is our priority, then we focus on neutralizing the warship or Gahren himself," Andizha tells me.

"Agreed," I reply. "If I get the chance, I'm going into the ship with you two. Sound good?"

They all agree.

"Let's get to it."

Everyone looks to one another for what we all know could be our last time. Nothing else needs to be spoken. Just a few silent nods are exchanged. Marukarn and Andizha leave the building, making their way through the streets of Duluth to a position of better opportunity. Free heads back to his post, double checking his rifle. Sasha remains with me for a moment longer.

As delicately as I can, I place my hand upon the side of her face gently running my mechanical and unfeeling thumb along her cheek. She leans into my gesture.

"You've given me a reason to live," I tell her, meaning every word with all my heart. "You've given me more than I ever thought I could find again."

Her eyes look into me, fathoming the depths of my being, holding me in their gaze as the man within the machine. "Same here, Nathan."

She pulls me to her, holding me tightly in an embrace that brings comfort even to a cybernetic entity supposedly incapable of a sensation like relief.

We share the moment much like we did before. But knowing we must act, we soon break away, taking one last look at the person that has come to mean so much to the other.

"See you when this over," she says to me.

I give her a nod, then turn to leave.

"Hey! Ferroc!" I hear Free call from behind me.

I turn to find him running up to me, weapon in hand. We regard each other for a moment.

"Take this," he says, holding his rifle out to me. "I don't know what you'll be up against, but it should help. You have five high velocity rounds in the mag. I've killed Rantir with them before so I saved the rounds for when it really mattered. Seems like it really matters today."

Normally I'd protest, arguing that he could do more than I could with his own weapon. But today, I know better. Today, I know I'm the embodiment of warfare, master of any weapon. It's time for me to unleash that against Gahren.

It's time to accept just how much of a machine I am. For the sake of those I know and love.

I accept the rifle, strapping it over my shoulder after handing him mine along with the extra magazines. "Thank you, Free."

He nods silently as he accepts my weapon.

"Take care of Sasha," I tell him. "Please."

He looks back at her, then to me, comprehending exactly what it is I've just asked of him. "I will."

I then extend my hand to him. He accepts without hesitation. He goes back to Sasha and lies prone next to her, taking up his spotting scope and calling out wind indicators and distance markers. Sasha is already consumed by her mental state, memorizing and acknowledging every one of his points of interest with surprising alacrity.

It's my turn to adopt such a mindset.

I don't know what today holds. Truth be told, I'm scared. But I feel a sense of peace amidst the tumult of fear. I feel like today is the day I find out who and what I really am because my purpose is revealed after all these years.

After surviving for so long, looking for the answer, I know what I stayed alive for at last.

I exit the building, walking in the open.

I'm ready for you, Gahren.

I get to the building laced with C4. The warship now hovers in front me, blocking out the morning sun and casting an ominous shadow upon the remains of the city. It's still advancing, so I work quickly. I gather the bricks and the grenade I'd left to detonate them. Then I climb to the roof as quickly as I can. Once I get on top of the building, I mold the explosives onto the straps of my pack, creating an improvised, volatile harness. Then, I set a charge in my arm and pull the pin from one of my grenades. I release the charge, hurling the weapon toward the gargantuan warship. It flies through the air with incredible speed thanks to my powered throw. It explodes directly in front of the vessel and in a clear sky. The noise can be heard even through the deep rumble of the ship's engines.

More importantly, I know no one missed it.

Indeed, the ship seems to close the gap between us even faster. The roars of the craft's engines grow increasingly louder as the vessel nears me. I stand unfazed and resolute. No display of power or intent to intimidate was going to work on me. As the ship slows and the engines fall silent, I know I have his attention.

Now it's time to see if he'll negotiate.

The ship stops above me. I look up and see a bay door open. Sensors indicate the craft is holding position exactly one thousand and twenty-three feet above my current elevation. I enhance my optics and discover there's a squad of drones being released from the bay doors as well. I'm surprised when I see them streak across the sky, looping around toward my location as they're powered by jets similar to those of Gahren's, Marukarn's, or Andizha's battle armor.

Looks like my enemy has been busy improving the capabilities of his forces. That'll make life more interesting in the next few minutes when all hell breaks loose.

I watch as the squad of eight drones makes their way to me. I know Gahren is watching somehow, so I make a very clear display of pulling the pin of another grenade but holding the lever. The drones land in full synchronization on the rooftop, weapons leveled at me. Some have actual rifles, others have wrist mounted weaponry, others have blades and swords integrated into their arms or held in their hands.

We remain still. Me with my grenade held openly before me, and they with their weapons ready. Eventually, two of them lower their armaments and approach me. Both hold out a hand. I step forward, understanding the intention and offering them an elbow. Apparently, Gahren knows better than to speak with me openly this time. The negotiations will occur on a platform of his choosing. But that's fine. Now I have a free ride into the ship.

They clasp my limbs and blast off, carrying me with them back toward the bowels of Gahren's vessel.

As we rocket upward, I gain a better understanding of the ship as I note each gun battery and turret. The exterior of the warship is riddled with such emplacements of both Rantir and human firepower. They actively rotate and scan, no doubt looking for any other threat besides me. I see now why Marukarn and Andizha would be hesitant to approach, especially if the enemy was ready. I knew if I was going to have any backup from them on this mission, I'd need to create one hell of a distraction.

...Of which, I was more than capable of doing.

I'm lifted up through the bay doors, revealing a massive staging area that rivals the size of a football stadium and is shaped like the ancient Coliseum of Rome. The difference lying in the descending layers leading toward the arena floor. The ship's were much larger and meant for equipment placement instead of spectator seating for the ancient Romans. But the design was very much the same beyond that. I try to take note of as much as I can, but there are so many details in such a vast variety even I have a difficult time processing all things. Human vehicles range from tanks, to automobiles, to helicopters. There are also several different types of Rantir vehicles I can only guess the properties of. Then there are blends of these two technologies. I do spot several of the fighter vessels like the one I'd battled before, along with a few other familiar weapons carried by the inhabitants of the vessel. But that's about all the information I can acquire that's of use.

I focus most of my attention on the swarm of personnel that now begin making their way toward the edges of the floors upon which they prepare for the coming battle. A host of Rantir watches as I'm brought to the center of the arena while the bay doors close beneath my armed escort and I. There are hundreds of drones going about tasks within the ship as well, but apparently they have other responsibilities than watching me. It looks like there's a lot of supply distribution and arming procedures going on.

I see no humans. Something I find odd, but I can't focus my attention on that now.

Gahren brought his entire operation with him. He means to utterly annihilate the humans below, any way he has to. And now, my mission is made clear. If I fail to neutralize him or the ship, everyone below is going to die.

There is no failure here. Everything rests in my hands. Hands that now hold a live grenade.

I'm placed upon the floor. The drones holding me release their grip. They back away and join an entire army in taking aim at me.

It's hard not to feel a little daunted. But a little flattered at the same time.

Then, as nothing but tension and the echoing footsteps of the working drones fills the air, Gahren himself, along with an entourage of four heavily armed and armored Rantir bodyguards emerge from the crowd. They bristle with weapons and blades and their armor looks to have more in common with Marukarn's or Andizha's. No lightweight versions for these guards. It was clear they had the best equipment available. And I suppose that made sense given they were guarding Gahren himself.

I wasn't sure how this whole situation was going to pan out. It certainly didn't look good for me. But then, I was achieving my goal. I was stalling him. Every second in which he wasn't bombing the humans below was a victory. Marukarn and Andizha had more and more time to play a part as well.

But this is where my plan came to an abrupt halt as I hadn't thought this far ahead. Now it was time to improvise.

Gahren emerges from between his bodyguards, approaching me but remaining a good ten feet from me at all times. I notice he seems to walk with a hunch and his breathing is labored. There's a strange wheeze coming from him every time he exhales. I look a little closer and notice more external power supplies on his armor in the form of glowing cores similar to those that power the drones he manufactures. Wiring runs from them into his armor, but I also notice tubes with liquid and what looks like Rantir blood flowing from the cores too. I wonder what the properties of his modifications are as well as what purpose they play in the function of his armor. I run a scan. What I learn is most unexpected.

Life support systems.

"You understand why I'm here," Gahren states, a sharp rasp in his voice that takes on a strange undertone when he speaks. It doesn't help that his helmet amplifies his vocal projections.

"And you understand why I'm here," I reply. "This is between you and me."

He growls. "Is it really? Where is the one you travel with? The human girl..."

I don't like him bringing her up. "Sasha has nothing to do with this."

"Your whole race has a part in this," he snaps back. "And now they have one purpose, just as I'd told you before. I know how much you wish to save them, and you know that's why I came here. How many are down there? A hundred? More?"

"I know you're using them as a bargaining chip," I respond, holding the grenade out in front of me. "You touch a single human or make one move against them, I release this lever. And I know you're aware I have a bomb strapped to my chest."

He laughs. Not a deep, bellowing laughter, but laughter with a curious nature to it.

"Your plan is to eliminate yourself, hoping to take me with you?" he asks. "Board my ship to save your humans with self-termination?"

"I know you want me alive," I snarl. "So you'll leave them alone, or we can all die here and now."

"Go ahead, Ferroc," he responds so quickly it's discomforting. "I'm already dead. My body just doesn't know it yet."

For a moment, I'm confused by his intention. Then I remember his life support systems.

213

He takes note of my moment of observation. "You and I have more in common than you'd like to think. Behold your own doing." He gestures to his body. "You're not the only one who blends the fabric of both the artificial and organic realms now."

I stay focused on him. "What?"

"Some fluke," he explains. "Perhaps just like you. My cells aren't evolving like yours, but they now require a host of micro-robotic organisms to sustain my body. Robotic organisms that have unforeseen and arguably beneficial byproducts." He begins to pace in front of me. "I must admit, I underestimated you and your human companion. That has rendered me in this present misfortune. My armor is now my tomb, just as your body is yours."

I remember when I interfaced with Marukarn's systems to give him the coordinates to New York. I recall that Rantir armor linked to their nervous systems for faster cognitive and mechanical collaboration. It was the closest thing to artificial and biological cohesion in the field of cybernetics aside from me that I was aware of. I wonder if that has anything to do with what he's referring to.

"You're not like me," I tell him, hoping I'm right.

"No," he confirms. "I'm not. I must still perform all the necessary functions of a living organism. A task made all the more uncomfortable by the shell that now confines me." His tone drops ominously low. "And I have you to thank for this hell. But, with the addition of artificial integration, albeit involuntary, comes interesting, new discoveries born of necessity. A nervous system fused with, but also enhanced by outside artificial technology is useful in many circumstances."

Before I can even register what's happening, something has sliced through my wrist. The moment my artificial body informs me of the structural damage with warning indicators and readouts of the destruction, something else has snatched my disembodied hand from the air before it could hit the ground.

I try to make a lunge for my C4, but something else shatters my legs. It hits my knees so hard from the front they literally break in half, hyperextending with a screech of bending metal and breaking valves. I fall to the ground, trying to catch myself on my one good arm but it's impaled through the shoulder by a bladed appendage. And only now do I discover what's been attacking me.

It's a scythe, the owner of which stands before me, proudly displaying my severed hand with the grenade still within its grasp, lever depressed.

"I may not be the next step in evolution like you Ferroc," Gahren states. "But even if the circumstances that bred my adaptation were artificial, I know how to manipulate this development better than any naturally occurring process ever could." He rips his scythe free, taking what was left of my shoulder with it. Warning indicators flicker across my screen rapidly and repeatedly. This is damage on a nearly disastrous level.

"Never threaten a life that knows suffering far greater than your own," he tells me.

My mind is racing, desperately looking for something, *anything*, I can do to get out of this. Thoughts of resistance and rage boil within me with as much intensity as my growing anxiety. I know the consequences of failure today. I know what will happen if I can't make some kind of distraction for Marukarn and Andizha.

But I can't move. I can only claw at the ground with the nub of my right arm. My legs are useless from the knee down. I try to move them under me, hoping to get some kind of propulsion. For what? I'm not sure. But doing something seems like a better alternative than doing nothing.

As I attempt to claw my way to some form of defensible posture, a foot stomps down on my back, pinning me to the floor. One of the Rantir bodyguards stands over me, weapon leveled for my head.

"Go ahead," I tell him, more out of defiance than anything else.

"No!" Gahren interrupts. "I want him alive. Bring him to the laboratory."

"What of the humans below?" the guard asks.

Gahren looks at me. I swear he's smiling beneath his helmet. "Mobilize. The drones will join you once the human prisoners are processed."

I take note of that. I'm not sure if I can do anything with the information, but it's something I can hang onto. And I need anything I can get right now.

Gahren keeps his distance but takes a few steps forward, gloating over me like I'm his wounded prey. Which, I suppose, I might as well be.

"Living or dead, you humans serve a purpose to me," he states. "At least you'll join your kind soon enough in oblivion, Ferroc."

215

I start with a snarl that grows into roar of uncontained rage as I try in vain to fight back against the crushing pressure from the Rantir pinning me. But that's the extent of what I can do. I assess the damage, hoping there's some way I can get my legs under me and at least realign my damaged limbs for any opportunity that presents itself. Diagnostics inform me that rotation from the hip is all I have left. The joints on my knees have been completely neutralized. Nanobots are being administered to contain fluid leakage, which is substantial. Hydraulics are compromised in all but my right arm, which ends in a seemingly useless nub suitable only for scraping the floor fruitlessly. My left arm has only the most basic of function from the shoulder down, and I drag it limply whenever I get the chance to struggle against my captor. There is still enough wiring to carry a signal through it for basic function. Since none of my power sources have been damaged, I have plenty of energy for the task, but a simple flick of my wrist isn't going to do much.

...Then I remember that's all I need.

There's no way Gahren could have known about the weapon I'd acquired from one of his drones.

A plan begins to form in my mind. It's something I know has the potential to fulfill the ploy Marukarn, Andizha, and myself had set into motion. In a staging area like this, it was sure to cause the kind of disruption we needed.

I lurch forward, dragging my left arm so that it lies under my hip. My forearm is pointed at some of the C4 molded to my pack. I know I don't have much time when a few other Rantir guards start stripping my weapons from me. They take Free's rifle and my sword first. I lament their absence, but wonder if I'm even going to need them after I enact what I have in mind.

A strange sense of peace washes over me like a warm blanket. It's a sensation I actually *feel* inside me on a strictly human basis. I've been fighting for a long, long time. Apparently, that's what I was built for. But now I had the chance to do something with great meaning. Something other than the fighting that has been my perpetual existence.

I find comfort in that. I'll be dying for a cause actually worth dying for. And there will be rest for my weary soul.

I think of Sasha...How I lament that I'll never see her again. Even though I can't feel it, I want to run my hands through her hair, hold her to me, and have her hand in my own.

...At least I won't have to watch her die.

216

I perform some quick calculations, estimating the amount of time my human brain can survive without oxygen or necessary nutrients.

It's all the confirmation I need. I know I'm not going to survive this even if my brain is left intact.

I activate the receiver Marukarn gave me before I left.

"I'm in the hanger bay at the center of the ship. Gahren's forces are mobilizing. There are over two hundred armed troops at my location. Rantir and drones."

The bodyguards strip my .45 from me.

"Status?" I hear Marukarn's voice in my head.

Surprisingly, it's not hard for me to say. "I'm not going to make it, Marukarn. Be careful when you confront Gahren. He's faster than anything I've ever seen, and apparently, he's adapted the technology of the nanobots in a way that's similar to me. I don't know what else he's capable of."

I hear hesitation in his voice. "Understood."

The Rantir grab my grenades next.

My last thoughts are of Sasha. In a second, I think of every fond memory I've had with her over the last few months. They've been the best days of this robotic life. And as I told her, she gave me so much to live for, even inside a mechanical shell. She means so much to me...

There's only one thing I can say...

A last request to Marukarn.

"Tell Sasha I love her."

And now with a calm and tranquil mind do I fully understand that I've always been the man beneath the machine. At long last, I have utter peace with my life. After twenty-three, long, painful years, I'm OK with everything I've done.

It comes down to this moment.

Soon, with one last act on behalf of my fellow humans, it will finally end.

My one regret is that right now, when I've finally found such an important reason to live, I must die to save her.

So be it.

I look up at Gahren, speaking with the utmost resolution. "I might have made you what you are, but there's a difference between us I never had a part in."

"And what is that Ferroc?" he asks, looking directly at me.

"You never deserved an actual life to begin with."

I send the signal for all remaining power to divert to my weapon. My integrated disintegration gun rises from my forearm. In less than a second, the weapon is charged beyond maximum capacity. Gahren, despite the impossible speed of mind and body he demonstrated moments ago, can do nothing. Were he to sever my arm, the weapon would still discharge.

I see him rocket backward, trying to create as much space between himself and the blast as possible. The combined destructive force of the already unstable disintegration weapon and the C4 create an explosion the likes of which I've never seen before. But it only lasts for a fraction of a second.

I hear the weapon fire. Sensors inform me of the concussive, destructive impact with my body for the briefest of moments before distortion renders them indecipherable. I hear the C4 erupt with the fusion energy created by my weapon.

A brilliant flash into a white void, then I…

…

Chapter 12

ERROR CODE: 114.E6-99Y7C
-PRIMARY FUNCTIONS COMPROMISED
-------------------------DAMAGE CATASTROPHIC-------------------------
--

-------------------------DAMAGE CATASTROPHIC-------------------------
--

ERROR CODE: 5595-V9/HZ1221
-POWER DISTRIBUTION FAILURE
INITIATE SYSTEM DIRECTIVE: FS906
-------------------------DAMAGE CATASTROPHIC-------------------------
--

-------------------------DAMAGE CATASTROPHIC-------------------------
--

WARNING. WARNING. WARNING.
-INTERNAL SYSTEM FAILURE
WARNING. WARNING. WARNING.
-SENSORY FUNCTIONS TERMINATED.
WARNING. WARNING. WARNING.
-RESTORATION PROTOCOLS TERMINATED.
WARNING. WARNING. WARNING.
TERMINAL SYSTEM ERROR.
---------------------------///<ANALYZING...>///---------------------------
.
.
.

INITIATING SYSTEM DIRECTIVE: FS906
-CELLULAR PROCESSORS ADMINISTERED
ERROR CODE: 66J.756-AB49/XX4
-ORGANIC PROCESSOR FUNCTION DECLINATION
INITIATE SYSTEM DIRECTIVE: CC11
-------------------------DAMAGE CATASTROPHIC-------------------------
--

-------------------------DAMAGE CATASTROPHIC-------------------------
--

WARNING. WARNING. WARNING.
-REROUTE ALL AVAILABLE ASSETS.

WARNING. WARNING. WARNING.
TERMINAL SYSTEM ERROR.
-------------------------TOTAL SYSTEM FAILURE------------------------------
-------------------------TOTAL SYSTEM FAILURE------------------------------
------------------SYSTEM TERMINATION IMMINENT------------------------
------------------SYSTEM TERMINATION IMMINENT------------------------
SYSTEMS TERMINATING.
SYSTEMS TERMINATING..
SYSTEMS TERM...
.

.

.
-------------------------///<ANALYZING...>///-----------------------------
--

.

.

.
PRIMARY SYSTEM OVERRIDE
INITIATING DIRECTIVE 717.23CR
CLASS 5 SYSTEM FAILURE PROTOCOL INITIATED
-------------------------///<ANALYZING...>///-----------------------------
--

.

.

.
-------------------------///<ANALYZING...>///-----------------------------
--

.

.

.
-INITIALIZING CELLULAR PROCESSOR OVERRIDE
-ALL NON-ESSENTIAL FUNCTIONS TERMINATED
-------------------------///<ANALYZING...>///-----------------------------
--

.

.

.
-CELLULAR PROCESSOR POWER GENERATION SEQUENCE
INITIATED

220

----------------------///<ANALYZING...>///----------------------------

--

.

.

.

-INTERNAL ENERGY STABLIZED
-CELLULAR PROCESSORS REROUTED TO ORGANIC PROCESSOR
----------------------///<ANALYZING...>///----------------------------

--

.

.

.

-ORGANIC FUNCTION STABLIZATION CONFIRMED
-ALL LIFE SUPPORT SYSTEMS STABLIZED
-ENERGY FOR ALL CRITICAL FUNCTIONS SELF-SUSTAINING
-BEGINNING CESSATION SUBROUTINE OF DIRECTIVE 717.23CR
WARNING. WARNING. WARNING.
USER INTERFACE ONLINE
----------------------///<ANALYZING...>///----------------------------

--

.

.

.

-RESTORING SYSTEMS TO HOST
-INITIALIZING COMMAND PROTOCOLS
----------------------///<ANALYZING...>///----------------------------

--

.

.

.

-EMERGENCY FUNCTIONS TERMINATED
-PRIMARY SYSTEMS ONLi...

It's almost like waking from the worst nightmare I've ever had.
It's jarring. Everything is so disorienting. My vision is blurry and only
appears in shades of gray. It wavers and shakes as if I'm being jostled by
an earthquake. I'm having a hard time sorting my thoughts. I see bits of
code and warning indicators. Most of my systems are malfunctioning.
Others are simply not responding. And only pieces of what happened
after I triggered the explosion are known to me.

What's scares me is that I only remember system functions and computer protocols. No images or thoughts.

Just coding...

It's foreign.

It's mechanical and artificial.

It's...unsettling.

But I'm alive! I don't know how, but I'm alive! I can't believe I survived the explosion, but I'm not going to question the results. I just hope I don't have to live through another nightmare like the one I just had.

"We must get to the laboratory!" I hear Andizha shout.

I hear what I think is Marukarn grunt. Then, there's a screech of metal followed by a few dull thuds. I hear the charge of a disintegration weapon, but this one is much louder and sharper than any I've heard before. As is the ensuing explosion. I can't see the blast, but I know it was huge.

"Go!" Marukarn yells.

Then I hear the crack of a bolt action rifle.

"Two more to the left!" I hear Sasha call out.

Sasha...

I don't know if I should be overwhelmed with joy or horror. I can't believe she's here, especially after everything else that's happened.

Was I still dreaming? Or was I still in that strange void I perceived as a nightmare? It's hard to tell. I have so many emotions running through me. Fear, resolve, elation...All muddled into a storm of incoherent thoughts. But even amidst that tempest, there's a calm center composed of a comforting realization.

Sasha didn't leave me. I'm so glad she's here, even if I can't see her.

I try to speak but discover I can't. A warning indicator flashes a blurry message across my vision but I can't read it. There's too much interference with the static clouding my sight as well as the continuous, jumbling motion to pick out anything other than blurs and flashes of hazy imagery.

It's only then that I wonder how I came to be with Marukarn, Andizha, and Sasha in the first place. How did they even find me? And why are we going to the laboratory?

I try to run a scan of structural damage. I receive a cryptic message.

"HOST VESSEL 90% DESTROYED. SYSTEM FAILURE. INCAPABLE OF ACQUIRING REPLACEMENT MATERIALS."

Ninety percent destroyed? Incapable?

I have an idea of what that means, but it frightens me.

What really happened when I set off that explosion? What did I do to myself? And have I chosen a fate worse than death?

I discover Marukarn is holding what's left of my torso. It's only a portion of my chest and neck, but it attaches to my head, which is still intact. They must have pulled me from the wreckage I'd caused in the hanger bay.

I've had limbs removed before. I've even seen my own brain exposed beneath my artificial skull after a Rantir attack took off part of my metallic casing. But this...

This is by far the most discomforting feeling I've ever had. To be this close to death, and to be able to *see* it but unable to *feel* it...It's the first time I've ever been this in touch with my mortality. And given how distant I've grown from it after years of wandering and fighting, it's terrifying just how powerful of an influence that sensation is.

I try to yell once again. This time, I'm able to produce something similar to a moan, but at the cost of various power fluctuations and several warning indicators. With my vision growing increasingly clear, I can now read that my systems are running on minimal energy, trying to conserve everything for life support and cellular functions. I need to be careful when I try to speak. I don't know if the functions are stabilized.

In truth, I'm amazed they're even working at all. I shouldn't be alive.

But then, I'm not exactly human save for the one part that's still intact. I'm most grateful for that.

Though my moan was nearly drowned out by the furious activity of combat and movement around me, I hear Sasha calmly speaking to me. I don't know if she heard me, but I'm so glad to hear her voice. I need it so much right now.

I'm scared. I'm truly frightened and helpless, but her words soothe me. They help me focus and remain calm.

"Nathan, we're getting you out of here," she says as she pants heavily. "Hang on. Don't you fucking die on me, OK? Don't you leave me."

I won't Sasha.

I won't.

I see we're running down a long corridor, the shape of which is much like a tall oval to compensate for the substantial height of a typical Rantir. There isn't much cover, so I hope my friends can avoid a firefight. As light passes by me, I try to count the number of fixtures with the hopes I can get some bearing of where I am aboard the ship. I could be anywhere, but the more I familiarize myself with my surroundings, the better off I'll be.

Even if I'm a disembodied head...

God this is weird.

"There!" Marukarn calls as we come to an intersection.

He rounds the corner and I'm afforded a glimpse of an attacking Rantir slamming into my large friend. I'm thrown loose from Marukarn's grasp, bouncing off the floor and rolling to a stop against the corridor wall. I land with my face toward the scuffle, realizing there was more than just the Rantir waiting to ambush my friends. Three drones have joined the fray.

Marukarn struggles for a moment with the Rantir adversary. However, the fight is short lived. As his opponent strikes Marukarn's thick armor repeatedly with a blade that can't penetrate the dense shell, Marukarn lurches forward, slamming his head into his opponent's in a powerful headbutt. Then, with his enemy's face thrown back, he strikes with his right fist, slamming into his enemy's gut while releasing a small burst from his wrist-mounted weaponry and doubling the force of the blow. The enemy flies back into the wall, bouncing off it only to be blasted from both of Marukarn's cannons attached to his scythes. With the enemy clear of him, he releases a final, devastating blast from each of his wrist and scythe weapons that completely vaporizes the enemy Rantir.

Meanwhile, Andizha has dived past him, bounding over her ally with an agile flip, scythes planting into the walls to assist in levering her over the fight between Marukarn and his foe. She lands behind two of the incoming drones and on top of the third, bladed feet and arms leading the way. She takes her foe from its feet, impaling it first through the shoulders and hips, then pinning it to the floor. Immediately after, her scythes detach from the wall, cutting from the right and left, aiming for the drone's exposed neck. Unable to block or move, the machine is decapitated cleanly. However, Andizha doesn't stop there. She continues the swing of her scythes, crossing them in front of her but curving them upward as well, once again planting them into the walls. She uses them as anchors from which she turns her body, the natural motion of her as she unwinds propelling four deadly strikes against an opponent that has only turned partially to confront her.

All four of her bladed limbs strike in succession. The drone is severed in half at the waist from the repeated slashes. Now, she releases her scythes from their anchor point, bringing them down vertically into her opponent's head. As the lower portion of the drone crumples to the floor, she holds the upper half aloft with her implanted blades as it spasms, its systems malfunctioning from the fatal damage. Then, with hardly an effort, she rips her scythes free, tearing the enemy's head in two as she does so.

Sasha deals with the last foe. She draws her pistol, firing a line of bullets into the enemy's chest. It's enough to slow the foe, but it's able to advance close enough for a swing of its sword. She jumps back and resumes firing, but a telltale clicking reveals her magazine has run dry. However, she's bought enough time. Having slowed the drone enough, she shoulders her rifle as the enemy closes in. As it makes a heavy slash for her neck, she rolls under the swing and gets to her feet past the drone, drawing a bead on her foe's head. One bullet is all she needs, and it's that singular round that tears through the robotic skull of her enemy. The drone spasms, collapsing soon after.

This all happens within a matter of seconds. Helpless as I am on the floor and stricken with anxiety over the lack of control I have in the situation, I can't help but be amazed at the potent team my friends have created.

I know I'm in good hands with them.

Of which, there are two reaching for me. Sasha quickly approaches me and scoops me into her arms.

"In here!" Andizha calls. "Hurry!"

Sasha carries me into what I can only presume is the ship's laboratory. As we cross the threshold, I catch a glimpse of Marukarn working with some kind of panel. My curiosity is sated when I see the door, a thick and reinforced slab of metal, slam down behind us.

"We don't have much time," Andizha states. "What are we to do with him?"

"We save him," Sasha replies. "There's gotta be something we can do. Can't his body repair itself?"

"His restoration functions are too heavily damaged," Marukarn informs her. "He has no method of utilizing replacement materials."

I'm set upon a table, affording me a view of a room filled with components and equipment, including parts for what I know are more drones. Some of the mechanical bodies are even fully assembled but have yet to be activated. Some lie on tables while others are hung from the walls. I also see that some are near what appears to be an orange, glowing power core of some kind in the far right corner of the room.

It's shaped like a sphere with interlocking and glowing circuitry covering it. It has been mounted into the wall with two large tubes leading from it, also illuminated by the flow of whatever power source it's connected to. I chance a scan of it, realizing its energy output is vast. Nearly two thousand times that of a typical drone's power core. It's also not just a core, though I'm not sure what the other function is.

Far more interesting than that and highly disturbing are the rows of human brains contained in round tanks and stacked on shelves above the power core. All have cords attached to what I presume is the source of preserving energy. Apparently these poor souls were next to be converted into Gahren's robotic servants.

It's a repulsive sight. It makes my anger boil all the greater. Humanity has suffered enough.

"His body is filled with those tiny nanobots," Sasha continues, breaking me from my thoughts. "Aren't they fixing him now?"

I can see a blue grid of lasers emitted from Andizha's armor as she runs some kind of scan on me. The light washes over me downward, then upward.

She takes a moment to analyze the data she's gathered. "They are all focused on generating enough energy to continue electrical functions for his brain. All others are gathering oxygen. His maker must have implemented some kind of stasis procedure in the event of catastrophic damage. But the secret for undoing the state he's in lies with Ferroc's creator. I'm uncertain of what we can do."

"There's gotta be something we can do here," Sasha reiterates . "If Gahren can get those things working, we can fix Nathan."

As a plan starts to form in my head, I chance another scan of the drone bodies, trying to find a replacement vessel for my severed head. It consumes a fair amount of my energy and I fear I'll return to my previous state of empty preservation functions. However, I cancel the scan when I find a drone with a decomposition chamber like my previous body's. I don't know if I'll be able to interface with the vessel. But I don't have many options. It's all I've got. And if my evolved micro-robotic cells can adapt to fulfill the needs of the host, I had to take it on faith that they could adapt to my need of a new body.

A warning indicator flashes across my vision, informing me my power levels are dropping from the use of non-essential functions. Since I'm not gaining energy any time soon from my own systems, I decide to take a calculated risk.

My friends need to get me to a power source.

I try to yell.

All that comes out is an unintelligible, two-syllabled garble.

Sasha immediately runs to me, filling my field of vision with her comforting but concerned face. "Nathan!"

Marukarn tries to transmit to me. "Ferroc! Are you there?"

I receive the message, hearing Marukarn's voice in my head. But the act of doing so drains even more power. Another warning indicator flashes across my vision, and...

...

WARNING. WARNING. WARNING

-POWER FAILURE IMMINENT

-ALL NON-ESSENTIAL Fun...

...

It feels like taking a breath of air after nearly drowning, but I return from a void reserved only for cyborgs or forms of artificial intelligence like me.

I'm frightened. More terrified than I've ever been. But I know I need to stay focused. I can't speak, yet I have to signal them somehow.

I remember the large energy core.

Digging deep into the schematics of my previous robotic form, I find the program that dictates the function of my visor. When I find it, I order its illumination functions to cease and reactivate repeatedly. When I do so, I can only catch intermittent glimpses of Sasha and the room, but my visor is blinking while I stay fixated on the power core.

"Nathan!" Sasha calls to me once again.

Look where I'm looking Sasha.

"How do we fix you, Nathan?" I hear her plead.

Please Sasha...See through my eyes. It's all I can do to signal you.

I'm agonized that all I can do is blink my visor on and off, and even that is draining my power levels. It's not enough. Just the lights going on and off.

Please Sasha!

...
WARNING. WARNING. WARNING.

-SYSTEM Er...

...

I'm back again, teetering on the precipice of death for a third time.

God damn it! Please Sasha! Look where I'm looking!

I make my visor blink again.

"Nathan," she pleads. "Please...Say something."

I wish I could Sasha. How can I tell you something when all I can do is...

...Wait...

I can blink on and off at different intervals.

A distant but fond memory comes to me...

"They also believed in being prepared for anything. They even taught me Morse code, but I've never used it," she once told me on a rooftop after convincing me not to kill myself.

I delve into my memories, recalling everything I've learned over the years and finding my salvation. Out of the hundreds of books I've been able to garner information from, there is one I remember in particular. And contained in that book was a section in which I learned a skill I had dismissed as something to learn for the sake of something to do. In detailing the events of World War II, it included an informative description on the implementation of Morse code between ships. It also had included an alphabet and guide to the code for the purposes of documentation.

A guide I now remember.

I start blinking the necessary patterns.

S.O.S.

Come on, Sasha. I know you see this.

S.O.S

Through the intermittent moments of sight I'm allowed, I see her looking into my eyes, tears welling in hers.

Keep looking at me, Sasha.

S.O.S

S.O.S

It's so subtle, but I've seen it in other humans before I'd met her. I can tell exactly what that dawning moment of comprehension looks like.

She sees it.

"Nathan!" she yells, daring a smile. "We're going to save you!" F.A.R.R.I.G.H.T.C.O.R.N.E.R.

She takes a moment to decipher my message, then looks over her shoulder.

She looks back at me. "What is it?"

N.E.E.D.P.O.W.E.R.

Again, just a second to interpret my message, then she turns to Andizha. "He needs power!" She points to the core I've indicated. "There!"

Marukarn and Andizha run over to the power core. Sasha scoops me up and brings me to them. Andizha then gently takes me from her hands while Marukarn works on exposing a panel. He seems to struggle for a moment while trying to undo some wires, but in a shower of sparks and blue, electrical flame, he's able to pry a section of the core open, giving us access to an outlet of pure energy.

Andizha carefully aligns the base of my neck with the exposed portion of the energy core. As what's left of my body connects with it, two things happen, both of which are highly unexpected.

Almost immediately, available power levels spike from ten percent to two thousand percent capacity. My nanobots are now functioning at a level beyond anything I thought possible, and already my vision is cleared. My systems are operating nominally and I have access to more than a few of them which can help in my present dilemma.

I also interface with more than just a power source. This core is actually a computer with detailed files and programs. I'm granted a full dossier of information detailing the function of the machine I'm now interfacing with. This power core, when connected to a drone and freshly implanted human brain, reignites the neural transmitters while simultaneously powering a host of nanobots and providing them with necessary molecules for system activation and manipulation. I come to realize the power required for this is enormous as the nanobots consume vast amounts of energy to assimilate the organic and mechanical materials. This power core actually attaches to the ship's primary reactor for necessary power consumption. Once electrical impulses in the brain are carried, the nanobots of the drone seize all electrical functions, effectively controlling the vessel with the singular function of serving the host. From there, a user can manipulate that purpose.

That's what I've come to expect from a creature like Gahren. However, it might be exactly what I need to restore my body.

I find something else buried inside this computerized core. It's a record of Gahren's transformation.

Gahren's transformation?

I dig deeper into the file to see what it means. I start to see what look like examination charts of a Rantir body that has been fused to a suit of battle armor. The skin, the nerves, and even some of the muscle tissue have adhered to the interior of the protective suit. It renders the wearer incapable of removing the armor because of the embedded nervous system.

I keep exploring the file, pulling up schematics of anatomical solutions for necessary bodily functions. Sustenance is pumped directly into his body through exterior methods, explaining the other containment units I saw strapped to him. It appears he's also in a constant state of pain with the armor continually interfering with his nervous system, which requires vast amounts of neutralizing agents to help manage the agony. It further expounds on why he wears the extra power cores and supply tanks. I also see there has been extensive damage to his lungs that his damaged nervous system hasn't directed his body to heal due to interference from the armor. A respirator has been implanted into his battle suit, explaining the strange wheeze and raspy quality of his voice.

There are other things though. Things that are beneficial to the one undergoing this state of perpetual misery.

With his nervous system linked to the artificial interface of his armor, the two of them have become a singular unit. Reflexes and reaction speeds have increased exponentially due to the integration of computer processing protocols. His muscles, while causing him pain to maneuver, have been molded and integrated with the armor's mechanically superior capabilities. It seems as if the suit can function of its own accord, requiring no more effort than a thought on the wearer's part to perform the directed motion. Gahren doesn't need to lift his own hand anymore. The suit does it for him at speeds only a machine can match.

I can see why he's so fast now. Whatever he thinks, the suit does. Every part of him has been mechanized, save for his thought processes.

He was like me. A different, serendipitous form of me. One wrought of pain and extenuating circumstances, but still a living creature trapped in a robotic shell.

The thought chills me for a moment, as my current state was something I would never wish upon anyone. But then, Gahren did want to harness the power of my existence and what my cells have rendered me capable of. He'd achieved a lesser form of that.

Be careful what you wish for. Now he knows what it's like to be me.

While this information is useful and highly insightful as far as Gahren is concerned, there are bigger things at hand. I have power again, and with my systems functioning at two thousand percent capacity, I'm more than capable of finally communicating with my friends.

And how glad I am to do that.

I look at Sasha. There's so much I want to say. There's so much I *need* to say. I wonder what she's feeling now. All of this and more are things I want to address, but I just don't know if that's what's right in this moment. Instead, I find myself growing increasingly grateful for the chance to say anything. And if I had lips to speak with, through a smile they would say...

"God, it's good to see you."

Everyone in the room, even Marukarn and Andizha behind their armored exteriors, heave a very noticeable sigh of relief. Marukarn and Andizha look to one another and nod. Sasha smiles widely.

My dear friend's eyes water and her breathing quavers with joy. "You too, Nathan."

And it's so good to hear her say that. To have her with me. To just be here with her, even amidst the tumultuous circumstances.

I can tell she's terrified for me. I guess I would be too if I were in her position. Looking at a dear friend's severed head was sure to be disconcerting, to say the least. But knowing that the person was still alive and fighting for their survival was a special type of unsettling to be sure.

She leans in close to me. "Are you OK?"

Despite myself, I chuckle. "All things considered, I couldn't be better."

She smiles, a tear rolling down her cheek as she does so. "How do we fix you, Nathan?"

I think about that for a moment. "There's a compatible drone body against the wall. My systems might be able to interface with it."

Andizha approaches the drone husk and runs a scan on it, the same blue laser grid analyzing the inanimate machine. "Perhaps Ferroc. But you have no method of atomization for particle distribution."

"I still have a few micro-robotic cells inside me functioning at two thousand percent capacity," I reply. "If they can make contact with enough replacement materials I think they can assimilate the new vessel."

"Then how do we do it?" Sasha asks.

"I need to stay in contact with this power source," I begin. "Bring the body over to me and connect it with what's left of my torso. My cells should do the rest."

"And if this fails?" Andizha poses.

Marukarn steps forward. "We haven't a choice. Gahren's forces will be here soon."

"Then do it," Sasha says.

"I need particle transport tubes running from my neck into this core and into the drone's body," I tell them. "Anything that can connect with my fluid transport hoses will work. Just make sure we're all strung together."

Sasha looks around for anything she can find, searching the laboratory walls for spare parts while Andizha and Marukarn bring the drone's body to me. Instead of joining the search for materials after their task is complete, they take a more direct route. Marukarn rips the head off the drone with his formidable strength while Andizha begins connecting fluid hoses and transport tubes.

I can't argue with the results.

Sasha continues bringing Marukarn and Andizha anything that could be of use. Fluids, scrap metal, hoses...Eventually we have quite the collection. My two Rantir allies put all of it to good use, and in a matter of minutes, we're almost ready to proceed with what I hope will restore me. I'm wired and attached where I need to be. It's time to see what my cells can do.

"We all set?" Sasha asks as she brings over some other spare materials.

"Ferroc?" Marukarn asks, ready to attach a cord that would connect me directly to the drone body and power core.

This was it. Nothing left to do but take a leap of faith.

"Do it," I say as I try not to think of the myriad of things that could go wrong.

The thoughts are wrenched from me as my vision fills with coding and information, warning indicators and urgent messages regarding system malfunctions and the restoration of others. Suddenly a schematic of the drone's body appears on my visor as my system tries assimilating the new vessel. I wonder if this is going to work, hoping and praying I was right. All systems seem compatible. I see protocols and coding I had no idea existed inside my subroutines, but that I swear I've seen somewhere before. It's almost like I dreamed them. At least that's the only way I can describe this eerie type of robotic déjà vu. Regardless, I watch as my computerized mind calculates all necessary procedures and reroutes the nanobots I have available to me accordingly.

I'm helpless as I hope and pray that my structure will overcome any interference from Gahren's drone. I can see the progress reports as my nanobots flow from my head down into the drone's body. Warning indicators fill my screen with reports of foreign bodies attempting assimilation of my systems as they enact their own predetermined protocols.

There is nothing at all for a moment. Only darkness. An endless void that I'm fully aware of and totally vulnerable to. Just like any other creature, I fully comprehend my own frailty in this oblivion.

Then, I begin to see the silhouettes of my friends all huddled around me. They look at me, pleading with all their hearts that I've pulled through this.

I see a diagnostic report as my vision clears.

SYSTEM ASSIMILATION COMPLETE. ALL SYSTEMS RESTORED. HOST FUNCTUNALITY AT 2000% CAPACITY.

It feels strange at first; commanding a new body. But I lift my arm and brush the side of Sasha's face with a hand similar to my old body's. She immediately catches my outstretched arm and holds it to her so tight I fear even my metal exterior will bend and break under her powerful grasp as pressure sensors spike.

I wish I could hold her just as tightly.

A brush of her cheek does just fine however, and I'm eternally grateful for that. I want to smile as I touch her face.

A face that smiles just for me. Only this time, it's a million times more radiant and beautiful. I've never seen a more lovely sight. This is an image I'll hold not just in my mind, but in the very fabric of my being forever.

Marukarn offers a hand. "Good to have you with us again, Ferroc."

I clasp his arm, allowing him to pull me to my feet. "Good to be back." I look him in the eyes. "I owe you my life."

He bows humbly. "We are even."

Andizha approaches. "Were it not for your efforts, Gahren's forces would have overrun us. You gave us the opening we needed to bring the fight to him." She extends her hand.

I grasp it, giving her armored limb a firm shake with the utmost respect.

"Then let's finish this," I say as I look to all of them. "We need to destroy that reactor."

"It may well destroy the ship outright," Marukarn points out. "But at the very least, emergency repair protocols will have to be initiated."

"Good," I reply. "What's the fastest way?"

"Near the hanger there is a passage that would give us the most direct access," Andizha replies. "We must work our way back there."

Sasha checks her rifle to make sure she has a round chambered. "A lot of bad guys in there."

"You have my back?" I ask, wishing I could grin while I do so.

Her smile grows devious, yet reassuring. "Always."

Before we leave the laboratory, I decide it's worth running a complete system scan since my new body is relatively foreign to me. After all, my first form was a prototype. Now, I didn't have the slightest idea what I was, but I wanted to know what I was capable of. After a few translations, it's made clear.

Restoration protocols online.

Gyroscopic systems functioning normally.

Sensory functions all online.

Optical programs functioning.

Audio functions online.

Targeting protocols functional.

Navigation systems online.

Power generation and storage systems at one hundred percent. Power cores stable and fully charged with surplus energy distributed throughout the host vessel. Two thousand percent functionality.

...So I have power cores now...Good to know.

Motor functions online and at full capacity. I discover that I no longer have hydraulics within my limbs. Instead, my mechanical form supports an integrated power surge system. I don't have to charge my body anymore. It instantly distributes power where I need to it to go.

Looks like hydraulics were obsolete. I just upgraded to a newer model.

Propulsion systems online...

...Propulsion systems?

I activate them with a thought out of curiosity. I immediately regret that decision as I blast off from two jets built into my upper back and two other thrusters built into each of my calves. I rocket upward on a collision course for the ceiling.

With a thought and with the utmost of panic, I disable my jets and brace myself for a hard hit.

But not this time.

And perhaps never again. My arms, suddenly powered by what I can only presume are my thoughts and the subsequent distribution of power, catch me with enough strength to gently ease me into ceiling. I dent the metal roof, but I press myself up and away from the point of impact with ease and grace, falling back to the floor and landing lightly on my feet.

If I thought I was a strange creation before, I'm downright bewildered by what I am now.

My friends all stare at me curiously.

"What was that?" Sasha questions amidst a cough from the smoke of my jets.

In spite of the situation and considering all that's happened within the last two hours, I just chuckle. "A learning experience."

"Any other surprises?" she presses.

Good question, Sasha.

I scan for any remaining systems. Every function is the same as my previous body's except for one addition.

Integrated weapons systems.

"You guys might want to stand back," I warn my friends. "'Integrated weapons systems.'"

After what happened a few moments ago, they all know better than to ask questions and just do as I say. They all give me some space, and I activate the function.

My forearms suddenly sprout two double-sided blades. They look like internally mounted short swords or punching daggers. The blades protrude forward and down my arm, offering protection for my wrist and a direct line of penetration should I choose to punch with them as they extend ten inches past my fingertips. They were perfect for jabbing strikes, and I wasn't about to question their cutting capability.

On top of this, an indicator appears on my visor which states, "Secondary weapon function on standby."

With a thought, I activate whatever that program is. The blades fold back into my forearms and are replaced by a set of cannons that I can only assume are disintegration grade. They hum with energy and their barrels glow orange, ready to discharge at my command.

Sasha grins. Marukarn and Andizha look to one another. Again, I swear they're smiling.

The moment of levity is short-lived as a blast of disintegration energy rips the laboratory door apart. Not a moment after, three drones burst through the smoke-filled opening.

I seem to move the moment my thoughts direct me. My body responds to the every whim of my mind, and as I visualize myself closing the gap to my enemies, I'm already in front of them with a powered sprint of my new legs. The first drone is almost moving in what seems like slow motion. I'm moving so fast and with such precision it doesn't even register my presence until after my bladed right arm slams into its face, my short sword ripping through the front of its armored head and exploding out the back. I'm still moving as I pull my blade free, leading with my left arm to the next drone in the doorway. I impale it through the torso and drive it back, following up with an attack from right that slices its head off at the neck. I lunge out with a powered kick that drives the body from my blade with such force, it flies backward down the corridor, bouncing and skidding off the floor for more than two hundred feet.

In order to dodge the flying body, an enemy Rantir ducks low, revealing itself from behind a layer of cloaking smoke as it crouches. I make note of it as I turn on the last drone. It's still moving in what seems like a state of slow motion as it attempts to square off against me, disintegration rifle leading the way. It hasn't even completed its turn when I swing low for its legs with a backhanded slash from my right blade, ducking under any inherent danger from its powerful weapon. I slice through its legs cleanly, severing them at the knee. Its body is taken out from under it, and as it falls toward the ground, I impale it through the back with an uppercut of my left blade. I keep my momentum going upward, turning as I do so and putting the body of my impaled enemy between myself and the Rantir who has yet to rise to his feet.

Again, I kick the body of my enemy off my blade with force that surprises even me, launching the improvised projectile at the Rantir. The alien dodges aside, giving me a moment to close the gap between us. He tries as quickly as possible to get to his feet in the center of the hallway but I'm already upon him. His scythes aren't fast enough to reach me and he has no defense against both of my outstretched blades. I impale him through the chest, then switch my weapon systems to their secondary function. I fire a blast from both of my cannons, the disintegration energy launching him backward, burning his body to ash as it's flung away from me.

All of this in a matter of seconds, and I've only expended ten percent of my overcharged systems, even with the disintegration blasts. It seems as if my internal functions can read my thoughts along the urgency of which I place them, prioritizing energy dispersal accordingly.

Were my nanobots reading my mind now? Had they always done that?

It was only a guess, but it was the best theory I could come up with given what just took place. And it fell in line with the concept of combined artificial and organic evolution. The two now seemed to be symbiotic within my form.

I turn back to my friends to find them staring. Marukarn and Andizha have managed to take one step in the time it took me to dispatch my foes. Sasha has only managed to bring her rifle to bear.

I'm starting to like my new body, mysterious and unpredictable as it was. I feel like I just reached a new stage of the development I was continually undergoing as a man and machine.

"I'm functioning at nearly two thousand percent optimization," I inform them. "Let's take advantage of that."

Right when I finish those words, we hear the footfalls of many more enemies approaching. I send a ping of sonar down the hallways, learning that there are over fifty drones approaching led by several Rantir warriors.

"Lots of them coming our way!" I tell my friends.

"Back Ferroc!" Andizha calls as Marukarn steps in next to me.

Knowing better than to question them, I give Marukarn the lead and watch as he kneels down, grinding his knees and toes into the floor. His scythe mounted cannons align with those on his wrists, all of them humming with charged fusion energy. I watch as the air in front of him simmers with heat, wavering as the molecules are displaced. It seems as if the four weapons are combining their energy; focusing it into a larger and I'm sure far deadlier blast.

The first of the drones round the corner, blades ready and charging fast for us. Others level firearms of their own, a few brandishing human weaponry and firing a volley of bullets at Marukarn. The projectile rounds glance harmlessly off his heavily armored shell as he continues charging his weapons, waiting for the right moment to strike.

When the drones have closed the gap to around twenty feet from us and more than thirty of them fill the hall, Marukarn releases a thunderous blast of focused disintegration energy. The recoil of the discharge launches him backward, his armored knees and feet skidding along the metal floor, leaving a trail of sparks in their wake. Meanwhile, a massive, fiery ball of destruction rockets down the corridor, vaporizing all within the passage and much of the wall as well. Ribbing and pillars of the ship are exposed amidst a thick cloud of smoke and steam, revealing no indication that the passage once held any residents. With no room to evade or hide, any that rounded the corner leading to the laboratory were eliminated.

Now it's my turn to look at Marukarn with surprise.

He turns to me. "I won't let a human surpass me."

I like his challenging attitude. "Not exactly a human, am I?"

He chuckles. "No. But I still won't let you win."

"Girls," Sasha chides. "You're both pretty. We gotta move."

Right you are, Sasha. Though the joke is lost on Marukarn. He looks at me for an explanation I don't have time to give him.

"Ferroc," Andizha begins, brushing past me and moving swiftly for the debris laden hall. "We're at the front. Let's go!"

I'm not about to argue as my powered legs bring me in step with her. As we charge down the passage, we begin to see more enemies that were fortunate enough to avoid the initial blast rounding the corner.

They've only ensured themselves a few more minutes of life.

I activate a burst of my jets, blasting past Andizha and into the first drone before me. I lock my elbows, slamming into it so hard I nearly rip through its metal exterior, depressing its chest with my crushing impact. I tuck my legs under me, kicking off my foe to slow my advance while launching the projectile that is the drone into its fellows.

In the narrow confines of the hall, they're hard pressed to move out of the way. As they try to evade and move around each other, Andizha leaps over me, scythes leading the way with a subsequent flurry of blades.

There are close to twenty enemies remaining in the corridor, but their superior numbers are no match for our maneuverability and prowess. Bullets bounce off us and bolts of disintegration energy are deftly avoided as we move around the passage, using enemy drones as cover. Marukarn and Sasha approach behind us, laying waste to fully exposed enemies with deadly and interspersed volleys of cannon and rifle fire.

I dodge a swing from a sword, countering by slicing the wielding arm off with a cut of my own. A rifle round strikes the head of my attacker, and I'm able to confront the next foe. Andizha jumps in front of me, impaling an enemy drone with her scythes before ripping its limbs off with her bladed arms and legs. I fire a blast from my cannons, sweeping away any foes that would think to land a blow on her as she dispatches her most recent opponent. My fire is joined by Marukarn's as he covers my left side, discharging another powerful salvo from the linked energy of weapons. The drones and an unfortunate Rantir have nowhere to hide as our twin fire consumes them and forces others back around the corner.

"Keep pressing forward!" I shout as I slice another drone in half, then stab into a second with an uppercut under its chin, lifting it off the ground.

In under a minute, the intercepting force meant to overtake us is driven back. With the combined blade work of Andizha and myself, along with the supportive fire of Marukarn and Sasha, we overwhelm our foes. It's not long before we find ourselves back at the coliseum that is the hanger. We're at the midlevel between the bottom and top floors and are confronted with a slew of new enemies, some of which are mobilizing vehicles. Amidst them on the bottom floor, I see a massive hole, exposing an opening that reveals the streets of Duluth below.

Andizha sees me noting the damage. "You compromised the ship's exterior with your actions. All defenses were focused on the imminent threat and the attack was delayed. We infiltrated from another bay entrance with help from Meredith and the human forces. They now fight below."

"Then let's not waste a good opportunity," I reply. "We shut down the reactor and we save the people below. How much would it take to neutralize the core?"

"I'm capable of doing so," Marukarn replies, shrugging to engage his cannons.

"Good," I tell him. "Let's get you there. Andizha, Gahren has a bunch of human prisoners. Where might he keep them?"

"Nearby," she tells me. "Any holding areas would be near the cargo bays for easy processing."

"Let's get them out," I say.

"What about getting them off the ship?" Sasha asks.

That's a good question. "We'll have to deal with that as it comes. Maybe we can get them aboard one of the transports."

We all know the tentative plan will have to suffice as we're forced to take cover from a hail of gunfire fired by our approaching enemies.

I turn to Marukarn and Sasha. "Get to the high ground. I'll take the fight to them in the middle. Once we get an opening, you head for the reactor. Andizha and I will free the prisoners."

The plan, quickly formulated as it is, gets sprung into motion.

Marukarn grabs Sasha and starts jumping up the levels with ease. I know the ride can't be smooth for her, but she won't complain when she's in a prime firing position. Andizha sprints off to my right, running on all fours and ducking behind vehicles and containers to avoid any incoming fire. She works her way behind the advancing thrall of enemies.

Now it's my turn to move. With Gahren's forces beginning to mobilize, I need to act quickly. The groups gathered here aren't as large as they once were, and I'm guessing the personnel I saw when I was first brought into the hanger weren't all for combat purposes. Some must have been support and engineer roles for the rest of this massive craft and would have since returned to their duties now that the staging of the attack was complete. I'm glad of that because it makes my job a little easier at the moment, though not by much. Still, every little bit counts.

I spot one of the fighter vessels beginning to lift off. There are other vehicles in the hanger preparing to take flight, but since I know the capabilities of the most imminent threat, I prioritize my efforts there. Between me and the vessel is a large group of drones and Rantir equipped with the modified lighter armor. Already I'm ducking to avoid a volley of gunfire and disintegration energy, so I know a frontal assault is out of the question in my attempts to reach the fighter. Instead, I opt to do a little crowd control.

I activate my thrusters and launch, this time familiarizing myself with the exhilaration of flight while simultaneously confronting the difficulty of it. Unprepared for the forceful launch once again, I'm heading right for the lip of a higher level floor. Only at the last second with help from gyroscopic guidance and trajectory calculations do I adjust my legs, realizing it's my lower extremities that dictate my flight path. I push off a wall with my right arm, showering sparks as I do so but avoiding a more direct collision. Near fatal experience aside, I quickly grow accustomed to the technicalities of flight and roll to my left on an arcing path toward the now airborne fighter.

As I fly over my enemies, I roll and weave, avoiding bullets and disintegration blasts. There are even a few rockets from drones equipped with human weaponry. The hanger bay quickly transforms into a chaotic battle zone as explosions and ricocheting projectiles fill the air around me. Small arms and assault rifle rounds bounce off my armored exterior while I avoid anything heavier with adjustments to my flight pattern, my focus still on the fighter which now turns to face me. All the while, I fire off charged blasts from my disintegration cannons, destroying helicopters, Rantir craft, and other vehicles that pilots are making their way toward. Adding to my destructive strafing is the supportive fire of Marukarn and Sasha. My foes are too preoccupied with me to notice my two allies, and they pay dearly for that. Marukarn's accurate blasts vaporize craft about to take flight or mobilize, while Sasha picks off potential pilots as they expose themselves running to their vessels. She never misses a headshot; a perfect example of the old sniper mantra, "one shot, one kill."

As I continue my flight, I see the fighter has completed its turn to confront me directly, revealing the cockpit of the vessel and the pilot within; a Rantir warrior attempting to track my movement. Again, time seems to slow as my jets initiate what I think is some sort of afterburner sequence, and I blast toward my opponent. I soar to my enemy, placing my legs in front of me to slow my approach at the last second. The pilot has no time to evade as I land directly on the nose of the craft, facing the windshield and my enemy. I latch my robotic toes and the fingertips of my left hand into the metal of the craft, bending and molding the alloy to provide perfect handholds. With my right arm, a powered punch breaks through the canopy of the cockpit. A second later, a blast of disintegration energy fired at point blank range neutralizes the helpless pilot and all but obliterates the nose of the craft.

I'm engulfed in a fiery explosion, but there's no damage to me. The only drawback is my external temperature is raised. Knowing there's a host of enemies behind me who now have a clear shot, I reactivate my jets, but maintain my grasp on the fighter. Its engines haven't disengaged, and while it's losing altitude, it isn't "crashing" yet. I use this to my advantage as my thrusters propel the craft, turning the vessel toward my foes while I'm protected behind it. With some improvised cover in front of me, I now stop the rotation of the fighter while keeping my jets engaged, driving it towards my enemies with a powerful blast of my propulsion systems. The engines of the fighter are shutting down, but it only adds to the speed of its descent.

It was a shield before. Now it's a missile.

The robotic foes, following their protocol to eliminate an enemy, don't process the threat like the Rantir do. Immediately, the alien adversaries begin running for cover, discovering my intentions. The drones continue firing at me, trying in vain to shoot me from the sky. However, the exterior of the craft holds strong, shielding me as I continue my headlong course for the heart of their group.

Again, time slows, and I release from the craft a few moments before impact, blasting skyward and away from the ensuing explosion. The fighter slams into the hanger bay floor amidst the group of drones. Their self-preservation protocols don't initiate until after I've released my missile. By then, it's too late. As the craft detonates, my foes are engulfed and torn to pieces by the force of the blast.

The hole in the floor has gotten a little bigger after my handiwork.

Power levels at one thousand six hundred percent capacity.

Good...I have some energy to spare.

There's no time to celebrate though. The Rantir have regrouped and are firing at me along with what's left of the drones in attempts to finish what their counterparts could not. I avoid a disintegration blast by rolling to my left, then swoop under a ground-to-air missile. I turn to recognize the threat just in time to see Andizha pounce onto the enemy who just fired at me.

The Rantir is blindsided by my ally as she barrels into him, blades leading the way. She stabs him four times in the chest, then impales him with her scythes, lifting him in front of her to shield herself from the fire of an enemy to her right. The body is destroyed by a blast

242

of disintegration energy, but it served its purpose. She's already moving, closing the distance between herself and her foe. The Rantir only gets off one more shot, but Andizha easily avoids with a dodge to her left. Now close enough to her enemy, she lashes out with a scythe, severing her opponent's weapon in two. She follows up with her other scythe, sweeping the legs of her adversary before unleashing a devastating kick to the Rantir's abdomen. The sweeping motion of her leg cuts through her enemy's armor and into the flesh beneath, eviscerating him. She isn't finished though, and continues with a series of slashes from her bladed wrists as the momentum of her kick continues to carry her. The first cut slices her opponent's throat. The second cut deepens the laceration. The third cuts the head clean off. Her enemies eliminated, she's on the move searching for a new threat.

Meanwhile, I've been flying toward her, trusting her to lead me to where the prisoners might be kept. I land next to her as she sprints forward on all fours. With powered legs, it's not difficult for me to land and keep stride with my alien friend. We jump over and weave between obstacles. Five more enemies appear in front of us; two drones and three Rantir. I ready my firearms as I duck behind cover, thinking to immediately retaliate after their incoming volley.

I don't get the chance. There's a massive blast of disintegration energy that comes streaking in from somewhere above me and to my left. It takes out a drone and one of the Rantir. Almost instantly after the blast hits, a rifle report erupts amidst the chaos of battle, and a round blasts through the head of the remaining mechanical foe. Before the Rantir can turn and face the new threat from sniper fire, another round is already in flight, striking one of them in the eye and passing through the creature's brain.

The last foe is already dead when I attempt to line up a shot. Andizha finishes a lunge of her scythes that has impaled the enemy and hoisted him skyward by the time I realize what's going on. She releases her deceased opponent, who falls to the ground in a lifeless heap.

"Are we close?" I ask as I approach her. Marukarn and Sasha keep us covered from behind as I listen to their echoing gunfire.

"There," she directs, coming to a halt and indicating the next passage.

I see her pointing at a large metal door, secured and locked from what I can tell. As I approach it, assessing a way through the threshold, I hear Marukarn's voice in my head.

"Clear, Ferroc!" he warns me.

I oblige my friend, backing away from the door. A few moments later a path is made crudely but effectively from another concentrated blast of Marukarn's combined cannon fire.

I turn back to him and Sasha, waving them off.

"We're going in!" I tell Marukarn through my internal communications chip. "You two get to the reactor!"

"Understood!" he replies as I watch him and my closest friend fall back down a passageway behind them.

I begin running down the hallway as fast as my legs can carry me, hoping to free the human prisoners before Gahren can mobilize the majority of his forces. As I run down the long, widening corridor, I begin to notice storage areas and holding facilities. They appear to be for supplies and weapons. I stop for a moment when I pass by what I discover is a weapons locker.

"Andizha!" I call.

She slides to a stop next to me. "We haven't much time, Ferroc."

I nod in agreement, trying to scan everything I can in the room for anything of use. There's hundreds of weapons, both human and Rantir in make. Two of which stand out as something familiar to me.

My sword is hung on the wall next to several other blades, and Free's rifle is set among others of its caliber on a gun rack. I grab both as well as a harness, strapping my blade to my hip and slinging the rifle over my shoulder after double checking the magazine.

Five high velocity rounds.

Good.

"Any of this useful to you?" I ask my friend.

She shakes her head. "My targeting systems are not calibrated for such weapons. Let us move on."

I nod, glad to have a little luck and some familiar items again.

We continue making our way down the passageway, discovering some of the holding areas had indeed been repurposed for human inhabitants. Quick scans reveal human blood or excrement on the floors, but no humans to go with them.

I'm growing more concerned by the minute.

I know they're here…But where are they? I know I heard Gahren say he had them aboard this vessel.

We pass more of the improvised holding cells, finally emerging into an immense bay area. The opening is large, though not nearly as vast as the hanger bay. This one serves a different purpose. As I scan the walls, I see what looks like machines and operating equipment for loading and unloading cargo.

And there, in the center of the bay area, stands Gahren. He presents himself in open defiance of the impending threat that is Andizha and myself. It's as if he hasn't a care in the world.

That's because, behind him, are the human prisoners. Some two hundred or so by the indications of a quick scan.

He's using them as a shield, and he knows I won't go through it to get to him.

He holds his wrist in the air, finger hovering very near some kind of control panel mounted into his armor.

"Last chance, Ferroc," he shouts to me. "Surrender yourself."

The human faces look at me in confusion, but pleading for their lives. Men, women, and children of all ages turn to me now, begging me for salvation.

And I intend to give it to them. For everything that I've fought for and endured all these years, this stands as a monument to that hope and perseverance. I can't let them down now. I have to get them through this.

I don't know what Gahren has in mind, but I know their fate hangs in the balance. I see no explosives or hidden adversaries, but I know he has something planned.

"This is between you and me!" I shout back, anger boiling.

"Very well," is his response. He presses a button on the remote on his wrist.

In an instant, I see nothing but his silhouette as a fiery detonation erupts behind him. The image is a macabre statement.

Just as he is the only focus of the portrait, so too is he its only living depiction.

The human prisoners are mostly vaporized within a sequence of explosions. Those unfortunate enough to have survived the initial blast find a worse fate as they are engulfed in the residual flames from the detonation.

The screams...The agony...The sheer, unmitigated carnage...

And the act of genocide caused by one creature's callous ambition...

...And my inability to prevent it...

Just a moment ago I was promising myself I'd save them because that was a crucial aspect of my purpose; saving the human race however I could. One of the few moments where my life would be so very significant. A defining act that would solidify my existence as one that benefited humanity.

Gone…Just like that. With nothing left but the quickly dissipating flames that leave only charred corpses.

I'm shocked. Too stunned for anything else but to fall to my knees as my mind won't allow me to accept the situation. It was so sudden. It was so quick. Gahren didn't even give me a chance. I feel as if I may break in this moment, so great is my failure.

But no…

Thoughts of anger and revenge begin to swell within me as I look back at Gahren, still standing resolute as if nothing had happened behind him.

I remember Sasha in this moment. I remember how she's made me feel every moment I've been with her. I think of how she's given me so much more than I thought possible. Of her comforting words and touch, even though I can't feel it. Of her wisdom and love and how she's helped me overcome the most difficult obstacle of all.

Myself.

No…This wasn't my fault. I'm not going to dismiss the human lives lost today. I know I'll always wonder if there was something I could have done differently. I'm glad I can't dream, because I know I'd have nightmares about this forever. It will always remain undecided if their blood is on my hands.

But it wasn't just me who would bear that burden.

Gahren pushed the button. And he was going to pay.

It may seem cold, resolute, or downright mechanical to rationalize the needless death and loss of so many human lives, and I own that. But there are more at stake even now amidst the wanton destruction of Gahren's actions. Now is not the time for mourning or placing blame.

It's time for revenge and justice.

"Murderer!" Andizha shouts, apparently more appalled than I am at what Gahren has just done.

He turns to her sharply. "You, my former student, are an utter disgrace! To me, to yourself, and to all Rantir!"

"You abandoned the Rantir, Gahren!" she retaliates. "You were once a hero. Now look at you…You play god with the lives of those we should embrace as family! This is not honor! This is not the way of the Great Creator!"

"And allying with the humans and this *thing* standing next to you is?" he snaps back. "I served our kind loyally, and when we finished the fight the humans started, suddenly the morality of our deeds was called into question? Someone had to take action."

My friend seems to be silenced by that, but she's no less furious.

"Was it the Archon who sent you?" Gahren continues. "Was it one of the Seraphs? Did *they* endow you with the right to determine that which the Creator deems necessary? Your cause is no more holy or righteous than my own. But at least I try to save my people and remember the simple concept of *loyalty*!"

Andizha growls a deep, feral curse I don't need to translate to understand, then leaps at Gahren before I have a chance to react. I'm still recovering from the stun of what just happened, and she's in motion faster than I've ever seen her move. Running on all fours with her scythes leading the way, she's aiming for Gahren's throat.

When she reaches him, I see him move with that same impossible speed I did before. One of his scythes bats away Andizha's bladed appendages, the other sweeps for her legs, knocking her from her feet. To her credit, she rights herself enough to slash with her wrists and once with her legs. Gahren takes a cut to side of his face as Andizha tries to claw her way to her feet, but nothing else. The laceration doesn't do much more than cosmetic damage to his infused suit of armor. He grabs her flailing arms with his and wraps his scythes around hers, rendering them immobile. He then sweeps her legs with his own and straddles her.

I'm in motion at a velocity I didn't think possible.

"I taught you well, my student," he states. "But you have much left to learn."

He releases one of her arms while a blade much like my own extends from a concealed chamber within his armored forearm. He's about to bring it down on Andizha's throat.

I'm about twenty feet from him, and once again, time slows for me. I activate my jets and explode forward, arms outstretched and blades leading just like Andizha a moment before. Gahren's speed matches mine, but that only means we're on an equal playing field. When he attempts to turn my outstretched weapons away like he did to Andizha's, I see the attack coming as if it were at a rate I'd been accustomed to my whole life. Not the superhuman level we both possess. I pull my blades back and wide, allowing his deflecting strike to pass by harmlessly in front of me. I slam into him at full speed, wrapping my arms around his waist and forcefully tackling him. Not wanting to get caught up in a tangle of limbs, I release him from my hold, tucking my feet under me and slowing to stop as he flies backward into a metal wall some eighty feet away. He strikes the surface with such force he creates a sizable dent several feet deep into the solid metal surface.

He extricates himself with a growl and squares off against me.

Andizha climbs to her feet, her scythes hanging limply at her sides.

"You OK?" I ask her.

She tries to move a scythe, revealing to both of us her appendages are broken. "I'll manage."

"I don't know how he's moving that fast," I tell her.

"Nor I how you are capable of such speed," she replies. "But this fight is no longer mine. I'll just get in the way."

"Then get back to the others," I tell her. "I'll deal with Gahren."

She nods, then falls back. I admire her discipline and acceptance of knowing when she needs to live to fight another day.

"You truly are the force of great change Ferroc," she calls to me. "Now change our lives for the better."

I turn and offer her a small bow of respect. She exits, and though I'm left alone, I feel grateful knowing my friends will be together and stand that much more of a chance of surviving with their combined strength.

"It's between you and me, Gahren!" I shout at him. "It always has been."

"Now that the other humans are no longer a factor?" he asks, jabbing at my soul.

"You're gonna pay for that," I snarl, drawing my sword.

He extends a second blade from his other forearm. "I have shown you what awaits the rest of your kind should you continue to defy me. How many more lives do you want on your conscience?"

I shake my head. "All you've done is really piss me off. And the only thing left to do is *end* you."

He bends his knees and takes a ready stance. "There is no more negotiating now, Ferroc. Your life ends here."

I *really* wish I could smile at him, because it would be a wicked display of anticipation.

Oh...I want to kill him *so* bad.

"Bring it."
I snap into motion.

Chapter 13

It's a blur of motion, steel, and sparks as our weapons clash and glance off one another. I make the first move, blasting toward him with two disintegration shots leading my charge. He spins out of the way and readies himself for me. Knowing I can't keep up such levels of power consumption, I switch tactics to engage him directly in pure melee. My sword and wrist blades against his scythes and similarly bladed arms will decide the victor.

The sense of speed or the slowing of time, while present, no longer applies. I know we're both moving at a rate that's undetectable by the standards of the human eye, but to us, it's a pace that matches the other. It seems he and I are suited and equipped perfectly to do battle with each other on a level where only sheer skill can prevail. I don't know what forms of training Rantir undertake as they're raised among their society. The details of their combat training have never been made clear to me. Those I've fought before seem to blend a sense of tempered strikes with pure, animal ferocity allotted them by their predatory bodies. The closest thing I can compare it to are the styles of martial arts that mimic animal movements or that are heavily influenced by the creatures after which the form was named.

Whatever Gahren was trained to do, he does so with a precision and focus I've never faced. Each of my blows is turned aside and countered, forcing me to think just as defensively as I do aggressively. A slash of his scythe followed by a parry of the other. A lunging kick delivered toward my stomach, defended by his two lashing appendages immediately after the strike is initiated. It all balances perfectly and flows with a sense of harmony and grace I haven't seen in any other Rantir. Even Andizha with her quick and deadly motions can't compare to Gahren's true potential, and it becomes clear to me why he was the teacher of my two Rantir allies. There's no doubt in my mind as to why he ascended to such a high echelon among Rantir society.

But I'm nothing like the Rantir have ever seen. I'm matching him blow for blow, block for block, and step for step. My mechanical body, performing at exceedingly powerful capabilities, has no trouble matching the best of Rantir warriors.

And I am facing the *best* of Rantir warriors.

He slashes diagonally from above, aiming for the side of my head with one his scythes. I duck under the swing, spinning as I do so to build momentum for a backhanded slice of my sword. Powered limbs charge my strike before I even extend my arm. The force behind the blow is substantial, forcing Gahren to block with a defensive brace from both of his arm blades. Immediately he counters with a stabbing attack from his left scythe, aiming to impale my face. I move my head left, allowing the scythe to miss me by a few inches as I extend my left wrist blade, countering his strike with a lunging stab of my own aimed for his head. His right scythe moves to intercept my attack, the bladed appendage catching my arm with a shower of sparks. Now in a deadlock and knowing his other scythe is still capable of striking me, I press my offense. Powered arms raise both of our guards, and I snap my leg up into his stomach with a heavy kick. He manages to brace for the impact, but takes a solid hit. As I attempt the maneuver again, he raises his knee, intercepting my strike.

Now it's his turn.

His free scythe whips around him, building tremendous force and coming in for my legs. I'm up on one foot, so a jump will only result in me exposing myself for an easy follow up slash. Instead, I activate my jets. With a quick burn of my thrusters, I rocket away from him, breaking away from the deadlock. The moment I'm clear of his deadly limbs, I fire a shot of disintegration energy from my left arm, hoping to catch him by surprise. He jumps to his left, avoiding the blast with an evasive roll. I land, and this time Gahren closes the distance. Blasting off with his jets, he attempts a passing attack with his right arm blade. I decide to meet the attack head on, swinging my sword upward in an attempt to intercept and block his offensive with a heavy strike, hoping to damage his arm. I'm putting a lot of confidence in my blade's integrity, and I'm right to do so as the weapon holds strong. I catch his slash hard, the impact of the forceful block rattling even me as I stand planted and unmoving. But Gahren is more cunning than to let me make such a bold move without paying for it.

He accepts my blow at a heavy cost to his shoulder as my sword knocks him off his predetermined course. But by rolling with the momentum of my swing, he's able to turn his body into a position that allows his scythes to strike at my exposed torso. I can't dodge effectively, and take a hit to my side that external indicators read as moderate structural damage. Meanwhile, his other scythe wraps around my leg, bringing me with him on his passing movement. He continues his roll, allowing the momentum he's generated to build enough force to throw me towards the wall of the chamber at incredible speed. Before he releases me, I activate my jets once again, blasting myself toward him even faster though I know I'll just pass by.

I'm looking to land a hit of my own, and I succeed in doing just that.

I lash out with my sword, slicing through the armor of his left shoulder with the combined power of my momentum and charged limbs. I hear him grunt as I pass, then I attempt to slow my approach to the metal wall of the cargo bay.

My speed is too great. Even with the assistance of my jets slowing me, I'm forced to catch myself against the wall with my hands and feet. Thankfully, I do so with no ill effect. The wall is left with an impression about a foot deep where my limbs make contact.

I quickly roll away from the surface and drop to the ground, ready to face him. He hasn't moved, standing where he'd thrown me and inspecting the wound I'd just inflicted upon him. He touches the slash, holding his fingers in front of his face to examine the bright blue blood now running down his arm.

I take this moment to inspect my own "wounds." What I find is quite the surprise, but a welcome one. I see my body piecing itself back together at a staggering pace. The metal is mending right before my eyes. I perform some quick diagnostics that reveal the cut in my side was only to my exterior. No fluids lost or system functions compromised. Restoration protocols are functioning at superior levels of efficiency, just like the rest of my body, which explains my accelerated healing.

He and I both regard the other, and though we're bitter enemies in this struggle, we seem to share a moment of respect for the other's capabilities. Even if that moment is just a tactical archive of those abilities.

This break in the fight doesn't last long as we begin circling each other once again. This time, we're slow in our approaches; cautious lest we create the opening our enemy would need to finish the bout. It's all a mind game now. We wait for the other to make the first move, ready to counter any advance they would throw our way. We also understand that there's a careful balance of available resources the two of us are managing. He has a limited supply of power in his armor just like I have finite amounts of energy to expend. In a battle of attrition, there's no telling who would emerge victorious.

With that thought, and not caring to find out who would win in such a waiting game, I decide to make the first move again.

I sprint toward him, pulling up short at the last moment to avoid a horizontal sweep from his left scythe. I take a step forward, then pivot off my foot, spinning away and to my right to avoid the downward strike of his second scythe. Now within range, I attack with a lunge for his torso. He turns my weapon aside with his left wrist, swinging for my neck with his right. I duck under the attack and step into him, catching his arm and locking it with my right by holding it to my side. My left arm blade emerges to block a scythe attack coming from above me, and I force us both to turn clockwise so as to keep further offensive strikes from his bladed appendages to a minimum.

We're in another deadlock. This time, Gahren decides to shift the tide to his favor. He begins to overpower me, driving me back and halting the spin I keep forcing upon him with his impressive strength. Even with my feet planted and fully powered body, I slowly start to slide backward. I sink my robotic toes into the floor only to peel the metal away that comprises the ground upon which we fight. Meanwhile, I'm too busy fending off probing slices and stabs from his scythes to regain any form of offensive momentum.

As I'm forced backward to the wall, I know he'll finish me off if he can pin me against the barrier. Instead of allowing that undesirable fate to come to fruition, I activate my jets, putting substantial amounts of power into them and blasting forward, launching Gahren back toward the opposite side of the room. He tries to initiate a blast of his own, but it's too late. I've caught him by surprise with the sudden launch of my thrusters. We're traveling too fast for him to do anything but brace for impact.

We careen into the chamber wall with such force we burst right through it into what appears to be a maintenance corridor. We slam into the passage's far wall, unable to penetrate the surface. Gahren takes a hard hit as the combined force of the collision and my body weight drive the air from his lungs. He's quick to roll out from under me before my feet can contact the ground, and I'm forced to withdraw as he swings both of his scythes at me in a defensive flurry.

With some space between us again, there's another pause in the fight, and it's in that moment of stillness that a new factor is introduced to this conflict.

Suddenly, an alarm beacon is sounded throughout the ship, followed by a series of announcements in the Rantir language. I activate my translation protocols and get the gist of what's happening.

"Reactor destabilizing," the announcement says. "Energy distribution compromised."

Looks like Marukarn is holding up his end of our arrangement.

Gahren and I both look at one another for a split second, then he activates his thrusters and blasts through the hole we just created on our previous flight. I'm quick to pursue. The chase begins.

I follow him as best as I can as he maneuvers through the cargo bay and down the tight corridors of the ship. He doesn't hesitate to blast aside drones and other Rantir going about their duties on his way to intercept the growing threat to the ship's reactor. As I follow, I'm forced to initiate every type of movement program and subroutine I possess to navigate the corridors at such high speeds. A quick reading from my internal sensory programs reveals we're traveling at over six hundred miles per hour. Quick adjustments are made at particularly sharp corners or intersections, bringing us both to significantly lower speeds, but we're just as quick to reach our maximum velocities when we get the chance.

It's all I can do to keep up while simultaneously avoiding the other drones and Rantir in the halls that Gahren plows through or blasts aside. However, I find I'm up to the task as my enhanced and overcharged body gets me through the scenario.

A normal Rantir might have made this journey. There's no way a human would survive the velocity and G-force required for such tight and dangerous maneuvers, not to mention the strain of reflexes.

But something like me?

I'm beginning to believe more and more that everything happens for a reason, even if my whole life has led up to this *one* reason for my existence. But I need to see this thing through and finish the fight. Otherwise it won't mean much in the end even if this really is my one reason for being.

We careen through the hangar bay, blasting over and past a new force of mobilizing soldiers. None of them have a chance to fire upon me. Our time with them is less than a second as we pass by. Gahren fires a blast of his weapons to clear a door that reveals the passage to the reactor, and I'm right behind him, never wavering in my pursuit.

"Marukarn!" I call over my communications systems. "He's coming for the reactor!"

"Understood!" my friend calls back. "We'll be ready for him!"

That's enough for me. I'm thinking that, with the four of us, Gahren will at least be driven back. Even if we don't finish him off today, we'll at least neutralize a ship capable of destroying the human colony below.

It doesn't take us long to reach the reactor from the hangar bay. As we near the entrance of the ship's core, I see bodies of Rantir and drones, some marred with bullet wounds, others slashed and chopped to pieces. We reach the threshold, then I see a massive chamber, even bigger than the staging area. There are several levels and bridges in the cylinder-shaped room, all leading to what looks to be a giant power core much like the ones I've found inside the drones. This one radiates with pure energy. So much that I can't get a reading on the power levels in any known form like Kelvins or volts. Connecting to the reactor are several of the tubes and hoses like the one I found in the laboratory, no doubt powering other essential functions of the ship. Several of the tubes have been destroyed in what I can only assume is the handiwork of Marukarn.

And speak of devil...

The moment Gahren blasts through the doorway leading to the reactor, there's my large friend, planted and locked in position, ready to intercept his former instructor with his most powerful weapons. A tremendous blast of disintegration energy erupts at the mouth of the corridor I'm now speeding down, engulfing Gahren and destroying the passage. Rather than chance a collision at Mach 1, I pull up short and seek an alternative route, hoping Gahren was destroyed lest he rip my friends to pieces.

I check my power levels...

Six hundred percent capacity...

I'm burning through energy quickly in this fight, and now I'll need to sacrifice a little more. If I'm going to get back in the battle and ensure the safety of my friends, I'm willing to take that chance.

I send a ping of sonar through the smoke, discovering that most of the debris blocking the passage is scrap metal and ribbing from the ship. The majority of it collapsed inward from above, rendering a path of lesser resistance should I opt to take a more vertical route to my destination.

That's exactly what I'm going to do.

I blast through the ceiling right above the flaming wreckage, then fire two more volleys that finally expose the way to the reactor. I jet through, tearing past any edges of metal that attempt to hinder my way. I take minimal cosmetic damage as I do so, emerging into the reactor chamber.

Gahren is already near the core, and I see he's charred and blackened from my friend's barrage. I'm not sure how he survived, but Marukarn is currently grappling with him and not faring well. I see my large friend attempting to claw his way out from under his enemy, but Gahren is easily outmaneuvering him with his combined skill and enhanced capabilities. I notice him lining up a scythe to spear my friend, and I know I can't get there in time even with a quick blast of my jets. Andizha and Sasha are still near the door, too far away to help.

Time slows once again, and even Gahren's movements are reduced. I sling Free's rifle to a firing position off my back, lining up a shot.

Though *I* can't get there in time, high velocity rounds will.

I run a calculation of the downward path of Gahren's scythe, lining up a shot and targeting his blade.

Five hundred and thirty-seven feet away...The round travels at nearly six thousand feet per second...

I squeeze the trigger.

His scythe descends. Marukarn can't even process the threat as Gahren brings down the killing blow. Right before the scythe skewers my friend's neck, the bladed appendage is nocked aside in a violent shower of sparks as the bullet connects. The projectile and blade fragment upon collision. Gahren is even knocked off balance by the force of the round, giving Marukarn enough time to throw his enemy from him.

As my friend clears himself from Gahren by activating this jets and moving back toward the rest of us, I see his stand against Gahren came at a cost. His armor has been pierced in multiple places, and blue Rantir blood seeps from his wounds. He appears to bear the injuries well, and while I'm no expert on Rantir anatomy, I come to the conclusion my friend possesses a very hearty constitution to manage such grievous lacerations so well.

We all reconvene as Gahren rights himself, standing to protect the reactor.

"What now?" Sasha asks.

I hand her my rifle. "Four rounds left. High velocity and it looks like they can get through his armor." I turn to Marukarn and Andizha. "Plan is the same right?"

Andizha nods. "Destroy or neutralize the reactor. If Gahren truly does wish to sustain this insurrection against the Rantir, he'll need to protect his resources."

"He has reinforced its container," Marukarn tells me. "I can't penetrate it, but the power lines could destabilize the ship."

"'Could?'" I ask, not liking the information.

"He anticipated our moves," Andizha tells me. "This is the best we can do."

The best *they* could do. What's the best a super powered cyborg with supposedly limitless potential can do?

An idea starts to dawn on me.

"Buy me ten seconds," I tell them.

They're all confused.

"Trust me," I tell them. "We're doing this thing together, but if you can get me that time, the fight ends."

Sasha lines up her shot. "Good enough for me."

Marukarn and Andizha nod, then ready their weapons.

I double check my power. Two hundred percent capacity. I don't have much, but what I do have left I'm going to put to good use.

I surge toward Gahren, the safety of my friends as my priority. I need to give them the perfect moment to attack, which will, in turn, allow me the precious seconds I need. The timing must be flawless.

I circle around to his right, then swoop low under a sweeping attack of his bladed scythe as I close in on him. I attempt to tackle him off the platform, but he dodges aside with a concentrated burst from his own jets, evading my grapple. I quickly adjust my flight with my own focused burst, correcting my course and somersaulting over him in a backflip that clears me from a harmful swipe of his other scythe. As I arc over my enemy, I slash with my sword while upside down, forcing him to block. I attack again for his left side as I land, pushing off my legs and driving into him. He blocks, then counters with an overhead slash from his bladed scythe. I dodge aside, abandoning my advance to protect myself. He tries to follow up with a slice of his right blade, forcing me further back. He continues his advance with a snap of his left wrist, jabbing for my face. I block the attack with my sword, then block another from his scythe as it whips down at me again. I catch the blade in another deadlock that drives me to my knees from the force of the impact.

A rifle report disrupts the clanging of our metal, and the ensuing round slams into Gahren's other blade, shattering it much like the first. He roars and jumps away from me, turning toward Sasha. Marukarn and Andizha close in front of her as she chambers another round, sending a clear message that he'll not so easily reach my friend.

I take the time to check my power levels.

One hundred and forty percent...

...I need to leave my friends to defend themselves at some point.

I put thirty percent of my remaining excess power into a blast from my disintegration weapons, letting Gahren see exactly what I'm doing and hoping he'll take the bait. I'm betting my friends will follow up on the opportunity I'm about to give them. As I make a show of lowering my arms to line up a shot, I see him tense and ready himself for a dodge. I quickly reroute all available energy into an afterburner sequence and line up a flight path to one of the remaining energy tubes above me.

I fire a distracting shot at Gahren at nearly half the power I used to charge the blast, wasting a good amount of energy but succeeding in my ruse as he keeps his attention on me. The energy destroys the ground where he once stood, but Gahren safely evades the attack. He dodges again as another more concentrated and far more powerful discharge from Marukarn streaks toward his new location. He's forced to take flight away from the explosion, and I'm already on my way to where I need to go, free of Gahren's interference.

I don't look back at my friends. I trust them to defend themselves. Even Sasha, who I know to be more than capable but highly vulnerable. Instead, I focus all my energy on the power tube I know will win the day for us.

I need every second, so I can't bother slowing down. I use what's left of my surplus energy to catch myself from a tremendous impact with the ceiling of the chamber, straddling the energy line. My limbs strain in protest against the substantial collision, but I manage to brace well enough from the impact. Soon after, with a strike from my mechanical arm, I break through the tube, connecting my body to the flow of raw energy within.

System indicators and energy readings flash across my vision faster than I can process as my body is laced with excess power. It doesn't take long for me to store even more than I had before, and not wanting to chance an overload of energy, I withdraw my arm after only a few seconds. I turn back to face Gahren, but find he's already upon me.

I'm impaled through the chest and pinned to the ceiling as Gahren crashes into me with his wrist blades leading the way. My systems falter for a moment, disrupted by the force of the impact and the damage received. Assessments inform me my decomposition chamber is compromised and a power core is ruptured. Power levels are more than adequate to repair the damage, but replacement materials are needed.

I'm still in the fight, though I know I need help.

Gahren withdraws one of his blades, twisting it as he does so to widen the damage. My power core was already disabled, so it's merely cosmetic destruction at this point. However, I do realize my energy levels are draining fast in order to contain the compromises to my functions. They're already down to one thousand five hundred percent capacity.

My enemy attempts to slice my head off, but I manage to raise my arm in time to block the attack. He tries again, this time with a backhanded swipe, but he's struck by another rifle round to the side of his head. The bullet doesn't penetrate the armor, but it does tear off a good chunk of his helmet. Amidst the shower of sparks from Sasha's shot, I see Marukarn and Andizha on their way to help, already mid-flight to intercept my assailant.

Sasha gives me the opening I need, and if my other two friends can give me a few more seconds, I'll make them count.

I tuck my legs under me, driving my feet between Gahren and myself as I hold his arm back from slicing into my neck. His scythes, while devoid of blades or weaponry, still lash out at my head, slamming down atop me and further disrupting my vision with their forceful impacts. I activate my thrusters to their fullest potential, initiating a burn sequence that causes massive jets of flame to erupt from my calves and into Gahren's torso. He screams in agony, releasing his hold on me and launching backward, but not before slashing down the right side of my face with his blade. The cut leaves a defined groove from the top of my head to my jawline. It tears through my visor and compromises my optics. Coordination and depth perception are unreliable at best.

That complicates things, but I keep moving, now at one thousand percent capacity.

Marukarn and Andizha intercept Gahren as he withdraws from me. Andizha makes strafing and passing attacks against him, occupying his attention while Marukarn fires at him with pelting shots, forcing him to focus on two separate attackers.

I fly back down to Sasha, landing hard in front of her and collapsing to my knees as I'm unable to calculate my landing. I'm fine, and quickly wave her off from helping me up.

I sheathe my sword and start overcharging my twin disintegration cannons, focusing all remaining power into them. My forearms glow red hot as the weapons try to contain the excess energy.

"I don't know what this is going to do to me!" I yell at Sasha. "But you're going to have to be my eyes after this!"

"I've got your back!" she shouts. "Do it!"

Just when they reach the point of internal destabilization, my enhanced systems kick in. My sense of time slows and I seem to be given a higher level of concentration, allowing me to focus on my shot at the reactor. In this slower world, it almost seems like my mechanical body is relinquishing all control to me; as if my nanobots are rerouting all of their energies to containing the power of my weapons and providing me the clarity of vision I need.

Man…Machine…

Evolution…

Everything happens for a reason.

Time to save humanity. Not many people get the chance to say that.

I release the blast. The concussive force of the recoil throws me backward with enough power that I slam into the back wall of the chamber, depressing the metal barrier once again. Sasha is knocked from her feet as I discharge the energy, but both of us are given a perfect view of the ensuing chaos as we sit up to watch the fireworks.

My blast connects squarely with the reactor, engulfing it in a fiery explosion. For a moment, there's nothing. An eerie echo from the shot fills the air. But that was only the calm before the colossal storm, for the reactor then erupts in pure, unharnessed energy. Unstable electricity arcs outward from the volatile core, ripping through portions of the chamber and rending the platforms and bridges all around us.

I'm disoriented and unable to get a reading from my systems after such a large expenditure of energy, but I break free of the depression I created on the wall, then run to Sasha as I note the danger she's in being this near to the core. I shield her from a tendril of electrical power, hearing her scream in agony as I hold her to me while blocking and absorbing the power surge. It charges my systems, giving me an extra boost to my drained energies, though my concentration is only on Sasha and why she's in pain. Once it passes, I quickly release her and she scrambles away from me. Amidst the static filling my vision, I see smoke rising from my still red hot arms.

I'm horrified at what I've done, but at least I saved her life. Sasha rises to her feet, grimacing in pain but not severely injured, though she does have a nasty burn on her left cheekbone.

"Sasha!" I call amidst the roaring noise of the destabilized reactor. I reach out to her in apology.

"I'll walk it off, Nathan!" she shouts back. "We've got to get out of here!"

Her words redirect my focus as I look up to see Andizha and Marukarn on their way back to us. Gahren is in pursuit behind them, and I think to blast off and intercept him, even with my compromised vision and draining power. However, Sasha beats me to the punch. She's got her rifle up and ready, firing a shot that soars between our two alien friends and connects directly with Gahren's chest. He's slowed significantly from the force of the impact, then enveloped in electrical energy as an arcing tendril of power lances into him. He's driven back into the far wall of the chamber, then disappears behind a wall of flame from another explosion of the crumbling reactor.

I turn to Sasha. "I ever tell you how amazing you are?"

She grins that special grin. "Still have one left."

God I want to smile!

Marukarn and Andizha land next to us.

"We must leave!" Andizha shouts. "This ship will soon initiate its failsafe sequence!"

"Which does what?" Sasha asks.

"All Rantir vessels are programed to respond to such destabilizations," Marukarn tells us. "In order to prevent a collision with a planet, it will reach a safe orbiting distance amidst the stars for repairs to be administered while power consumption is minimalized."

"We're going into space?" I inquire amidst the confusion.

"Not if we move, now!" Andizha shouts back.

"I can't carry Sasha!" I tell them, holding out my smoldering limbs.

Marukarn obliges and hoists her into his arms. All four us then blast off through the opening I created upon my initial entry into the reactor chamber, rocketing down the hallway as fast as Sasha's body will allow. I keep close to Marukarn and Andizha, relying on them to guide me. At our reduced speeds to ensure Sasha's safety, I navigate the corridors, albeit at great effort through distorted vision. Still, I get the job done.

We continue to hear the thunderous explosions sounding from the reactor chamber as we wind through the corridors of the ship. We soar past more inhabitants of the vessel, most of which are happy to move out of our way as we travel at such high speeds. Those that don't are skewered and discarded by Andizha as we move unerringly forward.

Getting to the reactor seemed to take far less time. After what seems like hours, we reach the hanger bay. The hole in the floor is still open, but is currently being sealed. Two large blast doors are closing off the room for what I presume is a precautionary step to prepare for vacuum. We hasten our flight as much as we dare, Marukarn and Andizha leading the way.

But we are not unnoticed in our attempt to escape. Suddenly, a drone piloting a helicopter rises into our path, a stream of machine gun fire spewing forth from its wings. Marukarn and Andizha quickly swerve away from the incoming fire and avoid the props as they do so.

I can't process the threat in time with my compromised optics.

I receive a hail of bullets as I fly forward. The projectiles bounce off me, but further disrupt any chance I had of avoiding a collision. I careen into the nose of the craft, breaking through the cockpit and rending the vessel with my high speed collision. I'm not caught up in the wreckage, but I'm thrown off course and land hard on the hanger bay floor, skidding to a stop shortly after.

More static fills my screen and diagnostics confirm damage to my gyroscopic systems as well as further destabilization of energy distribution.

As I attempt to rise, I'm granted a view of Andizha and Marukarn escaping through the closing blast doors. I also see Sasha's longing gaze as she disappears through the opening.

"Nathan!" I hear her scream as she fades from view.

I reactivate my jets, blasting off with what power I have left.

Fifty percent capacity...

It isn't much, but it's enough to escape. And I have to do it now. Gahren's forces are mobilizing around me. Some are even firing at me and I lack the capability of avoiding their volleys effectively.

I soar for the opening, ready to readjust my flight and deactivate my jets when I reach the opening to simply fall through. When I'm above the quickly sealing gap, I come to a halt and shut down my thrusters, trying to conserve what energy I can and pass through the opening. I discover the ship's failsafe measures are being enacted at a faster rate than I'd anticipated. Already it's climbed a few thousand feet skyward and is accelerating. However, I'm clear of the retreating vessel. Below me, I catch a feint and blurry image of my friends returning to me from what I think is about a half a mile away.

That's good, because I don't know if I'll be able to sustain flight much longer with my power draining so quickly.

But it doesn't matter much when something wraps around my neck, holding me aloft and attached to the craft. I look up to discover Gahren, even more charred and blackened from whatever explosion had engulfed him, but still very much alive. He wheezes heavily and rasps with each breath, but I can tell he has a lot of fight left in him. One of his scythes has looped around me, and as I attempt to pry myself free, his second scythe binds my left arm. I think to burn him with my heated limbs, but his armored appendages are undeterred.

I draw my sword with my right, but he pulls me to him and seizes my right arm with his left hand, holding me fast. Without a powered strike, I can't break free as he holds me over the opening that's fast closing.

"You are not the 'Avenging Hybrid,' Ferroc!" he shouts at me. "You are not the vessel of the Great Creator! That is my destiny now! And you will be the instrument of my conquest!"

I try to kick at him with my legs, but as I dangle below the craft, held aloft by Gahren's firm grasp, I'm rendered immobile.

Then, when I'm helpless to do anything but accept my fate, Gahren is struck on the side of the head by something. Again, his armor isn't penetrated, but it bursts into a shower of sparks and tears his right hand from mine as he roars in pain.

The telltale report of a rifle round marks Sasha's prowess once again. The target nearly half a mile away, on the move, ascending...Only the last remaining high velocity round; a bullet that travels much faster than sound or even Gahren himself, would suffice for such a shot.

And she made it count.

I don't waste the opening she's given me. With what energy I have left, I place all my effort into a powerful strike of my sword, aiming for Gahren's armored scythes.

Again, time slows and I'm given a level of clarity and concentration similar to what I experienced inside the reactor chamber. I watch as my arm, fully powered, strikes, arcing the blade into Gahren's restraining appendages.

The weapon cuts through clean, a shower of blue Rantir blood raining down on me as I'm released from my enemy's grasp.

"Not today!" I shout as he cries in pain. He disappears inside the ship, clutching at the bloody stumps where his scythes used to be.

The blast doors close completely, and the ship rockets upward into orbit. I allow myself to fall, turning my body in time to see Andizha on her way to me.

"I don't have any power left," I tell her over our communications system.

"You have done enough, Ferroc," she tells me, granting me great comfort. "We have you."

Andizha soars up to me, taking me in her arms and intercepting me from my fall as I accept her embrace, holding her as tightly as I can. From there, we fly together, one next to the other. Marukarn gently cradles Sasha while Andizha does the same for me. I look over at my dear friend, who wears a tired, burned, but fully serene smile upon her face. She looks back at me.

"One hell of a shot," I shout to her.

She doesn't shout anything back. Instead, she mouths it to me.

"I'm not leaving you."

And I'll forever be grateful you won't, Sasha.

Epilogue

"So what do you think?" Sasha asks me, completing a full turn.

I admire how she makes light of a fashion model on a runway as she showcases her new fatigues. After our battle aboard Gahren's ship, her old clothes were too burned and torn to be of any use. Fortunately, the colony had plenty of standard issue military clothing to spare. They were more than happy to offer some to the woman that played a vital part in saving humanity's new beginning.

"What do I think?" I ask, surprised. "I think you look beautiful."

And indeed she does with most of her strawberry blonde hair up in a ponytail with the rest in braids. Even the burn scar on the side of her face, put there by me when I saved her from the lancing electricity, only enhances her beauty. Her body, covered in the olive green of the fatigues and riddled with straps from her vest and holsters, was the picture of loveliness to me. Everything about her read "survivor" but in a way that just as openly read "Sasha." Mind, body, soul, and now clothing, and all that comprised her, was perfect to me.

She smiles that smile that's meant only for me. "Takes a special kind of man to admire a woman in cargo pants, I think."

I laugh. "Not exactly a man, am I? I think my taste in fashion might be a little skewed."

"Or maybe you're starting a new trend," she counters.

I shrug. "Maybe."

She giggles, then approaches me. "I'm going to see Meredith and Free. Everyone else is enjoying the celebration. Figured I go join in."

"Good," I say, nodding in admiration of the situation. "I'll be down in a little bit."

She tilts her head. "Something on your mind?"

"Nah," I reply. "Just want a few moments alone. That was a lot we went through."

She nods, growing a little solemn. "Yeah. I hear ya. Do you even know everything that happened to you?"

I contemplate that for a moment. "No, I don't. But I think it was nothing more than was meant to."

"That all that you're thinking?" she presses.

The lives lost from Gahren's execution still occupy my thoughts. I know they always will.

As always, she knows my contemplations. "It wasn't your fault, Nathan. You did everything you could."

I nod. "I know...It just seems so...helpless."

"Then focus on the people here," she replies. "You can still help them the way you've helped me. The way you still do."

I look up at her, reaching out and holding the side of her face gently in the palm of my metal hand, thumb avoiding the burn wound on her cheek. It's healing well.

"I don't think I'll ever be able to stop thanking you," I tell her.

She holds my hand in hers, looking back into my eyes with the deepest sincerity and gratitude. "You're not the only one who has someone to be grateful for."

I love you so much, Sasha.

We stay like that for a long while. So long I wonder if time has stood still for us within the underground shelter beneath Lake Superior. It's just her and I; two survivors who have found family in a very unlikely counterpart. But a family that will never be broken or disrupted. A family that has withstood more trials in the span of a few months than most do in a lifetime.

I'm not leaving her. She's not leaving me. And we face everything from here on out together. For now, that meant going to celebrate with the other survivors. Later...?

We'll get to that in due time.

"I'm gonna head down," she says. "Don't be too long, OK? I really want you there."

"All right," I agree as she pulls away from me.

She lingers in the doorway for a few moments, looking at me lovingly, then heads off to join in the celebration.

Now it's just me. I'm alone with my thoughts, much like I was just a few months ago and just as I've been for so much of this mechanical life I call my own. And for the first time ever, I honestly don't mind. This moment of solitude isn't about reflection or meditation. It's not about longing or remorse or sorrow. It's about something so much better. It's about basking in the moment, grateful for the chance to *live*. Not just exist.

I cherish every second. It's truly the proudest time of my life.

I never thought this is where I'd be, or even *what* I'd be in my lifetime. But it's...

...Nice. Real nice.

Even if my face can't smile, my soul is wearing that expression from proverbial ear to proverbial ear.

There's a knock at the door.

"Come in," I bid them.

Marukarn pokes his head through the threshold. He still wears his armor, save for the helmet. "Ferroc?"

"I'm here Marukarn," I tell him. "Just taking a moment."

"The festivities of your fellows does not interest you?" he asks.

I shake my head. "It does. I'm just enjoying the silence before the party. It's going to be a wild night for a lot of them. Does Free really have that stash from the liquor store they found?"

He nods. "It seems to have inhibiting effects on your kind, though none of them mind. In fact, it releases higher levels of endorphins into human bloodstreams."

"Is there a Rantir equivalent to being drunk?" I ask.

He looks confused.

"Intoxicated maybe?" I attempt to clarify.

He shakes his head, not understanding. Apparently Rantir soldiers are too disciplined for inebriation.

"I'll try to explain it to you later," I tell him. "Why did you come?"

He takes a moment to consider his words. "As a warrior, I'm never to celebrate a victory that hasn't been won."

I nod, understanding his point. "You're thinking about Gahren."

"He is still out there," he says. "This fight is far from over."

I rise from the cot I was sitting on, looking out through an underground window that reveals the marine environment of Lake Superior. "I know. He'll be back."

"And we must be ready," my friend adds.

Again, I nod in agreement. "The next step is New York. He has an operation there. That's where he'll return to if he means to keep this war between us going."

"I have a feeling he won't be alone next time," Marukarn informs me. "Reports from our superiors tell us that more are rallying to his cause, believing him to be the Avenging Hybrid given his current, combined form."

"Nothing we can do but deal with that as it comes," I tell him. "There's an expression among humans you might like. 'Eat, drink, and be merry. For tomorrow you may die.'"

He contemplates that for a moment, then nods in approval. "Very applicable, given our circumstances."

"Then let's go do just that," I tell him as I clap him on the shoulder. He returns my gesture, but holds me at the door.

"Before we go, I must tell you something," he informs me.

"What?" I ask.

"I didn't tell Sasha your last words."

That stops me cold. If I had a heart, I know it would have skipped a few beats.

"Why not?" I ask.

"Because that is something you should tell her yourself," he replies, shaking my shoulder affectionately. "I think, my friend, you are capable of recognizing this now as you begin your nascence."

"My nascence?" I question him in my bewilderment. It's a whirlwind of emotions for me at this moment, so recognizing commonly unused words isn't easy.

"You are unfamiliar with the term?" he poses.

I search some memories, recalling it after a momentary pause. "'A coming into being.' Why do you say that's what I'm accepting? Or doing?"

"Because this is your life now," he replies. "And after the stand you've made against Gahren and the good you've done for both our kinds, I think you're beginning to see the existence you live isn't as forlorn as you once believed. You are a being capable and meant for great things, Ferroc. And you've only begun to embrace a life that exhibits this." He heads back to the door, stopping in the frame to say one last thing. "When you think the time is right, tell Sasha what you told me, knowing that she too is a very important part of this life you now live, whatever the circumstances. At least, that's my say in the matter."

I simply look at him for a moment as he lingers in the doorframe, perhaps waiting for me to reply. With no response forthcoming, he taps the frame and offers me a nod of encouragement before leaving me to my thoughts.

In that moment, it seems strange to me that I can face down Gahren's combined might without a trace of fear, but the thought of Sasha finding out how I truly felt could shake me to the bone. Or metal core, as it were.

I didn't know how I could ever tell her something like that, especially after what I'd said before our final confrontation with Gahren. And would there ever be a point? It would only cause her pain.

...Or would it?

It was a mystery I knew I wouldn't be able to solve any time soon. And maybe, there were some things that, no matter what our level of comprehension, would always remain unanswered.

Was this what it meant to be human? Or me?

I'm not sure...

But I'm glad I have the chance to find out.

Made in the USA
San Bernardino, CA
15 February 2016